Martin turned the d[...] in the same motion and let himself in. His heart stopped. His pilot was lying on the floor, the lower half of his body hidden behind his double bed. His face was turned away from Martin, his eyes closed.

Martin thought of the briefcase and whirled to look down at the grill as a searing blow smashed the back of his head, numbing his limbs instantly. He fell softly through an ever darkening space filled with the heavy fragrance of gardenias and the far away yapping of a dog.

This was only the beginning of his torturous journey into hell. A journey scheduled by that master assassin, Tony Sleep.

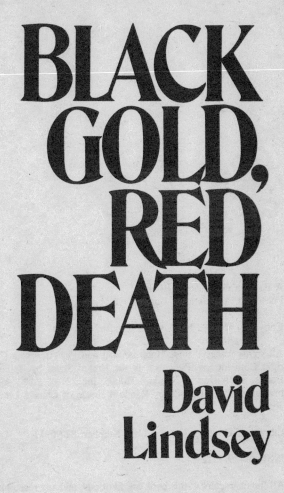

BLACK GOLD, RED DEATH

David Lindsey

FAWCETT GOLD MEDAL • NEW YORK

A Fawcett Gold Medal Book
Published by Ballantine Books

Library of Congress Catalog Card Number: 82-90911

ISBN 0-449-13121-1

Manufactured in the United States of America

First Ballantine Books Edition: May 1983
Second Printing: December 1986

For Joyce
A pearl of great price,
Of value beyond my deserving.

Chapter 1

Coatzacoalcos, Mexico

Buck Shimer flipped on the lights as he reversed the rusty trawler out of its slip. When he felt the solid bump against the stern he swore, cut the engine, and reached for the stout wooden pole that lay against his foot. With the pole he probed the murky water and shoved aside the corroding oil drum that had drifted across the mouth of the slip. As it bobbed into the light thrown from a freighter off-loading a hundred yards away, he saw the word "Pemex" stenciled on the end of the barrel.

Coatzacoalcos was a filthy damn port and getting worse every day. Its harbor stank more than any other on the Gulf, and Shimer had long since lost his ability to smell anything but diesel smoke, sour gas, and sulfur. Unconsciously he worked the muscles of his unshaven jaw as he turned the *Lucille* away from the brightly lighted docks where giant cranes and power machinery strained in a deafening roar to unload three grimy freighters. Out in the bay to his left, he saw the winking beacons of four more ships waiting their turn to disgorge an endless stream of cargo destined for the Reforma oil fields scattered around the Bay of Campeche.

As he eased the trawler away from the heart of the warehouse district, the harbor brilliance gave way to the muted, low-voltage blues and reds of the *zona roja* which was strung along the waterfront from the wharves to the edge of the city. The bars were the last things he could see before he turned his boat toward the deeper water of the bay and headed for Sanchez Magallanes, a rotting fishing village twenty-five miles farther down the coast. There was nothing there, but that was where his charters wanted to go. He had had stranger requests. Hell, it was nothing to him. They had paid him enough to go all the way to Campeche. This was one night's sleep he wouldn't mind missing.

The cabin door to his left opened, and one of the passengers emerged from below and joined him on deck. He was a young Mexican, early twenties, Shimer guessed, as the youth lighted a cigarette illuminating his face in the glow of his cupped hands.

They were an odd bunch. Four of them, two dead-assed drunk

and holding each other up as they came on board. The boy had done the talking. He had paid for the trip himself from a roll of American cash he drew from his khaki pants. But the wad of bills wasn't all that unusual in this part of Mexico, anymore. You saw a lot of unusual things, but you never let on what you thought. A poker face and deaf ears were invaluable in Coatzacoalcos.

They picked up speed, and the Gulf breeze whipped the back of Shimer's denim shirt, drying the sweat that had drenched it while they had sat in the foul stillness of the harbor. He kept the trawler close in to the shore for the first five miles, avoiding the network of buoys farther out that marked the freighter lanes to the busy port. In keeping this close to the mainland, the crusty old boat moved in the powerful glow of an infamous scene well known to those who plied these coastal waters at night.

Across fifteen miles of dark vaporous marshland dotted with flickering fire pits for burning off chemical waste rose the monstrous spectacle of the refinery of Minatitlán, a glittering castle in the mouth of hell. Surrounded by giant flares burning excess raw gas, it belched clouds of leaden smoke which hung in the night sky like brooding volcanic smog reflecting the lurid oranges and reds which themselves were mirrored on the glassy surfaces of the stagnant lagoons. It was an awesome sight, a billion-dollar conflagration in the poverty-stricken marshes of southern Mexico.

Swinging the trawler farther out into the bay to avoid the long tongue of a sandbar at the mouth of the Pedregal River, Shimer switched his attention from the landward side to the bay, where the sparkling towers of the offshore drilling rigs were scattered across the water toward Campeche. A cabin launch that had been gaining on them for the past five minutes veered off to their left toward the nearest rig, its wake leaving a widening V behind it. These launches maintained a constant ferrying service from Coatzacoalcos, carrying shift crews and supplies to the isolated rigs.

The cabin door swung open again and an older man came out onto the deck. In the brief splash of light that fell across the man's face, Shimer noticed his strained features were glistening with sweat. Though it was no doubt stuffy inside and the rolling trawler couldn't be comfortable on a belly gorged with *cerveza,* there seemed to be more than the discomfort of a drunkard's nausea portrayed in the man's expression. The older Mexican glanced at Shimer and then turned his back on him as he took a cigarette from the young man, whom he engaged in an earnest conversation inaudible to Shimer above the trawler's rumbling diesel.

It was none of his business, Shimer reminded himself as he caught a whiff of the resinous-sweet fragrance of marijuana, none of his damn business that these *bobos* wanted to go to that reeking coastal village. He tried to think of the money and how soon he would be back to Coatzacoalcos. He thought of the engine overhaul the *Lucille* had to have and how her hull needed scraping. There was no problem about getting those things done now, and all he had to do was lose one night's sleep. A goddam bargain.

But it wasn't a bargain, and Buck Shimer knew it. He sensed it, despite his forced optimism. He could feel the little bundle of folded money in his pocket, and for some reason he couldn't believe they would let him get home with it. He glanced around at the two men talking behind him. The kid was as nervous as a cat, and Shimer got the impression he was in something way over his head. The older man was right up in his face giving him a tongue-lashing he wouldn't soon forget, and the kid was looking him straight in the eye as if he was afraid to look anywhere else.

When the man had vented his spleen to his satisfaction, he turned to Shimer, wiping his face on the shoulder of his shirt with a shrug.

"How much longer is it?" he asked in Spanish.

Shimer looked toward land, catching familiar lights, simple landmarks. He used to use the rigs in the bay for markers but he soon learned they couldn't be trusted. They moved around, shifted positions if the locations weren't suitable to the geologists and drillers.

"I guess we're 'bout halfway," he said, nodding toward the shore. "There's the microwave tower at Politos."

"Time. How much *time* is it?" The Mexican didn't try to hide the impatience in his voice.

Shimer looked at him. "I'd say fifteen minutes. Not long."

The man ran his fingers through the rancid curls of his oily hair. "Pound on the cabin just before you head in to shore," he commanded. He was careful not to open the door too wide as he stepped back inside.

"Damn!" Shimer said to the young man without looking around. "Drinkin' sure sets 'im on his ear, don't it?" He knew the man wasn't drunk.

The youth didn't respond but sat despondently on the gunwale.

3

"Hey," Shimer said, turning to him. "You sick? They're not throwing up all over my cabin, are they?"

The boy jerked his head up angrily. "Shut up!" he yelled. "You shut up or—"

Suddenly a strident scream burst from the cabin, a scream of unmistakable agony. Shimer whirled around to face the youth, who was already on his feet, both arms extended straight out in front of him, his hands gripping a revolver pointed at Shimer's stomach. As they stared at each other, a second scream jolted them both, a sustained high pitch abruptly cut off by a blow Shimer could hear clearly from where he stood.

Ducking and spinning around, Shimer whipped the trawler's steering wheel, causing the craft to dip sharply as it sheered, flipping the boy backward over the gunwale. As he fell over the side he flung out his left hand and grabbed for the railing; the reflex action of his right hand jerked the trigger, firing a shot into the air.

Shimer righted the trawler, shoved the throttle on full speed, and headed for the nearest drilling-rig platform. He recognized the older Mexican's voice calling "Marcos! Marcos!" as he grabbed the wooden pole and stepped to the blind side of the cabin door to wait for what he knew would come next. When the door burst open, Shimer slammed down the pole with all his strength across the Mexican's neck.

Jerking the door back, he stepped over the body into the doorway. In an instant his stomach went hollow. Spread-eagled on the cabin floor with his wrists and ankles tied to pieces of furniture with nylon fishing cord that was cutting into his flesh with each convulsive jerk lay a middle-aged American dressed in business clothes. His shirt was pulled up under his arms, exposing a soft white stomach. His trousers and underwear were pulled down around his knees. Between his legs a briefcase lay open, revealing a dry-cell battery with wires running from it to the man's testicles.

Crouching over the man's stomach with an icepick and a bottle of dye, a third man gaped up at Shimer, interrupted from his task of scratching a crude tattoo in the American's soft flesh. The American's eyes were open but glazed over. Shimer knew he had gone beyond what he could endure and still be expected to live. Blood from his nostrils had caked around his mouth and run into his shirt collar.

In a single swift movement, the third man came to his feet flipping the icepick end over end at Shimer, who saw it coming and fell back over the body of the Mexican on the stairs. The

4

icepick whistled over his head into the water. As the Mexican lunged at him, Shimer kicked out with his right foot and caught the man in the throat, a lucky blow that sent him sprawling over the American on the floor. Shimer scrambled up the stairs and slammed shut the cabin door and barred it with the wooden pole. As he raised himself to the steering wheel a gunshot splintered the top of the door. It had come from behind!

He whirled around to the stern of the trawler and froze at the unbelievable sight of the young Mexican clinging to the gunwale railing with one arm and aiming the pistol at him with the other. He saw two flashes, then a third. He didn't feel the slug smash into the corner of his eye, and he didn't feel the back of his head blow out. He didn't feel anything at all.

San Antonio, Texas

Martin Gallagher was awakened by the sun streaming through the tall casement windows of his bedroom. He knew he was late. When he pulled Saturday shifts it put him in a bad mood even before he got out of bed. He threw back the cover and swung his legs onto the floor. It was already hot outside, and he could hear the cicadas droning in the Spanish oaks along the street. For a moment he sat half asleep on the edge of the bed fighting the impulse to fall back into the cool sheets. Instead, he turned his head to the windows again and opened his eyes. The burst of direct sunlight blinded him for a moment, making his eyes water. He stood up.

He pressed his feet against the cool hardwood floor as he selected his clothes from the wardrobe, then plodded into the bathroom for a cold shower. He hadn't slept well, and he knew why. On his desk at the office were half a dozen slips of yellow notepaper reminding him his sister had called repeatedly the previous day. He hadn't returned her calls.

The two of them had never understood each other. They were as different as two people could be, and, in many ways, he believed their long-standing alienation had been inevitable from the very beginning. And yet he couldn't help feeling that somehow they had let each other down. But if Stella felt anything similar she hadn't expressed it, and it was highly unlikely that she did. Wavering indecision wasn't a part of her makeup.

Though their personalities differed dramatically, that in itself hadn't been the cause of their alienation. Stella's impetuosity and hot temper were attributes Martin had always taken in his

5

stride, even when they were children. He had accepted them early on, and had even found them admirable when they took the form of righteous indignation. She was seldom wrong when it got to that point.

The serious differences had come much later when they were in college together at the University of Texas. It was during the rampaging sixties, and Stella had become embroiled in the radical politics of La Causa, a league of human-rightists who fought the long fight against police repression in the Mexican countryside. In those years there was a large contingent of students from Mexico at the university, and Stella had readily embraced their fiery causes.

But Martin steadfastly refused to become involved and accept what she insisted were his moral responsibilities. She badgered him unmercifully throughout graduate school trying to draw him into various political movements. Like so many of the radicals during that hectic decade, she couldn't tolerate benign silence.

The ultimate split came shortly after they both had completed their graduate degrees. Martin was already a rookie reporter working for his father at the San Antonio *Times*, and Stella was teaching at St. Mary's University while devoting what money and time she could to Mexican revolutionary causes. They were home for Easter Sunday, and Stella, having arrived in a foul mood, began haranguing the family and goading Martin during the course of the dinner. She accused him of having no affection for his own blood. She called him a drone, an albatross around the neck of human decency, because he didn't care for his own people who suffered injustice in their homeland while he took for granted the easy ride fate had given him.

It was the kind of rhetoric he detested, and finally he retaliated. By now he had forgotten his own words, but he remembered they had raved at one another, flinging curses and indictments across the table until his father had stopped them. But he was too late; they had said too much. In their anger they had gone too far, spoken words that would always hurt, that never could be canceled out with apologies or tears. They could never see each other with the same eyes again, and never did.

Then, later that same year, his parents were killed in a car wreck on a crooked caliche road north of San Luis Potosí during their annual trip into Mexico to visit his mother's family. He and Stella went down together to bring back the bodies. They drove from San Antonio to Laredo and then took the train to San Luis Potosí. They rode south in silence.

Coming back on the night train with the bodies of his parents in the baggage car behind them, they talked. He and Stella had been badly shaken by his parents' death, knowing how grieved they had been over their recent split. It was clear to him Stella was feeling guilty, though she would never be able to find the words to express it. They sat together in the empty coach drinking her Passport scotch from an aluminum thermos and watching the desert float by in the moonlight. Stella drank heavily, even then, and instead of becoming reticent as she usually did when she drank, she grew loquacious.

She admitted, as Martin had always suspected, that she resented being a stepchild to his parents. It didn't matter, she said, that they had been reared exactly the same. It really never could have been the same and never was.

"It's ironic," she said, holding her cup of scotch close to her mouth with both hands but not drinking, "I'm Mexican—Anna's cousin; we've the same blood, she reared me from infancy as her own child, and she loved me as much as any mother could. But temperamentally, spiritually, I'm Brian's daughter, and I haven't a drop of Irish blood in me."

Martin didn't reply. She had been talking endlessly, cathartically.

"You're like Anna," she continued. "Thoroughly Mexican, dissimulating, reticent, moody. But I'm like Brian: impulsive, fervent, explosive. I think he recognized that and it amused him. There's always been an abyss between you and me. You know that."

"Yes," he had said, staring out the window, "I know that."

"I loved her, dearly, but *he* captured my imagination. Those books he read to us when we were kids! He could have been an actor. Hell, he *was* an actor! He played the lead in Life, right up to the end." She smiled, then let it fade and sipped the Passport. "It's hard to think of them mute, back there in those boxes."

"Don't think about it," he said.

"Don't think of an elephant!" she snapped, then caught herself. "Shit. Anyway, I'm glad he saw us both through graduate school. That meant a lot to him. He was strictly bourgeois in that respect. Thought education would save the world. Well, he made us literate, by God, and he taught us to think. Poor Anna, she didn't look good, did she? I can't stop thinking of her slamming into the dash and what must have happened after that. She was the handsomest woman I've ever seen. Everyone said that, didn't they? Damn, they were wonderful."

Martin listened to her talk. He would rather have been alone, but Stella was taking them on a tour of the past. She remembered what his parents had been like when he and Stella were small children; she remembered the annual summer trips the four of them took to San Luis Potosí to visit his mother's family and Stella's aunts and uncles. She remembered high school when she decided to assert her independence and began calling them Brian and Anna, and how his mother had been hurt by what she believed was an act of rejection and how Brian had laughed at her spunk. She remembered the fat years when Brian had won national notoriety for his coverage of organized crime in San Antonio, and how the New York *Times* had tried to hire him and he had refused. She talked about the college days, not so far in the past. It had been a night train through Stella's memory, and Martin had felt sorry for her that it had been no less dark than the Mexican desert outside their window.

That had been ten years ago. He saw her seldom in the intervening decade, dinner together once in a while, birthdays, Christmas, and the anniversary of their parents' death. But they had never again talked of her work with La Causa. She had gone underground. She was even more serious now, the stakes were higher, and she had seen the wisdom in discretion.

Then, lately, she had been calling him under the pretense of "needing someone to talk to." They had had dinner together a few times, and she had alluded occasionally to her work with a group in the city who supported "certain political movements" in Mexico. She was subtle, subdued, less inclined to rhetoric, and he found her obvious desire to talk dispassionately with him about her great passion a touching show of deference uncharacteristic of the Stella he had always known.

For whatever reason, she was trying to lay to rest the past ten years of their strained truce. Their awkward dinners together two or three times a year had not been pleasant for either of them, and he had often wondered why they kept it up. Now she was wanting to close the gap that had grown between them, and he found himself holding back. He was suspicious, and angry at himself for his cynicism.

After shaving, he quickly dressed, locked the front door, and began jogging the three blocks to the bus stop. He had been late to the office three days (including today) out of the past two weeks, and he remembered with relief that his car would be ready at Sammy's garage at noon. He got to the corner just in time to put his foot on the bench and tie his shoe before the bus heaved to a roaring stop beneath the palm trees.

Martin stepped in the door, and the driver pulled away from

the curb as he dropped his coins in the change box. Grabbing the upright chrome posts, Martin hesitated in front of three dumpy Mexican women clustered at the front of the bus. They stopped talking, a concerted reflex action, and waited for him to choose his seat. He swayed past them down the aisle and sat near the back door.

The only person on the bus besides the women was a middle-aged man sitting two seats up from him across the aisle. He was small, pear-shaped, and wore light gray serge pants and a suitcoat with a yellowed white shirt open at the neck. His hair was oiled, dyed black, and parted high near the center of his head. Puffy bags hung under his eyes and a simpering upper lip sported a black pencil-thin mustache. Cradled in his arms, an aging Chihuahua with its nails painted red salivated profusely, smearing and streaking his coat. The man let the dog rest its chin on its paws in the crook of his arm as he stroked it gently, kissed its knobby head, and toyed with his little finger inside the dog's ear. With a ringed middle finger he daintily wiped a string of dribble from the thin canine lips.

The bus followed the boulevard to Market Street, where the three Mexican women got off with their webbed shopping bags. A discount record store blared bouncy *música norteña* from a storefront speaker where young Chicanos lounged in the shady doorway staring passively out to some distant, more romantic way of life.

New passengers got on: a platinum blond in a waitress uniform with a ruffled pink plastic apron, two cocky Mexican teenagers who leered at the waitress from behind designer sunglasses and nudged each other in a worldly manner. A solemn-faced street-walker found an isolated seat, leaned her head against the window, and closed her eyes.

The stops came more frequently as the streets grew busier and the selling, buying, and arguing of the downtown day dictaed the pace of the traffic.

The bus stopped on the southeast corner of St. Mary's Park at Trinity. At the other end of the block the tall wooden doors of the cathedral were thrown open, and a frail, wizened black man sat on the steps of the church tossing stale popcorn to the pigeons which came sailing in from the park across the street.

The pear-shaped man with the Chihuahua slid out of his seat and stepped into the aisle. He looked the other way as he brushed past Martin on his way to the back door. The dog yapped once

9

as they stepped out onto the sidewalk. Martin turned to look and saw the man put down the dog. With his hands on his hips, he strolled onto the gravel pathway which led into the park, where the morning sun was streaming through the trees.

Chapter 2

Lake Travis
Austin, Texas

The single mercury-vapor lamp threw a hoary light over the dock and the water, and on the lush summer vegetation that crowded the narrow path leading up the densely wooded hillside to the lake house. Two men maneuvered their rubber dinghy along the bank, staying under the overhanging trees as they used the limbs to pull themselves toward the light-washed landing. When they had gotten as close as they dared, they tied the dinghy snug against the bank and climbed out.

It was a still, clear night. An outboard motor coughed from one of the inlets formed by the converging hills that came down to the shore. Summer homes, the white banks of their hillside pools shimmering like ivory balconies in the moonlight, nestled in the hills, their lights twinkling across the water like stars in a black rippling sky.

When the first man gained his footing on the bank, he raised his infrared binoculars toward the house a hundred yards up the path. The second man collected his cameras and lenses and draped them around his neck. The numerical readings on the lenses had been meticulously recoated with phosphorescent paint. The cameras were loaded with Agfa Isopan high-speed film.

Together they started toward the house, making slow progress as they stayed off the path in the thick undergrowth and abundant mountain laurel. The first man was careful to hold on to the resisting limbs to prevent them from slapping back in his companion's face. When they were nearly halfway, the man with the cameras tapped the other on the back and indicated he wanted to try it from there. The first man hesitated, then slowly lowered himself to his stomach so the photographer would have a clear view. While he lay in the grass studded with pebbles, he put the binoculars to his eyes again.

Behind him the camera clicked and whirred in rapid-fire action, but he could tell by what he saw through the binoculars that the photographer wasn't getting anything significant. Several

11

figures moved back and forth in front of the windows, but none of them stayed long and none of them showed so much as a profile. That was good. Better than he expected.

"Dammit," the photographer swore in a whisper. He tapped the first man again. He wanted to move up.

The first man looked around at him. The photographer's eyes were still glued to the house, his camera poised under his nose ready for the perfect shot. He was a young man—the *norteños* recruited them even younger than they did in Mexico—and he wore a thin gold wedding band. The *federale* wondered how long it had been there. He wondered how this young man's wife would take it when they told her. Damn! He turned again toward the house. He never thought about these things in Mexico. It struck you differently when you were away from home.

Wiping off the tiny pebbles from the palms of his hands as he rose to a crouching position, he moved up the hill, placing his feet more carefully on the ground as the slope steepened. After twenty yards, he stopped once more and returned the binoculars to his eyes. Behind him the camera clicked and whirred. He saw the prone figure immediately. He was lying on the deck attached to the lake side of the house, his body aligned in the shadow cast by a potted palm.

The Mexican couldn't suppress the chill at the back of his neck as he looked through his binoculars at the marksman staring back at him through his own infrared telescope. He knew the marksman had picked him out, that he was now nudging the rifle over to the young agent, who was oblivious to his presence as he clicked away at the lighted windows. The Mexican lay as flat as he could against the hillside and waited.

What the hell was the rifleman doing? A trickle of sweat oozed out of the *federale's* hairline and ran down the side of his face, past his cheek, and into his black mustache.

The dull *chunk!* from the silenced rifle and the sickening explosion of the young agent's head occurred at the same instant, followed by the rush of expunged air as he lurched forward in the grass, then rolled back several yards before he stopped. The *federale* stood up—there was no need to check the body—and scrambled up the path to the house. He took the deck stairs two at a time, and when he reached the top the rifleman stood up from the shadows and opened the door to the house and followed the *federale* inside.

He walked quickly into the living room, where he found a woman and a man on their knees in front of the fireplace frantically going through stacks of papers and throwing most of them into the roaring fire. The man stood when the *federale* came in and grimly motioned for him to come to the far side of the room. The woman, olive-complected and strikingly attractive, looked up briefly but continued feeding the fire.

"You'd better leave something significant," the *federale* said, pausing beside her. "It won't look right if you don't. It's a long shot as it is."

"Some of these people have already gotten into Mexico. I'll leave the references to them," the woman said without looking up.

"You may have to compromise one or two. It's a hard decision, but it won't look right if you don't."

The woman ignored him.

The tall man who had stood up spoke. "We're almost through. We can't have thought of everything, of course. We've been using this place too long and we haven't had time."

"It doesn't matter. We're only buying time anyway. And not much time at that."

The marksman was now helping the woman feed papers into the fire. They did so without speaking, their faces flushed. A summer night was not the best time for a fire.

The two men sat opposite each other, a coffee table between them. The tall man crossed his legs at the knees and looked steadily at the *federale*, who loosened his tie and lit a cigarette.

"I'm sorry you had to do that," he said. His distinguished voice portrayed genuine regret.

The *federale* shrugged. There was nothing to say.

"We were lucky," the tall man said. He spoke in Spanish.

"Very. We were notified only two days ago they wanted us to cooperate. The border has been thrown wide open. I arrived only last night. This was the first thing breaking, and I got them to let me do it this way. The FBI will never forgive me. I'll be the stupid greaser who screwed up the best opportunity they've had so far." For an instant he remembered the eagerness in the face of the young agent. "Yes, you couldn't have been luckier."

"I suppose they will be moving fast now. What the hell happened in Coatzacoalcos, anyway?"

"It was the Brigada Blanca. I didn't know anything about it until it was over, which worries me. It was a decision made very high up. An effort to put the pressure on Washington. I can't understand why they fell for it."

"Maybe they didn't," the tall man said cryptically.

"What do you mean?"

"Washington is very clever. They have ulterior motives. We have the documents."

"I don't believe it!"

"It's true. Despite everything, the FBI, the CIA, everything. Greed is a remarkable vice. They cost us a fortune in the end, but that's nothing compared to what they will buy us in return."

"I can't believe it." The *federale* was allowing himself a faint smile. "Where . . . what have you done with them?"

"They're here."

"Here? In this house? You're a fool!"

"That may be, but not because of that. The courier was delayed. I had just received them when I learned of your mission here tonight. Things had to be cleared away here. I didn't have time for any other arrangements. But that doesn't matter. We're going to need your help now more than ever. You're going to have to buy us time until we get the documents over the border and down to Oaxaca."

"Buy you time! I'll be in no position. I'll be lucky if they don't ship me back to Mexico in a cattle car."

"Do what you can. Give us a safe number where we can contact you while you are still in San Antonio. We will be going back there tonight."

The *federale* ground out his cigarette and took a pen from his pocket. He wrote a number on a piece of paper the other man had handed him. "It may have to be changed, but I'll let you know first."

"Thank you, my friend. We'll move as quickly as possible. We'll let you know when the documents are out of the country."

"You must go now," the *federale* said, standing up. "I'll take care of the rest of the papers."

The tall man clasped the side of the *federale*'s neck with the palm of his hand. "Be careful. We have stirred the serpents."

There were a few things the *federale* had to do after they left, and he tried to think of them now as they packed the last-minute items in their briefcases and satchels and load them into the car waiting in the driveway. In ten minutes they were gone.

He walked back through the house, down the deck steps, and down the path to where the young agent lay in the weeds a few yards from the path. He located the exact spot where they both had crouched when the agent was shot, and got down on his knees and faced the house. With his own Browning magnum equipped with a silencer, he took careful aim and fired at the house. Twice through one of the windows, the sound of broken

14

glass lingering in the still night air, then three more times in the general area of the deck where the marksman had lain.

When he finished he reloaded his magnum and put it back in its holster under his suitcoat. Resisting the temptation to look in the grass behind him, he walked back up the path to the house. From the living room where the fire in the fireplace had died to embers, he placed a call to his FBI contact in San Antonio.

Chapter 3

The San Antonio *Times* was housed in an ancient building which occupied an entire triangular city block. Its entrance opened from the point of one of the angles of the triangle onto the wide intersection of Navarro, Medina, and Houston streets. Above the double front doors the name of the newspaper was etched in the glass transom in a rising-sun pattern.

Both secretaries smiled at Martin as he stepped out of the elevator into the reception area of the editorial department on the third floor. The secretaries and a PBX operator sat at a long curved desk of dark wood surrounded by tropical plants. One of the girls held up a yellow message note between her second and third fingers with her elbow resting on the smooth surface of the desk.

"Telephone call and a vi-si-tor," she chimed and nodded toward the newsroom. "A Mr. Cue-vas."

Martin cringed at the mispronunciation and looked through the glass wall into the newsroom, an acre of desks in the fluorescent gloam. Ramón Cuevas sat with his hat in his lap beside Martin's desk.

"How long has he been there?" he asked, not taking his eyes off the old man.

The secretary looked past him at the clock over the elevator doors. "Almost an hour."

"Jesus." He took the yellow note from her, saw that it was Stella again, and went into the newsroom. As the noise of telephones and typewriters hit him, he glanced again at the note in his hand and noticed the call-back number wasn't Stella's office at St. Mary's University or her apartment. Where the hell could she be long enough to have left this number for him? He thought of his two days off starting tomorrow, and he wondered if he would be able to spend some time with Susannah. She had told him there was a chance Francisco would be leaving town for the weekend. He would call her after he had talked with Cuevas.

As he angled through the maze of desks and brown metal

trash cans, he caught the city editor looking at him from the far side of the room. Dimmit raised his eyebrows, looked toward Cuevas and then back at Martin. Martin ignored him and rammed the yellow slip into his outside coat pocket.

"Ramón! What do you say, my friend?" Martin smiled and reached out his hand to the little man.

Cuevas stood, smiled too, and shook Martin's hand. "Nothing, nothing. And you?"

"Well, I'm working too much, but it doesn't matter. I'm getting richer every day." Humorless banter.

They both laughed, Cuevas tilting his head back and saying, "Ahhh, ahh, ahh." Martin knew Dimmit was watching them, and he saw a couple of other reporters look away discreetly as he glanced across the room.

"Sit down, sit down, Ramón. It's been a long time. You should've called me first. I'm sorry I was late."

"It was nothing. I looked around. It's not the same without your father, uh? Well, who expects it to stay the same? This man goes, that one goes." He smiled. "Then you go," and he raised his hands to indicate a disappearance. His felt hat dangled by its brim from one hand.

"How is Ovidia?" Martin took a pack of Camels from his desk and offered one to Cuevas. The old man nodded gratefully and took one, leaning forward as Martin lit it for him. He sat back then and crossed one leg over the other and put his hat on his knee. Martin settled back too, resigned to the rambling visit he would have to endure before the old man would get around to revealing why he had come by to see him.

"Oh, pretty good. She is strong but she has the cataracts." He squinted, and with the hand that held the cigarette he motioned in the air before him as though he were wiping something from a window, "Her eyes, they get cloudy and she feels around. She goes to the *curandera* and she gets some damn grass tea or something. I say, goddam, go to the doctor. We are civilized people, we can afford it. Go to a real doctor. But she goes back to the *curandera*. The old *bruja* gives her some cactus and tells her to sleep with it on her eyes. Goddam." He shook his head and took a drag off the Camel.

Martin listened to him attentively. Cuevas wore a brown pinstriped suit with a white shirt and no tie. The suit was expensive but baggy, and from a little distance it looked shabby. Martin knew the old man believed in the *curandera* himself, but he was in Anglo territory now and Cuevas knew what Anglos thought about such things. His manners were impeccable, and he could chat like this endlessly. He had put on a little weight since Martin last saw him but he still wore his hair slicked back with Seven Roses hair oil. Martin had caught a whiff of the cheap fragrance when they shook hands.

Ramón Cuevas had been one of his father's underworld acquaintances. He had been a big man years ago in the drug wars that raged continually on San Antonio's south side, and his involvement in the distribution of the *carga blanca* within the city was well known. But it had been Brian Gallagher, with his nose for the big story, who had discovered that Cuevas' barrio mom and pop business was only the front door for an organization that stretched down to the Mexican border, to Guatemala City, Managua, Bogotá, Lima, Cochabamba, and finally to the poppy fields of Paraguay and Argentina. From his little icehouse on Prado Street in Palm Heights, Ramón Cuevas controlled a multimillion-dollar pipeline for "dirty" Latin American brown heroin.

Brian Gallagher had been an investigative reporter too long to innocently turn over his information to the Drug Enforcement Administration. During the last phases of his investigations, he had involved a DEA agent who had the authority to make deals independently of the regular Bureau channels. They sent word to Cuevas that they wanted a meeting.

On a Sunday afternoon in a fly-ridden café one block off the main street of Castroville, the four men (Cuevas had brought along a "cousin") laid their cards on the table. The Bureau wanted Cuevas to give them enough information on his South American counterparts operating out of the States to burn them. They were willing to make an arrangement: Cuevas would be given three weeks to put his affairs in order and to feed them the information. The Bureau would look the other way during that time while Cuevas laid aside a *clavo*, a nest egg for his old age. At the end of three weeks the Bureau would move, but Cuevas would be overlooked. He wouldn't have to serve a day in jail or even be brought to the stands during the trials that would follow. He could drop out of sight. However, if he was ever caught in the business again, they would forget about his favor and he would be fair game.

Ramón Cuevas was in his early fifties then. He wasn't a stupid man. He had three sons and a daughter. He made the deal and he survived, and by his own scale of values that was what counted. His *clavo* had been considerable, and he knew people who made good investments for him. He kept his ear to the ground and his mouth shut. And he never forgot the favor. He stayed in touch with the Irishman who spoke Spanish like a Mexican, and he would do a little favor for his *amigo* now and then. Gallagher became the best-informed reporter in the state. And he kept his mouth shut too.

So Cuevas sat with Martin now, and they talked about the city council elections. Martin began wanting a cup of coffee. Ramón smoked another Camel. There were some little things about the elections Cuevas didn't like. The damn politicians. You couldn't trust them. He made a few predictions about how things would turn out. Martin listened and laughed to himself when he caught another glimpse of Dimmit watching them. The old man hadn't been by in years, and Martin knew Dimmit thought he smelled the makings of a good story.

Suddenly Cuevas stopped. "Listen," he said. He screwed up his right shoulder and tilted his head with a squint. "There are some things. A few matters. Is this a good place to talk?"

"What do you think?"

"Pino's has good coffee."

"Yeah, I think so too," Martin said, and took the Camels and slipped them into his coat pocket with the yellow telephone note. "Let's get a cup."

The two men stood and threaded their way past several desks to the main aisle that led out of the newsroom. At the elevator Martin told the secretary who had given him the note that he wouldn't be back until after lunch. She jotted this down on the log sheet.

"Telephone?" she asked.

"I'll call in."

She looked up at him. "Sure," she said cynically.

As they waited for the elevator, Cuevas smiled at the secretaries, who were used to being smiled at.

Pino's Diner was only a block from the front door of the *Times* building. It had been built in the 1930s in the purest Art Deco style, mostly of chrome and glass and with rounded corners instead of right angles. It sat on a corner and was open twenty-four hours a day, and newspaper people could be found there any time of the day or night.

As Martin and Cuevas entered the front door the diminutive Pino stood behind the counter stacking bananas, apples, and oranges on the cabinet top in front of the mirrors. He saw their reflection as they came in and waved without turning around. They took a small table next to the windows that looked out on Medina Street, and Martin signaled to the waitress that they wanted two coffees, which she promptly brought in detached silence.

From a little glass barrel which came on his saucer, Cuevas poured cream into his coffee until it was the color of his beige hat. He stirred, looking out the window.

"It's going to get sticky like a damn jungle and then it will rain," he said. "No doubt about it."

Martin nodded casually and blew on his coffee. It would be a mistake to seem anxious. He looked out the window too and wondered what kind of information this old man would have for him. It had been nearly two years since Martin had handled the cops-and-robbers stories on a regular basis, and Cuevas knew this. Whatever he had in mind was either unrelated or so big he would trust the information only with someone he knew well.

"That newspaper was noisy," Cuevas said. "I couldn't work in a place like that. This is better. Not many people, either." He looked at Martin and sipped the muddy coffee.

"I have some frens who do a lot of traveling in their work," he began slowly. "They go here and there in Mexico and south from there to *Sudamerica, America Central.*" He wobbled an open hand over his cup to indicate a generality. "They know many people in these places and they hear many kinds of news. Some of it is good information; some of it is not so reliable." He smiled. "But this that I hear recently I think is pretty good, and I think to myself that maybe Martin Gallagher would like to hear this thing too."

Martin remembered the Camels in his pocket and casually took them out and put them on the table. He was trying to stop smoking and was doing pretty well at it, but he carried the cigarettes anyway and kept a pack in his desk. He had learned a long time ago that some people talk better when they are smoking, and especially when they are smoking other people's tobacco.

"Two boys I know have been down in British Honduras looking around," Cuevas said, taking a Camel. "Some business, some vacation. I wouldn't go there on no vacation. I was in Belize City once and was so miserable I thought I had the malaria. Fever. But it wasn't so. I was just hot. I never cooled off. I sweated like a whore all the time. Nights. You couldn't sleep nights. No air. Nothing to breathe but mosquitoes.

"These boys got tired of it too, so they went to Oaxaca to spend some time. They drink a little, they visit aroun', and soon they hear some very interesting things."

For all his relaxed manner Cuevas betrayed a reluctance to

20

tell his story. He sipped his coffee, took a long drag on the Camel, and let the smoke leak slowly from his nostrils in wispy curls. Martin didn't try to make it easier for him; he simply waited.

"Well, you know Mexico's history. The discontent of the *peón* who works the land but does not own it. You know the revolution. Those are old stories. Oaxaca was a very important state in those stories about the revolution. The *campesinos* played hell with the *pistoleros* and *federales* in the mountains there. That sort of thing still can be seen. My frens tell me that in the state of Oaxaca there is today a revolutionary organization that is growing very strong. It is called El Gobierno Agrario Tradicional de Oaxaca. GATO. Cat." Cuevas smiled wanly at the acronym.

"It is about land, they say. It has always been about land, but the boys tell me that the *campesinos* and their cry for land are only part of the story. They say that GATO is a front for a much stronger organization that gets its money from some of the wealthiest families in Mexico—and from international sources too.

"Oaxaca, of course, is close to Veracruz and Villahermosa. Those are very busy cities these days, and the police cannot see everything, uh? The ports are busy. Everybody's busy. A crate from the states marked 'Pemex' is something for the oil fields, no? Or something for the building of the refineries.

"The boys say that is not always the case. For a long time now GATO has been getting guns through the little ports along the coast south of Veracruz, and even through Veracruz itself. Also in Veracruz and Villahermosa there are now living large numbers of revolutionaries. Not those like the *campesinos,* but those with educations who sit in the air-conditioned hotels and the boardrooms of the industries. These people mean business, and they have more to help their cause than the brave little guns of the *campesinos.*

"In Oaxaca the boys hear that in the States there is a very strong group that supports GATO. It is underground, of course. Its headquarters are here, in San Antonio, and it is run by a strong-arm called Paco. That is all anybody knows of him: Paco. He is legendary in Mexico. There are unbelievable stories about him, like Zapata." Cuevas raised his shoulders and gave a shrug with his mouth. "The people like stories."

The waitress appeared at his elbow and poured more coffee for both of them. She replaced his empty glass barrel of cream with a full one and left. Cuevas again poured the cream in his coffee and stirred it casually as he squinted at the sun-bright street. His spoon chinked against the rim of his cup. He was deliberately taking his time.

Martin took another cigarette from the dwindling pack. It was his third. He had promised himself he wouldn't smoke more than two before lunch, if he had any at all, but now he didn't care. Cuevas was leading up to something unpleasant.

Cuevas laid his spoon beside the cup in the saucer. "This man Paco has a woman who is as famous as he is. The people call her La Luz because they say she has kept the light of the poor shining in the darkness of Mexico with her support of their revolutionary efforts from up here. These two have gotten things done. They pull strings. They have organized bank robberies and a smuggling network that is to be envied. They have been very clever, very good with their covers. Always they are the organizers and have never been known to participate in these things themselves.

"But things are changing. These two have become too big for the state police. The Mexican government has long ago put the *federales* onto their trail. For a long time the FBI has been snooping around here for the same reason. What about this? What about that? Then there was this kidnapping in Coatzacoalcos a few days ago. An American was taken from the club in the Hotel Margón, and they find him the next morning on a beach thirty miles away very dead and bloated and covered with the jellyfish. On his stomach"—Cuevas put two fingers on his vest—"there is a tattoo of *un gato negro*.

"The Mexican government blows up. 'Goddam,' they say, 'these people are financed from the States and they kill an *americano* down here. It makes us look very bad. You must stop the flow of money to this GATO or things will get very sticky.' So the U.S. gets excited and puts on the pressures."

Martin had heard of the kidnapping-killing. He knew of the underground organizations, the revolutionaries. Things like this, as Ramón had said, were part of the history of Mexico. But the old man was leading to something specific, and Martin's stomach was beginning to roll with a sense of foreboding.

Cuevas stared intently into his cup. "A big gun from Washington has been put on the problem. His name is Anthony Wyndham Sleep. The boys say this man is good and has done most of his hunting in South America. Because of the oil situation, the States don't want anything to get out of hand. This Sleep is going to stop it."

Cuevas pushed aside his coffee cup and laced his fingers

together in front of him on the table. His voice grew softer with a tone of compassion. "The boys tell me Paco is so deep he is only a rumor to the federal police on both sides of the border. He is just a name. But I am afraid, my fren, it is not the same with the woman Luz. She has been too bold, trusted too many people. They say Tony Sleep has leads on her and that it is only a matter of time. Maybe she does not know the whole story about this man Sleep. Maybe she needs to know everything I have heard from the boys. This is pretty fresh information."

There was silence. Martin could not believe what he found himself thinking as he looked at Cuevas' fingers, dark and leathery and sporting a diamond ring so gaudy most people would be embarrassed to wear it.

Martin didn't want to misread the message. He played the innocent, a guise he knew would be immediately apparent to Cuevas. He knew also it was the custom to approach such things obliquely.

"Is this a tip for something I can put on the front page? Do I get more?" He wanted it spelled out. Cuevas had told him a great deal already. He could tell him more.

With a casual air of disinterest, Cuevas took in the few people in the restaurant, then looked again at Martin. "I thought maybe you could get this information to her. You know lots of people too."

This time Martin's throat tightened when he spoke. "Would this woman know what to do with this information? I'm going to be sticking my neck out."

The instant Martin uttered these words he wished he hadn't. He knew this was exactly what the old man was doing, and it wasn't even any of his concern.

Cuevas' eyes went flat and emptied of pretense. His face took on an expression of gravity, and Martin knew the bullshit was over.

"This Sleep flew into the international airport the night before last. She does not know this. For the past several days she has been contacting people, people she shouldn't be talking to because they are small-time thugs, *pachucos*. She wants something moved, something too hot for anybody to touch except the shitty *pachucos* who don't have no brains and will do anything for the kind of money she is offering. They will also turn her in if they get a better offer. They don't give a damn. She is desperate and forgetting to be careful. If she keeps it up she won't last more than a few days. She is very hot property now."

Cuevas stopped. His old eyes were wrinkled deeply at the corners. "Do I need to tell you they are watching you too?"

Martin was dumbfounded. What the hell was happening? Suddenly the yellow slip of paper in his coat pocket was enormously significant. He thought how right Cuevas must be about Stella's desperation. She must have been near panic to have left the telephone number with the receptionist at the newspaper.

As the magnitude of what was happening sank in it showed on his face. Cuevas watched him with interest, then reached out and gripped Martin's wrist.

"Listen, my fren. I remember your father. If I can help, call me."

Taking his hat from the windowsill, the old man stood and laid two dollars on the table. He hesitated a moment and then walked away.

Chapter 4

Martin sat at the table in Pino's and looked out to the street where mirages were already shimmering over the pavement. The sidewalks were now giving off heat like fired kilns. He thought of Stella's situation as Cuevas had described it, and he tried to make himself believe everything he had heard the old man say.

He took the yellow telephone message from his pocket and looked at it. If what Cuevas said was true, it was incredible that Stella should have left such an open message for him. Now he understood her persistence in trying to contact him during the past several days. La Luz, for Christ's sake. It was bigger than life, but Cuevas had made it sound real enough.

Martin got up from the table and went through a pair of louvered doors to a phone booth in the hallway outside the restrooms.

A quarter got him a dial tone. He dialed the number on the yellow notepaper and the telephone rang at the other end.

"Hipp's Bubble Room. This's Ray." It was a damned tavern.

"Is Stella there?"

"Hell, I don't know. Who's this?"

"Her brother." He didn't want to leave a name. He could hear music.

"I'll take a number."

"How soon will she call back?"

"If she don't call back in five minutes she ain't here. Come on, fella. I got people waitin' for me. I'm workin'."

Martin took a chance and gave the number on the telephone and hung up. He opened the booth door so the overhead light would go off and waited. He reached for a cigarette and realized he had left them on the table. In the middle of a curse the telephone rang and he grabbed it reflexively to shut it up.

"Hello."

"Who's this?" It was a man's voice, different from the one before.

"Stella's brother."

"Who's Agapito Santoy?"

Martin was taken aback. What the hell kind of a question was this? Agapito Santoy? It was familiar. He was aware of the waiting silence on the other end of the line. Agapito Santoy. He remembered. In San Luis Potosí.

"It . . . he was a boy we played with in San Luis Potosí when we were kids. We visited there in the summers." He tried to remember more. "He lived on Clarín Street . . . had a sister, Chicho, and they—"

"Okay, okay. Call Woodlawn 6-3431 tonight at eleven o'clock."

"Wait!" Martin had to think fast. "I can't do that."

"What do you mean?"

"I've got to see her before that."

"You can't."

"Tonight may be too late. I know what's happening, and I've just learned something she's got to know. It's urgent."

There was a moment's hesitation at the other end of the line. "Where're you callin' from?"

"A pay phone."

"Okay. It'll be a few minutes. Don't leave."

Martin hung up and slumped against the wall of the booth. He was aware of beads of sweat prickling to the surface of the skin on his top lip. He took a pencil from his inside coat pocket and wrote the number the man had given him on the yellow slip. He waited, dreading the jangling he knew would surprise him.

He didn't have to wait long. Again the voice was a different one.

"Who're you calling?" it asked. There was no music in the background.

"Stella."

"You just talked of someone. What's the name?"

"Agapito Santoy."

"I don't know anybody named Stella. Just a minute." The man covered the mouthpiece and Martin could hear someone else taking the telephone.

"Hello." It was Stella.

"Stella, what in the hell's going on?"

"Martin, thank God."

"Where are you?"

"It doesn't matter. We've got to talk."

"Listen, I just heard a lot of stuff you're going to have to clear up—"

26

"Not now, we need to meet somewhere." She was tense, hurried.

"When? I need to see you soon."

"This afternoon, during rush-hour traffic . . . five o'clock. Go to Brackenridge Park and put your car in the lot on the hill overlooking the Chinese Sunken Gardens. That'll be at the west end of the skyride that goes across the park. Walk down the trail to the pagoda. Walk slowly so my people will have time to spot you. Don't go down into the garden, but follow the main trail past the pagoda and turn off to the thatched observation point that juts out from the cliffs below the pagoda. I'll be there."

"Will you be alone?"

"Yes. And listen, check your car. It may be bugged. Your telephone is tapped for sure, and you're probably being followed. Don't bring me trouble."

She broke the connection before he had a chance to reply.

Martin walked out of Pino's, stopping by his table to pick up the half pack of Camels. He was dazed. He wished he had had the presence of mind to keep Cuevas longer and to grill him. The old man knew more than he said.

He looked at his watch. It was noon and his car would be ready at Sammy's, a converted Mobil station within walking distance of the *Times* offices.

At the garage Martin wrote out a check while Sammy talked nonstop as he pawed through a stack of parts manuals looking for his receipt book. He gave Martin his receipt and continued telling him how he could make his engine run cleaner as they strolled out to the driveway.

"And, oh yeah," he said, stopping and wiping his hands on a red rag. "Your friend came by 'bout half an hour ago to pick up his sunglasses, but I don't think he found them. He looked in the side pockets but didn't turn nothin' up."

Martin stopped and stared at Sammy, who was squinting in the sun, then he looked at the battered Triumph TR-3 sitting with its top down in the front row of cars waiting to be picked up.

"Damn," he said weakly.

"What?"

Martin shook his head and got into the car. The cracked leather seats were hot. He took his own sunglasses out of the driver's side pocket and put them on. Pulling onto McCullough Avenue only half conscious of what he was doing, he headed north, preoccupied with the question of whether or not he dared believe his car had just been bugged. After the conversation with Stella he would be a fool to discount the possibility.

It suddenly occurred to him how threatening these developments were to him and Susannah. He didn't need anybody using their affair as blackmail. That would make a hell of a story, and there would be an apparent, but totally erroneous, connection between Stella's involvement with the revolutionaries in Mexico and his own affair with the Mexican ambassador's wife. What a damn coincidence. No coincidence at all, they would say.

He turned west on Olmos Drive and went down into the laurel-wooded canyons of Olmos Basin. The stonework of the embankments along the winding drive was covered with ivy, and up above him to his right he saw the big homes shaded by the forests of Spanish oaks. He slowed as he approached Olmos Dam and looked down to his left at the green expanse of the basin. The old dam, a wall of stonework resembling the Roman conduits in Spain, stretched across before him to the cliffs of Alamo Heights. Behind him the wooded ridges grew a richer green as the sun reached the meridian.

On the other side of the dam, Martin pulled sharply to the right on a dirt road and drove a hundred yards into a little cove in the trees. He turned off the motor and began searching the car. He had always thought of the old Triumph as small, but now it seemed to have an enormous chassis with an infinite number of places where a device could be hidden. He searched the obvious places first, with no luck. Then, taking a flashlight out of the car pocket, he lay on his back on the floor and looked into the maze of wires and switches behind the dashboard.

When he found it, he was surprised at its size. On the back of his speedometer casing, a lozenge-shaped aluminum disk as small as a digital watch battery was stuck with adhesive. Martin pulled it off, sat up in the car seat, and stared at it. For a sickening instant he wondered if they could tell he had found it. His first impulse was to throw it as far as he could into the canyon. Then he had a better idea.

He backed the Triumph around and drove out of the grove. Traveling slowly, he searched the quiet streets for a parked car that wasn't visible from one of the big homes. Finally, he spotted a station wagon with its windows rolled down parked in the street. He pulled up beside it and, leaning across to its open window, jammed the tiny monitor into the air-conditioning vent on the dash. He drove away.

Staying off the main streets, Martin worked his way back to his apartment. He drove the Triumph into the driveway and pulled it as close to the hedge as possible. It would be visible to a passing car for only a second. He didn't see any use in making it easy for them.

As he was putting the key in the front door, the telephone rang. He fumbled with the lock and by the time he got to the telephone it had stopped. Cursing, he flung his keys on the floor and walked into the bedroom and sprawled out on the bed.

His head was bursting, and he had to think. He wanted to talk with Dan Lee. He was on his way up in the Bureau. They had had a back-scratching arrangement for years—information for information, a news break for a lead. But if what Cuevas had said was true, Lee might be a risk he couldn't take. In fact, as Martin thought about it, Lee was most likely involved. What Stella was doing was sure as hell within his jurisdiction. He would have a file on her, probably had had one for years. Jesus Christ, what a mess. It threw a strange light on his friendship with Lee over the years. Lee would have to wait.

But there were other ways. He could talk with Susannah; she would be able to put her hands on her Francisco's files. The special ambassador would have information. And there were Martin's own underworld connections, his string of informers. That whole world traveled in the same shadows. They would know if a smuggling offer was on the streets, and they would know the background.

Martin got up and walked into the bathroom for aspirin. He took two and washed his face with cold water. While his face was buried in his cupped hands the telephone rang again. This time he caught it, his hands and face dripping.

"Yes?"

"Gallagher?" It was Jack Dimmit. "You taking the day off?"

Dimmit talked slow, too slow for most people, and Martin found it particularly irritating now.

"I was just coming in."

"Don't bother. We just got a homicide downtown. At the Alameda. Gill Millar's on his way over there now. But it's his first one and you're going to have to take him through the paces. I don't know anything about it. It just happened. Better make it fast." Then as an afterthought, "What did Cuevas have to say?"

"Nothing. Small stuff. I'll tell you later."

Martin hung up the phone and dried his face. He was in no mood to do this, and he wished he had told Dimmit he was sick and couldn't go. But he hadn't, and if he had to break in a rookie he was glad it was Millar. He was a good reporter, and eager.

The Alameda was one of the oldest theaters in the heart of

29

downtown. It was the largest in the city that played only Spanish-speaking films and therefore had an exclusively Mexican clientele. The facade of the theater was garish yellow tile with the name inlaid in green on the floor under the marquee. The billboards around the ticket booth portrayed all-Mexican casts in histrionic stills from films of adventure and romance.

When Martin arrived, the Saturday-afternoon crowd, which consisted mostly of children, was milling around the edges of the entrance, kept back by two policemen. An ambulance was parked at the curb in front of the ticket office, and two patrol cars sat across the street. He recognized the unmarked car of the two detectives.

Martin knew the uniformed policemen and spoke to them as he went into the jade-carpeted lobby dominated by two curling staircases which ascended to the left and right and joined over the concession area in the center. On this landing a homicide detective was talking to the theater manager while a loose group of theater employees, mostly serious-faced teenage girls, stood solemnly behind them.

Stepping past a life-size poster of a grinning Cantinflas in baggy pants, he started up the stairs holding on to the chrome rails supported by glass panels etched with gaudy flowers and vines. Dim colored lights glowed from behind hidden cornices overhead, lending a surreal atmosphere to the setting.

Martin spotted the city coroner on the far side of the balcony lobby talking softly to a reporter from another newspaper. He heard other voices murmuring to his right. The body would be somewhere in the balcony. As he walked toward the center ramped doorway, Martin was struck by the peculiar caramel smell of the theater. It took him back to other Saturdays, childhood Saturdays.

A cluster of reporters crowded around the entrance, and a white strobe lit the dark doorway once, twice, three times. He could tell the body was three or four rows away from the door and that most of the men were holding back. They had already seen the corpse and were hanging around waiting for a few words from the coroner or one of the detectives. He caught a glimpse of Gill's face just as Gill spotted him. Martin thought he looked particularly grim, and strangely puzzled. He hadn't been to his share of these yet.

Martin shoved past the men at the door and saw the two detectives looking down between the rows of seats. Hooper was leaning over the back of the seats and his partner, Montoya, was straddling the victim's leg, which stuck out in the aisle. He was bending down between the rows. Douglas Latham, the coroner, had come in the other door after talking with the reporter on the landing and was making his way between the seats to the corpse and the two detectives.

As Martin approached the men, Montoya looked up and spoke to the coroner.

"Hey, Lath. This looks like something out of a Charlie Chan movie. What's the deal?"

Martin was close enough now to see the leg in the aisle. It wore oxblood leather shoes and brown pin-striped pants. Stunned, he lurched the last couple of steps in a throbbing fog and looked over the theater seats into Cuevas' flat glassy eyes.

He watched, trying to keep from fainting, as Latham took a flashlight out of his hip pocket and shined it down between the seats. He let the beam rove across Cuevas' ashy face and then reached down and turned the head to the side. A long sliver of shiny stainless steel protruded from Cuevas' old leathery neck. There wasn't a single drop of blood. Martin noticed, with the unusually clear perception that often accompanies shock, that the needle had carried some of the loose neck flesh into the wound with it, causing a curious concavity around the steel quill.

"Yaw'll want it, I guess," Latham said, and reached down with his handkerchief and slid it out of Cuevas' neck. He laid it in a white envelope Hooper was holding open. "Acupuncture needle. The old man never knew what happened."

"That's not exactly the kind of hit I'm used to in this business," Hooper said, peering down at the needle.

"No shit," Montoya said, shaking his head.

"It was done so smooth his grandkids thought it was a heart attack," the coroner said. "He just slid over. Didn't know it was a homicide until we got down here. The hit man must've sat down behind him in this row of seats here. Real slick."

Both detectives nodded.

Martin turned away from the body and made his way back up the aisle. Gill stepped out onto the balcony landing with him and stood by him in silence. After a moment Martin collected his thoughts enough to speak.

"I'm sorry," he said. "You're going to have to handle this yourself, Gill. I can't deal with it." He turned and went down the stairs.

He tried to reason things out as he drove up Houston Street toward Alamo Plaza. The narrow street was a furnace and the sidewalks were thick with weekenders: a collection of tourists,

31

short-haired airmen and soldiers, and barrio toughs. Although the needle would throw them, Martin was sure the police would connect the murder to the drug world. They would assume someone had finally paid off an old debt, that, after all these years, the business had caught up with Ramón Cuevas. But Martin knew they would be wrong. There was a hell of a lot more at work here than Cuevas had told him. He was not surprised by that. He knew enough from his years on the narcotics beat to know that the plots, counterplots, and betrayals in the underworld were more complicated than anyone could sort out. He would be a fool to try to figure out what had happened to Cuevas now that the specter of revolution was an added factor.

How should he act now that he knew he was being followed? He had to assume the Triumph was dirty again. It would have been easy for someone to slap another monitor on it while he was in the theater. He could never again be sure about the car. His home phone was out. He knew Stella was right about that. It would take him an hour of evasive action before he could be relatively sure he was going to meet Stella alone.

He drove into the broad intersection at Alamo Plaza. The dun-colored mission that gave the plaza its name stood off to his right surrounded by flower gardens and smooth green lawns. Tourists milled about the mission's compound, pausing to snap pictures of each other beneath the palm trees or under the archways of the trellised arcades.

Circling the plaza, he parked the Triumph in the shade of the pecan trees across the street from the Menger Hotel. He sat for a moment watching the traffic coming into the square. It was impossible to say which of these cars might be tailing him.

Or was it? At that moment a blue rental Torino darted into the intersection from Houston Street, barely making it through the amber light. After it entered the square, it hesitated about its direction, then slowed as it drove into the tourist parking area in front of the mission. It eased toward Martin behind a row of cars, then suddenly came into view as it rounded the end of the row. The driver braked abruptly and threw the car in reverse. But instead of leaving the parking area he pulled into one of the slots. As Martin watched tensely, a man and a woman got out of the car, slung cameras over their shoulders, and walked across the flagstone courtyard to the mission. He would remember them.

After they disappeared into the chapel, Martin hurried over to the car and wrote down the license number, then crossed the

32

street in front of the Menger and entered the beehive coolness of Joske's Department Store. Its maze of aisles and display counters would be a good place to lose his tail. But first he would call Susannah.

Chapter 5

Martin walked to the men's department and asked the clerk if he could use the telephone in the dressing rooms. It was in a blind nook which couldn't be seen by anyone passing through. He waited a minute or two, then dialed. Susannah's Mexican maid answered.

"Is Mrs. Lyra in, please?" he asked.

"One moment." After a short wait he heard another receiver picked up in what he knew would be a different part of the house, then the first telephone clicked back on the receiver.

"This is Mrs. Lyra."

"Susannah."

"Well, good afternoon." Her voice was light, happy. "I was hoping you'd call."

"How does it look for tonight?"

"He's in Austin until late. I don't know how late, but his office called and said he wouldn't be leaving there until after midnight. What time tonight?"

"Earlier than that, I'm sure. I don't know yet. I'll have to call you again later."

"Martin, are you all right?"

"I'm fine. I just wanted to make sure about tonight."

"You don't sound fine. What is it?"

"I'll tell you later. I'll call you," he said, and hung up.

He left the dressing rooms and stood for a moment in the doorway scanning the crowd. The store was enormous, and the bottom floor where he stood was almost entirely open space. People were constantly shifting, standing, sitting, bending. Nothing remained the same.

Without warning he started toward the door, walking fast, then broke into a run, bumping shoppers as he came into the main aisle and burst out the side door. He cut to his left as he hit the sidewalk and stopped abruptly against the brick wall of the building, facing the Hemisfair complex. He didn't think the tail would come out the same door, but he waited for someone to round the corner at a run. Nothing happened.

He began to feel foolish. Had Stella's warning and his own gut feelings been overreactions? Now he even doubted his suspicions about the couple at the Alamo. No one was following him. Even so, he felt obligated to carry his fantasy through until he met Stella. He calmly went back into the store.

He milled around in the crowd until he reached the Spanish-tile fountain in the center of the store, where he turned down the long aisle to the Bonham Street exit. There was a bus stop there.

He waited in the shaded entrance with a small group of shoppers. When the bus pulled up he hung back watching the group queue up until he was sure he would be the last in line, then he stepped forward and got on. The pneumatic door swished shut behind him and the bus moved away from the curb. As he paid the driver he bent down and looked out the window. His heart stopped.

Running away from him down the narrow, alleylike Blum Street was the driver of the blue rental car, the man he had seen go into the Alamo a few minutes earlier. He was heading toward the parking lot.

"Stop!" Martin slapped his hand down on the bus driver's shoulder.

"Hey, man! Whatsa matter?"

"Stop, dammit! I've got to get off. Emergency."

The astonished driver slammed on the brakes, and Martin got off in the middle of the block behind the Menger Hotel. He angled across the intersection and hurried into a bookstore behind the Alamo compound. He stopped at a table of sale books next to the front window and picked up a volume, his eyes glued to the street.

Two cars passed on Bonham, then the blue sedan rounded the corner, keeping the two cars between it and the bus. He recognized the two tourists.

Jesus Christ, they *were* following him! He was dumbfounded. He had spotted them. It was luck. He might never have known. He felt his body grow sticky under his suitcoat and recognized the phenomenon of an instant cold sweat. He hadn't experienced it since Vietnam.

He was not so naive as to believe that was the end of it. They would know soon enough what had happened. And if they didn't, there would be others. They believed he would lead them to Stella; it would be a miracle if he didn't.

From where he stood he could see the cabstand at the side of the Menger Hotel . Quickly scanning the streets, he left the bookstore and ran across to the stand. As he opened the back door the cabby put down his paperback and flipped up the red meter flag.

"Geneseo Road," Martin said, "by way of New Braunfels."

New Braunfels street ran straight as an arrow from downtown to Geneseo Road. It was hilly, and a car would have to stay close to the cab if it didn't want to run the risk of losing it if it turned off on a side street at the bottom of a dip. It was a ten-minute ride and he would have plenty of time to spot a tail. If it was there, he couldn't miss it.

By the time they reached Geneseo Road, he had seen nothing to cause suspicion. But he wasn't satisfied. Geneseo also ran straight before it turned into the winding drives of Terrell Hills. The homes were expensive. Traffic was infrequent. Martin asked the cabby to pull over to the curb and told him to make a few blocks and come back for him in ten minutes. Then he got out and stepped behind a tall hedge to wait.

The only car Martin saw was the cab coming back for him at the end of ten minutes. When he got back in he told the driver to take him to Brackenridge Park.

Stella had chosen the time and the place wisely. The traffic was heavy and the park teemed with afternoon picnickers and tourists. When they finally reached the center of the park, Martin got out between the miniature railroad depot and the entrance to the zoo and moved across the intersection with the crowd to the eastern terminal of the skyride. He bought a ticket and glanced at his watch as he climbed into the first vacant gondola. By the time he reached the other end he would be on time.

As the gondola climbed the cable, he looked down into the park at the narrow white trails that occasionally came into view through gaps in the heavy woods. The lush vegetation was mixed with Mexican agave and yucca plants holding their clusters of creamy blossoms on rangy stalks high above the lower brush. Abruptly the gondola swung over the enormous well of the sunken garden. A waterfall cradled in the limestone cliffs fed a network of streams and ponds blooming with aquatic plants and bordered with stone walks.

At the western terminal, he got out of the gondola and walked down the path to the shade of the pagoda. He lingered there, his hands in his pockets in an effort to appear casual. After a few moments he ambled farther along the main trail until he came to a wooden bridge which led out to the thatched observation hut. The hut was small, and once he got on the bridge he spotted Stella standing with her back to him staring out across the treetops toward the city.

As he entered the shelter, she turned toward him. She didn't smile, and she seemed frightened even behind the dark lenses of her sunglasses. As she spoke he was saddened to catch the familiar musky aroma of scotch on her breath.

"Real cloak-and-dagger stuff, huh, Martin?"

"Real cloak-and-dagger," he said.

"We should have some time to talk here, I think. No rush just yet."

They sat facing each other on the wooden bench which ran around the inside of the hexagonal hut. Stella returned her gaze to the city's skyline beyond the enormous sprawling park.

"Why don't you start by telling me who your visitor was and what he had to say?" she said with affected detachment.

"I'm not sure I'm the one who should be talking. You need to clear up a few things for me too. I'm a little touchy," he added pointedly.

Stella turned her face to him then and smiled behind her sunglasses. She was a handsome woman, like her cousin, Martin's mother. She was thin, with strong Indian features molded from smooth olive skin. Her hair was as black as carbon, and wiry, and Martin noticed fibers of brittle gray fanning out from the crown at the peak of her brow. She wore a simple sundress and sandals.

"A little touchy," she said in a throaty half-laugh. "Well, I can understand that. But you're going to have to go first."

Martin watched her closely. He wanted to see how she was going to react. He wished she would take off the damn sunglasses.

He laid it out flat and quick. "This morning just before lunch a man came to the office wanting to talk to me. He told me about El Gobierno Agrario Tradicional de Oaxaca, about bank robberies, about a body on the beach at Sanchez Magallanes, about Paco and Luz and how Luz was desperate to get something smuggled out of the States. So desperate that she was risking her neck contacting nickel-and-dime *pachucos* because she was too hot for anyone higher up to touch." He paused for a three-count, then said, "And he told me of a man named Anthony Wyndham Sleep who arrived in town the night before last."

Stella's face was rigid when he finished, and she didn't reply for a moment. When she did speak her voice was dull.

"You have a remarkable friend. Did he go into details?"

37

"No, but it wasn't difficult to make a few deductions."

"And Paco?"

"He hadn't any idea, and he said no one else did either."

Visibly relieved, Stella took a cigarette from her purse and lit it with an expensive gold lighter, which she began turning over and over in her hands.

"We had nothing to do with the engineer's death in Coatzacoalcos. That was the Brigada Blanca. The tattoo was a stupid and crude effort to indict us. It had a certain degree of success."

Stella swung her dangling foot nervously. "Look, I'm not going to give you a lecture about my politics, but I do want to put some things in perspective for you. Mexico is on the brink of tremendous changes. We've gone from being a nation with unlimited hope because of its oil reserves to a nation with no hope because a corrupt government could not deal effectively with a crisis they should have been able to foresee. All that big talk about how the oil was going to turn Mexico into the Kuwait of the Western World has come to nothing. Instead things are worse, much worse. Most of the nation still consists of Juan Pedros who'll wash your gringo windshield with a wadded newspaper for a couple of centavos or work their asses off all day for less money than you'd spend for a hamburger and a movie.

"The U.S. smells blood. With the help of the CIA and the multinationals, it has its fingers in things behind the scenes. The carpetbaggers are working overtime and, unfortunately, they're getting a lot of help from Mexicans who are willing to sell out their own people for a Swiss bank account."

Stella paused and removed her sunglasses, as though she wished to remove the distance they created between what she wanted to say and Martin's perception of it. Her eyes, as dark as the amber resin of the mesquite tree whose lacy leaves hung in the stillness behind her, glistened from wells of flesh purpled by strain and exhaustion.

"Then there're the Marxists. Ever since Cuba they've been watering at the mouth over Latin America. Now the Sandinista junta in Nicaragua has finally accepted Soviet-Cuban technical and economic assistance. Thousands of Soviet 'advisers' have made homes there. Honduras is a major conduit for Soviet arms smuggled to Salvadoran leftists. El Savador is doomed. In Guatemala leftist dissenters have dangerously weakened the government. All these countries are the back door to Mexican oil fields.

"But for Mexico, there are other alternatives. We want to keep the U.S. *and* the Marxists out of our politics. All we want is to be allowed to make our own decisions about our future without foreign coercion."

She stopped and looked toward the trail that led to the sunken garden. The sounds of the crowded park drifted up the wooden pathways to them. The trees were alive with whistling and screeching birds, obscuring for Martin whatever signal Stella received from across the narrow footbridge. He looked too as she turned her head and saw a man walking away from them.

"Stella," he said, turning back to her, "What's going on? What's this all about?"

She ground out the half-smoked cigarette with her sandal and glanced toward the pathway again, seeming more tired than ever. "GATO is a powerful organization. It's grown silently but quickly, and what you're seeing now is a last-ditch effort to stop us before we topple the Mexican government."

Martin had expected it. "You're insane! This isn't 1910. Those days are gone."

"Listen to me! I haven't got much time," she snapped. "Limón is the most corrupt Mexican president in decades. His government is Byzantine. The whole world is watching to see what Mexico is going to do. If this resource slips away, if the wealth continues to disappear through corrupt hands into foreign bank accounts, there will be no second chance. Limón is leading us down a familiar dark street, and we don't want to go. For a while Mexico was actually developing a middle class. There was hope. But for a long time now things have grown worse, like the old days. The gap between the rich and poor is awesome. The Juan Pedros find themselves in a corner of despair, and the once-developing middle class is furious at having it all jerked away from them. Rebellion, real killing in a real civil war, is on everyone's lips. If a sensible government cannot be formed to give the masses hope for the future, the people will take the future into their own hands. It will set Mexico back a hundred years and give the U.S. the chance to tighten its grip. The Marxists will retaliate and Mexico will become a battlefield of the superpowers. Regardless of who eventually wins, Mexico will lose."

Stella was speaking rapidly now, one hand tightened into a small fist emphasizing her words with sharp thrusts to her thigh.

"It *must* not happen. There are those who will not *let* it happen. Limón knows, and he's scared."

Martin watched her whip her anger to a white heat that could be cooled best with a hefty glass of neat Passport. No, Stella had not changed in a decade, not in a hundred years or a thousand even. She was a born revolutionary; the passion for it had always driven her, the fervency had been there even as a child. As he looked at her now he could almost see the high-strung little girl behind the mask of tension.

"What's going to happen to you?" he asked. Suddenly the more spectacular questions were meaningless to him.

Her face softened, and she smiled as though she knew it would be this one, of all the questions he could ask. "I'm trying to leave the States," she said. "I've done all I can from here. I've been found out by the people who count. It's time to go . . . if I haven't waited too long."

"Sleep?"

She nodded. "We've known about him, of course. Tony Sleep is infamous among Latin American dissidents. We had heard rumors he might be put onto us. Little pieces of information were adding up, but I didn't know for sure until you told me. I suppose it was inevitable."

"How much does he know? Obviously he's got enough to pick you up on sight."

Stella looked at him evenly. "He's not going to *arrest* me, Martin," she said coldly. "Tony Sleep is an *assassin.*"

Martin gaped at her in disbelief.

"It's true. You see why I was surprised you even knew his name? The man is very deep. Your visitor who warned me through you was taking a big risk. I hope he knows his business very well."

"Stella, I can't believe this," Martin said. He stood, walked to the railing of the hut, and looked out over the park, where the late-afternoon sun had stretched the shadows of the trees into spreading pools of blue and purple.

"You'd better believe it," she said.

"What do you mean by 'very deep'?" Martin asked, but he already knew the answer.

"I mean *CIA.*"

Martin turned to face her again. "How in the *hell* did you get into something like this?"

Stella reached for her purse and fished out another cigarette, which she lit with trembling hands. It sobered Martin to see those hands. He didn't attribute the trembling entirely to the scotch.

"There are two kinds of revolutionaries," she began. "The terrorists, who want to draw attention to their causes with kidnappings and assassinations. The media are their weapons as much as bombs and guns. Faced with this kind of approach the legal authorities have no choice but to make every effort to capture them and bring them to trial. They've got to prove to the public they can deal with these people. Public crime, public justice.

"The second kind of revolutionary operates silently. They believe far more can be accomplished behind the scenes. That's the way we operate, or did. But secrecy compounds the danger. Since there's no public anger to assuage, no public justice is required. Assassins are brought in. Their prey is unknown and their work is unknown except to a small number of intelligence branches. Silence becomes a double-edged sword."

Stella paused to let this sink in, then added, "There's one additional thing that makes Sleep so dangerous. He has numerous contacts with the secret police of most Latin American countries and has worked with the government death squads in Argentina and Chile. They're all scum like him. In Mexico he'll have the cooperation of the Brigada Blanca, the Mexican equivalent of the Gestapo. They're ruthless predators who specialize in 'controlling' dissidents. They're such animals the Limón government denies their existence. With their help, Sleep will be going about his business like a mad dog."

Martin shook his head incredulously. "You've been in this for years, haven't you? You're up to your neck in it."

"You're impossible, Martin." Her voice was tight, almost strident.

"All right! Fine! Do you know anything about Sleep except that he's deadly and he's after you? You have a photograph? Anything?"

"Of course not. Nothing like that ever exists. We hear he works with two other people. They're a team. They're all fluent in Spanish. I don't know. You hear a lot of crap. Apparently they're easy to underestimate. They're supposed to be the best."

"Do you remember Ramón Cuevas?" Martin asked.

Stella nodded.

"He was the one who told me of Sleep and all the rest of it. That was late this morning. At two-thirty he was killed at the Alameda Theater. I saw him afterward. He had a twelve-inch needle sticking out of his neck."

"Oh, my God!" she gasped.

Martin stood looking at her as she gazed into the woods momentarily lost in thought.

"Why did you want to see me, Stella?"

She raised her head, not even trying to hide the fear in her eyes. "I told you I was leaving the States. I could go tonight except for one thing. There's a package, a briefcase; I've got to make sure it gets into Mexico safely. It's important, too important for me to take out with me. There's a good chance I'll be caught, and we can't afford to have the briefcase intercepted. I can't leave San Antonio until I know it's been taken care of."

"You want me to take it?"

"Take the responsibility for making the arrangements." She stood, not giving him time to respond. "Martin, listen to me. We've spent months and hundreds of thousands of dollars getting this together. The whole thing might as well have not existed if I don't get that package to Mexico. You're mobile, you can arrange things. You know people outside the underworld who wouldn't be automatically suspect."

"What's *in* the briefcase?"

"It's just *papers*." Her tone pleaded for him to understand.

"Oh, you're incredible! You're asking me to involve innocent people in this damned game and you won't even tell me—"

A sharp whistle stopped him. At the end of the narrow bridge that led to the path, a stocky Mexican stood in the light-dappled shade and motioned to them. He wore dress slacks with a short-sleeved shirt hanging loose at the waist.

Stella waved him back impatiently. It was clear she was staying too long.

"Martin, listen quickly," she said. "Here's a new telephone number. Don't write it down, memorize it." She quoted the number to him twice, slowly. "Call me at this number just as you did before, only call on the quarter hour. We won't answer it otherwise. This number will be good until noon tomorrow. You'll have to contact me before then to get the new number."

She turned and picked up her purse from the bench, then faced him, pausing before she spoke.

"One last thing. About the ambassador's wife . . ."

Martin's stomach knotted and he braced himself. It seemed impossible that she should know.

"It's no secret. Don't kid yourself about that. She's all right; I'm not saying she's not. But that house is wired from top to bottom. There have never been any secrets there. Be careful."

She put the purse strap over her shoulder and brushed back a wiry strand of brindled hair that had fallen across her face.

"Get in touch with me soon," she said. "There's so very little time now."

He didn't have a chance to reply before she turned and started

42

across the footbridge. When she reached the trail she was joined by the man Martin had just seen. Before they were out of sight, a second man fell in behind them. He was the last to be swallowed by the closing shadows and the woods.

Chapter 6

Too much had happened too fast. The questions were coming to him rapid-fire as he pushed past the late-afternoon strollers on the narrow trail leading down to the center of the park.

How did Stella know about his affair with Susannah? And how did she know about the bugs in the Lyra home? It sounded as if the place had been tapped by everybody, GATO, the FBI, the CIA, maybe even the Mexican government itself. Mexican-U.S. relations had deteriorated seriously. Martin found GATO's plans for Limón terrifying. Whatever they had in mind, military coup, assassination, blackmail, the briefcase played a crucial part. But the pieces of the puzzle were scattered. And a lot of them were missing.

Martin was walking in the crowds again as they poured out of the zoo and the sunken garden toward the parking lots. The sun had fallen and dusk was covering the park in shades of mauve and gray, turning the trees black and making silhouettes of buildings. He crossed the bridge that spanned the canal and heard the caretaker chaining the paddleboats for the night. The park was emptying fast, and the headlights of cars threw broken cones of light through the woods as they meandered out in docile winding lines.

He wanted to see Susannah, but he decided it was useless to go back and get the Triumph if he wanted to keep his movements secret. There was a Ford agency with a rental service that stayed open until ten o'clock across the street from the Witte Museum. It was only a few blocks away.

At the agency a college student begrudgingly moved aside his chemistry texts to let Martin fill out the leasing papers. He got a Mustang and pulled onto Broadway and headed north to Alamo Heights. For the second time that day he crossed Olmos Dam and looked down into the sequined depth of the basin. The lights of homes sparkled along the cliffs as he turned into El Prado Drive and followed it until he entered Paseo Encinal.

Even in the dark he could make out the spacious lawns and the cultivated hedgerows that provided privacy barriers between the estates. Hefty stone walls covered with vines ran beneath the sprawling Spanish oaks, and everywhere the odor of freshly mown grass and watered lawns hung in the summer air.

Martin downshifted the Mustang and pulled through a pair of iron gates that opened off the street. He cut his lights and followed the familiar curve of brick drive along a rolling lawn to an elegant Tuscan home, its white walls and red-tiled roof lit by spotlights hidden in the shrubbery next to the house. Instead of continuing on the drive to the front door, he turned through a gap in the privet and drove into an arbored niche. He parked the car in his usual place among the garden tools and locked it.

As he came around the corner of the gardener's shed a figure stepped out of the shadows in front of him.

"Hold it," the man said.

Martin's heart stopped. He couldn't see the man's face, but he could tell he was wearing a business suit and tie. His hands were held chest-high, palms open to show they were empty. Martin heard a slight noise behind him, and he spun around as a second man stepped out slightly crouching, anticipating an aggressive movement.

"We just want to talk," the first man said cautiously. "There's no problem. Everything's legal. You'll be back here in an hour. We'll let you out at the gate and you can walk up to the house as if you had just arrived."

"Who are you?" Martin's voice was hoarse.

"It doesn't matter," the man said. "You coming?"

It was an absurd question.

The three of them walked through the gap in the privet and headed down the brick drive to the front gate. At the gate the first man took a penlight out of his pocket and stepped into the street and signaled. Two blocks away a car parked under a palm tree turned on its lights and started toward them. When it got to the gate Martin saw it was a late-model station wagon with a driver and one man in the back seat. As it stopped, the back door opened and Martin got in beside Dan Lee.

"Oh, shit," Martin said, relieved, and slumped down in the seat as the car pulled away, leaving the two agents behind.

"Sorry for the dramatics," Lee said, a slight smile reflected in his oriental eyes. "But we couldn't find you all day. So we . . . well, I knew you sometimes came here."

"Yeah," Martin said sourly.

"Don't worry about the Mustang. You'll be back before the ambassador. I'm sorry to intrude this way, but there was no choice."

Lee pulled a fortune cookie out of a small paper sack in his lap, broke it open , and popped half of it into his mouth. It was a habit. He faithfully read every fortune, then carelessly left these little tags of his personal destiny lying around behind him wherever he went.

"Want one?" He held the sack out to Martin.

Martin took one and cracked it open. He had known Lee since he had been a new street agent for the Bureau and Martin was a college-fresh reporter. Their highly successful agreement had evolved naturally as each became wise to the real world of their professions. Martin had inherited a gold mine of snitches from his father, and when their information was coupled with Lee's from the other side of the fence, he began to break good front-page copy.

As for Lee, he could well afford to leak a breaking story in exchange for first-class street tout. His sources soon became the envy of veteran agents. His arrangement with Martin became more sophisticated as the years passed and the two men developed a genuine friendship. They knew each other well, too well for either of them to be comfortable now.

Lee finished his cookie and set the sack behind their seat. He dusted his hands of crumbs, folded his arms across his chest, and turned to Martin.

"We're in a bit of a tight spot, Gallagher."

Martin had been wondering how Lee would start it off. It wasn't particularly graceful.

"Why don't you set the scene for me, Dan," Martin said sarcastically.

"That'll be easy: Your sister's in a hell of a lot of trouble."

Martin was suddenly furious.

"Goddam you! What is this? What kind of a friend are you, anyway? You muscle your way into my private life like Elliot Ness, throw out a cheap apology, offer me a fortune cookie, tell me my sister's in trouble, and then say 'we' have a problem. I'm not sure I like the way you're handling this.

"You say Stella's in trouble?" Martin's voice was quavering with anger and he was trying to keep it down. "Well, we've known each other *ten* years and you never said a word about it up to now. Maybe something could have been done about it if you'd spoken up a little sooner. Where have you *been,* 'friend'? If she's in trouble you ought to feel like the original Chinese Judas."

"That's all right," Lee said quickly, making a pacifying gesture with his hands. "That's all right," he repeated, this time catching the eye of the agent behind the wheel, who was staring hard at Martin. The tension was thick enough to smell.

"I understand," he said. "I apologize for the lack of tact."

"How are you going to apologize for ten years of buggering?"

"You've got it wrong, Martin. I didn't know anything about GATO until two years ago, when I got the promotion to field supervisor and they put me on special to counterintelligence and internal security. It was incidental stuff at first, but it grew. By the time my agents had worked their way up to Stella it was too late for anything like a warning. That was just six months ago."

"I don't believe you."

"It's the truth. I was shocked when we finally peeled back Luz's identity, but there was nothing I could do. I'll level with you. I had to put you through the treatment. There were some anxious weeks while I went about the touchy work of investigating you too. Washington wasn't going to take my word for it."

Lee paused and glanced out the window. The driver was taking them along the ridges of Contour Drive. Martin saw Lee's hooded eyes and his smooth, beardless face in the beams of an approaching car. He was looking at the homes. He turned back to Martin. "It was during that investigation that I learned about you and Susannah Lyra."

Martin turned away and shook his head.

"Look, Martin, I'm sorry, but we have to talk about this. It's best just to come out with it. Okay? When I found out about that it scared the hell out of me. It looked, you know, like you could be doing it for ulterior motives. Mrs. Lyra would have access to a lot of information GATO would find useful."

"Come on, Lee."

"Look, I'm just telling you how it built up. I'm trying to level with you, okay? You've got to admit it's an unfortunate coincidence. It took a while but we finally cleared it up. That wasn't easy, because nobody could believe you really didn't know what was going on with your sister. I mean, you're an investigative reporter."

Martin gave a cynical snort, but Lee ignored it.

"So we closed the file on you. Everybody was pretty satisfied until today. You had a fast day today."

No kidding, Martin thought. He wondered how much Lee knew. Maybe he didn't know as much as he wanted Martin to believe. Maybe he was hoping Martin would fill in some gaps. If that wasn't it, why had he picked him up? Martin would make Lee pull it out of him, and in the process he might find out some things himself.

"Where'd you go after you left the Alameda Theater?" Lee asked.

"I took a bus to a car-rental agency."

"You took a bus all right. My people followed it all the way to North Star Mall before they realized you weren't on it. You got a couple of agents in hot water."

"I didn't know you used women."

"What?"

"Women agents."

"I don't have any. What'd you do, pick out some gal in a crowd and think she was a tail?" Lee smiled.

"I guess I did," Martin conceded, and mentally noted that that cleared up one question. The pair at the Alamo weren't Bureau agents.

"Did you meet Stella after our people lost you?" Lee asked the question as if he really expected Martin to respond.

"If you picked me up to grill me, this is an odd way to do it."

"How much do you know about GATO?"

"Very little."

"What'd you and Cuevas talk about this morning?" Lee asked patiently.

"He's always giving me tips."

"It's a little awkward for you that he was killed just a few hours after you had a long talk with him, isn't it?"

"He lived longer than anyone could have expected considering his business."

"He'd been out of that business for years."

"You're never out of that business."

Lee sighed. He leaned forward, "Ben, pull off in the woods when you find a nook."

The station wagon slowed as it came around a curve above the canyon, then pulled off on the caliche shoulder on the canyon side of the street. The driver edged into the trees as far as he could, then stopped. Without saying a word he got out and closed the door, leaving them alone.

Lee reached forward and folded down a little table built into the back of the front seat. A light automatically came on, illuminating its surface. He took a manila folder from his briefcase and pulled out several 8 × 10 black-and-white glossies and laid them on the little table.

"Look at these," he said.

In the stark, documentary style of police photography, the pictures were of a man's water-bloated body wedged into the sand at the frothy rim of an ebbing tide. They were repulsive photographs, showing the swollen corpse nearly bursting the seams of its death clothes, its arms like tight sausages, its face cherubically fat with its mouth opened in a perfect circle. In a few of the photographs Martin could see glimpses of a tropical shoreline. The last three pictures were close-ups of the victim's abdomen. Clumsily tattooed across the top of the distorted navel was the sprawling figure of a leaping cat.

Martin's heart sank.

"The victim is Charles Boren," Lee said. "He was an internationally respected chemical engineer who had been acting as a consultant to Pemex. This picture was taken Monday morning where his body had washed ashore near a little fishing village in the southern Mexican state of Tabasco. The autopsy showed he had been tortured, his genitals were discolored from electrical shock, and that he died from heart failure. He'd been dead less than forty-eight hours when some Mexican fisherman found him."

Lee was silent until Martin stopped looking at the photographs and leaned back in the seat.

"Martin, I'm going to give you more credit than you're giving me," Lee said. "I'm going to tell you as much as I can about what's happening, from my perspective. I'm not a sentimental man, but I wouldn't be doing it for anybody else. It's as far as I'll be able to go in this situation before it turns to strictly business."

There was nothing for Martin to do but listen.

"First of all, we don't believe for a minute GATO is responsible for what you saw in those photographs. It's not typical of the way they operate. They've always steered clear of that sort of thing. We believe it was a set-up by Limón's Brigada Blanca to bring U.S. resources to their effort to wipe out GATO.

"Normally the murder of a U.S. citizen in a foreign country doesn't move mountains, but there's nothing normal about what's going on here. The Limón government reacted vigorously to Boren's murder. Obviously it was GATO, they say. These terrorist activities make Mexico look like a two-bit banana republic, they say, and it's largely our fault because we're allowing GATO's major financial resource to operate with impunity here in Texas.

"On Tuesday, the Mexican ambassador in Washington requested an emergency meeting with the President and the Secretary of State. Speaking for President Limón, he suspended their petroleum negotiations with us until we, in his words, 'clean up' GATO north of the border. When the meeting was over, the President was livid and the Secretary of State rattled the chain that shook up both intelligence agencies all the way down to the janitors."

Lee reached back and retrieved his sack of fortune cookies. He cracked one open, leaned over to the light, and read the fortune. Shaking his head ruefully, he put the tag of paper in his pocket.

"Washington wants scalps down here, lots of them," Lee continued. "As usual when the administration gets involved in field projects, they screw up everything for the guys who actually have to run it. This time they did two things: First, they ordered the CIA and the FBI to 'cooperate' in the GATO affair. Share intelligence briefs, data, approaches, in order to bring this ordeal to a close as soon as possible. That caused some heart attacks among the rank and file. Of course, the paper jockeys in both agencies are making it look good on paper, but the competition between the two agencies is worse than ever now. The important thing is, the CIA is now able to operate legally in domestic affairs. It's a damn circus.

"Second, the State Department arranged for the FBI to work closely with the Mexican *federales*. We've had to bring them into our organization as advisers and consultants. Everybody's bending over backward to cooperate with everybody else.

"But the most unusual thing that came out of that meeting in the oval office is that both governments agreed to throw the border wide open to the three intelligence agencies. Each can operate, under the auspices of the host agency, with full legal jurisdiction on either side of the border. There are no diplomatic restraints until GATO is wiped out."

Martin thought of Stella's trembling hands and began to understand. She, like Cuevas, had known more than she told.

"That's the background," Lee said, chewing the last of the fortune cookies. "You have any questions?"

"Is that all?"

"No."

Lee gathered the photographs, put them back in the envelope, and returned the envelope to his briefcase. He closed the folding table and turned off the light. "Let's go for a walk."

As Martin got out of the station wagon, Lee stepped out on the other side and said a few words to the agent leaning against the front fender. Then he came around the back of the car, and they walked together back to Contour Drive, which at this point ran its winding course several blocks without streetlights.

"I have that car swept for bugs about once a week," Lee

confided as they began walking, "but I'm never comfortable in it. I've planted too many of them myself.

"What I'm going to tell you now will make your life worthless if the wrong people find out you know. But if you keep your mouth shut and use the information right, it could save your life."

Martin wondered what kind of emotional strain this was costing Lee. Whatever the stress, it wasn't showing. They could have been walking down the block for a hamburger. He wondered too if Lee was setting him up somehow.

"About three months ago a CIA cryptanalyst monitoring Soviet communications in The Hague was startled when he came across an incidental reference to 'the Tabasco Plan.' The cipher system used in the reference was not normally employed in his sector, so he sent it to the Latin American office, where it was cross-referenced with those systems occurring most frequently in Mexican exchanges. They hit a gold mine. The Mexico City/Moscow communications yielded an entirely new system they hadn't known existed. They also uncovered a remarkable exchange between the two governments.

"Moscow has made overtures to Mexico City regarding the purchase of huge volumes of petroleum on behalf of the Soviet satellites. The price offered is considerably more than the OPEC scale and guarantees certain trade advantages for Mexican-produced commodities. The financial exchange between Mexico and the Soviet satellites would be an enormous boost to Mexico's outsized trade deficit. The advantage for the Soviets of having a 'most-favored' trade relationship with a U.S. common-border nation is obvious.

"Unbelievably, President Limón responded favorably to the Soviet proposals. Last week a meeting took place in Havana between representatives of both governments, and a preliminary trade agreement was drawn up. At a tremendous risk, the CIA was able to obtain a copy of that document. Its possession would have been invaluable to us in terms of . . . diplomatic leverage."

"Would have been?" Martin asked.

"The papers were intercepted before they even got them out of Havana," Lee said. "Even more incredible is that GATO agents ended up with them. When the documents left Cuba a few days ago they didn't go to Mexico, but to the GATO people here in San Antonio. We're sure of this. We think they engineered the whole thing from here, which means Paco is one hell of an intelligence operator."

This was the first time Paco had been mentioned, and Martin

51

noticed that Lee assumed he knew who he was. Was Lee testing him? He decided to let it go.

"Do the Soviets, or the Mexicans, know the negotiations have been copied?"

"No. Which makes our cooperation with the *federales* all the more delicate. Not only are we trying to squash GATO, we're also trying to recover the documents without letting the *federales* know what we're doing."

Martin was trying to keep up with the ramifications of what Lee was telling him in light of what he already knew from Stella.

"I assume the State Department wants the documents for some kind of blackmail to force the Mexicans into an oil agreement. But what value do the documents have for GATO?"

"It's not 'blackmail,'" Lee corrected, "it's 'diplomatic leverage.' The State Department could confront the Mexicans with the documents and suggest they back away from the Soviet proposals and offer us a very comfortable arrangement in return. If they didn't, they would risk our diplomatic and economic wrath, which can be considerable. It could be disastrous for them at a time when they need to proceed cautiously.

"GATO's intentions are not so different, except where we're concerned. They want to force Limón to resign. They know that with the right kind of enticements, he will sell himself to either the U.S. or the Soviets. As far as they're concerned, it's a losing deal either way. The U.S. knows that if GATO replaces Limón with their own man, he won't be someone the U.S. can deal with. Most likely he'll be uncompromising, independent. Not good for us."

They had walked until they saw the first streetlight ahead of them. Lee guided them across the street so that they approached it in a long shadow cast by a row of pecan trees.

"The point of all this is that you're in the middle of a hotbed of cutthroats," Lee said, stopping where the edge of the shadow met the spill of the streetlight. "The CIA has lost face by being outwitted in Havana. They're going to pull out all the stops to correct that. The FBI feels the competition keenly and resents the CIA's operating on their turf. They're not about to let themselves be outmaneuvered in their own territory. In addition, both agencies have to work with the *federales*, actually the Brigada Blanca, a very rough bunch of agents by anybody's standards."

Lee looked at Martin. "I just wanted you to be aware of the scope of this. If you're . . . involved, I don't want there to be any misconceptions about where everybody stands. You can be on

52

the wrong side, or the right side, or you can stay out of it. But after tonight, it's wide open. Nobody gets special treatment."

"And how the hell am I going to stay out of it?" Martin asked.

"Just stay *out* of it. Keep your hands on the table. Quit trying to shake tails like some kind of superspy. You're going to have to live with them and a lot of other shit until this blows over. I'm telling you so you'll know." Lee was speaking earnestly.

Martin could tell he didn't want to have to work against him; it was a bizarre conversation.

"What do you know about Cuevas' death?" Martin asked. He wanted to be sure he knew what had happened.

"Martin." Lee's voice betrayed impatience for the first time. "*I* didn't talk with him for two hours before he was shot. *You* tell *me!*"

"Shot?"

"Or stabbed, or choked, or however they did it. I don't know! I've been out of the office all afternoon. I just heard about it. I haven't seen the report yet."

Martin hesitated. "Then you don't know what happened to him? You don't know who did it?"

"What do you mean? Of course not."

Martin didn't know what to think. It was incredible that the CIA had kept the Bureau in the dark about turning loose their Latin American hit team. Should he tell Lee what he knew? Lee would put two and two together when he saw the lab report anyway. He would know in the morning. But should Martin let Lee know that *he* knew? What were the advantages? The disadvantages? He had to decide. Lee had already sensed something and was waiting.

"What is it, Gallagher?" he snapped.

Martin tossed the coin. "You ever hear of Tony Sleep?"

Lee looked at Martin, stunned, his oriental eyes expressionless as the glass eyes of a mannequin.

The headlights of the station wagon rounded the curve toward them. Lee saw them and quickly grabbed Martin by the arm, gripping it with a fierceness that surprised them both.

"Listen," he said sharply. "If that's true, you'll have to make up your mind tonight which way you want to play this. I can't give you any longer. You know too damn much!"

The tires of the station wagon crunched in the gravel as it pulled up beside them and stopped.

Chapter 7

They rode back to Paseo Encinal in silence, each staring out his window at the dark street. Lee had plunged into somber preoccupation, and Martin could not decide if he had done the right thing telling him about Tony Sleep. It complicated the situation for both of them.

As the station wagon stopped at the gate of the Lyra residence, the two agents stepped out of the shadow of the wall and opened the door for Martin. He put one foot out of the car, then turned to Lee.

"Thanks," he said. "I know you didn't have to do it."

Lee nodded. "It's okay."

The heels of Martin's shoes clacked against the red bricks as he followed the curving driveway to the front of the house. He stood at the arched front door between two orange trees in enormous terra-cotta urns and rang the bell. Susannah's maid, Victoria, let him in, told him that Mrs. Lyra was by the pool, and disappeared. He stepped up from the entranceway into the sprawling main room with white walls and vaulted ceiling. A hazy glow fell from an octagonal skylight across the center of the room, where a woven rug of white llama's wool was the centerpiece for an arrangement of silk parchment-white sofas. The only other light issued indirectly from tall display cases filled with pre-Columbian artifacts on glass shelves which loomed on either side of the room, testimonies to Francisco Lyra's devotion to the past.

Across the room a sparkling glass wall revealed a wide arched gallery running the entire length of the U-shaped house. Martin walked to the wall and looked across the lighted lawn to the pool which hung on a cliff overlooking the slopes of the basin. Next to the pool's edge, wearing only the bottom half of a white Brazilian *tanga*, lay Susannah Lyra, trailing one hand back and forth in the limpid water illuminated from the bottom. Her light taffy hair fell across a smooth tanned back toward the two shallow dimples above her buttocks. Her long legs were extended full-length against the blue Mexican tile that rimmed the pool.

He pushed a section of the glass wall and the panel swung open, letting him step out onto the flagstone walkway of the arcade. Without warning a caged cockatoo beside one of the arches shrieked a sustained wild cry, which was immediately taken up by five others in separate cages along the gallery. Martin hated the damned birds. They cried as if they were dying every time he got around them.

He moved quickly away toward the pool.

"One guess who's walking across the grass preceded by the cry of the pink *cacatúa*," Susannah said without looking around as he approached.

Martin took off his coat and flung it over the back of a bamboo chair. He loosened his tie and sat down beside her. She kept her head turned toward the water. The *tanga* revealed the cleavage of her buttocks and a trail of sun-bleached peach fuzz going up the small of her back.

"Good evening," she said lazily.

"That's debatable," he said, taking off his shoes and socks. He saw now the sweaty glass of gin and lime cradled next to her hip near the edge of the pool. Tossing his shoes back toward the bamboo chair, he rolled his pants up to his knees and swung his legs over the edge of the pool into the water.

Susannah sighed and slowly raised herself on her elbows to look at him for the first time. She shook her hair from her face and smiled as she offered him the sweaty glass. The top of her *tanga* lay small and white beneath her breasts. He candidly surveyed her body and then looked into her eyes. They had never seemed so green as they did now beside the pool.

"Have a sip," she said. "Victoria's going to bring out cold fruit and melons before she leaves. She's got tonight and tomorrow off. It'll be just the two of us until..."

Martin drank from the cool glass and looked past the lighted shafts of the palm trees toward the sparkling blue lights in the basin. A soft breeze came up over the ridges of the valley and gently rattled the palm fronds as it drifted across the lawn.

Susannah looked at him. "Tie this thing before I get up, will you?" He did, and she sat up and swung her legs into the pool beside his. She put her hands down on either side of her and moved her legs back and forth in the water.

"Are you hungry?" Susannah asked. "Have you eaten dinner?"

"Yes," he said, "and no."

The tone of his voice hadn't been right, and out of the corner of his eye he saw Susannah glance at him questioningly. She looked away to her feet in the water as he turned to her. She was a delicious woman, he thought, and the years had done nothing except enhance her beauty. When they were in college he had thought her beauty could not be surpassed. The intervening thirteen years had not proved him wrong.

The cockatoos had quieted down, and Victoria came from the house with their trays. She put them on an umbrella table a little way from the pool and returned to the house.

"Come on," Susannah said. "I'm famished."

They stood and walked to the table, where Victoria had thrown a silk robe over the back of a chair. Susannah slipped it on, gave it a quick cinch around her waist, and they sat down to eat.

From a liquor cart beside the table Susannah replenished her drink and made an identical one for Martin. They ate in silence for a few minutes before Martin leaned back in his chair and stared at her. She looked back at him with a slice of avocado poised halfway to her mouth.

"What are you thinking about?" she asked.

"About how you should have married me instead."

Susannah put down the bite of avocado and took up her drink. Martin knew she was collecting her patience. She knew what was coming. Actually he hadn't intended to bring it up, but as he watched her he found the anger difficult to suppress. He was finding it increasingly difficult to "share" her with Lyra. In the beginning of the affair, he had felt he had finally stolen her back from Francisco after all these years, but the triumph had gradually faded as he realized there was no end in sight for the secrecy they were obliged to keep. The relationship had not progressed beyond its initial desperation.

"We've been over this so many, many times," she said wearily.

She was right. They had, and Martin still didn't understand it. He never had. He had understood the choice she had made between them thirteen years ago, even though it hurt beyond telling. She was young, they were all so young, and Francisco had been irresistible: a handsome, cultured foreign student from a prominent Mexico City family. He would inherit influence, power, wealth, and it showed. Martin couldn't blame her for that, and he didn't. Unfortunately, it had gone sour almost from the start. Nearly two years ago the Mexican government had posted Francisco to San Antonio as special ambassador, and Martin and Susannah had met again after more than a decade apart. The affair was inevitable. They were in love and they knew it, but Susannah wouldn't leave Francisco. She wouldn't even consider it.

"Is that what you were upset about when you called earlier?"

"No," he said. "It wasn't. But now that it's out ... what *are* you going to do?"

Susannah folded her feet up under her in the chair. She put the cool drink to her temple and the green in her eyes picked up the color of the lime in the frosted glass.

"Martin, why do you want to go into it now?" Her voice betrayed a sadness. "We have a few hours together. Let's don't do this."

"That's the problem," he persisted. "A few hours is all we ever have. It's degrading."

"It wasn't his fault, Martin," she said softly. "I went into it with my eyes open. The man himself eludes me, and I'm sorry. Twelve years of sorry. But his life was planned before I met him. I just didn't have the intelligence to realize I would be incidental until it was too late."

"You don't have to be a martyr, Susannah. You don't have to stay with it the rest of your life."

Susannah tried to steady her voice. "If I leave, it will ruin him. The formality of this marriage, no matter how much of a failure it may be in reality, is the one thing he needs from me. It's the one thing I can give him."

"What about *you?*"

"I just told you."

"No, you just told me about Francisco."

"You weren't listening. I'm not going to leave him, Martin. Not for anything."

"Not even me."

"Oh, please." She buried her face in her hands.

She wasn't going to cry, he knew that. She was too tough in her own way to cry over it now, but it didn't mean she didn't want to. He knew that too. He hated himself for pushing it this far. It was a coward's tactic. He didn't have the guts to walk away from their affair himself, so he tried to harass her into leaving Francisco. But the needling was only poisoning their own relationship. It would kill him to lose her a second time, so he never forced the issue. And yet, as things stood, he didn't really have her at all.

He felt sorry for her now, and guilty, as he always did. They seldom got this much time together, and even tonight he would have to sneak away before Francisco returned from Austin. He looked past her at the caged cockatoos along the lighted gallery. The drone of the cicadas came up from the basin, and he wished the two of them could have been a thousand miles away and that Francisco Lyra had never existed.

Susannah began brushing her hair with long deliberate strokes.

"I'm sorry," he said. "I'm honestly sorry I got started on it again."

"Forget it. It'll work out somehow. Let's don't think about it."

She reached for her drink and finished it off, holding her hair back with one hand; then she stood, untied her robe, and dropped it in the chair. With a smooth stride she walked to the edge of the pool and dove in. Martin watched her long legs and hair rippling under the powder-blue water as she crossed the pool. When she surfaced on the other side she turned and faced him across the water. They looked at each other, their eyes saying all that could be said between them that would offer any reprieve from the sadness they could not escape.

"Come on," she said. "Come on, now."

They lay on towels on the grass a little way from the pool and Susannah toyed with the claret petals of a bougainvillea as Martin rested a limp arm across her bare hips and watched her face in the soft glow of the pool lights. The yard lamps had turned off automatically an hour earlier, and they lay under the dim Milky Way of the city lights reflecting back from the clear black canopy of the night.

Martin blew softly against her temple, feathering a straw-colored wisp of hair, and cupped the flesh above her hip in his hand. Without looking at him she responded by pressing her naked thigh to his, a slow, lazy movement.

"I've got to go soon," he said.

Susannah put the small blossom next to her cheek and spun it softly with her fingers.

"But we've got to talk first," he added. "There's enough ice over there for one more drink. Want to split it?"

She smiled. "Sure. Go heavy on the gin."

Martin got up and walked to the liquor cart and mixed the last gin and lime. He slipped into his clothes, leaving his shirt unbuttoned, and grabbed his shoes and Susannah's robe. He sat the drink between them and draped the robe around her shoulders as she sat up. They each took a drink from the glass, and Susannah held it while he began slipping on his socks.

He wasn't sure how to begin telling her what had happened

or if he should even tell her at all. But somehow he felt that he couldn't do anything without her.

"I came across something this morning that I've got to know more about. I think you can help me. A few days ago an American engineer acting as a consultant for Pemex was kidnapped from his hotel in Coatzacoalcos and brutally murdered. The murder is being attributed to a revolutionary group that I don't know much about—"

"GATO."

Martin stopped with one sock half on and looked at her. "Maybe you're going to surprise me," he said.

"I doubt it." She laughed. "That was an educated hunch."

"What do you mean?"

"They've just been in the Mexican news a lot in the past six months. Don't you know anything about them?"

"Nothing."

"You just want something general . . . story background?"

"Yeah."

"What kind of story?"

"Something on this murder, I guess. Dimmit just wanted me to look into it. Don't even know if there's a story there. Is there?"

Susannah shrugged. "Depends on your perspective, I guess. By Latin American standards they're rather unusual revolutionaries. The only thing I know about them is what I've heard in the diplomatic social circles, where they aren't exactly popular, and from what I read in the Mexican publications Francisco subscribes to. Two of these, the daily newspaper *Uno Más Uno* and a weekly news magazine called *Proceso,* are pretty gutsy. They aren't afraid to report on Limón's opposition as it really is. It was *Proceso* that first mentioned GATO publically.

"As a political entity GATO is difficult to tag except that it's anti-Limónist. I think it's pretty well established too that while its philosophy seems to embrace the grievances of the great masses of peasants there's far more to it than that. First of all, it's a middle-class organization. By that I mean an educational middle class, not necessarily an economic one. It also appears to receive substantial support from some of Mexico's political elite, people who traditionally support the incumbent president regardless of who he is. Because of this, and even though their numbers are few, GATO is a big embarrassment to Limón as well as a considerable threat."

"A threat?"

"Yes. GATO wields power, but it's not the ordinary sort you usually associate with revolutionaries. The real core of the or-

59

ganization is found in the power circles of politics and Mexican business and industry. It's like a secret society. You know they're among you. Your best friend may even be a member, but you can't prove anything. Things happen; you know it's there."

"What are they after?"

Susannah took the lime from the glass and squeezed the juice into her mouth. "They simply want things cleaned up. The oil money isn't filtering down to the general population, which is really no surprise to anyone. More than half the population of Mexico is under twenty, and they see what's happening. Their patience has run out. They're going to get their chunk of the petro pesos if they have to burn down the country to do it. They see no contradiction in that kind of thinking. They're angry; reason has nothing to do with it."

"But what about GATO?"

"Well, Limón is getting tougher to suppress the growing dissidence. Violence is swelling like a boil, and the 'South Americanization' of Mexico the politicians keep talking about is actually coming about."

"You mean Limón's having to use Gestapo tactics to hold the country together?"

"That's right. GATO knows that once Mexico is pulled into that spiral nothing but chaos can follow. I think they see themselves as mediators in a strange sort of way. They want to head off the flames of total revolution by building a backfire of their own. I know that sounds like one kind of madness in exchange for another, but I don't think it is. The ingredients are different."

"You'll have to convince me it isn't the same old story we've heard since 1910," Martin said. "Nothing ever comes of these rumors."

"But this time there's a major difference," Susannah said, a trace of something more than a casual interest in her voice. "In the past the issues involved only the Mexicans, who were a hopelessly poor and uneducated people. It was their household, and if they wanted to squabble among themselves the world community didn't care. But the oil has changed all that. When your oil reserves rival those of the Saudis, what happens to you becomes everybody's business whether you like it or not."

Martin dug the toes of his socked feet into the thick grass, his forearms resting on his raised knees. "Did you ever hear anything about GATO's getting financial support from a State-side branch?"

"Yes. As a matter of fact I first heard of it in connection with Francisco's appointment nearly a year and a half ago. Most of the decisions at that level are made behind the scenes, like the presidential nominations. But in Francisco's case there was considerable debate."

"About what?"

"It was a question of whether or not they should withhold the ambassadorship, which the U.S. was eager to establish, to protest the rumors that GATO was receiving significant support from a Texas-based operation. The anti-American feeling is pretty strong in some quarters of the government. He never would talk about it, and I was only interested in the final results anyway, being able to come back home."

As Martin suspected, Lyra would know everything. Would he also know about Luz? It was ironic that Lyra should possess so much of the information Martin wanted. It might as well have been on the other side of the globe. It was unquestionably out of reach.

Martin had one other question. "Have you ever heard of a revolutionary named Paco?"

Susannah laughed and tossed the lime out into the grass. "The modern Zapata. The brains behind GATO. I sometimes wonder if the man really isn't two or three people. Whatever the truth, he's definitely the new people's hero of Mexico. Mexicans love legends, and GATO and Paco have become full-fledged legends.

"But once again, it's not the same as 1910. The new heroes don't strap bandoliers across their chests and carry rifles. They wear European designer suits, sit on the directing boards of banks and international industries. They're educated, impatient, and determined to make the world change its stale image of the slow-witted, lazy, and incurably poor Mexican."

"And what do you think their chances are of doing that?"

"They'll do it."

Martin looked sharply at her. "You're hoping GATO will succeed?"

"Things could be a lot better. I'm sympathetic."

Martin was silent. The muscles at the back of his neck had been drawing tighter as he listened to her talk. He needed her. He could use her. He knew he *would* use her.

Susannah bent her head down and looked into his face. "Martin? Okay, level with me. Something's wrong. What's this all about?"

Martin slipped his feet into his shoes and stood, then reached his hand down to her and pulled her up.

"I'm going to tell you something you may find difficult to

believe," he said, putting an arm around her waist. "And then I'm going to ask you for help you may find difficult to give."

They walked together through the cool grass to the low stone fence at the edge of the cliff. As they stood there, looking down into the sequined basin, he told her everything.

Chapter 8

Martin sat alone in a Steak & Eggs diner and nursed a warm glass of orange juice as he watched an Iranian student in a chef's hat cook his hash browns and two eggs over easy. He had been awake only half an hour and it was closer to lunch than breakfast. He had awakened a hundred times during the night reliving the conversations with Stella, Lee, and Susannah. Each time he dreamed them over they became more sinister, more urgent.

Susannah, of course, had been shaken by what he had told her, but she had quickly agreed to help him in whatever way she could. He had told her only to wait, to be aware of what was happening and to pass along any information she might come across that would help him. He hadn't asked her to look into Francisco's affairs. She could do that if she wanted to, but he wasn't going to ask her, not yet.

It had taken a load off his mind just to be able to talk to her. She had been stunned to learn of the electronic surveillance in the house. Both of them knew how extensively they had compromised themselves. He suspected Susannah felt foolish, as he had, like an adolescent who suddenly realizes how carelessly he has played being an adult in a world far more sophisticated than he had realized.

On the way to the diner that morning he had stopped at a telephone booth and called the number Stella had given him. It was the quarter hour, but he got no answer. Later, after he had drunk the first warm orange juice and the solitary Iranian was getting him the second, he called again from the telephone outside the diner. It was essential that he get word to Stella about his conversation with Lee, but there was still no answer.

As he ate the eggs and sipped his first cup of coffee he made up his mind to see Jesse. He needed to know what was happening on the streets. If the news of the smuggling job had been offered as freely as Cuevas had said, there would be details with it. Jesse would know those details. If Stella couldn't be contacted through the number she had given him, something had gone wrong.

Maybe, though it was a long shot, he could get to her from the other end. The street offer would involve a contact. If Martin could find him he would work his way up from the bottom.

He watched the clock approach the quarter hour again, paid the Iranian, and went outside to the phone booth. He put in his quarter exactly on time, only to stand listening to the other end ring incessantly without being answered.

He drove to the *Times* parking lot, left the car in his regular slot, and walked the four blocks to Houston Street. Heavy traffic formed an endless line down the street's narrow corridor as Martin worked his way impatiently through the sweaty tide of pedestrians. Three small, barefooted Mexican boys, called "river mice" because they seemingly made their homes in the crooked streets along the river, darted past him jigging painfully on the shimmering sidewalk. Taking shelter under the marquee of a pinball arcade, they lingered before the fading photographs of topless strippers before they scuttled again onto the sunbaked concrete, jostling the crowds as they ran.

At St. Mary's, Martin came to the sprawling block-long awning of the old Woodbury Hotel. It was on the approach to the river, and its long wrought-iron-and-canvas awning covered the entire sidewalk, casting a cool blue shade in the relentless heat. In this shadowed gallery, newspaper vendors lined the curb side of the sidewalk across from potted palms that stood like sentries against the facade of the hotel.

Among the vendors were a black named Ross and a legless dwarf named Jesse who worked as a team. They were Martin's chief sources of street news, and their information was impeccably accurate. Like Cuevas, they had known Martin's father from the old days. As Martin stepped up on the curb into the shade, Ross spotted him and watched him approach with heavy-lidded eyes. His long hands hung from limp wrists draped across his knees as he squatted on a low stack of newspapers.

"Well . . . look who draggin' inta the shade," he drawled.

"Hello, Ross," Martin said as he removed his coat and straddled a folding canvas chair the black had shoved toward him.

Ross looked at him, expressionless.

"Where's Jesse?" Martin asked. He took his handkerchief from his hip pocket and wiped at the oily sweat that had begun to trickle down his temples.

"Havin' a san'wich with Curtis at the Alamo Café. He oughta be back any little bit. Where you bin keepin' you'self?"

"Here and there. Just been busy." He looked over his shoulder at the white heat of the traffic and grimaced at the glare coming off the chrome and glass.

Ross watched him. "It's Awgust, dawg days."

Down the sidewalk a basso profundo bawled, "Buy the *Light*!" and fell silent. He was the only vendor who hawked his papers, a blind Mexican named Benito.

"Jesse been wonderin' 'bout you," Ross said, shaking an unfiltered Chesterfield out of the pack and taking it with his lips. He leaned over and struck a wooden kitchen match against an iron lamppost and rolled the freshly lit cigarette back and forth across his lips with his tongue before he took it out of his mouth and held it in the cup of his hand.

"He thought maybe you was sick," he added. "I tole him you was jus' busy. Ever'body busy these days. Life eatin' 'em up."

Martin put his elbows on his knees and leaned toward Ross without looking at him. "You heard about Cuevas already?"

Ross bobbed his head. "Oh yeah, we heard. Weirdo shit. Wadn't right, the way it happened."

"Yeah, I know. I don't think the cops have anything. I'll bet the word on the street's a little confused too."

Ross bobbed his head again.

"I don't have any idea what's going on either, but I have some hunches. Cuevas did me favors. We had a long visit yesterday, then this. I don't like the way it went down either."

"There's not much to know," Ross drawled.

"I don't want anything on Cuevas. I've heard talk that someone's looking for a *fayuquero* for a trip into Mexico. I hear it's a big job. I want to know who's making the offer, who's turned it down, who's thinking about taking it, and what it pays." Martin waited. "You think I can get answers to those kinds of questions?"

Ross looked up and down the sidewalk. "They's been a lotta wild tawlk," he said cautiously. "Somebody's gonna get shot up on account of that. Jesse knows. It's big money but it's bein' throwed aroun' an' some people fallin' all over theyselves to get at it. Some people fallin' all over theyselves gettin' away fum it. It ain't dope. It's somethin' bigger'n that."

"What is it?"

"I don' know nothin' much. Jesse, he knows 'bout it."

That was it. Martin would have to wait. Jesse did the talking. He made the judgments about how much to tell, who to tell it to, and what it would cost. It had been a good team for a long time. There was protocol.

Martin stood and threw his jacket over his shoulder.

"I'll tell you what," he said. "You tell Jesse I'll be waiting for him at the cathedral. I won't leave until he gets there."

"I'll tell 'im. He won't be long. You wait there."

He left the tall black gazing lazily down the shady walkway and walked back to Navarro Street and into the laserlike sunlight. He turned left, and in the next block he could see the western wall of St. Mary's Cathedral rising sheer and monolithic toward the glaucous blue sky.

He crossed Navarro at Travis and stood in front of the cathedral which faced the ancient trees of St. Mary's Park. Pigeons milled about on the limestone plaza, jutting their necks forward with every step like mechanical toys. The church loomed above him with black moisture stains seeping from the cracks in its gray granite walls. Two spires shot up like gothic stalagmites on either side of the massive rose window set in the stone above the double wooden doors at the entrance.

He stepped up the single stone slab into the vestibule and stood at the mouth of the nave. On either side of him tiers of votive candles burned red in tiny glass cups. It was quiet. He walked past the basins of holy water and looked up at the vaulted ceiling, ran his eyes the length of it to the transept before the altar, to the shimmering white statue of Mary standing on a pedestal which elevated her above everything in the apse.

He passed two dozing winos close to the back with their paper bags beside them. A nun, businesslike and small, stepped out of the altar gate and disappeared into the east transept as a woman, neat and attractive with a trim figure, rose from a pew near the altar and turned into the aisle. She wore a navy-blue dress with a single string of pearls, and though a veil covered her face it did not conceal her handsome features nor obscure a surprisingly seductive smile. As she passed him, Martin caught the sweet scent of gardenias and could not resist turning to watch the movement of her hips as they pumped to the beat of her footsteps, clean and precise upon the stone floor.

Slipping into the last pew but one before the altar, where he and Jesse always sat during their weekly meetings, Martin looked up to the complicated groinwork and then back to the rose window. The pews and the aisle were washed in the colored light coming from it and from the towering windows set deep in the stone walls.

He turned back toward the altar and barely had time to collect his thoughts before the muffled opening and closing of the cathedral doors echoed softly in the cavernous church. Silence followed, then Martin heard, faintly at first, then more distinctly, the rhythmic squeak of a wheel on its axle, the coasting sound of Jesse's wheelchair, and then the dwarf was beside him in the aisle.

"That didn't take long," Martin said.

"You were impatient. You'd been gone only a few minutes when I got back." Jesse's voice was deep, mellifluous in cadence and tone. It would have been the envy of any Shakespearean actor, and its effect was even more startling when one saw that it issued from a body remarkable for its mutation. Jesse's body stopped just below his waist and his legless torso was strapped into his wheelchair by a canvas strap that stretched tightly around his midriff beneath a swollen and cartilaginous ribcage. His arms and hands were extraordinarily long and wraithelike. His dwarf's head, too, was long, with closely cropped hair that grew far back from his broad forehead. One hand always held a wadded handkerchief with which he continually dabbed his bulging red eyes, which swam in a serous fluid. His nose was beaked, his mouth sensuous and curling above a cleft chin, and his entire face was the tender crimson color of scalded flesh.

Jesse had spent his life vending papers on the streets of San Antonio, and Martin had known him since Martin worked with the vendors during his high school summers. Jesse and Ross had worked together even then, and the little dwarf, graying now and ageing fast, still received the selfless devotion of the black who had taken care of him for years. Martin's relationship with these two was almost familial, for Brian Gallagher had endeared himself to them in the early years by one of his expansive Irish favors that, once done, were never spoken of again. But it had enriched a friendship that had lasted beyond his death and extended unquestionably to his son.

"Ross told me you could be enlightening," Martin said, turning a quarter turn in the pew to face Jesse.

"Without a doubt." Jesse smiled. "Ross got the impression you thought this might be connected to Cuevas. I'd been wanting to see you anyway. I'd heard about the *fayuquero* job and thought you might be interested. Turns out you're ahead of me. I'll tell you what I know." He fingered the handkerchief in his skeletal hands and began.

"About five days ago a couple of FBI agents were snooping around one of those classy hillside homes on Lake Travis in Austin. It was night and they were trying to photograph through the windows. Something went wrong, they were discovered, and one of them got his face blown off. The people in the house got away.

67

"The surviving partner, who turns out to be a special agent with the Mexican *federales*, called the FBI here and two agents go up there and all three of them go through the house with a fine-tooth comb. The lake place was a safe house for some kind of radical group connected with revolutionaries down in Mexico. This U.S. bunch has been sending support in a big way to Mexico . . . guns, money, whatever. The house belongs to a U.S. senator who had leased it for the summer to a man whose credentials were very good . . . on paper. They checked out to be a scam. A dead end."

"What was the senator's name?"

"Oh, uh, Kahan."

Martin whistled.

"Yeah, no kidding."

"And the people in the house?"

"A couple of men and a woman. That's all I know. Anyway, three or four days ago word was out on the street that this *fayuquero* job was up for grabs. Hell, the border's like a sieve and everybody's done a little smuggling, so there's no shortage of applicants. But the thing is, this job turns out to be an offer from this underground bunch that blew the agent away. This is big-time moving. But when this gets around the real pros won't touch it. Too damn hot. Nothing but *pachucos* applying now, after the big dollars. In fact, the dollars were so big the little people were swarming, then suddenly the contact for the job drops out of sight. The thing dries up."

"Who was the contact?"

"Guy named Suarez. I understand he's a Mexican national. Even though he was offering this real sloppy deal on the street, I understand he's a cautious sort."

"What kind of money were they offering?"

"Well, I know it was going for twenty-five thousand dollars on the street. Don't know what was being offered the pros."

"That's big money just to take it to the border and dump it in the cactus."

"It's not that simple. The mover has to take the package all the way to . . . some said Veracruz, some said Oaxaca. Mexican and U.S. feds are as thick as roaches from El Paso to Brownsville. They really pulled out the stops. So the bad guys have set up checkpoints. There's a timetable to follow, a flight in a small plane or something like that."

Jesse stopped and held his handkerchief against his eyes for a moment. The constant irritation seemed to have worsened.

Martin wondered if Jesse had seen a doctor. He would have to talk to him about it.

"So that's it?"

"No, there's something else." Jesse finished wiping his eyes and shifted his position in the wheelchair. "I just got through talking with Curtis Gallela. We talked about Cuevas. Speculation is running wild. Nobody can figure it out. Old Ramón had been as straight as anybody can get after leaving that business. Everybody's spooked. It was a crazy hit.

"After we dealt with that Curtis said he had talked to Sully Greene earlier this morning. Said Sully had a guy in his office trying to make contact with the revolutionaries. The guy had all the earmarks of a pro and was from out of town, Houston, he thought. Anglo, dark blond, dressed in a business suit."

"Why was he talking to Sully?"

"I imagine he was just touching base, making the rounds, trying to spread the word he was interested. But here's the thing. Curtis said that after a few minutes he got the feeling it wasn't such a good time to chat. Sully was a little antsy with this guy in the office. So Curtis left. He said he could have sworn Sully was going to put the guy in touch with the contact. Like maybe Sully had had some inside information on this deal all along."

"When was this?" Martin's mind was racing.

"This morning, like I said. The guy was in Sully's office this morning." Jesse thought a second. "I guess it must have been just before I met Curtis for lunch, because it was after he had learned about Cuevas. Couple hours ago, maybe three."

"Did Curtis think Sully knew him, or had the guy just wandered in?"

Jesse shook his head. "I don't know."

From the corridor of the east transept an organist began the daily practice for Sunday mass. Faint pieces of Bach's *Passion According to St. Matthew* wandered along the transept into the nave. The organist went a short way into the mass, stopped, and started over. Again and again the musical phrases were interrupted and repeated, foretelling the monotony of the mass itself.

Martin sorted the pieces of the puzzle. The man in Sully's office had surely been Tony Sleep or one of his men. Or an FBI agent. The Mexican *federale* who survived the lake-house shootout would have to be a member of the Brigada Blanca. The woman inside would have been Stella. Maybe Paco was one of the men. And Sully . . . damn, where did Sully fit in?

The organist's labor continued, then, slowly, as though a

massive door were closing somewhere out of sight, the music became fainter until its litany was squeezed to silence.

"Why would Sully want to put this guy in touch with the revolutionaries?"

Jesse pursed his girlish lips. "Maybe he's going to get a little piece of the action for his services."

"Maybe he's connected with the revolutionaries."

Jesse snorted. "Not too likely."

"How about the FBI? He could be informing."

"If he's helping the feds, it's not for pay. More likely he's been blackmailed. His string of porno houses are his 'respectable' occupations. It gets worse."

"If Sully's not connected with the revolutionaries how did he have access to the contact?"

"Hell, lots of people had the contact's number at one time or another during the past week. The number kept changing. There were lots of people with stale numbers. Maybe Sully smelled a good chance for a deal and dealt everyone out but himself. Told Suarez he could get him a safe *fayuquero* for a little fee. I don't know. Maybe Sully's access isn't good anymore and he doesn't know it."

"Maybe Gallela was reading things into what he saw."

Jesse smiled. "Or maybe Gallela was right and there's a lot about Sully we don't know." It was the safest assumption.

Martin didn't have a lot of time to hedge his bets. He looked at Jesse and decided he had to tell him. He knew the risks of telling too many people, but he needed the dwarf. He could be his eyes and ears in a way nobody else could. Besides, Susannah and Jesse were only two people. Two out of more than a million. He started talking.

Jesse listened with increasing anxiety. He dabbed his eyes, he looked away and groaned, he shook his head. Martin brought him up to date on everything, including his long-standing agreement with Dan Lee. He wanted Jesse to see all the angles. He didn't want to have to spell out the possibilities.

When he finished, Jesse sat silently looking at his hands and the wadded handkerchief in his lap. By some acoustical quirk, the smooth burble of a pigeon rose and fell in the church's vaulted spaces.

Finally Jesse said, "It was bound to happen. She just couldn't stay out of it. I thought she had let it go back before your folks died. She just went underground. Too deep to get out."

"They're going to kill her, Jesse."

"God Almighty."

"I thought about taking the damn package so she'd get out of the city. I could dump it somewhere."

"Sure. You'd last maybe twelve hours before they got to you."

"I don't have a lot of choices."

Jesse heaved an enormous sigh. "This guy at Sully's. He's either from Sleep or from Lee, and you're going to have to find out which before you can do anything else. Go see Sully."

"What am I supposed to do, beat it out of him? I don't have anything on him."

The thought of trying to wrestle information out of Sully made Martin's heart pound. A fiercely loyal Jew, Sully Greene made his living cutting deals in the predominantly Catholic population of the Mexican underworld. In a personal crusade not totally lacking in humor, Sully touted the Jewish symbols of faith, the menorah and the Star of David, as flagrantly and recklessly as the Mexicans used the cross and the plastic statues of the Holy Virgin. He wore a necklace and a ring engraved with the six-pointed star, and in a gesture of gaudy Zionist pride inspired by pure *pachuquismo*, he had the candelabrum tattooed on the inside of his right wrist with the yellow flames from the seven candlesticks reaching up into the palm of his hand. This theological eccentricity won him the title El Judeo from the *pachuco* clans. Sully's cunning and brutality were widely known and respected. Martin had little confidence in his ability to get what he needed out of this graying old Lion of Judah.

As if he could read Martin's mind and knew his fears, Jesse touched the sleeve of Martin's coat with his long spidery fingers. "Listen," he said. "If you're willing to make threats I can give you the dope that'll open his mouth. But you can't weaken with Sully. Convince him you'll burn him to the ground if he doesn't cooperate. Make it foolproof. If you don't, he'll come after you when it's over."

Chapter 9

Martin waited five minutes after Jesse left before he got up from the pew and walked out of the church. Outside in the bright sun an old Mexican woman was sweeping the broad sidewalk in front of the cathedral, scattering the pigeons with her broom and a vengeful "Sshhht, sshhhht, sshhhht!"

At a telephone booth outside a service station he placed another call to Stella. Again no answer. She had said the number would be good until noon the next day. It was twelve forty-five. He didn't know if it made any difference. He hung up and dialed a second time. The telephone continued to ring.

He started back to Houston Street. He didn't know how Stella would get in touch with him even if she wanted to. Since his home phone was out of the question he supposed she would use the office. But that seemed improbable now. Rather he expected a personal contact through a third party. That was logical. He had to concentrate to be logical at this point. Every nerve in him pulled toward a desperate pessimism. Stella's disappearance, her failure to respond to a contact system she herself had devised, were black omens.

Martin stayed to the shady side of St. Mary's Street past the strip joints and taverns with their dark doorways open to the sidewalk and the odor of soured beer seeping from their somnolent interiors. Now, in the white midday heat, this part of the street near the river was only a sad ghost of what it became at night when the neon and jerky music transformed it to a surrealistic view of the good life.

Sully Greene's office was on the third floor above the Eros and Stag theaters in an age-stained building adjacent to the San Antonio River. At this point in its course through the city the river was quite narrow, more like a canal, and a stone stairway to the riverwalk curled down from a street bridge just outside the theaters. The bridge and the riverwalk below were favorite hangouts of *pachuco* gangs.

Squeezed in between the two theaters was a cramped and

stale-smelling lobby. A building directory on one of its plaster-cracked walls said the offices of Metro Theaters, Inc., were located in Suite 306. Martin pushed the yellowed button by the elevator and heard the metal doors close a few floors up. It was an ancient machine operated by a frail Mexican woman who, when she was not going up and down in the groaning carriage, dozed on a little wooden stool in the lobby.

The elevator bumped to a stop, and Martin heard the crone slide back the brass accordion inner cage and then the metal door was pulled open by her bony arm. Martin stepped inside.

"Third floor," he said.

"Ah." She nodded, and pulled at the door to close it, then slung shut the accordion cage. She maneuvered an antique lever and the elevator engaged with a bump and started up. They stared together through the cage as the raw guts of the building passed downward before them with the number of each floor painted in white on the cement girders. The machine wheezed to a stop, and Martin stepped onto the gritty floor of the hallway. Behind him the elevator doors closed and the old woman began her mournful descent.

The unmistakable odor of rat urine hung in the fetid air. Martin was careful to stay away from the grimy walls as he walked toward an open window at the end of the corridor that overlooked the riverwalk. Next to it was a door with its top half of frosted glass bearing the name Metro Theaters, Inc., in tarnished gold paint.

He turned the handle on the door and went into an empty receptionist's office. As he closed the door behind him, he heard voices coming from another office through the doorway across the room. Old issues of *Billboard* were scattered on a coffee table in front of him, and on the opposite wall a Texas Theater license hung beside a garish oil painting on black velvet of a bullfighter leading a charging bull through a contorted *paseo*. He sat on a turquoise Naugahyde sofa to wait.

Shortly the receptionist came into the room. Shirley was in her late forties and dressed like a girl half her age. She had been with Sully for years. She wore a straight black skirt and a pale yellow blouse with buttons straining to the bursting point against her tightly packed breasts. Her hair was an off red, nearly orange, and she wore an expression of excruciating boredom. She smelled of chewing gum.

"Can I help you?" she whimpered, throwing some papers on her desk.

"I'd like to see Sully," Martin said, standing.

Shirley knew him, but it was an eccentricity of hers, perhaps born of overzealous caution, never to remember anyone who came and went through Sully's offices. Therefore she demonstrated no recognition of him now.

"Who shallah say is callin'?"

"Martin Gallagher."

"And what about?"

"Just tell him it's Martin Gallagher."

"Oh, well . . . awright." She looked at him and scratched her cleavage between buttonholes with a long coral fingernail. She hesitated, seeming to want to ask another question, then turned and disappeared through the door to the next office. She came back immediately.

"You may go in," she said with cool formality.

"I guess you're slummin', huh, Gallagher?" Sully barked as Martin came through the door. He was standing behind his desk with his hands on his hips, grinning. He was short and stocky and wore a short-sleeved shirt with half-moons of sweat stains under the arms and an olive-green necktie that was so old it looked like discolored khaki. His broad smile revealed a row of flat, even upper teeth with wide spaces between the two front incisors.

"Why not?" Martin said.

"Yeah, why not?" Sully echoed cheerily, and came around the side of his desk motioning for Martin to sit in a chair. His well-worn suit pants were baggy, with the wadded crotch hanging absurdly low between his thighs. He went past Martin and shut the door, then came back and perched on the corner of his desk. A stubby hand ran over the bristles of his graying crewcut. He conducted his business with impatience, so Martin decided to get to the point.

"I understand you had a man in here this morning who wanted to get in touch with some people looking for a *fayuquero*."

"You're kidding." Sully was still grinning.

"No, I'm not."

"Then you been misinformed."

"I just want to know two things: Who was he and what was the number of the contact?"

Sully's grin faded and his face began to color. Abruptness was his trademark. He didn't like other people usurping his style.

"Look, Gallagher, I 'preciate your spunk but somebody told ya wrong."

"I understand the man was from Houston. Did you put him onto this or did he come over on his own?"

"Hey, don't get cute with me." Sully tilted his head forward and looked at Martin from under wild bushy eyebrows. "I tole ya, I don't understan' what you're talkin' about."

"Did he pressure you? Maybe he called in some old chits," Martin persisted.

Without warning Sully jumped up from the corner of his desk and stood with one fist clenched at his side and the other pointing a pudgy finger in Martin's face.

"You pigeon shit," he bellowed. "Who you think you are, bustin' in here like this, demandin' names and numbers? You newspaper turds are gettin' too fuckin' cocky. Somebody needs to take you guys down a notch!"

Martin stood too, ignoring the outburst. "I'm in a hurry, Sully. This is personal. It's got nothing to do with the newspaper."

"You dummy! You could *disappear* talkin' like this. You're not dealin' with your two-bit junky bums."

"I'll make it easy on you," Martin said, looking squarely into Sully's wide-eyed, indignant stare. "In my office there's a locked filing cabinet. I keep one key with me, one key hidden, and one key stays with the managing editor. In that file I have a series of folders pertaining to you and Metro Theaters. Here's a sample:

"The lovely wife of a prominent San Antonio citizen has a part-time job her husband doesn't know about. She likes what she does and her clients pay a healthy sum to the guy who makes the arrangements for her. You. One of these clients was conveniently wired when he made his appointments on three separate occasions. Those conversations reveal some surprising facts about a high-class stable that even the vice detectives never heard of . . . on file.

"Sample: Some of the porno theaters in San Antonio and Houston can't get the features they want because of pressure on the distributors. The pressure comes in the form of percentage inducements from the theaters where those films *do* play. Your theaters. Somebody who got cut out way up the line is pissed and has provided me with a lot of helpful inside information on the porno vendor business . . . on file.

"Sample: A couple of aspiring actresses who seem to have gotten into something way over their heads are pretty upset about the 'wife-beating' death of Elena Canellas. They say Elena got that way in front of camera lights in a warehouse on South Presa, not in her home where she was carried after she died. These girls say you own the cameras and the film, which is now a nice little S&M feature traveling underground. Details in my files.

"Sample—"

"Forget it. You're making a fool of yourself."

Martin's voice was even. "You don't mean anything to me, Sully. Absolutely nothing. I don't care what happens to you one way or the other. I'm trying to stop a murder, and if you don't give me the answers to my questions I'm going to deliver the goods on you. *Today.*"

Sully's square face glared at him. A thick hand flew up and breezed across the bristles of his head.

"You better know what you're foolin' with, birdbrain," he said evenly.

Martin didn't know if he was threatening him or cautioning him.

"If you slip up it'll be the last thing you do. These guys are like nothin' you've ever seen before. You don't—"

"Just give me what I asked for."

Sully slammed his hairy fist down on his desk in frustration. He walked around behind his desk and looked out the window, his hand feathering the top of his crewcut. He thrust his hands into his pockets and walked back over in front of Martin.

"You're goin' ta get us killed, you dumb twat." He stared at Martin, but neither of them spoke. "Come here," he said.

Martin followed him through a door that led to his private apartment. It was a long room furnished like a bedroom and adjoining sitting room. Here, too, windows looked onto the river. Translucent yellow curtains covered the windows, and the sun streaming through them onto canary walls flooded the room in a brassy glow. A frothy lemon carpet covered the floor, and a painting of sunflowers hung over the bed. Without looking closely Martin was aware of a woman's lingerie scattered about the room.

Sully walked to a console television in the sitting area and flipped it onto a midafternoon wrestling match. The picture was rolling. He turned the audio high and the announcer followed the blow and growl of the sweaty wrestlers in a near scream.

Getting close enough to Martin's face for Martin to feel his breath, Sully said, "You say this is a personal thing. Fine. With me it's just money. I got twenty percent of what those damn revolutionaries was offerin'. In advance. That's pretty good for just handin' over a phone number." He snapped his head matter-of-factly.

"This guy just drops in here this mornin' and says he hears I know where he can get a movin' job. I tell him I don't know, who is he? He says he's from Houston an' he drops a few names that sound okay ta me. Doesn't sound like a cop, so I tell him what I know about the job and—"

"Dammit, Sully," Martin yelled above the television, making the shorter man flinch. "Cut the bullshit!"

The rage in Sully's face was unmistakable. Contempt curled his lips. Martin was allowing him no room to slide by, and Sully wouldn't forget it.

Sully sucked air between his gritted teeth and started talking rapidly. "Look, what's happenin' is happenin' fast, and if you go stumblin' into it be ready ta get blown away. Okay? Yeah, I gave the guy the phone number and I gave him Suarez's name and the story behind the way these radicals are tryin' ta move their package. I would've give him my grandmother's address and the layout of her bedroom if he'd asked for it! You bet your skinny little ass I would.

"I was sittin' here and he just walks in, Shirley right behind him lookin' wall-eyed. He tells Shirley ta go answer the phone, which ain't ringin', and then he shuts the door and says he's John Doe and wants ta ask me some questions. I say who the shit does he think he is bustin' in this way and he just sits down and crosses his legs an' says he'd like ta know about the movin' job. He sees I ain't anxious ta help him, so he names some names. Says these guys will be glad ta call on me if that's what I want.

"I tell you, the guy's *connected!* He named the dirtiest people in the business. Anybody can name names, I know that, but on the other hand this guy's for real, and who the shit are the radicals to me? I start tellin' him what he wants to know. Suddenly Gallela comes waltzin' through the door. I don't know why Shirley let him in, but there he is and this guy just stands up like some kind of insurance salesman and introduces himself by somethin' other than John Doe, which I forget, and says he's from Houston and he's tryin' to find out about the movin' job 'cause he wants the money. I couldn't believe it."

Sully paused to scratch under a sweaty arm. His eye caught the rolling picture on the television screen. "Look at it," he snapped with a gesture of frustrated disgust. He turned to Martin again.

"Gallela chats a few minutes, gets the drift I ain't overjoyed to see him, and leaves. So I give the guy all the dope I know on this job. When he's satisfied he says politely, 'Thank you very much for your help,' and then he shakes hands and just walks out cool as a cucumber! That's it. That's all I know."

Sully narrowed his eyes and poked a stubby finger in Martin's chest. "I'll tell you this, though. I don't think he wanted ta move no package. I don't know what he wanted, but I wouldn't want him tryin' ta get in touch with *me*. Know what I mean, Gallagher?"

"What do you know about Suarez?" Martin asked.

"He's just a *puto*. Been aroun' town a coupla years. A nobody."

"What's the name of the organization?" Martin watched Sully closely.

"How the shit do *I* know? La Causa. He's always talkin' about La Causa. Hell, you know how many La Causas there are in Mexico? A dime a dozen. Those people!" Sully jerked his head in disgust. "Suarez has done some deals with me. Works cheap, so I'm a little surprised when he comes ta me with this *fayuquero* thing. I mean, he ain't big-time material. But the dough he was offerin'! He flashed some of it ta let me know he wasn't shittin' me. He had it, all right. That's all I know. Just a small-timer who's hit a big deal."

"You know anybody who works with him? I understand it's a big operation." Martin caught a brief scent of perfume. The television announcer was screaming that one of the wrestlers had fouled and the audience was going wild.

"I don't know nothin'. I was just spreadin' the word for the mover. *Everybody* was spreadin' the word. This kind of shit goes down all the time. Everybody makin' deals. I don't know no details. It's just money to me."

"Did the guy pay you in cash?"

"You bet your sweet ass."

"How much?"

Sully looked at Martin, their faces still close, and thought it over. "Five thousand." A slow grin spread over his face. He couldn't help it; even humiliation couldn't squelch his pride at making an easy take.

"What was the number?"

"Laurel 2-4278."

Martin's heart sank. The same damn number right here for the taking. They might as well have handed it out on the street corner. He couldn't figure it out.

"That's all I know," Sully repeated.

"All right," Martin said. Without further comment he opened the door and walked out of the room.

"Not so fast!" Sully grabbed Martin's arm and jerked him around. "What about the little items you mentioned? What about assurances?"

"If you didn't lie to me you don't have anything to worry about."

Sully's eyes expanded in disbelief. "What? That's it? Who the hell you think you are? Moses?"

"I've had those files a long time and I haven't used them yet. I figured I'd need collateral someday. I did. I may need it again." Martin could see a blood vein swelling at Sully's temple like a fat blue worm.

"You fucker," Sully said slowly.

Martin stared at him a moment, then turned and walked out of the office past Shirley, who was craning her tangerine head to see in Sully's office, and closed the door behind him in the hallway. He pushed the elevator button. The television went off behind the doors of Metro Theaters. Laughter and the splashing of paddleboats on the river floated through the window at the end of the hall as he waited for the old crone's journey up through the dark shaft to get him.

Chapter 10

Dan Lee didn't want to jump the gun. At first he believed without a doubt that Tony Sleep was indeed in San Antonio looking for Stella Gallagher. Then he had second thoughts. It was such an incredible shift in events. There was little time to check it out, and even if he had more time, he had no agents to spare. He was spread dangerously thin.

Still, he had to act one way or the other. After he dropped Martin off at the Lyra home he returned to his office, which, since the kidnapping in Coatzacoalcos, had been fully staffed around the clock. He sent for the lab report on Cuevas and double-checked with the listening post monitoring Lyra's house. He didn't think the tag put on the Mustang would be of much benefit. Gallagher would expect it.

Lee did as much as he could on his own without having to move against the information about Sleep. At two in the morning he went home and slept until six. He drank a wake-up cup of coffee with his wife, helped her get the girls up and off to school, and was back in the office on the fourth floor of the Federal Post Office Building across from Alamo Plaza by seven-thirty going over the autopsy reports once again.

By midmorning Lee had accepted Sleep's presence in the GATO affair, after deciding that to believe otherwise would be wishful, rather than rational, thinking. The polished steel needle taken from Cuevas' neck yielded no information under laboratory scrutiny except that microscopic examinations indicated this was probably not the first time the quill had been used. That was the curious part. Why hadn't it been taken again to be used another time as it had been in the past? It had been left in Cuevas' neck, a gross misstep no professional assassin would be guilty of committing no matter how rushed or crowded for time his execution might have been. Unless it had been deliberately left behind. But professionals are never clever in that way. Theatrics show a lack of discipline.

And then there was Gallagher. Lee trusted his information,

if not exactly his motivation. Lee had stuck out his neck there too. He didn't pick up Martin as he had said he would. Instead he decided to let him go a little longer to see what he would do. He needed more leads, and Gallagher might be able to give them to him.

He glanced at his watch. It was eleven o'clock. Twelve o'clock in Washington. He would teletype the query now. They could skip lunch up there. Taking a pencil and pad from his desk, he crossed to one of two doors that opened out of his office and walked into the communications room. There were two desks in communications, occupied by young women who busied themselves with various consoles of chattering computer systems. One of the two, an intelligent and fast-talking brunette who had been in Lee's office only a few months, was intently transcribing the reams of tapes which poured in daily from the various listening posts that had been set up since the Coatzacoalcos kidnapping.

Lee pulled a chair up to the second desk and waited patiently for Elinor Lederer, a simple-faced woman with a complicated mind and cornflake-colored hair, to complete keying information into one of the four consoles surrounding her desk. He began jotting down his message while he waited.

When she was through, Lee was ready.

"A little note for Washington," he said to her, and she reached for another of the consoles. "This can't go teletype," he said. "It's too important and we haven't got time. It's got to go directly on line with encrypted clearance."

Though this was the Bureau's highest level of classified communication and was used so seldom that Lee had seen the system in use only once and had never actually used it himself, Elinor simply reached for a different console without changing expressions, keyed in the clearance program as though she did it every day, and looked at Lee for the message.

He tried the simple approach first, hoping to circumvent an explosion of bureaucratic panic from the beginning. He requested the Blue file on Anthony Wyndham Sleep from the administrative security index, known as ADSIX, and held his breath.

When the acknowledgment didn't return within five minutes, he knew he had blown it. SOG had been caught off guard. The request was jangling the chain of command. Lee went back into his office and returned with his paper sack of fortune cookies and sat down. He offered one to Elinor, who accepted it without expression and discarded the fortune without looking at it. She stared patiently at the display screen of the computer as she ate it. Lee looked longingly at the unread fortune in the trash.

After twenty minutes a response burst onto the green screen. They wanted "motivation" for Lee's request. Lee swore and tore off the second sheet on his pad and gave it to Elinor. His reply was terse:

COLLEAGUE OPERATING TOWARD CON-
FRONTATION WITH GATO. DOUBT YOU HAVE
BEEN INFORMED. REQUEST COMPLETE SIS
FILE ON SLEEP. ADVISE.

The Special Intelligence Service had been the FBI's clandestine intelligence-gathering operation during World War II. It functioned primarily in Latin America, with the majority of the activity occurring in Mexico, where the Bureau still maintained more agents than in any other country. This was mainly because one of the primary bases of Soviet intelligence operations against the West was headquartered in the shrub-covered Soviet embassy at Calzada de Tacubaya 204 in Mexico City.

Lee and the young woman anxiously watched the blank screen for a response. In a few moments it appeared: STAND BY. He should have sent the request directly to Colin Weathers. It would have saved time. He was one of the few who would cut through the red tape. He wasn't intimidated by SOG, the Seat of Government.

"Let me know when it starts coming in," he said, standing and offering Elinor another fortune cookie. "I hope it makes it before lunch. If it doesn't, we'll send out."

She nodded and smiled for the first time and turned to another console for the interim. Lee returned to his desk, but before he could sit down Elinor quickly opened the door and motioned for him to come in.

The fluorescent green computer screen glowed with a brief message:

READY SR-TS FOR IMMEDIATE COMMUNI-
CATION.

Elinor was already attaching the Bureau's equivalent of the White House hotline to the computer in the event portions of the conversation needed to be recorded. The computer could be activated only from Washington once the telephone was attached to the system. After completing the hookup, Elinor left a clean tablet and a pencil on her desk, switched off the surprised brunette's transcriber, and motioned to her to follow her out of the room. When they closed the door after them, Lee sat at Elinor's desk and stared at the telephone.

He drummed the pencil on the paper pad. When the telephone buzzed he knew who it would be. Colin Weathers was assistant director of the intelligence division in Washington. He was seven years Lee's senior and had been a sharp, seasoned agent when Lee was a rookie in Chicago. Lee had served with him for a year, then, as Weathers was promoted, under him for four more. Weathers had gone to all the right schools, possessed a master's degree in criminology from Stanford, and was totally dedicated to his career with the Bureau. His advancement was inevitable, and because he liked Lee and thought he showed promise, he had given him all the breaks he could. He was responsible for Lee's having been appointed special agent in charge at a younger age than most men in the other field offices around the country. In a situation like this, Weathers would go straight to the man who owed him.

The telephone buzzed and Lee answered.

"Dan?" Lee recognized Weathers' voice. The connection wasn't as clear as he would have liked.

"Yes sir," he answered.

"This is clean," Weathers said, his voice fading in and out but never completely out. Lee imagined him in a similar room, also alone. "You can say anything you want. You alone?"

"Yes sir."

"When did you verify this? I assume it's verified."

"I first learned of it last night. I went on line as soon as I was sure about it."

"Jesus Christ, those bastards. How does it look? Are they ahead of you?"

Lee hesitated. "I'm not sure." Then he quickly added, "I can make a dozen arrests today, and it would give you some nice headlines, but it would be premature. Stella and Paco would go so deep we'd never dredge them out. It's bad enough as it is. Stella knows about Sleep."

There were long pauses between their responses to each other while the technology did whatever it was supposed to do for security.

"This really puts on the pressure. You're going to have to pull out the stops, Lee. Pull more agents out of the other field offices if you have to. I don't care if you drain the whole damn Southwest. I'll clear it. Work Mexico like it's home territory. If the CIA is sending in people like Sleep we can sure as hell step on a few toes too. But cover yourself as best you can. There's always something to answer for when it's over."

Suddenly the computer screen flashed a row of symbols and began filling with words as the printout mechanism kicked into action and started peeling out the back of the console.

"You should be getting Sleep's SIS file and ADSIX," Weathers said. "Do you have them?"

"They're coming," Lee replied.

"Okay. There's been a change in the reporting system to the Mexican government. The State Department and the Limón government have agreed to circumvent Ambassador Lopez here in Washington in the interest of time. You're to use Francisco Lyra instead. He's been cleared. Any questions on that?"

"No sir."

"How's it working out with the *federales?*"

"Nobody likes it."

"That's not what I asked."

"We're trying to keep them out of the way as much as we can. Sometimes they know it and it causes a little friction. They're kind of high-handed anyway and our men have a tough time holding them in. There's resentment on both sides. The lakehouse thing didn't help. It's touchy."

Weathers' voice was sober. "It's a hell of a situation, Dan. You're in no-man's-land on this operation, but the State Department put you there and everyone knows it. If that's any comfort. I'll back you to the hilt. I know what you're going through and I won't let you down."

Lee appreciated Weathers' saying so. It would make what he was going to do a lot easier.

"Okay, Lee. When the computer finishes the printout this system's dead. Good luck."

Weathers was off the line and Lee was left holding the receiver and watching the computer, which was steadily spitting out a long scroll containing everything the Bureau knew about Tony Sleep.

Anthony Wyndham Sleep was born in 1940 in the city of Belo Horizonte, capital of the Brazilian state of Minas Gerais nearly two hundred miles north of Rio de Janeiro. His father, Wyndham Markham Sleep, was a career bureaucrat in the British diplomatic service, and his mother, Ligya, was a native Brazilian from São Paulo. Stocky and seemingly languorous like his father, he nevertheless demonstrated his mother's strong will and ability to spot an advantage and then make the most of it.

After studying history and languages at the Federal University of Rio de Janeiro for four years, Sleep left for England in 1962 for postgraduate study in political science at Cambridge. It was here he first demonstrated his proclivity for the homosexual life. His studies fell off as he dived into the garish Soho student life, shedding his parochial training with remarkable ease. He lived a schizophrenic life, keeping his Cambridge and Soho friends apart with only a close few knowing anything about the other.

In 1966 Sleep took a master's degree from Cambridge and, with help from his father, took a minor functionary's position with the British embassy in Washington. After a year he asked for and received a transfer to the embassy in Mexico City, where his language skills were a considerable advantage to his advancement. Here he became a frequent figure at the diplomatic social functions, which he seemed to enjoy with an air of detached amusement. He got on well with the Mexican bureaucrats and his career was developing nicely until he was arrested in a raid on a notorious homosexual partyhouse in the city's elegant Chalco district. In the wake of the scandal that followed, Sleep was quickly relieved of his position and asked to return to London for review. He resigned instead, and disappeared.

What the British diplomatic service had not known at that time was that Sleep had been heavily involved in criminal activity since his early days in Soho. His diplomatic traveling had enabled him to cultivate a varied coterie within the criminal community, which ignored international boundaries and was much the same whether in Rio, London, New York, or Mexico City.

After his disgrace and disappearance, Sleep made no effort to restore himself to "respectable" society, but plunged into the seamier side of Mexico City's criminal life. This didn't mean, however, that he left all his acquaintances behind, for he had become close to a high-ranking officer in the Investigation Division of the Department for the Prevention of Deliquency, the oversight agency of the Brigada Blanca. FBI files contained several photographs taken on the night of the infamous 1968 Olympic demonstrations in Mexico City when hundreds of students were killed by the Mexican army in the green glow of flares dropped from military helicopters in the Plaza of Three Cultures. Sleep could be seen in the crowd shots, one arm holding a collapsible AK-47 and the other directing *brigadistas* against the unarmed students.

In the furor that followed the Olympic killings, Sleep disappeared again and was said to be an interrogator for the *brigidistas* at the dreaded Campo Militar Numero Uno in the heart of the city. This prison was the site of most interrogations conducted by Mexico's secret police against the government's political enemies. Often people taken there for questioning were never seen again and became a part of the expanding lists of *desaparecidos*, "the disappeared ones." Nowhere in the Western Hemisphere, except in Argentina, did so many dissidents "disappear" without government explanation.

There was a gap in Sleep's file from 1969 to 1973, when he was spotted by a CIA operative in Havana in the company of a high-ranking officer in the Soviet-dominated Cuban secret service known as Dirección General de Inteligencia, DGI. After cautious inquiries the CIA agent learned that Sleep was a mercenary with Castro's death squads. He lived apart from the military organization itself in Havana's best hotel and was thought to be something of a hedonist in Castro's austere Cuba.

At this time the CIA began an active file on Sleep. In Cuba, Sleep apparently won the admiration of Castro's Soviet overseers, for he was the first "outsider" ever known to have been invited to the Soviet's spy school at Stiepnaya on the northern border of the Kazakh Soviet Republic, the training center for Soviet agents destined for posts in Latin America.

It was not known whether Sleep received training or gave it in Stiepnaya, but when he emerged eight months later it was clear he was no longer just another enforcer for the police states. He immediately orchestrated two remarkable assassinations of CIA Latin American agents in the space of nine weeks, one in Argentina and one in Chile.

Here the files became sketchy because the CIA stopped sharing its data with the Bureau. Agent assassination was a closed book to all but those in the highest level of the Company. It was believed, however, that at this time Sleep became the subject of an unprecented occurrence in the annals of East-West espionage history.

There was considerable difference in the way the CIA handled the discovery of foreign intelligence agents and foreign assassins operating within their jurisdiction. Assassins, when they were identified, were simply "taken out" by their opposite number in the U.S. agency. In Sleep's case, however, the CIA seemed to have gone to the trouble of "turning" him just as they would have an intelligence agent. In 1975, just six months after he had killed his second CIA agent in Chile, he was identified by FBI sources at "the farm," the CIA covert actions training camp at Camp Peavy, Virginia.

In March, 1976, Anatoli Budanov, attached to the Soviet

embassy in Santiago, Chile, was killed by shots from a passing car while drinking in a small neighborhood bodega. He was the KGB's chief security officer in Chile. He had trained with Sleep in Stiepnaya in 1973–74.

In July 1976, Oleg Yukalov died of an apparent heart attack in his home in the comfortable Mercedes district of Buenos Aires. He, too, was chief SK officer with the Soviet embassy in Buenos Aires. In 1973 he had been stationed by the KGB in Havana and had recruited Sleep for his brief study at Stiepnaya.

In September, October, and November 1976, Sleep was seen regularly in Buenos Aires with the death squads of the Anti-Communist Alliance (Triple A), which flourished under the military presidency of Jorge Rafael Videla. These squads, driving unmarked Ford Falcons, could be seen frequently on the highway to La Tablada Infantry Regiment, an army installation on the outskirts of Buenos Aires. The "operating rooms" of La Tablada became an international disgrace, and Sleep was a regular "surgeon" in that environment.

After December, Sleep did not surface again until the summer of the following year, 1977. He was seen in Rio de Janeiro during the same week a third Soviet SK chief was killed by three gunmen who pulled the Soviet's car to the curb early one morning while he was on his way to his embassy. The Soviet, the driver, and a bodyguard were all killed within a matter of seconds, their bodies riddled by 7.12mm bullets from Czech-made AK-47s.

By 1978 it was clear that Sleep was a mercenary working solely for the CIA and right-wing military governments throughout Latin America. For the next three years he surfaced in Guatemala City with agents of the government's Mano Blanca, counterpart of Argentina's Triple A and Mexico's Brigada Blanca; in Santiago with Pinochet's secret police, DINA; in Managua, Nicaragua, in the bloody days preceding the ultimate takeover of the Sandinista junta; in Bogatá, La Paz, and Montevideo.

But the nature of Sleep's involvement was changing. He no longer indulged himself in terrorist-type assassinations like his classic 1977 murder in Rio de Janeiro with its cinematic drama. He grew more cautious and reclusive. No photograph of Sleep could be found after his sojourn at Camp Peavy in 1975. He formed a permanent team instead of relying on his underworld resources in each city, and in his executions he employed more subtle means of extermination than the gun and the bomb; prussic acid, which, when sprayed into the target's face and inhaled, contracts the blood vessels and causes death in the same manner as a cardiac arrest; injections of curare causing death by suffocation; stainless-steel quills which, when properly slipped into the target's neck, can kill in seconds without leaving a visible puncture wound. He had entered a sophisticated business and had learned his craft to perfection.

By 1979 the FBI was relatively sure Sleep's team included a woman and another man besides himself. The three of them had been seen together and positively identified only once, in late May 1980, in La Brasserie restaurant in New York. The unsuspecting agent was unable to get a photograph. There was nothing in the files after that date until Martin's mention of him the night before. The ever meticulous ADSIX researchers had already included that "rumor" at the end of the data that was now ticking over the computer. Lee noted it was an open-ended entry.

Chapter 11

The three of them sat at a picnic table in the lacy midafternoon shade of an ebony tree. The table, one of half a dozen surrounding the deserted cement dance floor behind a barrio café on Zarzamora Street, was cluttered with wadded wax paper from the tamales and tacos they had ordered from the dark cramped kitchen inside. A Mexican girl about eleven backed carefully out the ragged screen door of the café carrying two bottles of beer by their long necks and sat one in front of each of the two men at the table. A half-grown mongrel followed her out of the café, its toenails clicking on the cement surface of the patio as it tagged along behind her to the corner of the building where the trees shaded a water faucet, which she turned on, letting the dog drink from a battered aluminum pan.

The men sat on the same side of the table, facing the woman. The younger of the two said very little in the three-way conversation, which alternated between Spanish and English. He was thin and wore a European-cut sailcloth sports jacket and beige pants. His hair was light brown and razor-cut by a stylist. His eyes were hidden behind St. Laurent sunglasses with reflecting lenses, and one leg bounced nervously under the table as he listened while folding, unfolding, and refolding a paper napkin. Occasionally he looked at one or the other of his companions. His name was Esteban Macias.

Raúl Suarez was a little older, maybe in his late thirties. His features portrayed Indian blood from northern Mexico, a long upper lip with a black mustache, dark hooded eyes, and thick straight black hair well oiled in the barrio tradition. With the palm of his hand he wiped the mouth of the sweaty bottle and took a mouthful of beer.

Stella was toying with her gold lighter.

"We should have stayed at the house," Suarez said.

"Too many people had the number," she said.

"We didn't have to answer the damn phone."

"Numbers can be traced to their addresses. We're safer sitting here. Besides, everything's set up now. It's just a matter of getting the package to Klein, then flying out."

"You keep saying that," Suarez said. "Getting out in that damn plane might not be so easy."

"That's no problem," Macias interjected. "No problem." Suarez didn't look at Macias but swallowed another mouthful of beer. "I don't like this deal. We haven't had time to check him out like we should. It don't feel right."

"I agree, Raúl," Stella said. She was tired, and it showed. "But time is running out. You saw what happened to Cuevas. You said Sully had helped you out before. We've got to trust him."

"This man, he's not Sully's type. I can't figure it."

Stella pushed her sunglasses up on her head and rubbed her aching eyes with her hands. She hadn't had enough sleep since that early-morning shooting at the lake house. Leaving Paco that night had been frightening and painful. They couldn't be sure when, if ever, they would see each other again.

In the aftermath of the shooting they had to assume the worst. Stella dropped out of sight with Suarez, and in rapid succession during the following few days four of their people had been killed or arrested as the FBI and the Brigada Blanca acted on the information that had been left behind in the lake house. Two others fled to Mexico, which left only herself, Suarez, Macias (who had been sent up from Mexico to take them out), and Paco.

The arrests and killings were done in total silence, of course. The small number of FBI agents involved had used the Mexican agents as bloodhounds in a freewheeling operation which had become a law unto itself. The odds were they would get them all. Except one.

Paco had not been heard from since the shooting. He would not contact Stella again as long as she was in the States, and the only news he would be able to get of her would be through the nearest Mexican contact in Tampico, who would place a long-distance call to Paco asking for himself when the *fayuquero* cleared the first checkpoint south of the border. The telephone call would only tell Paco that Stella had been successful in getting the package out of the States. It would not tell him if *she* had been able to get out too.

As the only GATO member in the States who knew who Paco really was, Stella was his sole line of communication to the organization she ran at his direction. The tight security surrounding Paco's real identity was the main reason for his tremendous success and continued anonymity, which frustrated the FBI, the

Brigada Blanca, and now Tony Sleep. Paco had to be protected at all costs. He was the only one who could build a new Stateside organization from the rubble of the one that had begun to crumble. As the week progressed and no further move was made to arrest him, Stella realized he was still a faceless name to the agents.

The decision to separate her from the briefcase of documents had been made after the shooting, when her chances of making it out of the city were greatly diminished. It was a delicate task, and she had relied heavily on Raúl. But now he was beginning to doubt his own contacts.

Pulling her glasses down over her eyes again, she said, "What are our alternatives?"

"Martin," Suarez said firmly. He pronounced it *Mar-teen,* in the Spanish way. "You should have nailed him to it yesterday. He's the surest, cleanest way out of this."

"I wouldn't call him 'clean.' They're clinging to him like fleas."

"But he can move around. He can disappear. We step out the door for this meeting and we're asking for it. Shit. I'm telling you if you meet this Klein tonight you'll be walking into a trap."

"You set it up, Raúl," Stella snapped.

"I know, I know, and I'm saying I made a mistake. I can feel it. This isn't the way we should do it."

"And how would you get in touch with Martin?"

"Personal messenger. Tell him to meet us at the same place we met yesterday at twelve o'clock tonight. We could give the briefcase to him and be in the air by two o'clock."

"He wouldn't do it."

"He would if we threaten Susannah Lyra."

"No!" Stella slapped an open hand flat on the table. "She's got to stay out of this. Don't make any mistakes like that."

"We're only bluffing. A threat!"

"And how do you think he'd react to that? You're dreaming, Raúl, and it's dangerous dreaming."

She sipped from her coffee cup, which she had filled for the third time in the past hour with Passport scotch and water. She had drunk too much in the last few days, but she felt all right, in control. She too had grave doubts about Klein. They would have to be careful, but she knew from experience you could never be careful enough. Nothing like this ever went off without mistakes. The problem was, you never knew how many mistakes you were allowed before it all added up to bad luck and you were defeated.

"Let's go over it one more time," Stella said. She spoke kindly, deliberately keeping the impatience out of her voice. Raúl was as tired as she was. He was doing his best, and he didn't deserve to be her whipping boy.

Raúl nodded resignedly.

"At five o'clock when traffic is heaviest," he began, "Esteban will take the car out Loop 10 to Castroville. He'll go straight to the landing strip, double-check everything, and wait. I'll leave with the briefcase and take a cab downtown and check in at the Palacio del Río, where I'll stay until it's nearly time for your meeting. I'll leave the briefcase under the bed and go to the river bridge next to the Club Carioca, where you'll be meeting Klein. I'll watch everything from there.

"Klein will meet you at eight-thirty. I gave him your description and said you'd be sitting alone with two red packs of un-opened Pall Malls on the table. If the deal doesn't make, leave by the steps that go up at the Crockett Street bridge and I'll meet you there. If everything goes all right, you take him to the hotel room, give him the briefcase, and lay out his instructions about checkpoints. When I see you go into the hotel I'll take a cab out to Mora's station and wait. After you've closed the deal, call and let me know you're on your way. Mora's boys will drive us to Castroville and the airstrip."

Raúl opened his hands. *"Es todas,"* he said and fell into a stubborn silence.

Stella was glad he wasn't going to argue with her anymore. He had wanted to be with her while she was with Klein, but she insisted they remain separated. If there was a trap, one of them needed to be free to retrieve the briefcase.

"You'll tell the desk clerk your wife and her cousin are going to pick up the key," she confirmed. "You'll use the Ramirez credit card."

Raúl nodded.

Stella turned to Macias. "Do you have any questions?"

The mirror-surfaced sunglasses looked up at her. "If nobody shows up by noon tomorrow, I call Mora's station. If nothing there, I can try your brother. If nothing there, I call the number you gave me. I leave the message 'Waiting alone,' and give my telephone number. I wait thirty minutes for a call back. The caller must first say 'Forgive me for being late' before he gives me instructions. If he doesn't say that I hang up immediately and return to Oaxaca. If there's no call back in thirty minutes, I return to Oaxaca."

"Good," Stella said. "But if we don't show up at the airstrip you'd better do your damnedest to find out what happened. Don't leave us stranded."

"No problem."

"All right." Stella looked back and forth between the two men. "If something goes wrong, you can reach a GATO contact only through that number. You'll have to leave a call-back number, so pick a place you can wait without attracting attention. When they call back they'll use the same phrase: 'Forgive me for being late.' If they don't say that, the phone's been blown and you're on your own."

Shortly after five o'clock, Esteban Macias drove away from Flaco's tavern on Zarzamora Street and headed toward Loop 10 and Castroville. A little while later a cab stopped in front of the bar and picked up Raúl Suarez and the briefcase.

Stella poured more scotch into her white coffee mug and sloshed water from a dirty glass into the mug. The urge had never been stronger to break with the discipline that had become second nature with her and call Paco. Just to hear his voice one more time before she had to do this. She faced it squarely now that she was alone; she had little optimism about what would happen between now and midnight. The odds were great against her.

The constant danger that had fired her enthusiasm for so many years had begun to lose its sense of excitement nearly two years ago and had taken on a pall of dread. The whole nature of her work began to change when Paco had returned to take over what she had doggedly built into a powerful organization. She had not seen him since college, where she had admired his work, though she had not known him well. According to GATO's long-term plans his return to Texas would bring to culmination her years of patient groundwork.

Forced to live four separate lives between them, they began to form a bond neither of them had anticipated. It was inevitable, Stella thought as she looked back on the past two years, that she should have fallen in love with him. At first she denied it even to herself, and when she couldn't deny it any longer she was horrified. When neither of them could ignore it, their affair took on the tortured grace of a dance in hell. They lived in a secret world. They hoped and dreamed and loved in secret. Their nights together, too few and too seldom, were furtive and unexpected, dominated by fear and anxiety. But they had endured the separations which, for the most part, were of their own making according to the lives they had chosen to lead. They were like many other lovers caught up in an affair that seemed never to end.

Now the prospect of a prolonged and uncertain separation frightened her. It was a fugitive separation that threatened a finality she was not prepared to face. Yet, she wouldn't make the phone call. She knew she wouldn't. The revolution had brought them together and it would separate them if necessary.

An occasional customer came out of the ragged screen door, letting it slap softly behind him as he sought a shady table around the dance floor. Stella saw the half hour approaching and knew traffic would be heavy until six-thirty or seven o'clock. The next bus going north would be in front of Flaco's in fifteen minutes.

She took a hairbrush out of her purse and brushed her hair, oblivious of the glances of the middle-aged men who had begun to collect around the tables in the late-afternoon shadows like idle flies. Draining her cup, she stood and closed her purse and walked into the rank shadows of the bar, where a domino game between four old men was the only sign of life.

Chapter 12

Stella stepped out of the murky bar into the glare of the falling sun and walked past the rusty chain-link fence of an automotive repair shop to a bus stop in front of La Renya Beauty Parlor. She leaned against a telephone pole shabby with tags of old posters and fanned the top of her dress to relieve the stifling heat. When the bus pulled up, it engulfed her in a gritty scud of diesel exhaust that she vainly tried to avoid inhaling as she stepped inside. The seats were full, so she joined the crowd standing in the aisles, sharing with them the tangy odor of sweat and discount-store perfume that weighted the air.

She got off downtown at Market and Broadway, where the broad stone steps led down to the clubs and restaurants lining the banks of the narrow and sluggish San Antonio River. She paused at the top of the steps and looked south across the city toward Mexico. Against the horizon the Gulf clouds were piling up like massive banks of spume, while directly above her the clean summer sky stood motionless in its own cobalt heat.

Descending to the riverwalk, she turned in the opposite direction of the Club Carioca. She had almost an hour to kill. She walked along the bank past the great armored scales of the palms, past the patios of the restaurants and clubs with ivy and palmettos growing near their doorways. Tourists and businessmen sat at the small tables on the terraces.

At the San Remo Bar, she took a table near the river bank and ordered Passport scotch and water. She drank the first quickly, hoping to bring back the buzz that had worn off since she left Flaco's, and then ordered a second. She thought again of the Gulf clouds she had just seen. They were moving north, and when they did that in the evenings it meant rain, either tonight or tomorrow. It didn't matter. Macias was good. He would fly in a hurricane if he had to. It didn't matter to him as long as he got his money.

Being low, the river fell quickly into the deep purple of dusk. A pale glow, the fading, timorous precursor of night, hovered over the street above, then died as the streetlights and lamps along the river flickered and came on. It was the slowest time of the day, the pause before the hectic partying of the evening. Behind Stella two Mexican waiters laughed and tried to pop each other with their towels as the aroma of food filled the watery air along the river.

At eight-twenty, Stella asked her waiter for two packs of Pall Malls and her check. She paid, left a generous tip, and started along the riverwalk the way she had come. She realized as she edged along the water that if she had stayed much longer she would have been too drunk to do this.

The stone sidewalk wound along the river, in and out of the patios of clubs and restaurants. Finally she heard the driving rhythms of the Brazilian *batucada* coming through a bank of bougainvilleas and she rounded the corner to the Club Carioca. Instantly her stomach tightened and the blood drove through her veins as fast as the music. She glanced at the half-visible iron spans of the Crockett Street bridge not fifty yards past the club in the darkness. Raúl would be there, watching.

She found a table with two chairs and took the two unopened packs of Pall Malls out of her purse and set them on the table. With an unsteady hand she took a cigarette out of her purse and lit it with the gold lighter. A waiter took her order and returned with the drink and a complimentary order of *tostadas*. She checked her watch and began toying with the lighter.

She hadn't anticipated waiting. After fifteen minutes she moved her chair slightly so she could see the bridge better, or rather, the darkness where she knew the bridge to be. If something had gone wrong, Raúl would signal her with his lighter or he would appear at the bottom of the stone steps. Another ten minutes passed. She had to order another drink, which, by this time, she really didn't want. It was too dangerous; she shouldn't drink more.

The traffic along the sidewalks picked up and the diners grew louder. A party boat churned past, and she watched its colored lights play along the surface of the rippling water. The lights caused a lump in her throat for some reason she couldn't remember, a reason far away at the edges of her memory, other colored lights, strung together festively, silently. Such a sadness. She started on the next scotch. As she was lighting her fifth cigarette the empty chair at her table was slowly pulled back and a man sat down.

"I'm Alex Klein," he said in a natural, relaxed voice, and Stella looked at him steadily, waiting for the pounding in her ears to subside. He was clean-shaven, round-faced, and blond. His hair was combed immaculately, with the straightest part she had ever seen. He was thickset but attractive and wore a vested khaki suit, a bone-colored shirt, and a dark brown tie. He looked like an accountant, Stella thought.

"Where the hell have you been?" She surprised herself with the bitchy tone.

He smiled and sat comfortably across from her with one leg crossed over the knee of the other.

"I'm sorry," he said pleasantly, but offered no explanation. Stella saw a monogram on the stiff cuffs of his shirt sleeve, but couldn't make out the initials.

"Is this the way you do business?" she demanded.

Klein didn't respond but looked at her, a cool smile resting easily on his thin lips. There was a small scar angling down at the edge of his mouth which, in a mental non sequitur, reminded her of a ventriloquist's dummy.

"I'm not sure you're the person I should be talking to," he said. "How about giving me a little assurance."

Stella felt a flash of anger. "Two unopened packs of Pall Malls. Sully Greene. Raúl Suarez. Stella Gallagher," she said acidly, bending a wrist toward herself.

"Very good."

"Look, I've been here too long already. Do you want the job?"

"Yes."

"Okay. This isn't going to be your regular smuggling job. There are checkpoints and there is a timetable. You'll be carrying a briefcase with the clasps soldered shut."

"Fine. Give me the details." Klein had never stopped smiling, which Stella found maddening. The waiter came over and he ordered "the same thing the lady is having," which Stella thought an absurd deferential gesture. After the drink arrived, Klein reached for one of the packs of Pall Malls, and shook out a cigarette. He reached over and took Stella's gold lighter and lit the cigarette, then blew a fine stream of smoke into the heavy night air as he examined the lighter.

"Very nice." He smiled and handed it back to her.

Stella put it into her purse, never taking her eyes off his. He couldn't have offended her more if he had put his hand under her dress, and yet he had done nothing but help himself to a cigarette.

"Here's the way it will go," she said. "After I give you the briefcase and the first half of your payment tonight, I'll notify the first checkpoint that you've got the package. You have four hours to get to each checkpoint. I don't care how you get from point to point—chartered plane or bicycle—but you had better do it within four hours. If you fail to make a checkpoint within the alloted time, someone's going to come after you.

"First stop is Brownsville. Cortez Boots and Leather Goods at 1603 Nunez Street. Buy a can of Cavalier black boot polish and tell 'Jimmie' you're going to see Luz in Tampico. He'll call Tampico. When you get there, go to the curio shop in the Hotel Inglattera and buy a miniature oil derrick souvenir from 'Vicki.' Tell her you're buying it for Luz in Veracruz. When you get to Veracruz, go to the airport. There are several small private airlines there. Go to the office of Aéreo Supremo and ask for Miguel Vanegas. Tell him you want to see Luz in Oaxaca. From there on you're in our hands again. Vanegas will take you to a little airstrip outside Oaxaca, and I'll meet you there with the last half of your payment. You'll be flown back to Veracruz and you'll be on your own."

Stella paused. "Do you have any problems with that?"

"None whatsoever."

"Repeat it."

He did, like a parrot, putting commas where she had put them, word for word. It was like playing back a tape recorder. The bastard's mocking me, she thought. She was conscious suddenly of the stifling heat. She ran a sticky hand around her throat, which was slippery with sweat, and in an instant she knew it had caught up with her. The loss of sleep, the drinking, the smoking, the tension. Something was happening to her body. But she couldn't let it happen now. Just another half hour, she thought, and Klein would be gone.

"I'm going to the bathroom," she said, "and then we'll go to the hotel for the briefcase."

Klein's smile stiffened.

"Dammit," she snapped. "It's just right there," and she pointed toward the edge of the patio as she got up. Her mouth was so dry she could hardly pronounce the words.

The lavatory entrance was on the outside of the club and opened onto an alleyway formed by a high wall of banana trees growing close to a narrow sidewalk. When she got there it was locked. She swore and leaned against the wall. In a moment the commode flushed and a waitress emerged smelling of powder.

Stella went in and closed the door behind her. She put the lid down on the commode and sat down. Resting her elbows on her knees, she put her face in her hands and tried to steady her trembling legs. The outside wall of the lavatory had a small rectangular window with bars across it near the ceiling, and through this opening she could hear the sounds of the kitchen echoing in the alleyway.

Her dizziness increased in the close ammoniac air of the lavatory. She knew if she got up now she would pass out. Summoning all her strength, she swiveled to her right and turned on the water at the sink. Without getting up, she put her hands into the yellow-stained basin and filled them with water. With burning eyes she hung her head over the edge of the sink and splashed water on her face and rubbed it into her eyelids. She wetted several coarse paper towels and wiped inside the front of her dress, letting the cool water run down between her breasts to her stomach. She took others and dried herself.

She had to go. Raúl had surely seen her go into the restroom and would be wondering if something was wrong, if he should do something. Slowly she stood, bracing herself with one hand against the wall. Looking in the mirror, she ran a trembling hand through her hair.

When she came out onto the patio she saw Klein sitting just as she had left him at the table. She walked over.

"Let's pay and get out of here," she said.

"I've already done that." Klein smiled. "I'm ready."

Stella cursed him underneath her breath as he stood. She glanced again toward the bridge in the darkness as she turned in the opposite direction toward the Palacio del Río. Klein walked beside her, his hands in his pockets. She had to concentrate on walking steadily, and inhaled deeply of the damp river air. A slaty fog was settling in, making halos around the lamps, and she remembered the Gulf clouds she had seen earlier in the afternoon. The muggy air would drive the tourists indoors early tonight.

They walked past several patios which were already empty, and Stella could see the dimly lit faces beyond the windows looking back at her in the mist. They left the club district, and the river grew dark except for the tall sidewalk lamps. They passed the amphitheater with its tiered rows of stone seats going up into the darkness and facing the empty stage across the narrow river with its footlights at the edge of the green water. The fog had invaded the permanent set of stone-worked turrets and stairs.

At the theater they took a small path which slanted upward and doubled back higher on the riverbank. The foliage was heavy along the trail, and moisture from the leaves dripped on them as they climbed the path. Once Stella looked back at Klein and saw, against the backlight of a sidewalk lamp on the river, tiny sparkles of mist clinging to his neat blond hair.

The path ended at a sidewalk cabstand beside the front of the hotel. Self-consciously smoothing her hair, Stella, with Klein at her side, walked through the double front doors into the lobby. She briskly approached the registration desk and identified herself as Mrs. Carlos Ramirez and asked for her room key, which the clerk produced from the wall of pigeonholes behind him.

When Stella unlocked the door to the room, Klein stepped past her and put his hand over the light switch.

"Leave it off and close the door," he said, walking straight to the French doors which looked onto the river. He opened the doors and stepped onto the balcony, flanked on either side by rubber plants in clay pots.

"Eight stories down," he said, his voice faint as it fell into the fog beyond the room. He spoke with his back to Stella, and she noticed his buttocks were plump. She looked away.

He turned and came inside, leaving the doors open and allowing enough light to filter into the room for them to see each other and the outlines of the furniture. He stepped to the stereo and turned it on to FM classical music. Stella recognized a Chopin nocturne, soft and delicate.

"I'm sorry. I have my precautions too. Do you have any signals to send your people out there?" He jerked his head toward the balcony.

"No."

"Then you won't object to our conducting our business in this dim light?"

"No. There's little left to do. I'll give you the briefcase, make my call, and we're through."

She walked past Klein, who stood in the middle of the room, and knelt down beside the bed and dragged out the briefcase. As she stood he turned so that the glow from the river lights was to her back. She could plainly see his smile.

"You can make that call a little later," he said, coming toward her. He took the briefcase with one hand and grabbed the wrist of her empty hand with his other. He tossed the case on an overstuffed chair behind her and drew her to him.

She was stupefied.

She knew instantly she had no choice. He knew everything, the code phrases, the checkpoints, the contacts in each city. She was sure she would not be able to kill him if she resisted. And yet she couldn't flee without the briefcase and without making sure he wouldn't be left behind to give them away. She would have to let him do what he wanted. She would even make it easy for him, but as she felt his lips move along the side of her face, she vowed that when he landed in Oaxaca he was a dead man.

Klein buried his face in her neck as his hands went to the back of her dress and found the zipper clasp. With one smooth stroke, he took it to the bottom at the base of her spine. She was braless, and when he brought the dress off her shoulders it fell to her feet and she stood before him in her panties. He cupped a breast in each hand and began to knead them. Despite herself, she grew rigid, and as Klein began to breathe heavily, tears burned at the corners of her eyes.

"Undress me," he said hoarsely, and she began, crying openly but silently. It was all happening in a blur of tears, and then they were on the bed. She opened her eyes just as he straddled her on his knees and she saw his body, soft as the belly of a toad and the color of whey. His face was rigid, expressionless, as he eased himself down in silence.

Staring numbly into the room lit only by the soft light coming from the balcony, she let him work as she listened to the piano, the clear precise notes falling like water from the eaves of a house on a rainy night.

After Klein had spent himself twice, Stella continued to lie still. She didn't know what would happen next; how would it end? He lay as heavy as death on her, and after an interminable length of time she thought he had fallen asleep. She tried to move from under him, but he began again, violently. Then he stopped. His arms moved out across hers and tightened. Reflexively, she began to struggle.

"Just be still," he said. "Be still." His mouth was next to her ear. "Don't scream. I'll ram my fingers down your throat before you get the first syllable out. No one to hear you anyway. Especially not Raúl. Raúl's sleeping. *La sueño de muerte*. That's the reason I was late for our little appointment. He's sleeping in the bougainvillea under the bridge. He was there the whole time we were talking, not fifty yards away . . . dead, dead, dead. Sleep tight, Raúl."

Her terror was absolute.

She felt his stomach jerk against hers as he laughed, and her mind was immobilized.

"Nobody left but you and Señor Paco." She felt his stomach move again. "You're going to tell me about Señor Paco . . ."

Her body convulsed and he pressed himself tighter against her.

". . . or I'm going to do things to you you never dreamed of."

She started to scream, and he rammed his fingers into her mouth with such force his fingernails cut her tongue. Momentarily her hand was freed, and she swung with all her might with cupped fingers against his ear. He grunted with a cough and for an instant loosened his grip, and she broke her other arm free. Reflexively, she dug the thumbs of both hands into his eyes and tried to tear them out of his head. He screamed and flew into a frenzy, breaking her hands away and covering her with rapid, sharp blows. She began to smother and swallow blood, and still he continued to beat her. He was screaming, cursing. She grabbed for something to fight with, a stray pillow, a Bible from the nightstand, and finally an ashtray. She struck him with it and it broke. With the sliver she had left in her hand she struck again, swinging from the side. As deftly as if she had been butchering a hog, she slit his throat.

Somehow she got out from under him and flung herself off the bed, vomiting and trying to wipe away the blood that had gushed over her. Illogically she crouched nude at the foot of the bed, her hands splayed out at her sides and her mouth wide open as she stared in disbelief at the mess in front of her.

She could smell it. It was all over the sheets, still oozing from him, blacker than the darkness itself. She hid from his corpse, scarcely allowing herself breath for life. He would kill her for this, she thought irrationally. He would rise gurgling from the sheets and kill her. She heard herself begin to moan, but she couldn't stop it. Slowly her jaw started to quiver.

She eased her hands down on the floor and crawled around to the chair where her clothes lay on the floor, never taking her eyes off the lump twisted in the sheets on the bed. Rising slowly from the floor, she summoned all her willpower and tore her eyes away from the bed and reached for her clothes. In the instant before she touched them she saw her hands and stopped. The maelstrom in her mind swirled to a standstill as she looked at the blood smeared over her arms and stomach, and tasted it at the corner of her mouth. She seemed to be covered with it, hers and his mingled together, indistinguishable.

In a stupor, she turned and walked around the bed again and went into the bathroom. She took a washcloth from the rack above the sink and began to wash herself. The blood came off easily enough, except for the clots matted in her hair. Several times she gagged at the odor. She looked in the mirror. She had never seemed so white. An elongated maroon lump had risen just above her right eyebrow. Her right cheek was already taking on a greenish tinge, and a raw, burning scrape ran from under her left jaw down to the depression below her Adam's apple. Seeing herself like this, she fought back another throb of panic rising from her stomach. The back of her knees threatened to buckle, and she braced herself against the sink.

You are rational, she said to herself as she looked into the mirror. You must think of everything. Everything.

Her clothes and the briefcase were in there with Klein; she had to get them. And the ashtray. There was no reason for it, but she wouldn't leave without the thing she had killed him with. She had to think of everything because she wanted to go back in there only once. Just her clothes, the briefcase, the ashtray. Taking a bath towel from the rack over the commode, she wrapped it around her and tucked it tightly up over her breasts.

Slowly, with deliberation, she stepped onto the carpet outside the bathroom door. For a moment she stood at the edge of the light, unable to make the step that would take her into the darkness. It was then she noticed the radio was not playing.

She grew numb with the fear that Klein was going to lunge at her from the bed. She waited for it to happen. Everything evil seemed to lurk in the violent disorder of the sheets. Then something glowing on the nightstand beside the bed caught her attention. She looked at it for the first time. It was a clock with a luminous dial and numerals large enough to be read from where she stood. It was twelve-fifteen. A simple fact which fell into place against other facts in her mind like the tumblers in a lock. She moved her eyes slowly to the stereo and looked at its dial. It was still on. The FM station had gone off the air at twelve o'clock.

This simple deduction cleared her mind. He was dead, and only the two of them were in the room. She was in control; she had to make it work the way she wanted it to.

Moving quickly, she went to the chair where she had left her clothes on the floor and took off the towel. She stood sideways to the bed as she dressed, not wanting to turn her back to it but not wanting to face it either. When she finished she picked up the briefcase and her purse and moved to the bed. Her foot bumped something. It was part of the broken ashtray. As she picked it up and put it in her purse, she noticed it had broken exactly in half. Where would the other half be? She tried to remember how she was lying, and how she had brought her hand across from left to right. She would have flung it over on the other side of the bed. His side. She rounded the end of the bed and searched the floor in the darkness with her foot. She found nothing. It was still in the bed with him.

With her foot, she shoved aside his clothes, which had fallen on the floor. She noticed with morbid relief that Klein had thrashed about and covered his head with part of the bedspread. She wouldn't have to see his throat. Carefully she pulled away the sheet from the bottom part of his body. The odor was unbearable. She couldn't see much in the darkness. Reluctantly she reached over and flipped on the bedside lamp.

The scene was unspeakably grotesque in the light, and she was struck by the tawdriness of it. It could have been a black-and-white photograph in one of the cheap detective magazines. She forced herself to move. Avoiding his upper torso, hoping she wouldn't have to take off all the cover, she looked at his feet and legs. Her heart raced as she saw the glint of broken glass protruding from under a pale ankle. Taking care not to touch him, she worked the piece out from under his ankle and put it in her purse. She flipped off the light and took the briefcase and the purse into the bathroom.

Anxious to get out of the suite, Stella raked carelessly at her hair, covering the white porcelain sink with rubiginous flecks of dried blood and loose hair. She turned on the faucet and let the water dissolve the flecks and wash them down the drain in a rusty swirl. She looked at her face; there was no way to cover her swollen bruises, since she never wore makeup and had none with her. She would have to let her hair fall around her face as much as possible.

Tossing the towel on the floor, she took her purse and the briefcase and went out of the bathroom. She listened at the door of the suite. She didn't expect anyone to be in the hall at this time of the night, but her mind conjured up simple and devastating coincidences. She took the "Do Not Disturb" sign off the inside doorknob and opened the door. The hall smelled musty as she turned and closed the door and put the sign on the knob. She tried the knob to make sure it was locked from the inside and then walked around the corner to the elevator.

As she stepped into the lobby she ducked her head, letting her hair fall over her face as she pretended to search for something deep within her purse. As far as she could tell the lobby was empty, and in a few moments she was out the side door and into the street, where a fine drifting mizzle caused the pavement to glisten in the dark.

Chapter 13

Francisco Lyra looked down at the rainy street in the gray midmorning light. His elbows rested on the leather-padded arms of his chair while his long hands, pressed together in a prayerful posture, lightly touched his lips in a reflective attitude. He wore a charcoal Armani pinstripe and a sparkling white Ruffini shirt that showed a glint of gold at the cuffs. The oval cufflinks were converted from pre-Columbian earplugs, as old as the memory of the Toltec jewelers who fashioned them for a priest-king, forgotten except for this crafted vanity. Lyra took the ancient links for granted, as he did so many precious things. So had his father and his grandfather before him.

Angling his wrist slightly, he glanced at the porcelain face of his watch. He sat in the chair comfortably, preoccupied. His eyes betrayed a man taken to the limits of his energies. He had not been home in three days, and the only sleep he had gotten in the past twenty-four hours had been taken in the back seat of his Mercedes 450 SEL in the early-morning hours while it sped along the smooth black ribbon that stretched from Houston. He had come straight to the office and tried to catch up on the messages that flew from Mexico City and Washington with appalling consistency. It was more than he could keep up with. Everyone demanding the latest in developments, everyone demanding the results he couldn't give them.

Today he would have to meet with the FBI agent in charge of the GATO investigation. Even as tired as he was he smiled wryly at the thought of that meeting. It should be amusing. Keep on top of Dan Lee, Limón had told him yesterday morning on the telephone from Mexico City. Lyra had been on the eighteenth floor of Houston's Hyatt Regency sitting in his pajamas and watching the yellow-gray smog move in from the back bays to the southeast. Limón was yelling, telling him to get every last drop of information he could squeeze from the FBI. And from Ruiz Campa. Ruiz had been working with Lee for over a week and should have something by now. The Brigada Blanca weren't idiots. Squeeze Campa. Lyra had smiled wryly then, too.

Francisco rubbed his grainy eyes. He needed six hours of sleep, at least, away from the charged atmosphere he had been moving in for the last few days. He wanted to go home and sleep, then have an hour after waking to collect his thoughts and to mend his frayed nerves. It was more difficult for him than for his staff. He had to appear unruffled. He did not allow himself to loose his temper.

Reluctantly he turned away from the window and the rainy street below and began putting papers into his opened briefcase. He would try to steal the time to do some of his paperwork in his study at home. Unexpectedly his telephone buzzed and Lyra picked it up as he held a sheaf of papers in his other hand. With a forced calmness he spoke in a chilling tone that always terrified his secretary.

"You were going to hold my calls, Miss Baranca?"

"Yes, sir, but this is Senator Kahan. Line two."

Lyra closed his eyes. "You were right. Thank you."

If Leonard Kahan wanted to talk about GATO, Francisco didn't know what he would say. No one was supposed to know what was going on, but there were bound to be leaks sooner or later. He jabbed the button on the black console and spoke briskly.

"Hello, Leonard. How's your morning?"

"Mornin', Cisco, you ol' dog."

Francisco could have shot him. Kahan knew Lyra hated that fractured version of his name. He had discovered that when they were in college together and he used it to needle Francisco whenever Kahan himself was feeling bullish. Kahan knew Francisco was too much of a stuffed collar to protest.

"I hear you were in Houston the past coupla days. Why didn't you call on me? I guess I don't rank high enough anymore, huh, Mr. Ambassador?"

"Word travels fast."

"You know it does, friend. Lotta top-secret stuff goin' on, I understan'." Kahan was shouting as he always did on the telephone. "Stuff you cain't talk about, I guess."

"I'm afraid not, Leonard. What have you got on your mind?"

"Well, I need a little favor." Kahan drawled this out in such a way as to let Lyra know that it wasn't a little favor at all. In fact it was probably sticky. Francisco was silent.

"I got some pressures coming on me down here in Houston,"

Kahan went on, "and money can cut me loose. Ready cash, I mean."

Still Lyra was silent.

"What I need is in your bank down there, and you boys have screwed things up so bad I cain't get it out."

Francisco was relieved. As long as Kahan didn't want to get his finger into the GATO investigation.

"Sure you can get it, Leonard. They've set up a system for foreign investors to recoup their funds. It'll just take a while, maybe four months. Everybody's in the same boat on this one."

"That's the problem. This isn't a usual situation. I need the money now."

"You can't put it off for four months?"

"Hell, I cain't put it off a *week*."

"How much?"

"Three separate accounts. Seventy-five each."

"You want it *all*?"

"I do."

"I can't do that, Leonard. That's two hundred and twenty-five thousand dollars. Over twenty million pesos!"

"That's right, Cisco."

There it was again. Kahan was cocky, and Francisco suspected he had good reason to be. The proportions of the request were commensurate with the weight of the senator's leverage. Francisco didn't like the way the conversation was shaping up.

"I can't do it," he said.

"What d'you mean you *cain't*? It's your bank, for Christ's sake!"

"Not anymore. There are certain restraints now. I can't do things like this as freely as I used to."

Kahan lowered his voice. "I can make it worth the extra effort to ya. I can afford to let go of a little percentage."

Francisco was instantly furious. Goddam him, the clumsy, bumbling politico. To Kahan and millions like him a Mexican was always susceptible to a *mordida,* a bribe. A little haggling here and there and a Mexican would eventually buy off for a little bit of pocket money. But there was more to it than that. Kahan knew it couldn't be that simple. He wasn't getting to the point. A *mordida* wasn't the leverage he was depending on.

"Leonard, it will be virtually impossible to keep this kind of thing quiet."

He could hear Kahan suck in a deep barrelchest of air and let it out. "I'll tell you what, Cisco. I don't like to call in old scores, specially from you, but I think you owe me one."

Lyra tightened his grip on the telephone. They held a world of secrets between them, but like prudent men everywhere each had wisely kept his own counsel, letting the other's indiscretions accumulate like cobwebs in proof of moral indigence. The skeletons in their closets were arsenals held in readiness, and now Kahan was threatening to drag one of them out in the open.

"What's that, Leonard?"

"You know what. I got involved in an uneasy situation 'bout a week ago 'cause of you. I didn't say anything. Just went at it straight and acted real surprised, which wasn't hard to do under the circumstances. But it cost me a little political hide. Nobody ever believes a politician in regard to such things. I don't want to be mean-spirited, my friend, but by God we got to stick together or the damn wolves will eat us up. Now I don't see how withdrawin' my money a little early from your bank can possibly make any waves that cain't be soothed reasonably enough. I mean, we got to work this thing out, don't you see."

Francisco did see. He saw that Leonard Kahan was desperate for his quarter of a million dollars. They understood each other, all right, but Kahan had overplayed his hand. He'd picked the wrong time to ask for this kind of favor; and he'd used the wrong piece of leverage to get it.

"All right. I'll do what I can. I'll do something today. When do you want to pick it up?"

"I thought the courier could bring it up."

"He's not due for another ten days."

"Well, damn, couldn't he just bring it up on the shuttle an' go back the same day? I mean, hell, as a favor?"

This was a blatant turn of the screw, something Lyra knew Kahan enjoyed doing and felt secure in requesting. Lyra didn't like it. He didn't like the way Kahan was handling it.

"I'll have it brought up within two days."

"Listen, I 'preciate it. I'll have something to redeposit in two weeks. It's just that I need it quick, you know. You been a lotta help, my friend. Look, I know you been courtin' some people down here. Let me know when you have time for a little dinner party and I'll arrange it with whoever you want to see. Hell, ever'body gets to Houston sooner or later. It's the goddam buckle on the Sunbelt."

Kahan's tone of jocular familiarity was repulsive. It was the sound of a man who knew he had the advantage, a tasteless magnanimity. It was the good ol' boy maneuvering that Lyra detested so much and that was completely foreign to his own precise style. It maddened him to be compromised by this kind of hokey, transparent manipulation.

The instant he hung up, Lyra realized he shouldn't have had that conversation over the embassy line. It was supposed to be kept clean, but he never assumed that it was, though he had it checked himself periodically. He wasn't going to worry about it; it was too late. He would call the bank from his study phone at home, which he *knew* was clean.

Tossing the last batch of papers into his briefcase, he remembered he hadn't spoken to Susannah in three days. When his trip to Austin had necessitated an immediate trip to Houston, he had called his secretary and told her to inform Susannah of his delay. It was easy to do and saved them both the effort of having to pretend to care.

He locked his briefcase and desk and asked Miss Baranca to call for the car. He took his Aquascutum from the cedar-lined closet and put it on. He tightened the buckle, pulled his suit sleeves down smooth inside the coat, and turned up the collar. With a sigh, he picked up his briefcase and walked out of the office.

Once he sank back in the cushioned leather upholstery, he thought he might doze off. His driver, ever watchful and obsessive about his responsibilities, was taking a longer, seldom-traveled route along Belize Boulevard with its file of palms standing motionless and sullen in the pouring rain.

But he did not sleep. Instead he thought of Susannah. Everything was gone between them. That couldn't be denied. He had known about her affair with Martin Gallagher from the beginning and had dutifully performed the part of the unsuspecting husband. It wasn't difficult to play. He didn't care what they shared between them or how this old lover touched his wife and used her body to satisfy himself. Their relationship was not something he was jealous of or felt compelled to rectify with recriminations or excuses.

And yet he was not without a sense of loss. There were times, rare moments, when his eyes met hers and both their thoughts were drawn from far away to then, that he could feel for one unsuspecting, flashing moment a last remaining passion that refused to die. But those were moments, too, of disappointment. Like the rain, they saddened, left him with a feeling of something final, something absolute.

The silver Mercedes slowed on the curving brick drive and stopped in front of the scalloped portico and flanking orange trees. The heavy wooden door Francisco had brought up from

Oaxaca was darkened by the rain on its bottom third. He looked at it a moment through the rain-streaked window, its wood rippling in veins that aged it still another hundred years. Reuben opened the door, sheltering it with an umbrella as Francisco slid across the seat and stepped out on the red brick to the portico.

Victoria was waiting inside. She took his coat and wiped off his briefcase with a white cloth and handed it back. He stepped up to the whiteness of the main room, intending to cross the corridor to his wing of the house, then saw Susannah watching him from across the room. She was sitting—waiting, he could tell—on the parchment sofa, her taffy hair falling rich and luxuriant about her shoulders. Her feet were tucked up under her beige caftan, and at her back, beyond the glass wall, the rain drifted in gray sheets across the cliffs of Olmos Basin.

He stopped, still holding his briefcase, and looked at her through the shaft of pale, hazy light that fell between them from the octagonal skylight.

"Hello, Susannah," he said.

"Hello." There was no meaning in her voice except the courtesy of acknowledgment.

He was trapped by his own code of civility and the training of a lifetime that demanded propriety. With secret resignation he walked through the column of light and sat in an armchair at the far end of the sofa. He leaned his briefcase against his leg.

"I'm sorry," he said. "I know I should have called you myself. The trip couldn't be avoided."

She smiled. An expression of tolerant amusement.

He didn't know what else to do. There had to be a conversation, though both of them would gladly have let it go. He took a thin cigarette case from his inside coat pocket, held it open for her to refuse, then took one of the handmade cigarettes for himself. He lighted it, inhaled deeply, and was surprised that it was exactly the thing he needed.

"Will it slow down for a while now?" She was doing her part.

He blew a stream of blue smoke up into the air, where it hung like a nimbus above them. He shook his head. "No. It's not going to slow down. I don't know if it will ever slow down again. It seems not."

"What's happening?" She had taken the lace hem of her caftan in her fingers and was lightly tracing the seams of it as though she were reading braille.

"Politics." It was a stupid thing to say, and he was struck that it had taken him only a few sentences to get around to it.

Susannah averted her eyes and nodded. It seemed she was

thinking the same thing. The conversation was a kind of dull ritual for dead spirits. A wake. And yet there was something else, too, something about Susannah's manner that was not so easily identified. Francisco watched her for a few moments and decided she had something she wanted to talk about. My God, why didn't she just come out with it?

"What's bothering you?" he asked.

Susannah's eyes darted to his, surprised. That amused him. She had thought he had lost all touch, all sensitivity to her. She couldn't have been more wrong. Only an absolute fool could be as detached as he had pretended to be these past few years. But it had to be that way. He was embarrassed for her, that she had been so thoroughly duped.

Susannah looked at him oddly, he thought, then stood and walked to the glass wall with her back to him. She wrapped her arms around herself in a hugging fashion. Francisco noticed the cockatoos were gone from the gallery. Gilberto would have taken them to the aviary because of the rain. He probably coddled them too much.

"What do you know about El Gobierno Agrario Tradicional de Oaxaca?"

Francisco's eyes froze on her back. He was stunned. Why? What was this going to mean? Damn, was there no end to the surprises? He suspected them from other quarters, but not from her. It angered him.

He forced himself to be calm. "I could write a book about them," he said matter-of-factly. "What do you want to know?"

She turned from the rain and came back to the sofa and sat down as she had been before. "I've heard rumors there's a crisis in Mexican-U.S. relations and that they're at the bottom of it."

"Our diplomatic community was never discreet," he said.

"I didn't hear this at a garden party," she countered. "I haven't been to one in years. But I don't live in a convent, either, Francisco."

How well he knew that. He wanted to smile.

"Yes," he said. "There are serious problems. And, yes, GATO is definitely at the bottom of it." He ground out his cigarette in a bronze dish. It had been uncovered on an archaeological dig in Yucatán. Like his cufflinks it was pre-Columbian. He used it for an ashtray.

"How serious is it?"

"Why do you want to know?"

"I want to know how it will . . . affect us." She was looking at him now. It was a straightforward question.

111

Francisco thoughtfully rubbed the graying edges of his receding hairline. "I'm not going to be recalled, if that's what you're worried about." They had never discussed it, but he was reasonably sure that when his time came to return to Mexico City, Susannah would not be going with him. The tenure of his marriage was exactly the tenure of his assignment in the States.

"I should tell you," he said, "that the trouble with GATO has caused some dramatic shifts in Limón's operations. It's been a complicated turn of events, but the result is that I've been appointed acting ambassador in the U.S. They're circumventing Washington for the duration of the crisis. It's an enormous responsibility . . . and opportunity. If it goes well I assume I'll be due for a move. I don't know where, but it will be a promotion."

"Congratulations," she said coolly.

He nodded in acknowledgment.

"I understand there's a massive manhunt," she said.

He nodded again.

"What happens to those who are caught?"

Francisco was surprised. Now she was getting down to the real reasons behind her questions. He sensed there was far more to her concern than she wanted him to know. Curious, he answered honestly.

"Some have been killed. Others, if caught, will be imprisoned. What happens to them after that depends on whether they are apprehended by Mexican or U.S. authorities. Even then it will be questionable. The U.S. is likely to extradite them. They want very much to accommodate us right now."

Susannah shifted on the sofa. Francisco waited and watched her. She was going to the heart of it. The preamble was over.

"A woman came here to see me yesterday. I didn't know her and she came alone, very distressed, crying. She's Mexican and has a son mixed up in GATO. She's terrified he's going to be killed, and she was wanting me to intercede with you. You could stop it, she said. You are an honorable man and could save her son. If he is caught she asked that you make sure he isn't extradited to Mexico. She didn't make excuses for what he had done; she just didn't want him in Mexican jails. I told her I'd talk to you."

This wasn't what Francisco had expected to hear. The story did not have the ring of truth about it. He watched her green eyes carefully and asked, "What's the boy's name?"

The eyes flickered. "Domingo. Esquivel."

She was lying! By God, she was *lying*. What was going on here? Then suddenly he *knew*. It was Gallagher. She was doing

112

this for Martin Gallagher. Francisco had feared he would finally get involved. Susannah's affair with Gallagher had been like a sleeping serpent as far as it influenced his career. Not many people in Limón's government knew about it, and those who did were so placed that Francisco controlled them. But if Martin became involved in the chaos around his sister, there would be no way to keep it out of the papers. It could ruin him. He had to know for sure.

But what was she trying to do with this absurd story? Was she trying to find out what would happen to GATO accomplices after they were captured? If Martin was now involved, was she trying to foresee his fate? Was she wanting to know if he, Francisco, could get him out of a legal mess if he was caught aiding GATO? He tried to play her game, see through the silly fiction she had contrived.

"How long has it been since the woman heard from her son?" he asked. He mentally put "woman" and "son" in quotation marks. As far as he was concerned they were ciphers.

"The night before last."

Could she be saying that Martin had talked with Stella at that time? Was Stella going to use him to help her smuggle the documents? She would have to be desperate, almost without any alternative, to involve him.

Hiding his irritation, he tried to appear genuinely concerned. "Is this . . . Domingo trying to flee the States? Is he in hiding?" He cursed himself for sounding like an interrogator.

Susannah hesitated. She seemed nettled by the question, maybe even sorry she had broached the subject. "I don't know. She just wanted to know what would happen to him. If you could stop it."

"Where do I get in touch with her?" he pressed.

"I don't know. She didn't leave anything but her name."

"Then what the hell am I supposed to do?" he blurted in frustration.

"I don't know," she snapped. "Forget it. Forget I brought it up."

She was freezing up, damn her. He wanted to walk over to her and shake her to pieces. What was she trying to do? She hadn't accomplished anything or learned anything. Instead she might have given information he could put to good use. More information, maybe, than the FBI even *knew*. Certainly they weren't passing anything of value along to him. The reports were formalities, bureaucratic double-talk. While a massive investigative machine raked the city from side to side, he had to pretend to be content with the humoring techniques of diplomacy and the condescending spoon-feeding from U.S. intelligence. Nothing was coming from the Brigada Blanca.

Francisco glanced down at his long hands. They felt moist and he wanted to get up and wash them.

"Look," he said, taking a deep breath and letting it out slowly. "The investigation's moving quickly, and there's probably nothing I could do anyway. Or *would* do if I could." He wanted to end this inane play-acting. Reaching down by his chair, he picked up his briefcase and stood up.

Susannah had flushed red. It was not embarrassment, but anger. She had done a clumsy job of whatever it was she had wanted to do, and she knew it. She glared at him, her thoughts unapproachable now that anger had clouded the face he had felt so confident in reading only a few minutes ago.

They faced each other in silence. It was a strange and cruel game they had played with each other over the years, and played still, like bickering children enjoying the discontent too much to stop. But poor Susannah, Lyra thought, knew so little about the rules. No one could know everything, though. Every man lived his life with certain things hidden from him which would change his destiny if he could only know them. It was this thought that preoccupied Francisco as he turned without speaking, and walked deliberately from the rainy gloom of her presence toward the seclusion of his study in his own wing of the house.

Chapter 14

When Martin left Sully's office he followed the grill-hot sidewalks along Houston Street to the newspaper parking lot. The tendons at the back of his neck were as taut as bowstrings, and he had the beginning throbs of a blinding headache. He stopped at a drugstore near Alamo Plaza and bought the strongest nonprescription relaxant he could find. He went back out into the suffocating heat and took a shortcut down an alley that brought him out on the backside of the newspaper parking lot. He was too tired to worry about monitors on the Mustang, and he didn't take the time to watch for tails as he drove through the congested streets to his apartment.

By the time he reached his front door he had developed a raging headache. The pulsing of the summer cicadas in the oaks along the street filled his head to the bursting point as he twisted the key in the lock and pushed his way into the dark coolness of the apartment.

He stripped to his shorts, took the bottle of relaxants into the bathroom, and swallowed the heaviest dosage allowable with a glass of water. The pain at the back of his head was now so severe he walked back to his bed stooped over like an invalid. Carefully, as though his spinal cortex would shatter if he moved too quickly, he eased himself down on the rumpled bed. The sheets were cool, and the last thing he saw through his bleary eyes was slivers of summer light seeping through the cracks in the closed shutters.

Martin rose to consciousness from the deep, black well of drugged sleep. He didn't want to wake, and fought the rocking sensation that was bringing his nerves to sentience, pulling him up from restful oblivion to the awareness of his body stretched out on his bed in the darkness. When he reached the surface he opened his eyes and saw a pewter-gray dawn glowing faintly through the glass panes of the windows. In the same instant that he realized the shutters had been thrown back, he sensed the huge figure beside him and felt the hand stop shaking his shoulder and clamp over his mouth.

He lurched up from his pillow but was flung back onto the bed with such force his head snapped, and then the upper torso of the big man fell across him, pinning him to the mattress. The hand stayed over the bottom half of his face.

In his quarter vision in the charcoal light, Martin saw the simian features of a broad face with a drapery of long hair. He smelled oil and gasoline, and he could feel rough, cracked fingers against his lips.

"Lissen," the giant whispered. "I ain't gon ta hurt yew." The man was Mexican. "Okay, man? Estella sent us. You sister. Okay?"

He loosened his grip slightly, letting Martin nod his head. "I'm gon ta let you up but you batter not make no noise. We gotta sneak outta here. Okay? Estella sent us, okay?"

Martin's heart was about to explode, and he was having trouble getting enough air to keep up with it. Again he nodded and the big Chicano eased his hand off Martin's mouth and raised himself slowly off the bed. Martin started to speak, but the man's hand flew up in the air to signal silence.

The giant stood and backed away from the bed and cautiously closed the shutters again. When Martin's eyes adjusted to the darkness he saw the man was holding his clothes for him. Martin threw back the cover and dressed. As he slipped on his shoes and checked his inside jacket pocket for his wallet, the big Chicano thrust something else at him. A pair of greasy overalls.

As Martin pulled them on the Chicano went to the bedroom door and held it open, waiting. Martin followed him down the hall to the opened back door, where he could see that fog and rain had moved in during the night. A second Chicano, thin and gaunt, stood just inside the door, and Martin realized they were all in identical grease-stained overalls.

With a deferential nod to Martin, the second Chicano stepped out on the back stoop. He shoved his hands into his baggy pockets and looked both ways across the adjoining backyards, then started down the steps into the light drizzle. Martin and the giant followed, and the three of them walked single-file across the backyard to the alley gate. They crossed into the backyard gate of the house on the other side, moving quietly, disturbing only the mist that swirled around them in visible eddies.

They circled the side of the house and stopped beside a toolbox and several pipes left under a sheltering magnolia. Each took something to carry and emerged onto the front lawn and walked briskly to a plumber's panel truck parked at the curb. The thin Chicano got behind the wheel. Martin sat between him and the giant, who rolled down his window and, with a log-sized forearm, bumped the outside mirror until he adjusted it to suit him. No one spoke. The headlights rippled on the wet pavement as the rattling truck moved through the lead-colored streets toward downtown.

When they reached the ornate and long-abandoned Southern Pacific depot near Hemisfair Plaza, the thin Chicano wheeled the panel truck into Shadrack Street and pulled under the shelter of a boarded-up service station. A new, mud-splattered pickup was waiting.

"We got ta shange trocks," the giant said, getting out. He took a screwdriver from his hip pocket and began removing the license plate on the panel truck while the other Chicano unlocked the pickup and started the motor. He motioned Martin to get in beside him, and they sat in the idling pickup while the giant finished.

They continued south through the city, bearing continually west through the barrios of Collins Gardens and into Palm Heights. There was a brief stop while the thin driver made a call from a battered phone booth, and then they swung north on Zarzamora and west again past San Fernando Cemetery. The giant kept his eyes fixed to the outside mirror.

Finally they turned into an unpaved side street lined with small frame houses painted in fading pastels. Most of the front yards were separated from the street by chicken-wire fences overhung with gnarled mesquites and fast-growing chinaberries. Banana trees nestled in the corners of the yards and next to the houses, giving a lush, cool feeling to the shanties. Tomato and pepper plants grew in coffee cans on the front porches, and the grassless yards with dirt packed hard as brick by long summers of bare feet had begun to puddle with yellow pools.

The truck turned quickly into an alley. They slowed, the driver anticipating the jarring *whump!* as the front suspension extended itself to capacity for a water-filled chug hole. They lurched forward and crept along the alley to the crate-cluttered back door of a neighborhood grocery. The thin Chicano stopped the truck and they waited in silence, hearing only the scrubbing of the rubber treads of the wipers on the windshield as they looked out the giant's window at the sagging screen door of the grocery.

Like the arrival of a reluctant ghost, a figure appeared on the other side of the screen, dim and wavering through the rusting wire mesh. The giant spoke: *"Estamos aquí."*

"Bueno," the figure said, and the screen was flung open by a young man in his early twenties carrying a shotgun cradled in the crook of one arm.

"Okay," the giant said and stood in the muddy alley holding the door open for Martin.

Martin got out in the rain and ran for the opened screen door as the truck disappeared down the muddy alley.

"You want to take off those things?" The kid nodded at the overalls, his youthful face somber with the gravity appropriate to a young warrior with a weapon. A mangy mustache was smeared over his top lip and drooped at the corners in the pre-scribed shape of the current style.

They were standing in the storeroom of the grocery, which smelled of Valley fruit, fresh and fragrant, mixed with the over-ripe odor of spoiled produce. A string of blackened lettuce leaves littered one side of the passageway where they stood, and the floor was gritty with mud tracked in from the alley.

The kid took the overalls and hung them over the top of a wire-mesh cage holding empty cardboard boxes. "Come on," he said, and Martin followed him to the end of the aisle, where they turned into a longer passage, their steps muffled on the cement floor as they passed by stacks of produce reaching over their heads to the low ceiling. Two bare light bulbs gave off insufficient light.

They approached the corner of the storeroom, which had been partitioned off with painted plywood to form an office. The kid rapped on the door twice and then opened it, standing back for Martin to go in.

He was not prepared for what he saw. Stella lay on a sagging cot against one wall on the small office. At the sound of the knock she had raised up on one elbow, her misshapen and dis-colored face turned toward him without expression and held at an awkward angle to accommodate a persistent pain. The hair around her face was matted and still wet from the washcloth she held in her hand, and she gazed at him with wide feverish eyes, the black irises watery and piercing.

"Oh, Jesus God." Martin closed the door behind him.

At these words an old woman sitting on a backless chair next to Stella snapped a glance at him and crossed herself, then turned back to Stella, whom she had been nursing with ice cubes wrapped in a towel. Beside her on a tiny table lay cotton swabs and a plastic bottle of peroxide.

"They didn't tell me," he said, gesturing behind him.

"It looks a hell of a lot worse than it is." Stella had to clear her throat before she spoke. Her voice was reedy, without strength, and the bravado of her words seemed inappropriate.

"Who?"

"I think it was Sleep." Her emotions were barely below the surface now that he was here.

Martin could see tears welling in her eyes. The old woman saw them too and placed a gentle hand on Stella's shoulder. *"Reposa, reposa,"* she cooed softly.

Stella laid back, and the old woman frowned at Martin and flicked her head at an office chair beside a battered desk. He pulled it over to the cot and sat at Stella's side as the old woman held her arm and bathed the inside of her wrist with the cool towel. A small oscillating fan shoved the air around in the room.

Martin looked at Stella. Tears seeped from the corners of her eyes as she bit her bottom lip.

"When did this happen?" He was stunned. He wanted to tell her it was his fault, to apologize, but he did neither.

"I tried to keep you out of it, Martin, I really did. After we talked I knew I shouldn't have asked you. I got Suarez to abandon the telephone number I gave you, and he arranged this other deal. But it was a trap... and they killed him... and did this. I needed you. I'm sorry."

"When did it happen?" he repeated.

"Last night. Early this morning." Her voice cracked and she stopped. She glanced uneasily at the old woman and then began her story in a brittle, even voice. Twice during her recitation the old woman crossed herself and whispered, *"Pobrecita,"* but she didn't look up from her lap. Stella didn't go into details, nor did she have to.

When she finished her story, he waited a moment, then said, "I don't think you killed Tony Sleep in that hotel."

Stella was taken aback.

"If he's a professional he wouldn't have handled it the way it happened. He would have killed you straight out. He wants the briefcase and your scalp and that's all he wants. It wasn't him."

"What makes you so sure?" she asked nervously.

"Look," he said. "I need to bring you up to date from my end now. Then there's a lot we've got to get straight." He took a crushed Camel from his coat pocket and lit it with a paper match from a folder he found on the desk. He started with his meeting with Lee and finished with his futile effort to pick up her trail through Sully Greene. He didn't mention his visit to Susannah.

When he was through, Stella said, "Lee shouldn't have told you."

"He was trying to scare me away. But actually I'm involved whether I like it or not, and he did me a favor. I'll stay alive a lot longer if I know what's going on."

"Did he give you any help with Sleep?"

Martin shook his head. "He didn't even know about him."

"What?"

"That's right. The CIA pulled Sleep off the bottom of the deck. I think Lee was furious. I'm sure the Bureau's doing something about it by now."

"Did he tell you who he was working with from the Brigada Blanca?"

"No, but he didn't seem happy about having to do it. And he let me know they were rough. Have you heard from your pilot? Is that still set?"

Stella looked away self-consciously. "When I got here this morning I had these people call Mora, who got a message to Macias about what happened. The grocery was not a part of the emergency plan. I knew these people were sympathizers, and I didn't want to take a chance on going straight to Mora. Those were his boys who picked you up this morning."

"And what are your plans for getting out now?"

"Essentially the same, but the plane's been moved to a country airstrip. Mora's men will take me out. Soon."

"How soon?"

"Today. This morning."

"In the rain?"

"It's better. Rain is the next best thing to darkness."

There was a silence while the obvious hung between them, no longer to be ignored. He knew he was irretrievably a part of what was happening. To pretend he could turn his back on it, even a part of it, could get them both killed. He had dragged his feet long enough.

"How do you want me to handle the briefcase?" he asked.

Stella fixed her eyes on him and shuddered, fighting back a sob. He spoke to relieve the tension. He had never seen her like this.

"I understand there's a schedule, a route. I'll need to know every detail you can think of, any help you can give me."

Stella shifted on the cot so that her back rested against the wall. She began by outlining the route she had given to Klein, including details she had not thought necessary then. She named sympathizers in each city, people he could count on in a bind.

"And what about here?" he asked. "What if something happens after I leave here? Do I contact Mora? This place?"

"No. Once you have the briefcase and I'm gone, you have only one contact here in the city. A black-box number."

"Black box?"

"A safety device. We've rented a room in a boarding house and installed the box, which is actually a one-number terminal. I don't know the details of how it works, but essentially the device diverts the three primary numerals in a dialed number so that the call is rerouted through a prefix other than the one dialed. The box has an automatic timer that disconnects the call after four minutes. It takes seven minutes to complete a trace. If someone should enter the room where the box is located while a conversation is in progress, it instantly disconnects. It's an expensive gadget."

"And what do I tell the 'control'?"

"You're only to call the number in an emergency. You'll know what to say," she said. She reached across to the desk and wrote the number on a piece of paper. She held it up to Martin. He memorized it, and she burned the piece of paper with her lighter. She leaned her head back against the wall, and the old woman gave her a fresh washcloth wrapped in ice. Martin waited.

Finally Stella said, "The briefcase is under the cot."

Martin reached under and withdrew the scarred case. As he hefted it onto his lap he noticed the clasps were soldered closed. It was heavier than he expected.

"How much paper you have in here, anyway?" he said. "It's unwieldly. Too heavy."

Stella started shaking her head, reading his mind.

"I can microfilm it," he continued. "I can get a camera tonight and shoot it myself. I could fit the whole thing in a ballpoint pen."

"No. Don't mess with the case. You can't. Part of the weight's an explosive. It's rigged. Anybody tries to open that without the proper tools and he'll be blown to hell."

"Plastique? There's plastique in here?"

"No. I mean, I don't know," Stella said. "But it's all right. It can't detonate unless you try to open it. It's all in the solder, in a grooved seal around the edges on the inside. You'd have to break that, practically have the thing all the way open, before it would blow. It's stable if you don't do that."

"Stable," Martin said, shaking his head. "And I suppose Paco is the one with the 'proper tools'?"

"That's right. Either he gets them or nobody gets them."

"All or nothing. That's the way this whole thing goes, doesn't it, Stella?"

She locked her eyes on him. "If I'm caught before I get out of San Antonio, the only thing that will keep me alive is the authorities' belief that that briefcase is still in GATO hands. If either government gets me *and* the documents, I'll be killed 'trying to escape.' But if the documents *do* get through to GATO and accomplish their purpose, I'll be safe. The U.S. will not want to be responsible for killing one of the 'heroines' of the new regime with which they must now bargain for their oil."

Her point was well taken. Martin had already seen enough.

Stella wiped her hair back from her swollen face with the damp cloth, leaned over the end of the cot, and picked up her purse, from which she withdrew a zippered bank bag.

"There's twenty-five thousand here," she said, handing it to him. "Half of Klein's fee. He was to get the other half in Oaxaca. If you get the papers there safely, that second twenty-five thousand will only be a down payment. Paco will see to it you receive a far more comfortable compensation."

Martin unzipped the bag and counted the money. Half of it was in large bills, half in smaller ones.

"It's a lot of money," Stella said. "But you'll be surprised how it'll melt away. Living underground isn't cheap. The farther under you go, the greater the cost. And if I were you, I'd use that money to buy invisibility."

There were two quick raps on the flimsy door and the young Chicano stuck his head in. "They just went by," he said.

Stella looked quickly at Martin, her eyes a mixture of emotions. "You'll have to hurry. Ramos and Garcez will take you wherever you wish in the city. When they drop you off you're on your own."

The boy opened the door wider. "Come on, come on."

Martin stood, gripping the bank bag and the briefcase. For a moment they looked at one another, Stella's eyes murky and dark, and then her lips began to quiver. There was nothing to say. Everything between them had been left unsaid, and anything they might say now to try to rectify that would seem trite. He turned abruptly and walked out of the office, following the young revolutionary down the long aisle the way they had come.

He stood inside the screen door watching the rain in the muddy alley. From the outside he knew that now he too looked like a ghost behind the ragged screen. Even more interesting, he felt like one. From here on everything would be as new to him as

122

dying, and it would require all his skill and imagination to avoid that, too.

He heard the pickup before he saw it, and when it pulled up to the cement slab at the back of the grocery the giant already had the truck door open and was climbing out. The boy flung open the screen and Martin dashed out and climbed in beside the thin driver, who nodded as the giant wedged in beside Martin as before. They drove him south on Nogalitos and picked up Military Drive to San Jose Heights and the Las Palmas shopping mall. It was done quickly. The giant let him out in the crowded parking lot, slapped him on the back as he said, *"Buena suerte,"* and was back in the truck before Martin could thank him. The thin driver had never uttered a word.

Surrounded by the mall's insulated atmosphere of canned music and summer sales, Martin found a department store and bought an inexpensive canvas bag. He bought an extra pair of khaki pants and another white shirt and stuffed them in the bag along with the bank bag. He walked out of the department store and headed for a bank of telephones near an island of tropical plants. He chose a panel phone situated so that he could see the escalators and both main corridors. He looked at his watch. It was midmorning.

When Susannah answered he told her immediately that he couldn't talk long. The tone of her response indicated she was alerted, that she hadn't forgotten the tapped lines.

"Look," he said. "I'd like to try to get together tonight. I'm on my way to meet someone for a late breakfast and I'm behind schedule. Why don't you call me there and we'll make arrangements."

"Where will you be?" Susannah asked. There was a slight edge to her voice.

"Same place you and I had breakfast together last week."

There was a pause on Susannah's end. "Okay," she said, her voice tentative.

Martin knew what she must be thinking. They hadn't had breakfast together last week, and she was trying to read his message. "You know, now that I think of it, that was probably the *only* time we've ever had breakfast together." He forced a half laugh.

"Okay," she said. "I'll call you in about fifteen minutes."

As Martin hung up he hoped she had understood him. Nearly six months before they had been lucky enough to wrangle a long weekend together in Monterrey. They had flown down, then decided to rent a car and drive back together. They had arrived

123

in San Antonio from Laredo early in the morning before daylight and had stopped at a JoJo's Restaurant where the Laredo highway intersects Military Drive. It *was* the only time they had had breakfast together in San Antonio. The restaurant was half a mile away.

He took a cab and was there in less than five minutes. He sat in the alcove near the cashier and waited, watching people come in out of the rain for late-morning coffee. When the telephone rang, a tingle formed at the back of his neck as he casually looked at the hostess. She looked up, saw him, and nodded as she spoke into the receiver, then motioned for him to take the telephone.

"Are you calling from a pay booth?" he asked as he pulled the flexible cord as far away from the counter as possible. He was straddling the bag and the briefcase on the floor.

"Yes. God, I'm glad to hear your voice. I wasn't sure about all that mumbo jumbo."

"You did great. Can you come get me?"

"Now?"

"Yes."

"What's the matter?"

"I'll tell you when you get here. Are you being followed?"

"I don't think so. It occurred to me and I watched, but I couldn't be sure. Not absolutely."

"I know. Just watch for it. I'll be waiting."

"I'm on my way."

It seemed an interminable period before the steel-blue Mercedes pulled into the drive and stopped at the front door. He got into the car dripping wet and tense. For a quarter of an hour they drove the rainy streets of south San Antonio as Susannah followed Martin's directions through a convoluted route in an effort to verify they were not being followed. For Martin the greatest strain of the last few days had been never knowing when he was alone and when he wasn't. He didn't talk as he watched the rainy streets.

Finally satisfied, Martin directed Susannah to a collection of smutty pink stucco cottages on a street that had been a main thoroughfare in the 1940s before modern San Antonio had squeezed it into back-street status. The pink neon sign flickering in the rain said they had arrived at the Flamingo Courts, VA-CANCY.

Susannah waited in the car in the gravel driveway while Martin got the keys to the cottage and paid an additional five dollars for a "secluded" cabin, an afterthought by the wheezy desk clerk, who had seen the expensive car and the blonde behind the wheel. The courts were in a gloomy thicket of hackberry trees, and their bungalow was situated at the far end of the courtyard, sitting at an angle from the others. They parked in a carport not visible from the street and let themselves into the musty room that smelled of disinfectant and forty years of smoky nights.

Martin hadn't said a dozen words since Susannah had picked him up. Weary from the tension, he locked the door and stretched out across the stained green bedspread. He rolled over on his back and looked up at her standing motionless at the foot of the bed.

"Can you believe this is happening?" he said softly.

No, she thought, she couldn't, and she couldn't believe it would end in anything good for them, either. But she didn't say anything. She stepped to the two windows covered with café curtains and shoved the flimsy material to the side, letting a pale leaden light into the room. She returned to the foot of the bed and hesitated, then while he watched her she began to undress. The only sound besides the muted drumming of the rain was the soft susurration of silk falling away from her body.

Chapter 15

"They *lost* him?" Lee leaned aggressively toward the agent sitting across from him. "They don't know where he *is?*"

"That's right, sir."

"Who is it?"

"Jameson and Bryan, sir."

"They're in trouble."

"Yes, sir." John Womack had known that when he walked into Lee's office. Jameson and Bryan knew it too.

"How could they *lose* him? A simple sight surveillance like that?"

"Apparently he left out the back way with someone else, sir. His car, the rental Mustang, is still there."

"Apparently? The back door? Don't Jameson and Bryan know about back doors? Are they specializing in front doors?"

"It was raining, sir. Ordinarily during a routine surveillance—"

"This is *not* a routine surveillance!"

"Yes, sir."

Lee took a fortune cookie out of his desk drawer and cracked it open. He didn't offer one to the agent sitting across from him as he angrily thrust half of it into his mouth. Damn, damn, damn. He had taken a chance on letting Gallagher run loose for just one more day to see what it would bring him, and this is what happened. It was a bad ending to an otherwise good decision. It was true they hadn't picked up any of the conversation between Martin and Susannah Lyra, but they probably hadn't missed much. There had been nothing to it in the past, and the odds were they hadn't missed anything significant this time either.

But now Gallagher had disappeared. There was no doubt in Lee's mind Martin was involved despite his warning, but the question was *how*. The *why* wasn't hard to understand. It would take a hard man to stand by and watch his sister being stalked like an animal and not do anything about it. Even though Gallagher had been alienated from Stella for years and disagreed with everything she stood for politically, he wasn't the kind of man to refuse her in a plea to save her life. It was messy, very, very messy.

Lee put the second half of the cookie in his mouth and read the fortune. It was an old one. Over the years he must have read every fortune in the fortune-cookie business a thousand times. Still, he read them. They were like the daily horoscope predictions in the newspaper; he didn't feel totally comfortable ignoring them.

"Signs of violence in the apartment?" He looked suddenly at Womack, who was nervously sliding a yellow pencil back and forth in the groove of his lips.

"The lab man is going over it now, but Jameson said everything looked normal enough to him at first glance."

Lee shook his head at that observation. The telephone rang. Lee put his hand on the receiver, waited for it to ring a second time, and answered with his last name.

"This is Hooper over in Metro," a husky voice said. "I think I've got something for you. You wanted to know the minute something turned up that looked like it might be related to the Cuevas murder. Well, we got it."

"What is it?" Lee asked, reaching for a pad to jot down the address.

"You're practically sitting on top of it. We got one male, Mexican, with one of those needle jobs in the neck. He's under the Crockett Street bridge down here on the river. Then at the Palacio del Rio we got another male, Anglo, in room 812. Looks like a slaughterhouse in there."

"How do you know they're related?"

"The guy in the hotel's carrying the needles."

"I'm coming right now."

Lee hung up the telephone and stood up. "Okay, Womack. Put on your slogs. We're going for a walk."

Though it had been raining steadily since before daylight, the heat had not let up appreciably, and Lee was perspiring under his raincoat by the time they had walked the four blocks to the Crockett Street bridge. The morgue van and the police cars had blocked the street from traffic between Presa and Broadway, and Lee and Womack had to push their way through the crowd that had gathered along the cement balustrade despite the inclement weather.

A uniformed officer guarded the stairs that led down to the riverwalk. Lee showed his identification, and the officer moved aside a temporary barrier to let them descend. As Lee turned the bend in the steps he saw a large sheet of opaque plastic stretched out beneath him like a canopy. When he reached the flagstone riverwalk, he saw that the plastic covered a cluster of palmettos and half a dozen men standing around waiting. Lee saw the corpse's legs first. He thought suddenly that it seemed that in ninety percent of the homicides he saw the legs first. He tucked it away in his mind to think about later.

A tall, bulky blond man broke away from the small group and met Lee at the bottom of the stairs.

"Hello, Hooper," Lee said.

The man nodded. "Everything's the same as we found it." He tilted his head toward an older, slightly stooped man in the group. "I've even held off Latham. It pissed him off but I thought I should."

Lee thanked him and walked to the shelter of plastic sheeting. Everyone nodded and mumbled greetings as Lee came up to the feet of the corpse. With his hands in his raincoat pockets he pulled the coat closer around him as he stepped into the clump of palmettos and looked down into the fan-shaped fronds. He immediately recognized Raúl Suarez, who was lying on his side, his legs slightly bent; he looked like a wino sleeping it off in the bushes. He saw the slight hole Hooper had referred to. It seemed such a little thing to have caused death. He squatted down and went through Suarez's pockets, slowly and delicately, as though he were trying to pick them.

There wasn't much. Small change, a hotel key to the room where the other corpse lay, a Bic lighter, a handkerchief, a comb. No wallet.

Lee stood up, backed out of the palmetto clump, and dropped the things into a plastic bag Hooper's partner, Montoya, was holding open for him. Hooper saw the hotel key and took the plastic bag and read the room number through the plastic. He flicked his eyebrows.

"Okay," Lee said to no one in particular. He turned to the coroner. "Sorry," he said and hoped his expression conveyed the sentiment that it really hadn't been necessary for Hooper to hold him off on Lee's account. The old coroner silently picked up his bag and strode into the palmettos with the deliberate attitude of a man not the least bit squeamish about doing a job which would have to rank as one of the world's most gruesome.

Lee looked at Hooper. "When did you find him?"

Hooper looked at his watch. "It's been about three-quarters of an hour. One of the city's park department boys found him. I'd been here about ten minutes when the dispatcher radioed about the body up in the hotel. I went right on over there, found the needles, walked back here, and called you." He spit out into the rain. "This's beginning to look like an epidemic. I hope you have a handle on it."

They started along the riverwalk past the closed restaurants. The rain glazed the flagstones and the uneven texture of the stones held pockets of water that soaked into the seams of their shoes. The river was green and mottled by the rain, which fell steadily. They walked in pairs, just the four of them, Hooper and Lee, Womack and Montoya, with the detectives carrying umbrellas for the two federal agents. No one talked.

As they approached the Commerce Street bridge, Lee peeped out from under the dripping edge of the umbrella and saw the crowd hanging over the bridge railing. What was it about violence that fascinated people? What was it that gripped them so genuinely that they would stand for an hour in a driving rain just to see a sheet-covered corpse strapped to a stretcher hauled up the cement steps and loaded into a morgue van? Not until the van itself drove off would they be satisfied there was nothing else to justify their morbid vigil in the rain.

They crossed under the Market Street bridge and found themselves at the riverside patio of the Palacio del Río. They stepped under the striped canvas awning, where the pounding rain was almost deafening. They quickly moved into the restaurant, which was empty except for two uniformed officers serving as a reception party. A busboy hurried from the kitchen with Styrofoam cups of steaming coffee and set them on a linen-covered table. They removed their coats, hooked the umbrellas over the backs of chairs to drain, and went through a passageway to the lobby and the elevators.

Room 812 was on the west side of the hotel, the river side. As Lee got off the elevator he saw the police photographer come out of the room with a handkerchief over his nose and mouth and crouch down in the hallway beside his camera case to change film. The two morgue men, dressed in white jump suits, were leaning against the wall talking to a policeman.

Hooper stopped by the photographer. "You through in there?"

"Shit! I wish I was," he said, standing. His thumb pumped the new roll into the barrel.

"Why don't you let us have a look before you finish?"

"Be my guest. If you have any special requests for party shots I'll be right here."

They set their cups on the floor next to the wall and went into the room. The musky odor of blood was overwhelming as soon as they walked through the door. Reflexively Lee took out his handkerchief, as did Womack. Hooper didn't seem to mind the smell; he callously strolled into the room sipping his coffee. As Lee walked around the bed, Hooper spoke.

"I think it was some kind of sex thing here. There's no luggage anywhere, nothing in the bathroom in the way of toilet articles. The desk clerk says a Carlos Ramirez registered here for the room late yesterday afternoon, using a Visa card. Ramirez said his wife would be asking for the key later on in the evening. Around ten o'clock, the desk clerk wasn't sure, a woman accompanied by a man fitting this guy's description called for the key and they went up to the room together."

"Did she have identification?"

"Another Visa card."

"Her description?"

"A Mexican. About five-seven or eight. Wore a peach sundress."

"And when did she leave?" Lee asked, raking aside part of the bloody sheet that was draped on the floor.

"Nobody remembers seeing her leave."

"How did they find the room?"

"Maid let herself in despite a 'Do Not Disturb' sign on the door. Said she had just this one last room before she left her shift and she wanted to get it out of the way. She knocked, tried the door, called, let herself in, called again, went in further and found it. Manager came, saw it, and locked it. The radio was playing on a classical-music station and the balcony doors were open. No lights on. Everything just like you see it."

"And the needles?"

Hooper set his cup on the dresser and took a pencil out of his pocket. He went to the pile of clothes at the side of the bed and laid back the suit jacket with the pencil. In the inside pocket a small leather scabbard protruded from the pocket, and the blunt heads of three needles stuck out of the top of the scabbard.

Lee circled the bed to the coat, crouched down, and delicately retrieved the scabbard with his handkerchief. Hooper put it in a plastic bag he took from his pocket. Lee put his hands in the side pocket of the suitcoat and withdrew a hip-pocket wallet. He found fifty-three dollars in cash and a Visa card for Carlos Ramirez. He checked the other side pocket and withdrew a long folding suit wallet. The driver's license said it belonged to Richard Klein.

"Looks like Mr. Klein lifted his target's wallet after he gave him the needle," he said. The second wallet went into another plastic bag.

130

Lee went through the other pockets, putting everything in the plastic bag with the second wallet. After he had finished he turned his attention to the corpse itself. With the tips of his fingers he tugged at the sheet wrapped around Klein's puffy midsection. The blood had dried and the sheet was a stiff as a canvas tarpaulin. As the sheet came away from the body Klein's rigid limbs resisted the unveiling as if to protect their nakedness in death. But Lee persisted until the body was completely revealed, and then he began to examine it.

The throat wound was enormous but smooth. It extended from one ear to the other side halfway past the jaw, causing the head to hinge low down. Klein's eyes were rolled to the top of his head almost out of sight. Lee turned and took the pencil from Hooper and reached across the distended stomach. He eased the pencil alongside Klein's neck and began probing. Carefully he hooked a gold chain over the end of the pencil, drawing it up away from the wound until he dangled a quarter-sized medallion from the end of the pencil. Pulling the chain tight, he laid the medallion on the sparse hair of Klein's chest.

Hooper and Womack came closer and bent over the corpse with Lee.

"There's nothing on it," Hooper said.

Lee caught the side of the medallion and turned it over to reveal a meshwork screen on its front side. They leaned closer.

"I'll be damned," Hooper said, squinting at the medallion. "Is that a *mike*?"

Lee nodded. "It's probably still live. Whatever happened here last night had an audience. It must have been a grisly transmission."

The medallion went into the plastic bag too. Lee scanned the body. The only thing left on it was a digital watch which pulsed off the seconds, an ironic symbol of the survival of the fittest. Dead man, living machine.

They heard voices behind them and the lab men came in the door with Latham and his assistant. They paused and backed out the door to let out Womack, Lee, and Hooper.

Lee looked at Latham. "What do you think about the guy under the bridge?"

"Just like Cuevas. Neat and simple. I don't think he was killed where he was lying. Looked like he'd been dragged in. Been dead about ten or twelve hours. Around eight or nine last night. No signs of trauma as though there'd been a struggle. The guy was probably nerve-dead in two seconds."

"Well," Lee said, bending down to get his coffee cup, "that one in there is going to look a lot different to you. I appreciate it, Lath."

On the way down to the lobby, Lee told Hooper that Carlos Ramirez was in fact Raúl Suarez and that he suspected the woman was Stella Gallagher. He instructed Womack to have a report to Hooper later that day containing all the pertinent information he would need to make the proper reports on the murders. From this point Womack would act as liaison officer with the Metro police. They could use them as extra eyes in search for Gallagher. Both Gallaghers.

Walking back to his office, Lee mulled over the dual murders as he hunched against the rain. It was his bet that Klein was one of Sleep's assistants. Judging from the photographs that had come in over the wire it couldn't be Sleep himself. It was easy enough to surmise that Klein had killed Suarez, but the circumstances of the two murders could have a dozen scenarios. But who had killed Klein? Stella? Paco? Martin? Jesus, he hoped not Martin.

Jameson and Bryan had followed Martin from Sully Greene's to his apartment at two thirty-five the previous day. When Lee had radioed for them to pick him up at eight-thirty this morning, he was gone. His bed had been slept in. But had he slept one hour or sixteen? His telephone was tapped and he hadn't made a single call during the time he was supposed to be home. Had Stella arranged to pick him up? Or had someone else? That brought him back to Susannah Lyra. He really couldn't put off talking to her any longer. Luckily he had a good excuse. He had not yet called on the ambassador.

Victoria took Lee's raincoat and disappeared with it around a bank of potted palms, leaving him standing alone in the entryway. He had phoned ahead apologizing to the ambassador for reaching him at home and hoping he would understand under the circumstances. Lyra had said Lee was perfectly welcome to come right over. Lee stepped up the few tiled treads into the bone-and-beige decor of the living room. His eyes caught the display cabinets of pre-Columbian artifacts and he walked over and began browsing the glass shelves.

Lee knew the ambassador had a fortune in collectibles. Like Moshe Dayan, he was in love with his past. And like Dayan, he had obtained these sacred shards of antiquity at considerable expense. Often the government's expense. Powerful men, even honored ones, sometimes misconstrue the breadth of their privilege.

"Are you interested in antiquities, Mr. Lee?"

Lee turned to see Francisco Lyra standing in the center of an arched doorway. He was dressed casually, wearing navy trousers and an immaculately pressed long-sleeved white shirt open at the neck.

"Only in a casual sort of way, I'm afraid. My history and my homeland are both remote." He nodded toward the cabinets. "Your own interest is obviously more serious."

"I've been fortunate in my collecting," Lyra said. He turned at an angle to Lee and extended an arm toward the hallway behind him. "Would you like to join me in my study? It's the only room in the house where I can guarantee some degree of privacy."

Lee could vouch for that. During the nearly two years Lyra had lived here his study had been the only room in which they had been unable to plant an effective bug. They had been able to place mikes there on several occasions, but none of them ever functioned after placement. Bureau technicians had never been able to solve the secret, and Lyra's study remained a sanctum. Lee was far more interested in seeing inside Lyra's study than viewing his pre-Columbian statuary.

As they walked together along the corridor beyond the arched doorway, Lyra spoke to fill the silence which is a social embarrassment for diplomats. "As you know, my wife and I have no children, and I'm afraid it has made us a little selfish and even eccentric. Each of us lives in a separate wing of the house. Our lives would appear rather monotonous to most people, I believe."

When they were halfway down the corridor they approached a door on their left. Lyra stepped back and let Lee precede him into the study.

A glass wall was opposite the door, made of huge modern panes, and Lee could tell from its sheen it was one-way glass. It overlooked the sloping lawn to the pool and the Olmos Basin below. The two end walls of the room were covered with overflowing bookshelves, and those adjacent to the door contained artifacts as well as books. A massive antique library table covered with working papers and lighted by two green-shaded lamps sat in the center of the room and served as Lyra's desk. It was flanked on both sides by wooden credenzas, one laden with a bank of the latest telephone and recording systems and the other with the usual paraphernalia of an office work area. A

133

modern beige sofa with matching armchairs and a glass-and-brass coffee table faced the work area.

Lyra closed the door behind them and offered Lee his choice of seats around the coffee table. Lee took an armchair and Lyra settled himself in the center of the sofa, where his tall, lean body looked comfortably at home in this plush atmosphere of authority and intimidating wealth.

Lee declined the offer of a drink. "I want to congratulate you on your recent promotion, Mr. Lyra. Washington informed me of your new responsibilities just this morning. I've assigned a special assistant to prepare your briefings. You'll receive a daily report."

Lyra smiled. "I appreciate your efficiency, Mr. Lee. I'm looking forward to working with you."

"I'm sorry for this imposition this morning, but there have been new developments which I thought should be communicated to you personally. Also, I may need your assistance in several matters."

Lyra nodded accommodatingly and waited.

"An exceptionally dangerous element has entered our search for the GATO leaders. It's been verified that a professional assassin is now involved in the search for Paco and Stella Gallagher." Lee was watching Lyra closely. "I'm not at liberty to say all I know about the origins of the assassin's assignment, but we do know he and the two people we think are working with him have a reputation for working quickly and efficiently. Their presence in this operation has put a tremendous amount of pressure on your government and mine to locate Stella and Paco as soon as possible."

Lee carefully outlined what had happened during the past two days since Cuevas' death, ending with his investigation of the two murders this morning. Lyra's face portrayed nothing but a cool attentiveness until Lee began describing the details of the Palacio del Río scene. Then the change in his expression was practically imperceptible, but certain, though Lee was unable to determine exactly what had triggered the subtle reaction.

"Was Luis Campa with you this morning?" Lyra asked as soon as Lee had finished.

"No, he wasn't. He'd gone with one of my agents to the international airport."

"Then he doesn't know these latest developments?"

"No."

Lyra considered this a moment before he asked, "Is there only one blood type in the hotel room?"

134

"That's being checked out."

"Of course." Uncharacteristically, Lyra momentarily forgot his guest as he let his eyes wander through the one-way glass to the sloping lawn. But it was only a brief lapse and he turned to Lee with his flawless composure intact. "And what is it I can do for you? You said you would need my assistance in several matters."

Lee was cautious. "Stella Gallagher's brother has disappeared. Although he hasn't been close to his sister and has little interest in her political activities, we believe he may possibly be with her now, trying to help her escape. He knows of the assassins. It would be an understandable thing for him to get involved for purely personal reasons."

Crossing one leg over the other, Lee continued. "I thought perhaps I might be able to visit with Mrs. Lyra. I know she's acquainted with Martin Gallagher, and it's possible she may . . . have an idea of his whereabouts. I know it's a long shot, but I've tried everything else."

Francisco Lyra regarded his visitor for a moment longer than Lee found comfortable before he spoke.

"It is not such a long shot, Mr. Lee. I believe we can be candid about that. I do not doubt that the extent of Mrs. Lyra's 'acquaintance' with Martin Gallagher is known to you, though I appreciate your discretion. Unfortunately Mrs. Lyra is not at home just now. She left to go shopping over an hour ago. She was, however, home all day yesterday and all last evening. That can be verified by persons other than myself. But I know that doesn't help you now. I can assure you I shall have her contact you or your office as soon as she returns."

Lyra leaned forward on the sofa and knitted his brow. His long hands took up a small clay figure off the coffee table, and he sat back again turning the figure over in his fingers.

"This is a delicate situation for me, is it not? If the extent of my wife's relationship with Mr. Gallagher were to become known to the general public, the newspapers would be merciless. It would be the end of my career, since I would be directly implicated with the GATO conspiracy. An unfortunate end for a career diplomat. An unjust end, I might add.

"In light of this . . . potential disaster for me, I would like to continue to speak candidly with you, and it is my hope that you will reciprocate."

Lee had not anticipated encountering the kind of frankness Lyra was obviously bringing them to, and he watched the aristocratic Mexican with increasing fascination and a combination

135

of wariness and empathy. A fine dew of perspiration had appeared on the diplomat's handsome upper lip, the only sign of the tension the man obviously felt.

Lyra continued, "This last upheaval with GATO is both a blessing and a curse for me. By virtue of proximity I have been entrusted with responsibility far greater than my position warrants, though no greater than I have always felt myself capable of handling. It's a rare opportunity for me to demonstrate my abilities, a shortcut to advancement. I have been at the right place at the right time, as the saying goes.

"On the other hand, I have the misfortune of my wife's unusual relationship that we have just referred to. Let me say before I go further that I do not blame my wife for her association with Mr. Gallagher. Our lofty claim to mutual fidelity made in our marriage vows was, from the beginning, a sad impossibility which neither of us recognized until it was too late. There were forces, social and political, destined to prevent it. No one is to be blamed, least of all Susannah."

Lee found it difficult to hold his eyes on Francisco Lyra.

"But I would like to salvage what is salvageable," Lyra said. "If not my marriage, then my career. The sooner the GATO affair is over the better. I want to ask you some straightforward questions. I hope you will answer them in the same manner."

Without giving Lee time to agree, Lyra said, "I am well aware that the Mexican government receives from you, through me, only a fraction of the information you actually possess about GATO and its operations on this side of the border. That is only expected. Were the situation reversed it would be no less true. While I will not ask you to betray particulars, I would like to have your honest opinion about the progress of the investigation. Is it being successful from your point of view?"

He stopped and looked at Lee. It was clear he expected a straightforward response, just as he had said. And it was easy to give him one on such a broad question.

"Yes," Lee answered. "Actually I think it's going quite well. It's obvious from our recent arrests that GATO's Stateside operation is crumbling. Of course, the assassins threaten everything. Paco and Stella are still free." And the damned documents are God knows where, he thought.

"But you *are* closer to Stella Gallagher? It is not a matter of weeks, but days?"

"Yes," Lee said cautiously. "I think maybe even sooner than that."

"Then she's still in the city?"

"I think so. Her organization is out of commission. Her closest subordinate, Suarez, is dead. Her possibilities for escape have shrunk dramatically."

"And Paco?" Lyra asked.

"He's useless without an organization."

"But he can create another. It only takes time."

"If he remains at large that's a possibility," Lee said. He hesitated a moment, then added, "But we have reason to believe Paco's hours are limited too."

Lyra's eyes came alive. "Then you know who he is?"

"When the time is right we'll take him."

"How soon?" Lyra's expression was that of a man about to lay a heavy bet, his last, and waiting for the tout's final word.

Lee examined the diplomat's face with mixed emotion, weighing the ballast of his response.

"Soon," he said. "Much sooner than Paco expects."

Chapter 16

Francisco shook hands with Dan Lee at his front door and watched through the window as the boxy green government Fairlane retreated down his brick driveway and disappeared through the pillars at the front gates. Then he turned and retraced his steps to his study, where he went directly to his table/desk and switched off the recording equipment in the credenza. He took a cigarette from a flat opal box on the table and lit it, then pulled a blank pad of paper toward him and picked up a freshly sharpened pencil. He doodled on the fresh paper as he smoked.

After a few minutes, he scratched a number one on the paper and circled it. Out to the side he wrote: "Call Gris about Kahan." He had not had time to call Mexico City about Kahan's account before Lee's office had called and asked if Lee could come over. The FBI agent had gotten there in twenty minutes, and Lyra had only had time to make sure nothing was out of place in his study and to set a new cartridge in the recording equipment before he arrived. Now he had to think through the new information.

Lyra wrote down the number two and circled it. "Call Campa." The investigation was critical now. It was unfortunate Ruiz Campa had not been with Lee to investigate the two murders. Campa would have to insist on sticking close to Lee whether Lee liked it or not. Lyra would complain to the highest authorities if Lee didn't cooperate, and Limón would raise hell that Mexican intelligence was being cut out.

Lyra was amused at Lee's refusal to discuss the source of the newly arrived assassin. The U.S.'s investment in Latin American politics, especially the Mexican question, was too heavy for it not to bring in its big guns when the situation became critical. Obviously the CIA had decided to use the all too familiar talents of Tony Sleep. Francisco could well imagine his simple and succinct instructions: Locate and confront Stella and Paco. "Confrontation" was the latest in a string of euphemisms like "extreme prejudice" and "wet operation."

The arrival of Sleep did not surprise Francisco. He was thoroughly educated in the rivalry of the CIA and the FBI. Mexico was the only country in Latin America, besides Puerto Rico, where the FBI had continued operations against the local leftists after the CIA took over foreign operations in 1947 following the war. Since then both intelligence agencies had been influential in Mexico's efforts to suppress leftists and communist movements, which would surface periodically only to be overwhelmingly crushed by the attention of three intelligence agencies and a vengeful federal police in the form of the Brigada Blanca. It was common knowledge to any Mexican diplomat or politician who had served in the government for any length of time that Mexican presidents received regular briefs from CIA chiefs-of-station, while American ambassadors often cooled their heels until the president deigned to see them briefly over a social Tecate.

He *was* surprised to learn, however, that Sleep had gotten so close to Stella so quickly. In fact, while Lee was describing the scene in the Palacio del Río, Francisco was uncomfortably aware of his own sweating palms and pounding heart. Like Lee, he did not doubt that Martin Gallagher had entered the already complicated plot and for this reason the silence from Campa was doubly frustrating.

He wrote down the number three, circled it. "Susannah and Martin." All he needed was three more days at the most. It would be over then and he wouldn't care anymore. He was sure it had gone beyond salvaging. He was convinced Susannah was involved along with Martin, was probably with him now as a result of the phone call that morning. But surely the FBI would have picked up the arrangements on their tap, and Lee would have known that Susannah had gone to meet Gallagher. God, what a disaster. If it worked, if any of it worked, it would be a miracle. It was such a tragic turn of events after all their careful planning. This was the critical time, and he needed Campa in place.

But there was one matter Francisco did not need Campa to clarify. That was Lee's quiet bombshell that the FBI was closing the gap with Paco. It was, of course, a lie. They might have formulated theories, educated guesses, but they didn't know who Paco was, and they wouldn't know until they captured Stella Gallagher. And maybe they wouldn't even find out then.

However, Lee hadn't told Francisco that they were close without a reason. Whatever Lee's reason was, it meant something altogether different for Francisco. For him, it was the first real alarm that the end of the affair was, indeed, imminent. He would have to move quickly now, without worrying about the other

139

developments over which he had no control. He would move blindly, having faith that the other events, also moving blindly, would work to his advantage.

With a slashing stroke of his pencil, Francisco struck through item one on his list. He turned to the bank of lights on his telephone console, picked up the receiver, and pushed a button. He listened while the technology of Southwestern Bell's most advanced engineering cleared a line for him to the Banco Federal de México in Mexico City. The connection did not ring in the bank's commercial offices, but in a top-floor suite that overlooked the tree-lined Paseo de la Reforma. A woman answered in a voice so clear she could have been in the next room.

"Banco Federal, 1212."

"Lupe, this is Francisco. Give me Gris."

Without responding, she plugged him into silence. He waited, but not long. There were two clicks.

"Francisco?" Gris' voice was firm, inquisitive. Lyra imagined his ample neck bulging over a white winged collar and Windsor-knotted tie. A glass with ice and Pepsi would be sitting in front of him, a napkin underneath it to catch the rivulets of sweat. "Where are you?"

"San Antonio. Everything is fine," he said quickly. "I need a favor, however, with Special Accounts. Do you have the ledger nearby?"

"Just a minute."

Francisco knew Gris was going to the safe. He knew the combination by heart and would be spinning the dial with a sure, firm hand. It would take five turns. The ledger for Special Accounts was bound with a red spine and would be the first of six colored ledgers standing upright on the first shelf of the safe.

"Okay," Gris said. Francisco could hear him breathing.

"Account 060408. Requested withdrawal of total deposits prior to term maturity to be paid within three days. I told him I would do what I could."

Gris made an audible grunt. Francisco knew his fat fingers had traced to the far-right column and pinpointed the figures.

Francisco continued. "Account must be paid within forty-eight hours . . . by night courier. I want a confirmation from you on the delivery. Anytime, day or night. I will spend as much time here in my study as possible. Any questions?"

There was a brief pause from Gris, then he repeated the information.

"Yes," Francisco said.

"Fine. Have you heard from Ruiz?"

"No. Moreover, we've got big problems with American intelligence. The two agencies were elbowing each other over the prize. I just talked with Dan Lee and learned that the CIA has turned loose our old friend Tony Sleep. Sometime last night he got Suarez. He's going to move fast. I would say the odds of the U.S. getting the documents have increased by quantum leaps. According to Lee, the FBI is poised to close in on Stella and has a solid lead on Paco. I don't believe what he says about Paco, though. I think he wanted to see how I would react. As for Stella, I think we will know within the next twelve hours."

"And have you talked with Limón?" Gris was somber.

"He called me yesterday in Houston. Gave me a pep talk. He puts too much faith in the *brigadistas*. They may rule in Mexico, but here in the U.S. the agencies are effectively keeping them at arm's length while pretending to let them in on all the big secrets. And if the pursuit of the documents should go into Mexico, I have no doubt the U.S. agencies will act with full authority. We'll have no similar advantage over them when they get down there. There's too much at stake."

When Lyra finally ended his connection to Mexico City, he turned off the desk lamp and leaned back in his chair. A flat, pallid light came through the windows from the rain-washed landscape, obscuring the details of the study, making them like the grainy images on the screen of an aging black-and-white movie. He took a slim Dunhill lighter from his pocket, reached for the cigarette box, then changed his mind and carefully stood the Dunhill upright on the lustrous surface of the rosewood table. The lighter's gold sheen was the only tint of color in the muted luminescence of the room. Fixing his preoccupied gaze on the solitary obelisk, Lyra thought about what he had just done.

Sending the night courier to Kahan had made his stomach roll over and left him feeling hollow. He knew the feeling and was more familiar with it during the past few years than he liked to admit or wanted to think about. He had learned though, not to struggle with the morality of it for he knew when he was once more faced with this necessary choice he would do it again. He would not avoid the responsibility he had long ago taken upon himself, regardless of the anguish he might wallow in afterward.

But at times like now, he came close to dwelling on it, unable to push ahead to something else, unable to block out the sound of his own voice intoning the foolish euphemism: night courier. He wondered what Sleep called it, and he wondered how Sleep felt about it afterward.

* * *

The rain fell steadily on Medina Street, and the gutters outside Pino's Diner ran gray with the oily scum that washed from the surface of the steamy asphalt. The neon lights came on early as the gray sky turned smokey, embracing dusk, then night. A dark blue sedan eased along the curb in the pelting rain and cut its motor opposite the café, its wipers stalling in the upright position. The rain on the windshield immediately obscured the two occupants sitting in the front seat. The passenger cleared a small space from the fogged side window and focused a pair of binoculars on two diners in the brightly lighted café.

Inside Pino's, Jesse and Ross were finishing an early dinner. They lingered over second glasses of iced tea and looked out to the rainy street when their conversation gave way to long familiar silences. A waitress brought their check and chatted with them as Ross stood and took his raincoat from an empty chair and put it on. He took a second coat and draped it over his arm as he grabbed the handles of Jesse's wheelchair and pushed him to the cash register by the door. They paid, and the tall black man draped the second coat over the dwarf's head and body. Jesse clasped the raincoat around his face and held it tightly under his chin as Ross pushed him out the door into the downpour.

The cherry neon trim that framed Pino's spilled onto the wet sidewalk as Ross pushed Jesse through the rain to the crosswalk. It was the same route they had taken every evening for years, across the street and up the slanting curb at the opposite corner, past Harper's Blue Moon Shoe Shine Parlor, with its nocturnal habitués staring silently out the doorway. Nearly a block farther on they stopped in front of an ornamental wrought-iron railing that bordered a doorway. Jesse opened the gate as Ross pushed him through. While Ross closed the gate, Jesse stuck his arms from under the raincoat and unlocked the door.

Down the street the dark blue sedan had started up and crept along the curb to the intersection. It stopped again and flicked its lights once. From the intersecting street a '67 Ford LTD lowrider slowly pulled around the corner onto Medina. There were four people in the car, two in the front, two in the back. They sat low in their seats, peering out the windows like ferrets with only their heads and gray fedoras with black bands visible above the doors. The driver glanced furtively toward the dark blue sedan as the LTD glided past Harper's Blue Moon and stopped in front of the door with the wrought-iron railing.

Quickly, two *vatos* got out of the back doors wearing the distinctive dark baggy pants hanging in folds over highly polished, pointed shoes. The taller of the two wore a mismatched suit vest over a too large long-sleeved shirt, buttoned at the wrist and neck, without a tie. His stocky companion sported suspenders over a T-shirt. The LTD moved away from the curb and disappeared around the next corner as the two on the sidewalk hunched their shoulders against the weather and thrust their hands deep in their baggy pants. They moved through the iron gate and rang the doorbell. When the door opened, they flashed chrome pistols in the rainy night and shouldered their way inside.

In the dark blue sedan, a chunky little man, holding a trembling Chihuahua in his lap, pushed the play button on his tape recorder. It was the third time he had listened to the tape that evening. The voices were low at first. He adjusted the volume, and Jesse's clear baritone was audible. Martin's voice was less distinct. When there was a brief pause in their conversation, the faint strains of Bach's *Passion According to St. Matthew* could be heard in the background.

Chapter 17

He stood in the dark at the motel-room window and looked across the puddles in the courtyard to the street where the headlights of occasional passing cars caught the angling rain and made it sparkle like shattering glass. He had been awake maybe fifteen minutes, smoking, thinking.

Susannah turned in the lumpy bed behind him and suddenly sat up. "What's the matter? What're you doing?"

"It's okay," Martin said softly, and ground out his cigarette in a little tin ashtray on the windowsill. He walked to the bed and sat on the edge of it. "I was letting you sleep."

"You're dressed," she said, hugging her knees.

"I'm going to walk down the street to an icehouse. I'll get a couple of barbecued sandwiches and beer and bring it back here. We'll talk then, decide what to do."

Susannah threw the sheet back and got out of bed, reaching for her clothes. "What time is it?"

"It's only nine-thirty. I won't be long."

"Wait," she said. "What if someone calls?"

"Don't answer it. But no one's going to call. If they find us they won't worry about calling first."

Martin looked at her standing beside the bed holding her underclothes, a furrow of tension wrinkling her forehead. He walked around to her and took her in his arms.

"I'm sorry," he said. He kissed her and held her tightly, smelling the fragrance of her body that had nothing to do with perfume. "This is a hell of a thing for me to do to you."

"I'll feel better about it when we talk it over. I'm just not sure what comes next," she said.

Martin kissed her on the inside of her neck and then walked to the door. "Keep it locked," he said, and she nodded. He put the room key in his pocket and went out.

He hitched the plastic raincoat over his head as he walked along the muddy pathway beside the street. He had seen the icehouse and barbecue pit earlier that evening when they came in, but it seemed farther than two blocks now as the overgrown weeds soaked his pants halfway up to his knees, and he watched with growing anxiety every pair of headlights that approached him through the rain.

Yellow insect lights cast a jaundiced glow over the open breezeway of Galindo's Barbecue, Ice & Beer. On one side of the breezeway a huge smoke-encrusted brick pit seeped tangy gray smoke into the heavy night air. Several neighborhood cronies sat in straight-backed wooden chairs around the edges of the pit talking and drinking Lone Star as they watched the cars go by. On the other side a clean-cut Mexican kid with a knit Izod manned a counter cash register. His attention was absorbed by a tiny television set.

Martin walked over to a refrigerated locker, took out two bottles of beer, and set them on the counter. He ordered two chopped-beef sandwiches and took two bags of corn chips off a wire rack. The kid rang it up while one of the Mexican men at the pit raised the lid on the brick oven and made the sandwiches on warm buns kept inside the pit. Martin slipped a newspaper from a cage beside the counter, and the kid put everything in a paper sack, which Martin tucked under his raincoat as he stepped out of the lemon glow of the icehouse and into the black-and-white rain.

Susannah let him in as he approached the door and took the paper and sat in the middle of the bed with it as Martin took off his raincoat and soaked shoes. Susannah, wearing only her bra and panties, unwrapped the sandwiches and tore open the sacks of chips while Martin opened the beer and unfolded the newspaper on the bed.

He read the front-page article closely and then thumped it with his hand. "There's what happened last night."

Susannah took it and read it slowly as she chewed her first bite of sandwich. When she finished she looked up at Martin, puzzled.

"Lee's running a tight operation," Martin explained. "The paper says the police 'think' there's a connection between the two murders." He took a swallow of beer. "Well, the man under the bridge was Stella's lead man. I think the guy in the hotel room is one of Sleep's people. Stella killed him."

Susannah sat in astonished silence as Martin related the events leading up to their meeting at the restaurant earlier that day. Martin knew that as he talked it was becoming obvious to her where all this was leading: If she got mixed up in this she could forget Francisco. If she wanted out she needed to get out now, before it went any further. At some point she would have gone too far, if she hadn't already.

She had finished her beer by the time he stopped talking and was tracing her finger around the mouth of the bottle.

"So from here you go to Brownsville?" she asked.

He nodded.

Susannah didn't take her eyes off the bottle. "It was unrealistic of me to think it could go on as it was, wasn't it?"

It was a rhetorical question. Martin looked at her caramel hair falling past her face.

"Actually, I made the choice nearly two years ago. Since then, I've just been stalling. I need you, Martin," she said, looking up. "Far more than you think you need me. I guess that should be enough for both of us, shouldn't it?"

"It is," he said. "It's more than enough."

"So what do we do?"

They sat in the dark, having never turned on the lights. A pale lamp glow came in the windows from the courtyard and fell across the bed where they faced each other. Martin let his mind run up and down the possibilities as he spoke.

"First, before I can leave the city, I have to see Jesse again. I know him. He'll have something for me, something that might save my neck. After that I can go. I want out of here by morning."

"We can go anytime. The sooner the better."

Martin looked at Susannah, her eyes wide, anxious.

"Not 'we.' I don't want you out of this room."

"Martin, be realistic. I'm not—"

"Susannah, listen, I've given it a lot of thought. They're going to be looking for your car. By now they suspect what's happened and they're going to be looking for the two of us. More than that, I need you right here. I've got to have someone I can keep in touch with during the next two days. Someone I can always reach . . . and trust."

"But how're you going to get to Brownsville?"

"You don't have to worry about that. The important thing is that once I get there I'm going to call back here and check in with you. I'll tell you how things have gone, the means and length of time I expect it to take me to get to Tampico. When I get there, I'll check with you again. The same with Veracruz.

"What I need is a lifeline in the event everything else fails me," he said. "If something happens, if my GATO contacts disappear when I need them, I want to be able to turn somewhere for help. You can keep me posted on what's happening here."

146

He tore a piece of paper off the sack and wrote the number Stella had given him. He handed it to Susannah.

"If something goes wrong—if I don't check in when I say I will—or if I tell you for some reason to call this number, then you've got to be free to do it. My life could depend on it."

"How long is this going to take?" she asked.

"I don't know. Several days. They're all going to be looking for you until they know either Stella or the documents are out of the city. Then all the searching will turn to Mexico and the pressure will be off here. Until then you've got to stay hidden. Send out for meals. If you absolutely have to go out, use a cab. Your car's useless until this blows over."

Susannah looked at the telephone number in the dim light. "Who are these people?"

"I don't know. Whatever you do, don't identify yourself or tell them where you are. The very fact that you *have* the number will be proof of your valid association with GATO."

"And if everything goes well?"

"Then I'll call you from Oaxaca and we'll decide what to do."

In less than an hour Martin stood on the sidewalk on Medina Street in the shadow of a dripping pecan tree. He watched the traffic approach him on the one-way street and was grateful for the old pecan's sagging limbs, which protected him from the wash of the headlights of the oncoming cars. Nearly three blocks away, Pino's Diner cast a carnival glow on the shiny sidewalk, and a block closer than that, Harper's Blue Moon threw its own sapphire gleam into the empty street.

Martin shifted the briefcase and canvas bag to his other hand, checked his watch, and moved farther back in the shadows. Something was wrong. He squinted his eyes to see more clearly the grill-protected doorway and window of Jesse's apartment. It was nearly eleven-thirty, and the light in Jesse's window should not have been there. Because they got up at three-thirty in the morning, Jesse and Ross seldom stayed up past nine o'clock and were more often in bed before that. Certainly eleven-thirty was out of the ordinary.

There was something ominous too about the solitary dark sedan that sat at the curb several blocks away. It was difficult to tell because of the rain, but he could swear there were two people sitting in its front seat. Waiting till a string of traffic on one of the cross streets obscured the line of sight between him and the sedan, Martin hurried across Medina to the corner adjacent to Jesse's doorway and stayed close to the brick wall of the building as he continued toward the alley entrance in the middle of the block.

To his relief, the alley was empty except for random clumps of battered trash cans stacked against the glistening walls and a mammoth dumpster bin sitting in a cove at the opposite end. Avoiding the dreggy gutter water that meandered a sloppy course down the center of the alley, Martin made his way to a gray doorway darkened by the loss of light from a shattered bulb above the lintel. He lingered a moment at the lip of the doorway, listening, tense, then stepped into its blackness.

The tunnel-like hallway ran both to his left and right, its narrow confines heavy with the sour odor of garbage trundled daily down its length to the alley door. Martin knew Jesse's kitchen opened into this hall. The wooden floor creaked beneath his feet as he cautiously approached the wedge of light that escaped from under Jesse's door. He held his breath as he leaned over and put his ear to the sticky wood. For a moment he heard nothing, then a deep sigh was heaved so close to the door that Martin flinched. Someone got out of a chair and walked around in the kitchen, pausing, then pacing, stopping several times at one spot.

"I think this little *puto* iss not goin' to wake up this time." The *vato*'s voice was whiny, high-pitched.

"Pick up hiss head," the second *vato* said.

"*You* do it," the first said belligerently.

There was the sickening sound of flesh slapping flesh, and then Martin recognized Jesse's deep baritone moan.

"*Enano!*" the second voice said. "Fuckin' freak!"

"It wass gonna be *sooo eeassy,*" the whiner mocked. "*Sooo eeassy!*"

"Break some more fingers."

"I ain't doin' *nothin'* more to this one," the whiner insisted. "That neeger's dead as shit, man. I ain't goin' to kill this little one too. No way."

Martin backed away from the door, his head swimming, the collar of his shirt wet with sweat. He kept a fierce grip on the briefcase and canvas bag as he lurched across the hall to the back door and burst out into the alley, slipping on the slimy cement steps and going down on one knee before he plowed a shoulder into the trash cans in an effort to break his fall. He got up, his ears ringing with the crash of the cans, and sprinted to the end of the alley and turned in the opposite direction of the way he had come, out of sight of the blue sedan. It was only half a block to a bus-stop kiosk with a telephone.

He dialed the police emergency number, and when the dispatcher answered Martin blurted, "There's a one-twelve at 208 Medina! One-twelve at 208 Medina! Do you hear me, for Christ's sake? Do you *have* it?"

"Got it." The dispatcher's voice was steady. "Hold on."

When Martin heard the dispatcher put the call code on the radio, he hung up. He spun around and raced straight across the street, flinging the briefcase and canvas bag into a hedge at the corner of an office building, then turned back to look across the street. The blue-and-whites came together down Navarro and turned in front of him, going against traffic on Medina. They jumped the curb at Jesse's apartment and mounted the sidewalk to the wrought-iron grill. From the opposite direction a third car screamed across traffic in front of Pino's and headed into the alley, as a fourth did the same from Martin's end.

The loungers in Harper's Blue Moon emptied onto the sidewalk, then fought to get back inside as the *vatos* in Jesse's apartment stupidly opened fire on the police. In an instant the sounds of gunfire and shattering glass filled the rainy night, the pop of small arms punctuated by the reverberation of a riot gun. Then gunfire erupted in the alley too, and Martin saw the lurid flashes from .38 Special muzzles leap toward the back door he had come out of only moments earlier.

Then it stopped as abruptly as it had begun. The sudden silence sucked people into the street again as if they had been pulled from their doorways and cars into a vacuum whose center lay in the spotlighted front door of Jesse's apartment. Two more blue-and-whites arrived with an ambulance, it's siren ripping a gash in the vacuum as the crowd separated to let the EMS van get as close as possible to the wrought-iron grille.

Policemen in flak jackets shouted at one another, cursing the crowd that swarmed around the police cars with their cherry and star-blue lights flashing and sparkling against the buildings in the rain. The shortwave radios crackled and the tinny voice of the dispatcher echoed stereophonically from the opened doors of the cars.

Appalled and jittery with the rush of adrenalin, Martin fell in behind two motorists who had stopped at the curb in front of him and were running across to the ghostly scene in front of Jesse's apartment. He bunched up in the gawking crowd and

149

pressed closer, shouldering his way to the cordon the police had managed to throw up with remarkable speed.

The first stretcher was emerging from the front door into the glare of the white lights provided by a television crew that had also muscled its way to the front. The cameraman followed the stretcher with ghoulish intensity, catching the gray pallor of shock on the *vato*'s waxy face, his arm threaded with an IV held aloft by an attendant who never took her eyes off the victim.

The second stretcher followed quickly with Jesse, a small grotesque hump beneath the starched sheet, an oxygen mask pressed over his discolored face by one attendant while another on the other side held the plastic bag of an IV. His eyes were not closed, but stared unseeing into the night sky. Martin coughed a stinging bilious taste from his stomach but managed not to throw up. He backed numbly into the crowd as the ambulance doors closed and the siren ushered it into the street.

He leaned momentarily against the open door of a patrol car where a boyish officer with one leg stuck out in the rain was talking with the dispatcher.

". . . some kind of torture setup. Yeah, that's right. Yeah, and a Chicano and a black still inside. No, both dead. The Chicano got it in the fire fight. The black was dead when we got here."

Unnerved, Martin made his way to the empty street. He could think only of Jesse's face under the oxygen mask and the sound of his moaning in the stench of the dank hallway. *Vatos!* It had to be Sully. Or Sleep. He would have known about Jesse's connection to Martin too. What in God's name had they done? Suddenly he thought of the sedan and looked toward Pino's. It was gone. Of course it was gone.

Quickly surveying the other streets in both directions, Martin recrossed Navarro and darted into the shadows. He scrambled through the hedge until he found the briefcase and canvas bag. Staying well outside the margins of the streetlights, he hurried to St. Mary's Street, where he turned toward the aging Blue Bonnet Hotel adjacent to the Greyhound bus terminal.

He stood just inside the door of the musty lobby and stared at the harsh fluorescent glare of the terminal across the street. He knew there would be detectives stationed there. It was a busy depot, with several heavily traveled daily routes to Eagle Pass, Laredo, and Brownsville. All on the border. But Martin's intention was not to go into the terminal at all.

The rain was heavier now, coming in sheets like a tropical storm. He looked at the line of cabs parked outside the depot coffee shop. It didn't matter which one. He stepped out in the rain and dashed across the street to the third cab in line. He yanked open the back door and threw his bags into the seat as he leaned sideways and slammed the door. The driver was gone.

Cursing, he slid across the seat and peered out the window at the plate-glass window of the coffee shop. He saw a khaki-uniformed man stand up at his table, take a hurried sip from his coffee, and wave at Martin that he was coming. He tossed some change at the girl at the cash register as he strode out of the shop and ran across the wet sidewalk. He got in on the curb side and pulled himself across to the steering wheel.

"Shit a'mighty," he whooped, rolling his soaked long sleeves up past the elbows. "Wooeeeee, oh! What a flood! What-a-flood!" He took a ragged towel from the front seat and wiped his face. "Monsoon. Mon-*soon*, huh?" Grinning, he turned to Martin. "Where we goin'?"

"I've got a proposition for you," Martin said.

The cabby looked at him. He had bushy sandy eyebrows, a long Nordic face. "No *shit!*" he said with sudden sarcasm.

"I need to go to Brownsville," Martin said. "Right now." He nodded toward the terminal, "It's a two-hour wait for the next one of these things to leave. No more commercial flights tonight, and the charters are grounded because of turbulent weather."

"Rent a car," the cabby offered matter-of-factly.

"I need the sleep."

The cabby looked at him closely, measuring him. "It'll cost you, buddy, and you don't look like no Lamar Hunt to me."

"No, but I can make a bundle if I meet my business partner there by breakfast. It'll be worth it to me."

"That's a six-hour drive. I gotta go the legal speed. Cabbies can't afford tickets."

"Your gas will be about fifty dollars. Covering what you'll lose in fares and paying for the trip . . . I'll give you three hundred."

"Three-fifty."

"Fine. Three-fifty."

"In advance."

Martin reached inside the canvas bag, produced the money, and handed it over.

The cabby counted it. "Okay, Jack, you got yourself a deal," he said. "We'll go by the garage and leave this thing. I'll say I'm sick, get my personal car, and we'll go. Shit, I'll be back by lunch."

Chapter 18

By two o'clock in the morning the faded green station wagon was plowing through the dense fog that blanketed the empty stretches of brush country between San Antonio and the Mexican border. They had run out of the rain altogether. For the first half hour the cabby tried to carry on a conversation with Martin, who refused the part of the talkative businessman from the beginning. He locked his door and pretended to nod off as he leaned against it, answering the persistent cabby's monologues with occasional grunts. After a while the cabby gave up and turned on the radio.

At three-thirty the cabby pulled into a roadside café in Falfurrias for coffee. Martin stayed in the car and tried to sleep. He was vaguely aware of the car starting up again as he tossed in the uncomfortable seat, wrestling with surreal dreams that pulled sweat from every pore in his body. When he finally decided to give up any hope of rest, he sat up and discovered they were already on the Valley highway between McAllen and Harlingen, their headlights picking up the columns of palm trees on either side of the straight dark corridor.

Martin looked at his watch and then concentrated on the horizon beyond the palms. It was almost six o'clock, and a pastel blue glow was beginning to show in the east beyond the Gulf of Mexico. To his right lay the broad sluggish sandbar-ridden Rio Grande and the brown brush country of northern Tamaulipas, Mexico.

By the time Highway 281 entered the outskirts of Brownsville and became Elizabeth Street, Martin was trying to remember what he knew about the layout of the city. He had the cabby turn off on Palm Boulevard and then again on St. Francis. As they cruised slowly toward the international bridge that crossed into Mexico, Martin could see Fronton Street at every intersection. He got out of the station wagon on Fifth, and the cabby drove away in the gray morning light.

Overhead, huge ash wads of Gulf clouds rolled in from the coast twenty-five miles to the southeast. It happened every morning, and Martin knew that by ten o'clock the swelling southern sun would have burned them off and a baking white heat would parch the earth on both sides of the border. He inhaled deeply, catching the fleeting dewish moisture in the air and the smell of the smoky neighborhoods of Matamoros just across the railroad tracks and the river only blocks away. The street where he stood now was *puro mejicano*, and the good odor of breakfast tortillas wafted through the mesquites and castor bean trees while the bells of the convent of Santa Teresa called the sisters to morning prayer.

In a neighborhood café, Martin ate an oily breakfast of *huevos rancheros* and lingered over several cups of strong black coffee, as he waited for the barrio pawnshops to open at eight o'clock.

When it was time, he paid, took his bags, and walked to the fringes of commercial downtown, where pawnshops and liquor stores proliferated all the way to the international bridge. He was the first customer of the day in Victor Lilas' pawnshop. A corpulent, acne-scarred Victor laid out three similar Colt .45 automatics on the scruffy glass counter at Martin's request. It was the only handgun he was really familiar with. Martin carefully worked the action on each one before choosing. Shit. Shades of Vietnam. The grip on the handgun felt depressingly familiar. He bought a shoulder holster, two extra clips, and a box of ammunition, put everything into the canvas bag, and walked out of the shop.

In a nearby service station Martin strapped the .45 under his left arm and checked in the mirror to see if the bulge showed under his suitcoat. It didn't, but the heavy-duty sidearm felt as big as a cannon. He was ready to contact the first check station.

Cortez Boots and Leather Goods was not what Martin had expected. The store was situated on a prominent corner of the center of downtown and was one of the most conspicuous businesses there because of a bigger-than-life-size sign of a smiling Mexican *charro* on a rearing horse. According to the sign the store was the Southwest's largest importer of Mexican and Latin American leather and specialized in handmade boots and shoes.

The spacious and elegantly furnished shop smelled richly of tanned leather and exotic dyes and was filled with displays of every conceivable product that could be made of leather, all crafted by Cortez artisans with Cortez imported hides. Martin was met at the door by a handsome and soft-spoken Mexican woman who obviously did not buy her clothes in Brownsville, Texas.

"Could I help you with something this morning?" she asked.

Her smile was pleasant, accommodating. Her expensive clothes and immaculate appearance reminded him that his own clothes had been repeatedly soaked by rain and were certainly no better off for having been slept in during the long ride from San Antonio.

"I'd like to speak to Jimmie, please."

The woman raised her eyebrows in query, still smiling. "May I tell him who wishes to see him?"

"Martin Gallagher." He didn't know what else to say.

"Just a moment, then," she said, and walked across the shop to a Mexican man in a dark sharkskin suit who had been talking animatedly to another man dressed in Western clothes. A woman, presumably the rancher's wife, was being fitted by one of Cortez's bootmakers.

The Mexican woman politely interrupted the two men and spoke softly to Jimmie Cortez, who glanced over his shoulder at Martin. After a few more words, he finished his conversation with the rancher with a raucous laugh and gave a slight bow to the woman being fitted. He strolled across the russet carpet toward Martin, his smile never fading but taking on a more formal demeanor as he took in Martin's clothes with the professional's worldly knowledge. You can judge a man's taste by the way he dresses, but you can't judge his bank account. No need to be hasty with this one.

"Jimmie Cortez," he said, approaching Martin with an extended hand. "What can I do for you?"

Martin took Cortez's hand and shook it, holding it a little longer than necessary as he said, "I need to buy a can of Cavalier black boot polish."

Cortez's smile froze and then in an instant thawed again. "Well, surely." He hesitated. "But I'm already engaged with a client. Perhaps Mrs. Nañez could get that for you."

"That would be fine," Martin said—he didn't know why he found it awkward to say. "I'm on my way to Tampico to see Luz. I thought you might want to know."

Cortez's smile fell away completely as he looked blankly at Martin. Then the corners of his mouth quivered slightly and the smile returned, though somewhat strained.

"I will get your polish, Mr. Gallagher."

Martin followed the sophisticated importer across to the sales counter, and Cortez pulled a can of polish from a wooden display rack where they were lined up like golden tins of tobacco. He placed the can on the counter and glanced around him.

"You'll need a taxi, of course. I'll get you one."

154

Martin tensed. "No, I can handle it from here."

"You will need a taxi," Cortez said meaningfully. *"This* taxi." His eyes stayed on Martin.

Martin nodded reluctantly. "Thank you."

"It is nothing." Cortez had completely recovered his entrepreneurial smile and manner. "If you would like to wait over here"—he indicated a small waiting area with leather chairs near the front window—"you will be able to see your car when it arrives."

Martin walked to the chairs, and Cortez made a call on the telephone by the cash register. He spoke no more than a few words, then walked over to Martin.

"I believe everything is set. Can I do anything else for you?"

Martin looked at him. He would have to get used to this. He didn't really doubt Cortez was his contact, but somewhere, sometime between here and Oaxaca, someone would try to hand him over to the wrong people. Martin would have to be smart enough to see it coming.

"What's the situation at the border station?" he asked.

Cortez took a boot from a nearby display and smiled as he pretended to show it to Martin.

"They are looking for a man and a woman. We were hoping you would be alone. That is a great help. We did not have time to prepare papers for . . . your friend. Of course, they are aware people can cross a border separately. It will not be easy, but you will be in good hands."

"Thank you," Martin said. He would have liked to hear something more specific, but he could tell Cortez was not inclined to give details and did not want Martin in his shop any longer than necessary.

Cortez reached his hand out to Martin again and bent forward deferentially. "Mr. Gallagher," he said, his smile softening, "it is I who should thank you. *Buena suerte.*"

Cortez turned and walked away, and when the cab stopped in front of the store only moments later, Martin did not look back to see if Jimmie Cortez was watching.

In contrast to the slick Cortez, both the cabby and his car were derelict. Neither of them gave the appearance they would be able to hold up long enough to get Martin across the international bridge. The driver had a hacking, consumptive cough that dredged up ragged kernels of phlegm that he flung out the car window with an angry growl. Red-eyed and unshaven, he hunched over the steering wheel as though he were using it to hold himself up rather than to guide the car.

155

They drove to the end of Elizabeth Street and turned right. A block ahead of them the international bridge and customs houses straddled a bend in the Rio Grande. Normally the routine traffic into Mexico was waved through quickly, but today cars were backed up almost all the way to Elizabeth. The cabby pulled up in line and cut his motor, then got out and raised the hood of the car. He stood by his front fender and waved the next few cars around him so that the line of cars developed a bulge where they sat.

He got in again and turned to Martin over the back seat.

"I come over this godawful bridge every day," he croaked. "Sometimes two, three times. These guys know me and they know my car. Breaks down all the time. It's going to break down lots this morning, and we're going to have to push the damn thing right through customs. You and me. Let me have the briefcase."

Martin handed it over the seat, and the driver started pulling rags out of the big slit in the front seat beside him. He shoved the briefcase into the cavity left by the rags and stuffed a few of the rags back in to hide the shape of the case. Then he pulled a roll of electrician's black tape from his pocket and sloppily taped up the slit, which would be next to his right thigh.

He turned again to Martin. "Give me your driver's license."

When Martin complied, he handed him another in return. Martin was astonished to see his photograph, though several years younger, on the counterfeit license. He looked at his new name, Louis Rankin, and tried to memorize the unfamiliar data.

"You got anything in that flimsy bag you don't want them pawing through?" the driver asked.

Martin felt sweaty. He reached into the bag and pulled out the zipper bank sack and handed it across.

The cabbie's eyes widened. "Oh, shit. Money?"

Martin nodded. "A lot of money."

The veteran bootlegger grinned slyly, testing the heft of the sack. "Now wouldn't the lizards like to find this." He laughed, and a shambling rattle knocked around in his chest. He turned around in his seat with his back to the steering wheel and ripped a piece of sweat-faded blue tape off a tear in the plastic seat cover. The bank bag replaced a few wads of foam rubber. He applied more black electrician's tape as he explained.

"I call 'em lizards, those Mexican customs. They won't hardly get out of the shade for shit. Just like a lizard. And they always wear sunglasses. Every damn Mexican you'll ever meet thinks there's something magic in sunglasses. They wear them inside and outside, day and night. Doesn't matter to them. I think it's sleazy-lookin' myself. Anything else?"

"No."

The driver turned around and got out and slammed down the hood. In a few moments he had muscled back into traffic. Both lanes were full now, and a stalled car could not be gone around. It would back up traffic until it was repaired or pushed on through by the car behind it.

The driver turned his head sideways and talked over his shoulder.

"Name's Brooks, Ronald P. Just so you'll know. We'll stall again in a few minutes, little more than halfway to the bridge. We'll be out of commission long enough to get those folks behind us to honking so the lizards will hear it. When I get close enough to the checkpoint for them to see me, they'll know what the shit was about."

True to his prediction, he cut his motor after a few minutes and got out and raised the hood once again. Martin opened his door next to the bridge railing for air and heard Brooks hammering and banging under the hood. After a while he came and leaned on the railing with Martin. His seemingly unconcerned attitude about his car infuriated the motorists behind them, and the honking he had predicted began. He let it go on until an angry Mexican four cars back got out, slammed his door, and started toward them. Brooks expeditiously slammed down the hood, miraculously started the car, and moved up in traffic.

After hacking and spitting out the window, he talked over his shoulder again. "Don't let this Easter-egg business in the front seat fool you. I'm not dumb. If they want something you got, you can't hide it from 'em. They'd take this old junker apart nut by nut. And they're good at it. Do it for a living. But you see, we just want the stuff out of sight. The trick is, they don't think old Brooks from Brownsville's got anything they want. I come acrost here every day and my car breaks down once a week at least. Fact is, I'm a nuisance. They just want to get me the hell out of the way."

Suddenly someone moved alongside the car next to the bridge railing, jerked open the door, and fell in beside Martin, who rammed his hand inside his coat.

"It's okay!" Brooks yelled over his shoulder to Martin. Then he spoke to the man now slumped in the corner panting and sweating profusely in a rumpled business suit, "Tippet, you asshole. I thought you wasn't going to make it. Goddam, this is no way to do it. Wanna get killed?"

157

"I had complications," the man said defensively. He was in his late thirties, and his brow was knitted fiercely, demonstrating he should be commiserated with, as his eyes zipped back and forth between Martin and Brooks.

"The law?"

"No, Lena. She just gives me hell for no—"

"Oh, shut up," Brooks rasped. "Goddam. Okay. This man's your business partner. You're a talker. Soon's we get up to the station you keep it going. Bitch about this junker breaking down, bitch about the heat, whatever. You two are just nipping acrost the border for some quickie shopping. Understand?"

The man nodded.

"Which ID you got?"

"Harrison."

"Okay." Brooks fixed his eyes on Martin in the rear-view mirror. "You get the drift of this? They're looking for a man and a woman together, or a man and a woman trying to cross separately. But not two men. Okay?"

"Fine," Martin said, looking at the fidgeting and disheveled man beside him, but he didn't feel fine about it at all.

When they were two cars away from the checkpoint, where a cement canopy stretched across the two lanes to create a thin ribbon of shade, the cab stalled for the third time. Cursing, his croak high-pitched with frustration, Brooks pushed open his door, got out, slammed it shut, and kicked it. He stalked around to the hood and jerked it up with such force it rocked the car. The cars in front of them moved up, and the customs officers turned their heads toward the stalled cab. One officer put his hands in his gunbelt and strolled over to them.

Brooks raised his head out of the motor and snapped at the officer, "You got any pliers? *Tenacillas!*"

The officer shook his head, and they talked together in Spanish, Brooks gesticulating, explaining what was wrong with his motor. When the other officer finished with the car in front of them he yelled at Brooks and his partner to hurry it up.

Slinging his body around in anger, Brooks stalked around to Martin's window and said, "You guys gotta help me push this thing through."

While the customs agents watched them through their dark lenses, Martin and Harrison got out, went around to the back of the car, put their shoulders to the dirt-caked rear fenders, and shoved the groaning cab through the band of shade while Brooks guided it to the Mexican side of the station. One of the agents stepped out into the sun and directed them to push it to one side. The next car pulled up and the inspections continued.

Harrison swore loudly as he wiped his dripping head with a handkerchief. He looked at the scabby car with disgust, then walked over to one of the Mexican agents and engaged him in a bitchy tirade about his ordeal with this cheapo taxi driver. The agent listened a few moments, then politely tried to move away, but Harrison followed him. He continued harping, drawing in the attention of the other agents as he talked. Could they believe the jalopy this old fart called a taxi? It had broken down four times since they left Brownsville. Four times! The inside was a damn junkyard. Jesus H. Christ!

The agents smiled, nodded their heads in understanding, and tried to ignore him. Harrison kept at it.

Meanwhile, Martin joined Brooks at the hood. As he came around to the front of the car, he saw two Anglos standing in the air-conditioned customs office looking out the window at them. Martin put his head under the hood.

"Did you see those guys inside?" he asked.

"Yeah. They're something new, all right. I told that lizard you were day-trippers. I think they'll just wave us on through when I get this 'fixed,' unless the boys inside want to snoop around."

He started taking the air filter off the carburetor, laying the pieces on the yellow fender of the cab. "I gotta kill a little time," he said. "Wouldn't do to fix it right away." His grease-stained hands prowled over the motor as he fiddled with every wire and nut.

Martin put his arms on the other fender and watched, resisting the temptation to glance back toward the office. The minutes moved like hours, and Martin wondered how the hell Brooks judged when this charade had gone on long enough.

"Having trouble?"

Both of them looked up into the clean, smooth face of one of the Anglos. He wore a lightweight gray suit with some kind of small institutional pin stuck in the buttonhole of its thin lapel.

"Yeah," Brooks said flatly, then jammed his face back down over the carburetor.

The man looked at Martin. "Your friend's pretty worked up," he said.

"He's hot-tempered," Martin said, looking over at Harrison. "He'll get over it." He tried like hell to seem he was taking all this in his stride.

"You going to be long in Mexico?" the man asked. His head

159

was at an angle as he squinted into the sun. His short haircut betrayed his occupation.

"Just today." Martin squeezed his upper arm against the .45. Why the hell hadn't he hidden it in the car too? This guy could probably recognize a gun bulge a mile off.

"Where you from?"

"Houston."

The man nodded. He bent down to see what Brooks was doing, watched him a minute, then rose up and said to Martin, "Could I see your driver's license?"

Martin gave him a questioning look. "What for? I've never had it checked here before."

"Just a different routine," the man said casually.

Martin shrugged, took his license out, and handed it over. The man examined it, looked at Martin, then at the license.

"You look a lot older," he said.

Martin managed a smile. "It's nearly five years old. It expires next April."

The man looked again and nodded.

Brooks pulled his head out from under the hood. "I think she might start," he said. His face was dripping with sweat.

He went around to the driver's side and got in and hit the ignition. Martin could smell gasoline and heard Brooks pumping the accelerator. He tried again and a dark ball of smoke belched from the exhaust as the motor caught. Brooks revved it to a shimmying scream that echoed unmercifully under the concrete canopy of the check station. Everybody looked at them. Brooks grinned up at the Anglo from the inside of the car.

"You just got to know how to treat her." He got out and slammed down the hood, leaving the car running. "Gotta take my customers shopping. Everything all right with those Mexican customs?" He hacked and sent a plug of phlegm whorling over the bridge railing.

"I think so," the man said. He walked up to the car and looked inside.

"You smuggling anything?" he asked Brooks, smiling. A serious man's idea of a joke.

"You betcha," the cabby said sarcastically. "How else you think I got where I am today?" He paused a beat. "What're you boys doing on this side of the river, anyway?"

"Sometimes they need a little help," the man said with an effort at understated self-importance.

"Sure they do," Brooks said.

"Might as well go on," the man said. He handed Martin's driver's license back to him and nodded.

Harrison had heard the car start and was hurrying over, still mopping his face.

"Goddam, got it started. Wonder how long it'll last this time." He looked at the man in the gray suit. "Hey, those guys over there . . . they didn't even check me over. You know, for customs. You need to see my license?"

"Not necessary," the man said, as anxious to avoid this obnoxious sweating gabbler as the Mexican agents were.

"Not necessary? What kind of customs check is this, anyway?"

"Come on, Harrison," Martin said, opening the cab's back door. They got in, with Harrison complaining loudly about the customs farce. Brooks nosed in front of the next car and headed down Calle 1, the main street into Matamoros, Mexico.

"He's just standing there staring at us," Brooks said, his eyes glued to the receding image of the Anglo reflected in the wobbling rear-view mirror.

Martin stood on the tarmac at the southern end of the Matamoros airport. To his left a lake of wild grass lay between him and the main air terminal, distorted by heat waves rising off the asphalt. To his right a single rusted Quonset hut sat alone at the edge of an abandoned runway. The hut served as hangar, office, and home for Paul Kennedy and his insolvent Coastal Airways. The hangar doors were thrown open, and Martin could see the three-bladed nose prop of a single-engine plane at the edge of the shadowed interior. There was no name on the tin hut, no windsock, no trees, nobody moving.

Brooks had parked a good way from the hut to unpack the briefcase and the bag of money. He reminded Martin to tell Kennedy he had come from Jimmie Cortez. That was all he said before he drove off, sharing a fresh bottle of Oso Negro tequila with an emotionally drained Tippet.

Martin started across the asphalt, which was already getting sticky in the ascending morning sun. The wind whipped a piece of loose tin somewhere on the back side of the hut as Martin approached the hangar door. He stood a moment in the sun, a bag in both hands, and tried to peer into the shade from the stark light outside. His eyes wouldn't adjust, so he took another few steps inside, blinking. As his pupils dilated he began to make out various features, a workbench cluttered with tools, one or two beat-up oil drums, a wheelbarrow. Suddenly he flinched

161

and froze as he detected movement only a few feet away. Still trying to focus his eyes, he looked down.

Sitting on the cement floor of the hut with their backs leaning against the tin wall were three men staring solemnly up at him. They didn't speak and didn't look as if they were going to: two Mexicans side by side and an Anglo next to them wearing khaki clothes and a khaki pilot's cap. All three were holding bottles of beer.

Martin singled out the Anglo.

"Paul Kennedy?"

The man looked at the two Mexicans and then back up at Martin. "Yeah."

"I'm Martin Gallagher. I came from Jimmie Cortez. He said you could help me."

Kennedy took a swig from his beer and regarded Martin as he sloshed the brew around in his mouth before swallowing it.

Martin could tell Kennedy was a big man. Big-boned and barrel-chested, with a stomach threatening to get out of hand. He was maybe in his early forties. His face was red, burned by too much sun from the outside and broiled to tenderness from too much whiskey on the inside. His hands were thick and strong, and the hair on his forearms was a wiry blondish-red.

"I need to hire your plane," Martin volunteered in further explanation.

Silence.

Then Kennedy said, "Get yourself a beer," and jerked his head toward a corner where a single chunk of block ice floated in water in a halved fifty-gallon oil drum.

Martin nodded, walked over to the drum, and hauled out an amber bottle of Mexican beer from the icy water. He came back and squatted in front of Kennedy.

The pilot looked at Martin. "I've been expecting you. I got word last night, but it was late and I was having a little drinky and a little nooky and I'm not sure I remember all the details."

"I need to go to Tampico, then Veracruz. From there it's kind of open-ended. Maybe two days in all. I'd like to reserve your services on a kind of retainer basis. I guess you know the coast well enough to keep us out of the big airports?"

Kennedy smiled slowly. He leaned forward and looked at the two greasy and sun-blackened Mexicans. "A little re-*tain*-errrr. Man wants me on a little re-*tain*-errrr." He was imitating W. C. Fields. The Mexicans laughed and nodded, and Kennedy laughed too. He turned to Martin again.

"Those two don't speak a word of English. Can you beat

that?" He laughed out loud. "I know that coast like . . ." He closed his eyes, searching for the right words. "Well, you just wouldn't *believe* how I know that stinking coast. I can get you where you want to go. I could fly you into a gnat's ass and out again and the creature wouldn't even know it. Jimmie Cortez!" He squeezed his eyes shut and leaned his head back and grinned silently, baring his teeth, then he snapped his eyes open and straightened his head, looking at Martin. "Oh, you *bet*." He nodded his head exaggeratedly.

"I'd need to leave soon. This morning."

"That's my plane," Kennedy said, thrusting his bottle toward the Cessna. "This's my ground crew. Faithful ground crew. The plane's the best for what I do and it's *always* ready to go. But about my retainer . . ."

"What's your fee?"

"Is this dangerous?"

"No more so than your regular work."

Kennedy's eyes widened in mock horror. "Oh, well, shit! That'll be one thousand five hundred American dollar bills per the day."

"Fine," Martin said.

"Fine?" Kennedy said. He eyed Martin narrowly, drained his beer, and rose to his feet, grunting and groaning. "Is that all you got to take with you?"

Martin nodded, standing too.

"Then we'll take off in exactly twelve minutes. Payment every day in advance."

"I'll pay you in the air," Martin said.

"Fair enough," Kennedy said. He turned to the Mexicans and told them in Spanish to get the plane ready.

"Do you have a phone I can use?" Martin asked.

Kennedy indicated a tiny office through a grease-smeared window. Martin stepped inside and placed a collect call to the Flamingo Motel in San Antonio. It took a long time before he heard the desk clerk and then Susannah.

"Martin! It seems as if you've been gone ages. Where are you?"

"I'm at the Matamoros airport. I'll be leaving for Tampico in a few minutes. Have you seen the morning paper?"

"Yes. It's all over the front page. How did you know about it?"

"I walked in on it and called the police. Is Jesse alive?"

"Intensive care."

"Those bastards. I can't believe it. Did they say who did it?"

163

"'Gangland grudges.' Something vague like that."

"I thought so. I don't know if it was Sleep or Sully Greene. One of the two, I'm sure."

"Are you all right?" Susannah asked, hearing an edge to his voice.

"I'm fine," he said. "I'm just not prepared for all this. It's as if it's happening to someone else. How about you?"

"Scared. Hurry back."

"I'll call you from Tampico." He hesitated. "I love you."

"I love you, too. I wish I could do something."

"You stay in that motel. That could have been you last night instead of Jesse." He paused. "I'll call you."

"Goodbye," she said.

Outside, Kennedy had already pushed the Cessna into the sun and had raised the cowling to check over the motor. Martin walked up to the plane and looked in. It was a new Turbo Centurion II six-seater, Fleet Blue trim. But there were only two seats in the plane. The back seats had been taken out, and Martin could see that nylon cargo straps had been mounted in the floor on both sides of the cabin.

Kennedy fastened the nose cowling and came around to Martin. He was wearing aviator's sunglasses. They climbed into the plane, and Kennedy took a moment to wedge his hunking body behind the controls, wheezing and breathing heavily as he checked over his instruments. He started the engine and let it idle while he and Martin fastened their belts.

"What you got here is a dream craft, Gallagher," Kennedy explained. "It's brand-new. Only been on two trips. It's turbo-powered, maximum cruise speed of two hundred and twenty-eight miles per hour, takeoff roll of just eleven hundred and fifty feet, uplifting climb of one thousand thirty feet per minute. Autopilot, three hundred navigational compass, Omni-Flash beacon, ELT, directional and horizon gyros, glide slope receiver, weather radar. All sorts of 'amenities,' as they say. Got it in Houston."

He smiled proudly at Martin from behind his sunglasses and shook his head in admiration of the technical resources at his fingertips. He coasted the Cessna out on the runway, checked with the nearby tower, and turned into the hot, gummy Gulf wind. Settling his back comfortably in the cushioned seat, he accelerated, and they hurtled down the runway until Martin felt the plane lift off the tarmac and heard the landing gear retract into the belly.

Kennedy quickly lofted the Centurion above the few remain-

164

ing clouds not yet burned off by the sun and banked south along the Mexican coast. To their right the tawny desert of Tamaulipas stretched its vast solitude toward the purple Monterrey mountains in the distance, and to their left the glittering water of the Gulf of Mexico disappeared over the horizon.

Chapter 19

The flight from Matamoros to Tampico took just over an hour. While they were still fifteen minutes north of their destination they spotted a long smudgy cloud produced by the Petróleos Mexicanos oil refinery located in Ciudad Madero, Tampico's twin city on the northern bank of the Panuco River where it empties into the Gulf.

Kennedy shook his head in disgust and veered inland to avoid the cloud that crept northward along the coast. Circling west and south of the city, he dropped altitude and skimmed over the oldest oil field in Mexico, still active with the monotonous rocking of pumping units scattered across the hazy marshland.

Tampico had been in its heyday when these fields were new around the turn of the century. It had been a lusty, brawling port with a strong international flavor right up to 1938, when Mexico's President Cárdenas expropriated the extensive foreign oil holdings. Though it remained an important port, petroleum exports dropped dramatically and the wild boomtown excitement that characterized the city abated.

But Tampico had once again found itself in the middle of an oil boom when the vast Reforma fields to the south had opened up within the last decade. It was once again a wide-open city, its harbor and docks crammed with oceangoing vessels, its population swelling.

As they flew over the lagoons west of the city, Kennedy banked sharply and circled over the sparkling pockets of water that shared the lowland fresh water with the Panuco River.

He straightened the Cessna and headed toward the city airport. "There's always a few private strips and hangar shacks that feed off the main runways in these airports. I'll put down at one of those. Those *taxistas* watch the little strips. They'll be at the hangar before I cut the engine."

Kennedy stayed with the plane while Martin, carrying the briefcase, endured a hot, crowded three-mile taxi ride downtown. The Hotel Inglaterra was the most modern downtown hotel in

Tampico, with a heliport on the roof and a top-floor ballroom that offered a romantic view of the city at night. It sat on the corner of Olmos and Miron across from the city's main square, the Plaza de Armas, a peaceful park shaded by oriental elms.

Martin stood in the pink Moorish bandstand in the center of the plaza and looked across to the Inglaterra as he went over the description of Vicki that Stella had given him. She was small, almost frail, but with a delicacy that was oriental, not sickly. She had dark Indian hair and eyes and would be wearing her long hair in a single braid that was doubled to make a loop at the back of her neck. He was to buy a miniature oil derrick for his girl, Luz, in Veracruz.

A long shrill whistle sounded on the Panuco waterfront five blocks away, signaling noon, as Martin stepped out of the bandstand and walked across the park to the hotel. He entered the air-conditioned lobby and the welcome blast of cool air that offered instant relief from the city's unrelenting humidity and heat. He headed for the telephones on one side of the lobby and pretended to place a call as he tried to locate the curio shop.

Three main corridors led out of the lobby. Two were on either side of the registration desk. The other was across the lobby from the telephones and led to the pool and an outdoor dining area. The curio shop was at the entrance of this third corridor. A large island of azaleas allowed Martin only a partial view of the shop, so he hung up the telephone and casually strolled to the stone curbing of the flower bed. He propped his foot on the curbing and tied his shoe as he cut his eyes across the corridor to the shop. He actually flinched when he saw the woman.

It was not Vicki. At least, not as Stella had described her. This woman was older, full-bodied though not heavy, with alabaster skin and dark chestnut hair worn shoulder-length, unbraided. Martin stared at her, wiping the bottom half of his face with his hand. He watched her as she crossed the shop to help a customer. She was a handsome woman, but there was something about her, about the way she walked, that gave him an eerie feeling. He had seen her somewhere before. Recently.

He turned, walked to the registration desk, and caught the attention of a young Mexican man in a gold blazer.

"I'm looking for Vicki Zubaran. I understand she works in the curio shop here, but she seems to be gone."

The young man raised his eyebrows quizzically and looked across to the shop. Then he remembered.

"Oh, yes, she called in sick this morning." He turned to another young man and spoke to him in Spanish, nodding his head toward the shop. He listened to the reply and then turned to Martin.

"That is her cousin. He thinks her name is Yolanda. Vicki asked her to fill in for her until she comes back. I'm sure she could tell you how to get in touch with Vicki."

Martin thanked the clerk and walked quickly out the front door of the lobby. Stepping around a sidewalk vendor selling candied fruit from a glass box tied to a rickety cart, Martin quickly ducked into an open-front drugstore. The telephone book listed only two Zubarans. One a Miguel, the other V. Zubaran. Martin deposited the proper change and dialed. A man, perhaps middle-aged, answered, and Martin asked for Vicki.

"I am sorry," the man said. "She is sick and cannot come to the telephone."

"I would like to come by the house, then," Martin said. "It is important that I talk to her."

"No. She is too sick. A doctor has been here."

"I have just spoken with Vicki's cousin at the curio shop. She gave me this number and said she was sure it would be all right if I came by."

There was a long silence, then, "She was wrong," the man said gruffly, and broke the connection.

Martin waited half a minute and dialed the number again. It was busy. He did not doubt that the woman at the curio shop was at this very moment trying to defend herself to the man at Vicki's house. It was all the proof he needed.

He stood in the corner of the drugstore looking out across the plaza. He must have been out of his mind to think he could do this. Anyone who had seen him enter the lobby could have followed him here, could walk in the door, blow his brains out, and walk away with the briefcase.

Should he go ahead to the Veracruz checkpoint and bypass Tampico altogether? That really would be cutting himself off. Stella had stressed following the route outlined and then checking back with GATO contacts if anything went wrong. Fine. He would do that. He would follow the contingency plan set up in case the Tampico contact was compromised.

Though they were only a block apart diagonally, there was a vast difference in the environs and atmosphere of Tampico's two downtown plazas. The Plaza de Armas was an elegant park surrounded by smart hotels, the city hall, and the Tampico Cathedral on its north side. There was a stately, dignified feeling about the plaza that made tourists feel they were experiencing the very best of romantic Mexico when they strolled along its shaded walks and lawns toward its famous centerpiece, the curious Tampico Monumental Kiosk.

The Plaza de la Libertad was a different matter. Only a block from the bawdy Panuco riverfront, this raffish plaza caught the overflow from the waterfront bars and the open marketplace a stone's throw from the railroad station. The flavor of older and better days lingered in the nineteenth-century buildings that surrounded the plaza, where the city's best seafood restaurants were still located. At night prostitutes strolled among the shadows in the park and languorous vendors and impromptu minstrels with guitars or saxophones wandered in and out of the open-front cafés and bars.

It was across from this plaza that Martin checked into the Hotel Ébano on the corner of Rivera Street where Madero made its steep drop down to the docks. He registered in the dingy lobby under the name León Blanco while an effeminate desk clerk with a menacing wire swatter and a wild bug-eyed stare protected the countertop from persistent flies. Martin made his way up the narrow stairs to his room, which looked out over the plaza from the third floor. He locked the door behind him, threw the briefcase on the bed, and opened the two windows. There were no screens, and the management had provided a rusty fan to pull in the dock noises and the river air heavy with diesel fumes and the pungent fragrance of fried onions.

Martin took off his coat and sat on the bed, where he could look out over the green canopy of palms in the plaza. He leaned over on one elbow and dragged the telephone across the bed to him. GATO "owned" the room and the telephone. When the organization needed a safe house in Tampico the contact registered as León Blanco, and he was assigned room 303, which was the only room in the hotel with a private trunk line that did not go through the switchboard. The line was regularly swept.

He dialed the number he had gotten from the airport hangar where Kennedy was waiting. It took the burly Texan a few minutes to come on the line, and when he did Martin could hear low-flying aircraft in the background.

Kennedy said, "You couldn't have called soon enough, good buddy."

"What's the matter?"

"We got 'inquiries' out here."

Martin tensed. "What do you mean?"

"I mean the *federales* were out here pumping me. They were checking all flights originating in the U.S., and they were being pretty damn thorough about it. As far as they were concerned Matamoros *was* the U.S."

"And?"

"Well, they didn't slap no restraints on me, but I'd bet money they're gonna come back. They acted like they were satisfied with my little fabrication, but I didn't suck in to that. Now, I'll do whatever you say, 'cause I haven't broken no laws yet and if they put me on hold it's nothin' to me, but if I hang around much longer you're goin' to end up without a pilot."

"We're in a bind then," Martin said. "My deal here didn't work out. I'm going to have to stay awhile, probably overnight. But I'm going to need you. I can't afford to let them put a hold on your plane."

"Okay. I can handle that. I got some friends with a little strip in the boonies outside town. Real safe. Use it all the time."

"Great, but somebody's going to have to come in and get me."

"I can do that."

"Fine. After you've got everything settled, come to the Hotel Ébano on—"

"I know where it is," Kennedy interrupted. "Can't say much for your taste in accommodations."

"I'm in room 303. Don't stop at the desk. Just come on up and knock on the door six times. If you get in a bind and have to call me, use this number." Martin gave it to him. "It's a special exchange, so don't let it get out of your hands. Understand?"

"Look, Gallagher," Kennedy said after a pause. "These diversionary tactics I'm gonna have to take, they're gonna cost you something. This ain't no ordinary routine situation."

"How much?"

"Let's level with each other," Kennedy continued. "Whatever you're doing is definitely not on the up and up. Now, I don't mind sticking my neck out, but I sure as hell don't want to do it for no charter-flight fees. I mean, there's more risk in this than you let on back in Matamoros. Right?"

"Okay," Martin said. He was willing to pay whatever Kennedy wanted. It was too late to change plans in midstream, and it was becoming increasingly apparent the pilot's savvy was going to be invaluable to him. He obviously had the kind of experience Martin could use, and his knowledge of Mexico's Gulf coast, its hideaways and backroads, could make him worth every cent he charged. "How much?"

"Three thousand American dollar bills per the day."

"That's steep."

"I'm worth it."

"All right."

"In advance."

"When you get here."

"Okay. Look, this place is across the Panuco. It's a little after noon now. It's gonna be the middle of the afternoon, maybe later, before I get to the hotel. Any problems with that?"

"I don't think so," Martin said.

"Okay, I'll see ya," Kennedy said and hung up.

Martin was wringing wet with sweat. The back of his shirt was soaked and the leather holster under his left arm was stained. He hung the holster on the back of a chair and then removed the limp shirt. He flipped on the fan and aimed it at the bed, where he sat down again and called Susannah in San Antonio. It had been only two hours since he had talked to her, and she was surprised to hear from him again so soon.

"I can't believe you're already there," she said. There was excitement in her voice. "If it's going this smoothly you'll be in Oaxaca by tonight. Why don't I go ahead and fly down there? I can be waiting for you when you arrive."

"Everything's *not* going smoothly," he snapped. Her spontaneous optimism angered him. "There's a problem. The Tampico contact doesn't fit the description Stella gave me. I hired a pilot to fly me down here, and the *federales* have already been out to the airport checking him over. Someone's on to me, and I don't have any idea who it is."

"What are you going to do?" Her voice was suddenly far away and tentative.

"I'll call the contact number in San Antonio. I don't know what else to do."

"What happens then?"

"Damned if I know. Listen, I'm staying at the Hotel Ébano on Plaza de la Libertad. I'm registered as León Blanco. I'm supposed to wait until their people contact me and give me further instructions. That's all I know."

"Is there any way I can reach you?"

Martin gave her the same number and information he had given Kennedy.

"Okay, I understand."

"I'll still need you to contact the GATO number for me if something goes wrong. I'm going to call now and report what's happened. As soon as I'm contacted by their people and something happens at this end I'll call you. But if you don't hear

171

from me in, let's say, four hours, call the number and tell them that I said something was wrong. Only don't use my name, refer to León Blanco. I don't know any other way to put a safety backup on this thing."

"This is getting complicated," Susannah said.

"If I'm in good hands I'll call you within the next four hours," he explained. "If you don't hear from me, call GATO. That's all there is to it."

"That's not what I meant. I've got that. It's just . . . well, I can think of so many ways this could go wrong."

"I know. Don't think about it."

After he hung up he called the GATO number. The connection was made remarkably quickly—something to do, he supposed, with the special arrangements on the line. He could tell from the trunk sounds it wasn't a normal hookup, and when the receiver was picked up at the other end there was a hollow humming noise that told him the voice he would hear would be camouflaged with a distortion device. Dan Lee had once demonstrated such a device to him after the Bureau had confiscated it following a kidnapping case several years ago. A soft whirring replaced the hum, and then a single word was spoken.

"Yes?"

Martin had thought it over beforehand. He allowed for a "worst case" situation at the other end and assumed Sleep was listening to the conversation. He didn't want to reveal any actual name or geographic location.

"Mr. Blanco has checked in according to the contingency plan for this circumstance."

The voice that responded was not unlike the croupy tones of a throat-cancer victim who has lost his vocal cords and has learned to talk by means of a series of controlled belches. Martin had to listen closely. He felt the hair on the back of his neck tingle.

"You have done the right thing. Excellent."

"Do you understand?" Martin asked. The mode of communication was tenuous, cryptic. He wanted to be sure.

"Perfectly. And the . . . center of attention?"

It was Martin's turn to interpret. "Safe with Blanco. At his place."

"Excellent."

Martin interjected quickly. "Any news?"

"None. Someone will get to you as soon as possible and identify himself by this conversation. In the meantime be patient. Be careful."

172

The connection was broken and the line went dead.

Martin set the telephone on the floor and fell back on the white sheets of the bed. He was waiting now. Waiting for Kennedy, waiting for GATO, waiting for the whole damn dream to end. Suddenly he was starving. He could smell the food from the cafés fronting the plaza and he thirsted for a cold bottle of Superior.

He went into the bathroom and took a cold shower, then let his body drip dry as he pulled the new khaki pants and white shirt from the canvas bag and dressed. He strapped on the .45 and slipped on his jacket to hide it. He decided not to carry the briefcase with him. He would have to hide it somewhere he could be sure it wouldn't be disturbed for at least another four hours.

Chapter 20

Dan Lee did not like Ruiz Campa. The *federale*, Lee knew, was a high-ranking officer in the Brigada Blanca and had a reputation for being an excellent intelligence operator. Campa was handsome and excessively polite. He had thin lips with a clipped mustache and black hair which he wore in a close-cropped military fashion combed straight back from his forehead. It was a severe style, but then Campa was a severe man. His cosmopolitan manners and easy grace hid an austerity of spirit that Lee found disconcerting. Lee had just seen a demonstration of Campa's ability to slip in and out of his two personalities, and he didn't like it.

They had been at the Santa Rosa Hospital across from Milam Park since two o'clock in the morning. Both Jesse and the Mexican kid had undergone lengthy operations, and the doctor hadn't let Lee and Campa see either of them until just after daylight. The *vato* was first. The doctor whispered to them as they were going into the ICU door that the kid was going to die. His abdomen was mush and he was staying alive on sheer adrenalin. As soon as that played out it would be over.

They pushed through the swinging doors and found the boy hooked to a network of catheters, IVs, and electronic equipment. He lay in the bed, his eyes wide open watching everything that moved: the nurse hovering over the equipment wired to his body, two sobbing Mexican women who appeared to be his mother and sister, a priest praying alone by a blipping cardiac machine.

The doctor stood at the foot of the bed, and the nurse moved away so Lee and Campa could approach. Lee looked at the *federale* and nodded for him to go ahead. Campa looked at the boy, moved in front of Lee as the boy's eyes caught Campa's Mexican features. In a voice too low for Lee to hear what was being said, Campa spat a sharp, taut sentence in Spanish. The boy's eyes rolled as the two women locked their startled eyes on Campa. Before he could say anything else the boy opened his mouth wide in a yawning seizure and began vomiting.

Before the first mouthful of blood and mucus had spilled on the sheets, the nurse yelled and the doctor shoved Lee and Campa aside as the priest pulled the two women away from the bed. The boy died while they watched the medical team work over him in a frantic battle to fight back the inevitable.

Campa stepped out into the hallway and lit a cigarette. He turned to Lee.

"I once knew a woman who looked remarkably like that nurse. She, too, was a nurse and exuded an enormous aura of sexuality without really being aware of it. I think proximity to death does that to some women. It's extraordinary."

He then walked down the hall toward the waiting room. Lee didn't ask him what he had said to the boy.

Jesse's situation was no different. The doctor didn't let them in to see him until there was no doubt the dwarf would die. There was no risk in questioning him. It was seven-thirty and the breakfast carts were moving along the halls in the wing outside the ICU, filling the sterile, polished corridors with the good odors of bacon and coffee, the smells of morning that promised another new day of hope and life, another beginning.

"This little guy's really suffering," the doctor told them as they stood in the hallway. "He already had complications before this, but he didn't know it. I doubt he'd ever had a true physical examination. Some of his internal organs are just as deformed as the rest of him. A real jigsaw puzzle. He's doped, but his senses are acute for some reason. His chemistry's really messed up."

The room was blue from low-wattage fluorescent lights located behind a ceiling sconce. Lee thought it was cold and then noticed the nurse seated beside the monitors near the bed was wearing a sweater. The doctor went to the bed, moved aside an IV trolley, and covered a plastic bag collecting fluid hanging at Jesse's side. He moved around to the far side of the bed.

Lee stood beside Jesse and whispered his name. The dwarf's eyes fluttered open and stared, then turned on Lee.

"I've got a few questions, Jess," Lee said softly, apologetically. For some reason the rhythmic pinging of the cardiac machine made his own heart pound. It depressed him, seemed to have more to do with moribundity than life. He tried to ignore it.

Jesse nodded.

"You know who did this?"

"*Vatos*," Jesse said. His voice, coming from deep in his arched chest, had shifted from a baritone to a rumbling bass.

175

"Yes," Lee said, leaning forward. "Who sent them?"

"No." Jesse rolled his head from side to side.

"We found a tape in your place. A recording of you and Martin. Where'd that come from? Was that yours?"

Jesse rolled his head again.

"Did Sully Greene do this?"

Another negative motion.

"Who?"

"Fat . . . short . . ."

"Did you know him?"

There was no response except for the negative head motion and then: ". . . Chihuahua."

Campa was at Lee's elbow with a notepad and pencil.

"Did he mention Chihuahua? Does he know about the route into Mexico, more than is on the tape?"

Lee repeated the question to Jesse, who rolled his head again and continued to roll it without stopping. Lee looked at the doctor, who only shrugged.

Campa put his hand against Lee's arm and politely moved into his place next to Jesse. He bent down until he was only inches away from the dwarf's head.

"Was the fat man alone?" he asked. "Did he participate in the torture himself? Did he ask you about any specific cities in Mexico? What about Chihuahua?"

Jesse's head rolled incessantly, his mouth falling partially open.

"Was he alone?" Campa spoke mechanically, as though somehow his persistence might trigger a response from the dying dwarf. "Did he mention *any* specific cities in Mexico?"

Jesse's head moved more vigorously and he began to cry, huge glycerol tears that wetted his flushed cheeks.

"We must know," Campa droned. "Specific cities in Mexico. Did he ask you about any specific cities in Chihuahua? Is that it?"

Lee turned away from this bullying, and the doctor moved to one of the IVs and opened it up. Jesse's head was slamming against his pillow, back and forth, back and forth.

"It's too late for you," Campa persisted cruelly, "but you can save others if you help us. We *must* know these things. Cities, places, anything!"

"That's enough," the doctor said. "I can't let you continue."

Campa looked at the doctor, then at the weeping dwarf. "Certainly. Of course. Thank you." He paused momentarily, then turned and walked past Lee out of the room.

The two of them walked the length of the hospital corridor without speaking. When they came to a waiting area with a glass wall that looked out over the front of the hospital to the park, they stopped. Campa lit a cigarette and inhaled deeply. He walked to the glass wall and looked out to the rain-soaked trees. He thrust one hand in his pocket and held the other chest-high and close to his face so that he constantly squinted through the smoke that rose to his face.

He spoke facing away from Lee. "So. What do we have? A little. We have a taped conversation between Jesse and Martin which was apparently taped by someone other than themselves. Not you. Not the *federales*. Obviously Tony Sleep. I would like to know how he did it. But that isn't important, is it?"

He paced back to where Lee was standing. "We know there was a specific route Stella Gallagher was going to assign her *fayuquero*. On the tape Jesse said that some of his informers said the destination was Oaxaca, others had said Veracruz. Just now he himself threw out the city, or state, of Chihuahua. We know she was trying to get her brother to help her. He refused but wanted to save her from assassination. So he began a little investigation of his own... to this Sully Greene. And that's all we know from that tape, isn't it?"

"You think the 'fat man' is Tony Sleep, don't you?" Lee said. Campa had already paced back to the window.

"I think so, yes."

"But that doesn't fit his description."

"Have you seen a photograph of him since 1975? No. No one has. That was six years ago," Campa said simply.

"Then he's still in the city."

"He was at midnight last night."

Lee watched the *federale* bury a cigarette stub in the sand of an ashtray and then light another. He found the Mexican agent's control not only remarkable, but even curious. A major shift in the operation had taken place last night when Lee and Campa arrived at Jesse's apartment. The ambulance and morgue van had already gone, and Hooper and Montoya were again waiting for them. When Lee saw the cassette tape in the middle of the torture paraphernalia he knew he was in trouble. He would be forced to listen to it in Campa's presence and it could blow the top off everything.

It did.

Lee had asked the two Metro detectives if they had listened to it, and when they said no, he asked them if they minded if he and Campa listened to it alone. In the middle of the tape

177

Martin began describing to Jesse his conversation with Stella in Brackenridge Park, and in the process he spilled the whole story about the Limón government documents.

Campa froze, seemingly mesmerized by what he was hearing. He knew what he had stumbled onto, and at the time Lee had given him credit for having a cool head. It must have been an astounding discovery. He had inadvertently uncovered an intrigue between his own government and the Soviet Union, a second plot between the CIA and the FBI to block it, and finally, the news that GATO now had the documents. It was of colossal importance to his government.

As they stood in the wreckage of Jesse's kitchen, Campa looked at Lee and said, "You *know* what this means?"

Lee nodded, angry and embarrassed at the same time.

"My God, what a revelation," Campa said. "I'll want a copy of the tape for Ambassador Lyra."

That had been shortly after midnight. It was now eight o'clock and Campa had not been out of Lee's sight a single moment and still had made no effort to contact the ambassador or his intelligence superiors in Mexico City. Campa was not the sort of man who forgot things. Certainly not these kinds of things. Lee watched the *federale*, wishing he could read his mind.

Lee walked to the window and stood beside Campa without speaking.

"We are at a crossroads, huh?" Campa said, exhaling a lungful of smoke.

Lee remained silent.

"Mr. Sleep has lost an 'associate.' We believe he still has a woman working with him, huh? Stella Gallagher has lost *her* close associate, Suarez. Martin Gallagher has disappeared. Susannah Lyra has disappeared. We think the route for the smuggled documents was to go through Veracruz or Oaxaca, but that could easily have changed by now. Perhaps through Chihuahua?"

"The big question is whether they've left the city or not, whether they've already crossed the border," Lee said. "Sleep's presence at Jesse's last night leads me to believe that *he* thinks the documents are still in the city."

"True," Campa said, looking at his watch. "But as I said, that was . . . eight hours ago."

Lee found a stray fortune cookie in his overcoat pocket and cracked it open. The honey sweetness tasted good. He had had too much coffee.

"His main advantage," Lee said, swallowing, "is knowing what passed between Stella and Klein. I don't know how Klein

178

could have gotten that close to her, in a room like that, without posing as a potential *fayuquero*. If that's the case, she could have revealed the route in detail. Sleep would have heard it via the microphone around Klein's neck."

Campa sighed and nodded. He turned to Lee with a slight smile on his thin lips. "And how do you think my government will react to the tape we heard last night? How do you think our intelligence agencies will cooperate now?"

Lee returned the slight smile. "I learned a long time ago I couldn't anticipate the moves or motives in Washington. They don't tell me everything. They never ask my advice."

"Well, we shall soon see," Campa said. "I must go now to Ambassador Lyra. And you must go tell Washington that the cat is out of the bag, if you will excuse an appropriate pun. If it should happen that your assignment takes you into Mexico, please be assured that I will afford you the same kind of co-operation you offered me here on this side of the border."

Lee felt the sting of the thinly veiled rebuke as Ruiz Campa extended his hand. Lee shook it, and Campa walked away. Lee went to the telephone on the coffee table in the lounge and called Womack at his office.

"Campa is just now leaving here. I imagine he'll be coming by there to get his copy of the tape, and then he's supposed to be on his way to Lyra's. I want you to put the best Mexican agent we have on him and tell him to be ready to follow Campa all the way to Yucatán if he has to. Call Mexico City and put all our agents on standby. Make sure they're receiving hourly teletype updates. I'll be in shortly."

Lee stared down at the rainy street and thought about the depressing turn of events. He had to admit he had lost whatever advantage he might have had over the *federales* and the Brigada Blanca. Campa also had sensed the shift. Lee had an animal fear of having to direct an operation in Mexico, but he knew that was what it was coming to. The series of deaths they had seen in San Antonio during the past two weeks would be like child's play compared to the carnage that would surely occur if they had to enter Mexico. The place was a tinderbox, and Lee's chances of being effective across the border were minimal under the circumstances. He had no leads in Mexico and could expect no help from Campa. It was the Brigada Blanca's game now. And Tony Sleep's.

Susannah began to struggle with the tension and the isolation of the tiny motel room long before the minutes of the fourth

179

hour had begun to diminish. It was now less than thirty minutes away from the deadline that Martin had given her when she should call the GATO emergency number. The gloomy weather had only intensified her anxiety. She couldn't believe Martin wouldn't call before the deadline.

He didn't.

Instead of calling the GATO number, Susannah tried the number at the Ébano Hotel. The connection was never completed. She tried four times, and each time the connection failed to go through. She called the operator, who, after an interminable search, could only report that apparently it was not a working number. Through information she called the hotel on its directory listing, but the lisping desk clerk insisted there was no León Blanco registered and that room 303 was not occupied. Her search had consumed twenty minutes.

Forcing herself to act precisely, she dialed the GATO number. She waited through the same hollow humming Martin had heard and then the whirring. None of the noises meant anything to her, so she was startled to hear the croaky voice that answered with a simple "Yes."

"I have a message," she said hesitantly. "From León Blanco."

"Please."

"He was supposed to call me within four hours of his call to you. He said if I didn't hear from him in that time something was wrong and I should report that to you."

There was no response, only silence.

"He called from the Hotel Ébano . . . he said you would be able to help him," she added. It was a plea.

Silence.

"Did you *hear* me?" she screamed into the phone. "Is anyone there?" She was fighting back tears.

"Yes. Yes, please be calm. I have the message. Where can I reach you again?"

Susannah froze. She listened carefully, wanting to hear every syllable, every nuance of the distorted voice. Her mouth was dry as she strained to listen.

"Hello? Where can I reach you?" the voice repeated.

Susannah was stunned. She *knew* that voice! It was disguised, but she knew it. How could it be? What had she done? She had told him: León Blanco, Hotel Ébano. The connection was broken as she held the receiver to her ear, immobile. Oh, God, what had she done?

She quickly redialed the number, but the connection was never made. There were the same trunk noises she had heard when she had tried to call the number at the Hotel Ébano. Suddenly the number simply did not exist.

She *knew* she had been talking to Francisco. She could not mistake thirteen years of intimate knowledge of that voice. Had she turned Martin over to the Limón government? How had Francisco gotten the GATO number? Had the Brigada Blanca actually succeeded in breaking into the system?

She knew Martin had not anticipated this possibility. He had assumed the secret number would be safe, that it would always be the calm in the center of the storm that had swept over them. There had been no contingency plan for this; she would have to act alone. Martin must not fall into the hands of the Limón government to become one of the thousands of *desaparecidos* mourned by bewildered families. She knew her only course of action. It was true that Dan Lee was looking for him too, that Martin was operating in the wrong theater of war. But they had been friends. That had to count for something. Something in the face of nothing.

Lee had returned to his office from the hospital feeling nasty from not having bathed or changed clothes in nearly forty-eight hours. Though his head felt thick and his eyes were grainy from the lack of sleep, he worked at his desk throughout the afternoon.

He had crypted a cable to Weathers that Ruiz Campa had learned of the documents, and the wires had been busy the rest of the day trying to anticipate reactions from Mexico City. But the Mexican government was ominously quiet, and Washington was nervous. Francisco Lyra's maid said he was not at home, and the agent who had been put on Campa had not reported in since he had left on the assignment.

When the telephone rang, Lee was totally unprepared for what he heard.

"Mr. Lee? This is Susannah Lyra."

There was a brief pause while Lee collected his thoughts before he said, "Are you all right, Mrs. Lyra? I'm sure you know you are considered 'missing.'" Lee pressed the buzzer to Elinor Lederer's office. When she came to the door he motioned for her to trace the call.

"I'm perfectly safe, Mr. Lee, and I'm well aware that you are probably tracing this call, so I'll make it brief." She quickly gave him the background of Martin's situation and her involvement, bringing Lee right up to the moment of her call to the GATO number and her recognition of Francisco's voice.

181

"I can tell you where he was four hours ago, Mr. Lee, but I want some assurances in return."

"What kind of assurances?"

"That he will not be prosecuted when this is all over. What he's doing he's doing for his sister, not a political cause."

"I'm aware of that, Mrs. Lyra. I can assure you only that I'll do everything within my power to protect him. However, I doubt if that will be necessary. Strictly speaking, what he's involved in is not prosecutable under federal law. He's engaged in a special action initiated by the State Department. It's not a black-and-white situation. Do you understand what I'm saying?"

"I'm not really sure. I think so."

"I can tell you one thing," Lee said. "If we don't get to him first, the U.S. government won't have anything to say about it one way or the other. We're going to have to move fast."

There was a silence, and Lee's heart was pounding so hard it rocked his entire body. She *couldn't* hang up on him. He looked at the big red second hand sweeping the face of the clock over the door opposite his desk. He needed another two minutes.

"I'm at the Flamingo Courts on South Flores. I don't know the address."

Lee couldn't believe it. "That's okay. We'll get there," he said quickly. "Listen carefully." He wrote the name of the motel on a notepad and handed it to Womack, who had come into his office with two other agents when Elinor told them who was on the line. "I'm sending a couple of men out to get you. I'm going to start arrangements to take a plane into Mexico. Will you go with me? I've got a million questions. You can help me enormously. It's the only chance we have to get Martin out of this," he added strategically.

"Yes," she said. "I'll go."

"Great. Just stay in your room." He motioned for the other two men to go, for Womack to stay. "They'll be there in a few minutes and will bring you directly to the airport. Okay?"

"Yes," Susannah said. "I'll be ready."

Lee hung up and quickly started jotting down notes.

"Womack, listen to me. I want you to clear the paperwork for the Bureau plane at the international airport. Get me the two best radiomen we've got available. See that they get the kind of equipment we'll need to set up a *strong* signal post in a hotel room and provide five or six agents with car radios. We'll need operational firearms for the four of us. The men from Mexico City can bring their own. Let me know as soon as the plane can be ready."

Lee looked up at the big agent. "This could be it, Womack. By God, I can't believe it. Right out of the blue." He tore the paper off the pad and gave it to the agent, who turned and hurried out of the room.

Lee quickly crypted a message to Weathers informing him of the turn of events and had Elinor send it. Then he got on the direct line to Jack Whitfield, the rangy Oklahoman who was the special agent in charge of the Bureau's Mexico City office. After giving Whitfield the background on Susannah's unexpected call, he told him what he had in mind.

"I want you to take half your available agents and go directly to Tampico as quickly as possible. That'll mean hiring a plane. Get to that hotel and get Gallagher out of there. Be careful. I can't imagine what's going through his mind, but you can bet he's scared.

"Send the rest of your men to Veracruz. Have them set up in a hotel, a suite big enough for all of us, and begin scouring the airport and outlying strips. Check out the farms and ranches and oil-field locations. If Gallagher has gotten out of Tampico his pilot has got to park that plane somewhere."

"That's a long shot, Dan," Whitfield interrupted in a sobering drawl.

"I know, Whit, but it's also the *only* shot. We only know Veracruz is a checkpoint. We don't have anything beyond that. Susannah Lyra is flying down with me, and I'm going to question her on the way. When I find out more I'll radio it down or tell you when I get there if it can't go over the air."

"And how about *federale* support now that they know what's going down? Can I depend on them?" Whitfield asked.

"I wouldn't try. But the last word we had from Washington was that our free movement in Mexico was still a part of the agreement. Do what you have to do."

Shallow puddles on the black tarmac reflected the lights from the twin-engine Beechcraft sitting at the end of an isolated runway at San Antonio's international airport. Lee sat inside the government car and watched Womack and the two radiomen load the equipment he had ordered into the tail compartment of the plane. He could see the pilot sitting in the bright lights of the cockpit sipping a cup of coffee and going over his charts. The weather continued to be nasty, but there was no turbulence that prohibited their taking off when they were ready.

At the far end of the field the headlights of a car turned onto the runway and started toward them. Lee got out of the car and stood in the mizzle and waited. As soon as the car stopped beside him and cut its lights, he stepped over to the back door of the sedan and helped Susannah Lyra out of the car.

"I hope everything is all right," he said.

"How long is this flight going to take?" she asked, ignoring his affability.

"Two and a half hours, maybe three," he said.

She hurried up the steps of the plane, and he followed.

The pilot fired the engines as Womack and the two radiomen finished loading the equipment and pulled up the steps behind them as they came into the plane. Within moments the pilot had secured clearance from the tower and the twin engines propelled the plane down the runway and into the murky night sky. They climbed out of the rain and flew in cloud cover until they were over the brush country of south Texas where the clouds began to break. By the time they crossed the border and entered the Tamaulipian desert, they had clear skies with stars sparkling like tiny pinholes in the dark canopy of the universe.

Chapter 21

"Gallagher! Dammit! You *in* there?"

Martin lurched up off the damp sheets of the sagging bed. He didn't know how long he had been asleep, but the sky above the palm trees in the plaza was purple, growing darker. A streetlight outside the window sent a pale beam into the room.

Once again Kennedy yelled and kicked the door with enough force that Martin heard the rip of splintering wood. He staggered across the room and jerked open the door.

Kennedy's meaty shoulders filled the doorway, and his shirt was blotched with sweat. His khaki pilot's cap was pushed back on his head, revealing sweaty matted hair. He stared hard at Martin.

"You been sleeping? You got a hangover?" he demanded.

Martin suddenly looked at his watch, and Kennedy, growling in disgust, pushed past him and slammed the door. He went into the bathroom and ran a sinkful of water to wash his face.

"I'm not hung over," Martin said, walking to the window and looking out. "After I talked to you I went down to the plaza to eat. Had a couple of beers, ate, and came back. I was going to doze just a few minutes. I guess I was exhausted."

"I guess," Kennedy said sarcastically, his face dripping as he splashed his forearms with cold water. "And I'll tell you what else I guess," he said, turning off the water and walking into the room without bothering to dry off. "I guess you got your ass in a crack."

"What's the matter?"

"You'll notice it ain't in the middle of the afternoon, when I said I'd be here. I ran into trouble. I got to my friend's little strip across the Panuco, tied down, borrowed his old Ford Ranchero, and headed into town . . . and ran right into a roadblock!"

Kennedy arched his shoulders back, his hands dripping at his side as he spoke. "Lookin' for a gringo. *Malo hombre!* They thought I was just the bad man they wanted. Took all my papers, put me in their rickety old Nash patrol car, and took me to the station, where I endured a little anxiety while they pissed away three hours and finally decided I wasn't the *malo hombre* they wanted after all. Apologies all around. They let me go, but I knew they were keeping an eye on me, so I went through a lot of rigamarole before I came here."

"They say who they were looking for?"

"What do you think?"

Martin swore. "They have photographs?"

"I didn't see any. They didn't *show* me any," Kennedy said. His eyes moved to the chair beside the bed. "You didn't tell me you were carrying a pop gun."

Martin turned from the window and looked at Kennedy and then the chair. He didn't reply but looked down to the plaza again. "Why didn't you call me? I told you to, if you got in a bind."

"I *did!*"

Martin's head snapped around.

"No shit," Kennedy said. "Your don't operate."

Martin reached for the telephone and picked up the receiver. He got a dial tone. He dialed a local number and when it answered he hung up. "Only outgoing calls?" he asked. He thought a moment, and then dialed the Flamingo Hotel in San Antonio. When the desk clerk answered, Martin asked for Susannah's room.

"She's gone."

"What do you *mean?*" Martin shouted, horrified.

"I mean *gone*," the clerk said defensively. "Coupla guys checked her out 'bout half hour ago. FBI guys. Agents. Showed me their badges and everything. Government paid for the room. First time that ever happened to me."

Martin slammed down the receiver.

Kennedy watched as Martin dialed another number. The system never made the connection to the GATO station. Martin swore, and Kennedy didn't miss the expression of confusion on his face.

"I want more money," Kennedy said flatly.

Martin's mind was working fast in another direction, and he gave the pilot a blank look.

"I want more money," Kennedy repeated. "It's taking me a little while to wise up, but I think I'm beginning to see the light now. You're in serious business. I want serious money for carting you around."

"What the hell is this?" Martin suddenly yelled. "You going to do this to me every fifteen minutes? And what are you going to do if I don't give you more money? You think you can walk out of here with what I've already given you?"

Kennedy eyed the gun slung over the chair. "Maybe I'm reconsidering the whole thing," he said evenly.

There was an awkward pause and Martin said, "Look, I'll give you ten thousand dollars right now. That's *all* I can give you. Stick with me until I deliver that briefcase in Oaxaca and I'll give you five times that."

Before Kennedy could reply, Martin continued, "Let me tell you something. I don't do this for a living. I'm a newspaper reporter in San Antonio. I got involved in something I can't get out of until I unload that attaché. Then I'm through. Clear. But I need your help and I'm willing to pay for it. Understand? I'm not playing games with you."

Kennedy was silent and looked again at the .45.

"I got that in a Brownsville pawnshop before I crossed the border this morning," Martin explained. "I haven't fired a gun since I was in Nam twelve years ago."

Kennedy started to speak.

"One more thing," Martin interrupted. "My sister's life may depend on my getting that briefcase to Oaxaca. I'm going whether you go with me or not."

"I can't turn that down," Kennedy said soberly. "Let me have—"

He was interrupted again, this time by two sharp knocks on the hallway door. He caught the startled look on Martin's face and knew he hadn't expected it. Quickly he moved to the side of the door so he would be hidden when it opened into the room.

Martin already had the automatic in his hand and was standing directly in front of the door on the other side of the room. The two men had not bothered to turn on the lights and had been standing in the deepening shadows that became increasingly obscurant as night settled over the city. Two slabs of weak light from the streetlight fell across the floor from the windows.

The knock was repeated.

"Mr. León Blanco." The man was Mexican. "I have a message from the man with the strange voice on the telephone. I must to discuss the 'center of attention' which you have at your place."

Martin recognized the words. "Are you alone?"

"Yes, *señor*."

"Open the door . . . slowly."

The door handle turned and the door swung open to reveal a

small, middle-aged man dressed in common, dirty street clothes. He was holding a scrap of paper in his hand, nothing else.

"Come in," Martin said, and the little man entered until he stood in the middle of the room, his hands at his side. Kennedy suddenly closed the door behind him, but he was not startled. It was as if he had known someone would be there. Kennedy moved up and took the paper out of his hand and went to the window to read it.

"It's only the message he just told you," Kennedy said.

"I did not want to make the mistake. I was told the words were important," the little man said simply.

The three of them stood in the pale light.

"Who sent you?" Martin asked, strapping the Colt under his right arm.

"Jorge Arango."

"Who's that?" Kennedy looked at Martin, who shook his head.

The little man put his hands together in front of him. "Jorge says to tell you he will talk to you at El Pelicano at eight o'clock."

"That's a bar on the docks," Kennedy explained. "A stevedore hangout."

"How will we know this Jorge?" Martin asked.

"I will remember you, *señor*."

"Good," Martin said. "We'll be there."

The little man bowed his head diplomatically, then turned and let himself out the door, which he closed softly behind him.

"You gonna trust him just like that?" Kennedy asked after he was gone.

Martin took a box of shells from his canvas bag and emptied them into his pockets. "He knew the right words," he said. "This is their safe house. I've got to play by their rules."

"Who's they?"

Martin looked at his watch. "Have you had anything to eat?"

"No. And nothing to drink, either," Kennedy added.

"Okay. Why don't you go down and get something and bring it back here. We've got nearly an hour before we have to be at that bar. I'll fill you in as much as I can. And I'll give you your money."

Kennedy returned shortly with a sack of sautéed prawns and four bottles of Superior beer from the Del Mar on the east side of the plaza. As he ate at a small wooden table in the room, Martin sat on the bed with his back to the wall and told the husky pilot a liberally fabricated outline of what was happening. It was enough to satisfy his immediate questions, and Martin knew that Kennedy wasn't naive enough to believe Martin would give him the full story anyway.

When the time came to leave, Martin slipped on his sports jacket and followed Kennedy down the narrow stairs to the hotel's entrance on Rivera. They turned away from the plaza and the lighted arched gallery of the restaurants and bars that surrounded the park, and headed through the darker streets to Fray Olmos, where they turned toward the riverfront. The street dropped sharply and was narrowed by the congestion of cluttered booths and stands selling trinkets and black-market goods smuggled in on the merchant ships. Kennedy elbowed his way through the crowd of sailors and peddlers to the mouth of the street where it opened onto the dockfront.

They turned left, away from the towering freighters berthed at the wharf and strung with sparkling lights that tinseled over their rusting hulls and bilge holes spilling sewage down their sides to the Panuco's muddy water. Ahead of them the bars lined the waterfront until they played out at the end of the harbor, where the darkness embraced the slums hidden in the jungle that flourished on the banks of the river. Beyond that a pink glow in the sky was a constant reminder of the Pemex refinery at Ciudad Madero.

El Pelicano was distinguished from the other bars by a neon sign over its doorway depicting a green pelican whose head jerked up and down in endless spasms. The bar was not crowded, but busy, and was unusual for its lack of the obligatory jukebox that throbbed with Latin music in most of the bars. Kennedy strolled through the tables and the sweet, smoky haze of marijuana toward a table against the far wall. They sat sideways to the doorway and ordered two beers from a one-armed *zamba* wearing a lowcut dress that threatened to spill her ample cinnamon-colored breasts glistening with sweat.

There was a comfortable murmur of conversation, an occasional laugh.

"If you're interested," Kennedy said, "there's a back door directly outside that curtain, past the toilets." He took a long pull on his bottle and sloshed the beer around in his mouth.

When they had come in the door Martin had noticed a solitary man sitting at one end of the bar. He had a shock of shaggy black hair which was unruly despite a liberal application of shiny hair oil. He was thin, with a face that bore an uncanny resemblance to the tight-fleshed and slack-jawed cadaver of King Tutankhamen. His eyes had unabashedly locked on Martin when he came in and had not left him. He was turned on his bar stool, staring frankly, and revealing a gargantuan tropical beetle crawling around on his shirt front and attached to his collar by a tiny gold chain. The beetle was encrusted with brilliant chips of costume jewelry and roamed the thin man's chest like a living bauble.

Kennedy touched Martin's forearm and tilted his head toward the door. The little man who had visited them at the hotel stood there a moment, then disappeared in the darkness. As Martin and Kennedy stared expectantly at the doorway, a young man rose from a table across the room and approached them.

"My name is Jorge Arango. May I sit down?"

He was in his middle twenties, Martin guessed, a university student or just out of the university, and determined to prove he was not a mere messenger boy. He was handsome, with fine linear features showing no trace of Indian blood.

He smiled happily and looked at Martin. "We checked out your suspicions and you were right," he said without preamble. "The woman, of course, was not Vicki, or her cousin. When we checked at Vicki's house, we were too late. She had been shot in the head. Then the woman disappeared from the curio shop. We don't know who she was." He took a package of French cigarettes from his pocket, offered them around. "So some changes have been made."

"Like what?" Martin was wary.

"You will not be taking the briefcase to Oaxaca," he said, picking bits of tobacco off the tip of his tongue. "By the way, I didn't see you bring it in." He raised his eyebrows.

"That's right," Martin said without explanation. "What am I supposed to do?"

"You will go to Veracruz and call a contact number there, and they will tell you."

"Veracruz will be as far as I go?"

"That's what I understand."

"Why can't I just leave it with you?"

The young man laughed. "I'm afraid I've been compromised."

"What?"

"The *federales* are trying to pick me up. I'm going to be worth very little after tonight. I'll give you the number in Veracruz. Pull your shirt sleeve from under your coat and fold it back."

Martin did as he was told, and the young man used a felt-tip pen to write the number on the exposed cuff. As Martin folded

190

down his cuff and began buttoning it, he felt an arm slide across his shoulders and around his neck.

"Aaahhh! Momia!" Arango forced an uneasy laugh and looked up at the mummified man from the bar, who was gazing doe-eyed at the top of Martin's head. Arango rose quickly and put his own arm around the man and pulled him away.

"You cannot do this to my friend. You will have to wait for someone else." He laughed again, throwing his head back and hugging the heavy-lidded Momia with one arm as he walked him back to the bar. Arango kissed him on the cheek, ordered another drink for him from the bartender, and loudly admired his beetle. Finally he came back to the table and sat down.

"Forgive him. He has strange ways but he can be very valuable. Actually he is quite cunning."

"I'll bet he is," Kennedy said. His toneless expression was meant to put Arango on notice that the situation had better not get too weird.

"What do we do next?" Martin asked.

"I am to make sure you get safely in the air . . . with the briefcase. The *brigadistas* are watching Mr. Kennedy's Ranchero, so you cannot return to the airstrip in that. I have a car"—he jerked his head to the side—"down in the barrio. I will drive you across the Panuco to the plane."

"How do you know about my airstrip?" Kennedy challenged. Martin could feel him tensing.

Arango returned Kennedy's glare for a long moment, then a slow, strained grin moved over his face. "Your friends the Stoward brothers have for a long time appreciated our interests. Just because they share with you the strip and some piece of your smuggling business does not mean they do not have other interests too."

"Son of a bitch," Kennedy said.

"What about the roadblocks?" Martin put in.

"I have bought the only one we must go through. They will not delay my car at the bridge."

Arango turned again to Kennedy. "There is a strip we would prefer you use on the northern edge of Veracruz. It is a packed caliche surface built by Pemex but seldom used now that the drilling has moved from that particular area. The caliche is white and will be easy to see in the moonlight as you approach."

With his finger he drew in the moisture left by their sweaty bottles on the black tabletop. "From the air you can be guided by three gas flares situated at the north end of the strip, two straddling it, one at its end. They form a perfect equilateral triangle with the north end of the strip beginning at its apex and running exactly between the other two angles."

He reached in his coat pocket and withdrew a piece of paper, which he handed to Kennedy. "Here is the compass reading. We have hired a man to wait near the strip all night and to take you into Veracruz when you arrive. He knows nothing and he is paid well to suppress his curiosity."

"How about a safe hotel?" Martin asked.

"Yes. The Colonial Hotel on the north side of the Plaza de Armas. A beautiful place, not like your unfortunate accommodations here." He smiled. "You will register as Carlos Rabassa. Again the telephone is secure but allows only outgoing calls. You can safely reach your contact on this line."

Arango looked at his watch, his face showing for the first time the stress that he was handling so gracefully. The soft flesh under his right eye quivered noticeably, and his smile betrayed a tenseness in his thin lips.

"Are you armed?" he asked Martin.

Martin hesitated, then nodded.

Arango looked at Kennedy, who shook his head.

"Then I have something with me you may have," Arango said. "And something more in the car. If neither of you has any further questions we must be on our way." He looked pointedly at Martin.

"It's back at the hotel," Martin said.

Arango stood and signaled with his eyes that they should use the back door. He went to the bar, paid for their drinks, and followed them through the doorway covered with a filthy organdy curtain. Kennedy fell into the lead as they walked briskly down the unlighted shaft that separated the buildings. At the end of the block he turned up the street that rose sharply from the docks toward the Plaza de la Libertad.

Instead of going to the head of the street to the plaza and front entrance of the hotel, Kennedy ducked into a narrow doorway that opened directly off the steep sloping street. When they got inside the doorway that was a rear entrance to the hotel, Arango reached around Martin and grabbed Kennedy by the arm.

"I think it would be best if you took this and waited here until we come down." He handed the pilot a compact handgun and a fistful of extra cartridges. Kennedy leaned toward the sidewalk and examined the gun in the streetlight, checking the action and the safety.

"It's a Czech-made M52," Arango said. "It holds eight rounds in the handle clip. If you use it, our chances of getting out are better if you use this also." He pulled a silencer from his pocket. They waited while Kennedy screwed it in, and then they passed him and continued up the stairs.

Arango followed Martin into his room and stood at the window overlooking the plaza while Martin threw his things in the canvas bag. Then Martin stepped across the hall, opened the cluttered janitor's closet, and bent over a cardboard box filled with red oiled sawdust used for sweeping the wooden floors of the hotel. He dug to the bottom of the box, grasped the handle of the briefcase, and hauled it out. Just as he stood and turned, Arango burst out of the room carrying Martin's canvas bag.

"Hurry! *Federales* are in the plaza. Hurry!"

They took the dark stairs in leaps, using the handrail to maintain their balance. When they rounded the last turn and saw the narrow rectangle of light that was the doorway below, they heard the muffled *phutt!* of Kennedy's pistol twice, then a third time. They got to the doorway just as Kennedy fired a fourth time from his kneeling position next to the wall of the sidewalk, both hands holding the pistol, which he pointed at the crest of the street above them. One *federale* lay across the curb and a second writhed in the street, grunting in agony from a stomach wound. They both had fallen in silence, their comrades in the plaza unaware of their failure to make it into the rear entrance of the hotel.

Arango hit the street running, followed by Martin and Kennedy. They turned into the first alley and stayed in it, half a block off the riverfront, for four blocks as Arango led them toward the slums adjacent to the docks. Soon they were in the shanty wilderness of the barrio, fighting their way along the dirt paths and gullies that fed through the district to the river. Here the jungle of the river delta had crept into the city, threatening to reclaim the sprawling warren of clapboard shacks and shanties whose dirt streets turned into unnegotiable mudways during the rainy season. They scrambled across junky backyards, twice scattering roosting chickens and rousing the ubiquitous curs that wailed like death hounds in the still night long after they had gone.

They ran, single-file and tiring, to a block of stucco buildings on the waterfront. Arango ducked behind the buildings which backed up to the jungle-covered barrio and dashed to a late-model Buick parked in the dark. He jerked open the door and got behind the steering wheel as Kennedy climbed in beside him and Martin piled into the back seat.

The young man started the car and flipped on the headlights.

In one brilliant instant the beams caught a surprised and sprad-dled-legged Momia standing paralyzed in the middle of the dirty alley. Suddenly Momia threw up a rigid arm and pointed at the car as he bellowed something Martin could not understand.

Arango screamed something in Spanish, and gunfire exploded from the jungle through his window, blowing the front of his head across the dash onto Kennedy's hand. In the trauma of violent death, the student's leg jammed down on the accelerator and the car shot forward, crushing the scrawny Momia and burst-ing from the alley out of control as Kennedy jerked Arango's still-quivering body over to his side of the car and took control of the wheel. From the floor behind the driver's seat, Martin emptied his Colt into the flashes coming from the undergrowth as Kennedy spun the car around and headed away from the docks.

"Jesus Christ!" Kennedy was screaming. "Jesus Christ!"

Martin was reloading the .45, his mind registering nothing but the mechanical effort necessary to ram a new clip in position without jamming the mechanism. It was the same single-mind-edness under fire he had experienced in Vietnam, and the smell of Arango's blood emptying onto the front seat revived every survival instinct he had forgotten since the war.

Martin and Kennedy both ducked reflexively as a burst of gunfire shattered the rear window, spraying them with glass, just as Kennedy turned the corner out of the line of fire.

"You okay back there?" Kennedy screamed.

"Yeah, I'm okay. I'm okay."

"God, this poor kid won't be still, oh God, this is terrible."

"You know where you're going?" Martin yelled. The Buick was weaving treacherously from one side of the street to the other, its headlights panning recklessly across the fronts of the buildings.

"You bet I do. They're gonna have to be good to catch my ass." Kennedy looked in the floorboard. "This poor kid."

They were well away from the barrio now, Kennedy maneu-vering the car onto better and wider streets as they left downtown behind and entered the main arteries that would take them to the river bridge and Highway 180 out of the city.

"I can't believe we got out of that," Kennedy shouted over his shoulder. "I hope this poor bastard wasn't lying to us about buying that roadblock at the bridge. I'm not so sure we'll have that kind of luck again."

Martin was looking through a ragged hole blown in the rear window. "I don't see anything behind us."

"You will," Kennedy said. "You will."

They came to a major intersection and Kennedy ran the light, taking the Buick into a power turn as he skirted around a flatbed truck and straightened the car out for the river bridge looming in front of them half a mile away. They both concentrated on the path of the Buick's headlights as they illuminated the long corridor of steel girders and the solitary police car blocking the road at the opposite end.

"*Son* of a *bitch*," Kennedy roared. "You can't trust these goddam people. Hang on, Gallagher."

The headlights were tracking the bridge's tunnel of girders so fast they blurred into a dizzying motion that seemed to double their speed.

Kennedy aimed the Buick at the rear end of the police car, which didn't completely reach across the highway, and pushed the accelerator to the floor. Martin knew what Kennedy thought he was going to do, but he didn't believe it worked except in movies. He watched the pilot hunch over the steering wheel as though he would break through by sheer determination. They saw a man standing on the side of the road, his features enlarged in anticipation of what he was about to see. Then, amazingly, at the last moment, the police car lurched forward out of the Buick's path and there was nothing left but black open highway.

"Oh, shee-it! I don't believe it," Kennedy yelled, "I don't believe it!" He kept his foot mashed to the floor as the Buick hurtled through the flat, treeless marshland dotted with glittering oil rigs.

But the triumph was short-lived as the headlights of two cars giving chase appeared at the far end of the bridge.

"There they are," Martin said.

"Yeah, I knew it," Kennedy said. "We've got seven straight miles before the turnoff. See if they gain on this stretch."

They did, and by the time Kennedy slowed enough to make a turnoff onto the dirt road, they were close enough for Martin to take potshots at them through the hole in the rear window with the powerful Czech M52 which Kennedy had tossed to him over the seat.

Once on the dirt road, Kennedy widened the distance between them again as the dust boiled up behind the Buick, obscuring the road for the pursuing cars as he gained precious seconds by anticipating the curves of the country road he knew so well.

Suddenly they broke out of the marshland and into an open stretch of fields. Martin saw the yellow glow of a ranch house off to their right in the distance as Kennedy swung the Buick across an unbroken field to a ridge of palms where the marshes began again at the edge of the farmland. Within a few moments they had stopped beside the Cessna and Kennedy had scrambled into the cockpit. He started the engine as Martin gathered the briefcase, the canvas bag, and the two pistols.

It wasn't until Martin was seated in the cockpit that he saw the strip, cleverly camouflaged as it ran congruent with the furrows in the field. Kennedy swore as he realized he would have to taxi out, then come back to take off over the Buick as he came into the wind.

He was pivoting at the end of the field when they saw the two pairs of headlights break out into the open. Revving the engine to a wail, Kennedy lifted the Centurion off the dirt just as the two cars slid to a stop beside the Buick, their doors flying open and disgorging *federales*, who fired their small arms into the plane's undercarriage as it passed over them and strained for altitude. Martin heard the sickening pock of lead in the thin metal of the plane as they climbed, and he kept his eyes glued to the orange flashes on the ground until they became mere sparks and disappeared.

Kennedy took the Cessna high enough to assure they would be detected on radar and headed straight for the nearest airport at Ciudad de Valles at the foot of the Taumin Mountains forty-five miles inland from Tampico. When the city was in sight he veered north, maintaining altitude. As he approached the lower reaches of the mountain range, he banked sharply southward and dropped below radar range as he headed back toward the coast, flying low over the trees.

Martin looked at the pilot's face washed in green from the instrument panel.

"That'll look like we took on too much lead and nosed into the mountains," Kennedy explained. "Radar just gives the facts. It ain't a reasoning animal."

Within half an hour they were skimming the coastline toward Veracruz, flying low enough over the water to catch occasional spray on the windows and to see the moonlit figures of night seiners as they waved their lanterns at the low-flying plane from the white cusp of the sandy beaches.

Chapter 22

For most of the hour-and-a-half flight south, Kennedy kept the Centurion over the water, not taking any chances on a compass course which might take them inland at altitudes detectable on radar. But ninety miles north of Veracruz they were forced to rise over the beaches and turn west over the vanilla plantations in order to intercept the airstrip heading given them by the luckless Arango. Still, Kennedy kept the plane low as he banked again toward Veracruz, skillfully hugging the trees in the smuggler's game of nerves.

Soon they encountered an occasional gas flare in the coastal plains between the Gulf and the mountains rising to the west. Arango's airstrip was far closer to the port city than they had anticipated, and the brilliant harbor lights of Veracruz dominated the horizon by the time they picked up the triangle of flares far to the north. Kennedy buzzed the strip once, banking sharply on the return lap so he could get a good look at the underbrush along the margins of the strip. When he turned to make the approach he put the nose of the Centurion directly over the point flare and set the plane down on the chalky runway. He taxied to the far end of the clearing and spun the Cessna to face the empty approach before he cut the engine.

They opened the doors of the cockpit and sat in the shadows fifty yards from the underbrush, listening for the sound of a car to break the silence and the stillness that surrounded them. Neither of them spoke for a moment, but Martin could sense Kennedy's anxiety.

Then the pilot said, "You got those guns loaded again?"

Martin handed the M52 back to Kennedy.

"There he is," Kennedy said, taking the gun and pointing in front of them. Halfway down the strip a pair of headlights flashed on and a pickup pulled onto the caliche strip and headed toward them. When the truck got close to the plane the driver cut his lights down to low beam and circled to a stop in front of the Cessna.

"Señores?" a voice called tentatively from the interior of the battered truck. "I am your ride to Veracruz. *Bien?*"

"Bueno!" Kennedy called back. *"Momentito, por favor."*

They gathered their things and climbed out, and Martin helped Kennedy lock the plane and block the wheels with rocks as best they could.

"Where do you want to go in the city?" the Mexican asked after they turned off the strip onto a country road that would take them to the main highway.

"Colonial Hotel," Martin said.

The hotel was one of the best in the city and sat on the north side of the busy Plaza de Armas in the center of Veracruz. Martin registered as Kennedy waited nervously in the lobby, and then the two of them went up to their room, which was again on the third floor, and looked directly onto the plaza with its five fountains sparkling with colored lights. Kennedy went straight to the balcony and stepped out into the cool night breeze blowing in off the harbor just a few blocks away. Below him and on two sides of the plaza the cafés and restaurants located under the arches of the sidewalk arcades were crowded with diners.

Martin was too tired, drained. He threw his things on one of the double beds and flung his jacket across a chair. Turning back the cuff of his shirt sleeve, he walked to the telephone. He dialed the number Arango had given him and waited, hearing the same familiar trunk sounds he had heard on the phone in the Ébano. Then a lazy voice answered.

"Hola."

"This is Carlos Rabassa," Martin said. "Do you have a message for me?"

"Please. One moment." The voice was crisp now, efficient. There was a brief silence, then the same voice was back on the line.

"You are calling from the Colonial?"

"Yes."

"Very good. Are you all right? We have heard of the trouble in Tampico."

"I'm fine," Martin said curtly.

"Very good. Tomorrow morning at nine-thirty you will walk from the *zócalo* six blocks east on Independencia to the Parque Zamora. There you will board the trolley marked Villa del Mar. This trolley goes to the beach and along the *malecón*. You will get off at the first stop on the beach at Hotel Villa del Mar and walk to the back of the hotel, where your contact will be dining on the terrace overlooking the Gulf. He will be wearing a white *guayabera* with a red poppy in the lapel. Introduce yourself to him as Rabassa."

"Look," Martin said. "Can't I meet this man tonight? I want to get this off my hands. Do you understand that? I want to give it to someone tonight."

"I am only giving to you this message, *señor*. That is all."

"I was told I would deliver the briefcase here in Veracruz. Is that true?"

"I know nothing of that."

"Well, who the hell *does*?" Martin shouted.

"I am sorry, *señor*. I have only these instructions. Nothing more. Do you remember the instructions?"

"Yes, yes, yes," Martin said wearily.

"Thank you, *señor*. Goodbye."

Kennedy walked back into the room. "What's the matter?" He too wanted to believe the worst was behind them.

"More meetings, more contacts, more of the same."

"Look, buddy," Kennedy said. "I'm worn out too, but there's no way in hell I could go to sleep without a few beers. I'm wired tight. Why don't we go down on the plaza and have something to eat? Soak up some beer, calm down a little."

Martin shook his head. "Go ahead."

"Gallagher," Kennedy said, "you'd be doin' yourself a favor to unwind down there in one of those cafés. Forget that poor bastard back there in Tampico. He understood the game. What can you say?"

"Go ahead," Martin said pulling off his shoes. "I'm going to shower, and then I'm going to bed. Knock six times when you want in."

Kennedy looked at him and shrugged. "You're gonna die young, Gallagher. You're gonna have to learn how to let off steam."

Kennedy pulled the door closed behind him, leaving Martin sitting dejectedly on the edge of his bed. He wanted to talk to Susannah. He wanted all this to be over so he could relax, so the tension would go out of his shoulders and he could think of something besides how to stay alive. This was no different from Vietnam. He couldn't believe it then and he couldn't believe it now.

He looked around the room, then picked up the briefcase and walked to the air-conditioning return-air vent at shin level next to the door. He knelt down, took a penny from his pocket, and began unscrewing the four screws that held the grate on the vent.

When they were out he pulled away the grate, slipped the brief-case behind it, and put the screws back in.

After a cold shower, Martin lay in bed with the balcony doors open and the ceiling fan pulling in the sea breeze coming across the plaza. The music from the cafés came over the balcony too, and the Caribbean rhythms of the *bamba* and *macumba* tangled themselves in his nightmares. Nightmares of Jesse, a look of horror and bewilderment on his blood-spattered face as he stared down in his lap at the jagged piece of Arango's forehead that had just landed there; of Stella slashing away at the swinish Klein; of Susannah floating on her face in a sea of blue water, her blond hair drifting out from her head like seaweed.

Sometime during the night he fell into a sleep of exhaustion, only to be awakened in the early-morning hours by Kennedy banging on the door. With his heart pounding and his Colt held firmly against the door at head height, Martin let the pilot in, and Kennedy staggered drunkenly to his bed, where he collapsed and was snoring before Martin could calm his own nerves enough to lie back on the damp sheets.

The next morning Martin waked as the first brilliant rays of the sun rose over the Bay of Campeche and burst through the balcony doors. He shaved, double-checked his .45 as he put it on, and left the fully clothed and unconscious Kennedy sprawled across his bed as he went downstairs to the Colonial's sidewalk tables for breakfast. The plaza was quiet, with only a few people taking an early meal served by slow-moving waiters.

Martin sat in the shade of the arches and read the local news-paper from front to back as he drank cup after cup of the strong Veracruz coffee. When it was time, he paid for his meal, walked the six blocks to Zamora park and took the trolley which rattled at a leisurely pace along a palm-lined boulevard through one of the main residential areas of the city. The sun was well into the tropical sky now and beat down on the Spanish homes with iron-grilled windows and white stucco walls that shimmered in the morning glare. The trolley continued into the barrios, where the Veracruzanos decorated their clapboard shanties in the mellow Caribbean colors of pale pink, ocher, salmon, and sky blue, with bright cherry or emerald doors that glistened in the early light.

Finally the open-air car jerked onto the *malecón* that ran along the seawall and stopped across the boulevard from the Hotel Villa del Mar. Martin walked across the street to the beachside hotel and followed a covered gallery around to the back, where a late continental breakfast was being served on the terrace above the beach.

The contact was not difficult to find. He sat at a table for two near the terrace railing, a little apart from the other diners. He was of middle height, with slightly Negroid features, a common trait among the Mexicans of the southern Gulf Coast. He was wearing sunglasses and eating with determined concentration. When Martin walked up and introduced himself, the man rose slightly from his chair, extended his hand while he continued to chew, and indicated that Martin should sit in the chair opposite. He neither smiled nor spoke.

He poured Martin a cup of coffee from the pot on the table and wiped his mouth.

"I trust everything is all right," he said. He was comfortable with English.

"Yes," Martin snapped. He was getting tired of answering that question.

The contact raised his eyebrows. "My name is Genaro Novo. I realize you are impatient, but the man you are to meet did not arrive in Veracruz until early this morning. He needed sleep."

"When do I see him?"

Novo looked at Martin steadily, his coffee cup poised halfway to his mouth. "Right now," he said, putting down the cup. "There is no reason to wait any longer." He placed a handful of pesos on the table and they left.

Novo drove them south along the beach highway to the small fishing village of Boca del Río at the mouth of the Atoyac River. The village consisted of a few open-air eating places with thatched roofs and three or four tawdry hotels and juke joints. Novo continued through the village's single sand-swept street, past the beached boats and drying nets of local fisherman, to a lonely stretch of beach where a solitary car was parked at the edge of the lapping surf. A man in a business suit without a tie was leaning against the fender of the car with his arms casually crossed as he watched them approach.

Novo stopped beside the car, got out, and spoke to the man, who was cleaning his fingernails with a small knife. On the hood of the car behind the man lay an unwieldly-looking Sten gun wrapped in plastic for protection against the salt wind and sand.

The man straightened up and extended his hand, open palm up, to Martin. Novo saw Martin's confusion at the gesture.

"He wants your pistol. You will get it back."

Embarrassed that it had been so obvious, Martin took the .45 out of its holster and handed it over. The man unloaded the clip and slipped it into his pocket.

"There is your man," Novo said to Martin, indicating with a

nod of his head a lone figure in hip boots surf fishing two hundred yards down the beach.

Martin started walking. A single gull drifted up over the sand dunes and hovered over him shrieking and bobbing down in the wind current, hoping for the tossed morsels it was used to getting around the village. When Martin was halfway down the beach the fisherman looked around and saw him and began letting out his line as he backed up in the surf and made his way through the foam to the dry sandy beach. By the time Martin had gotten to him he had put his rod in a holder jammed in the sand and was lighting a cigarette as the Gulf wind ruffled his straight, closely cropped hair.

"Good morning," the fisherman said. He held his cigarette close against his chest and extended his right hand. "My name is Luis."

They shook hands, and Martin saw that Luis' eyes were red and swollen. He had indeed needed sleep and probably still did. He wore a white starched shirt and tie beneath his rubber hip boots.

Luis saw Martin's glance, and his thin lips formed an easy smile.

"Business and pleasure," he said. "I have too much of the former and too little of the latter." He looked into the shallows of the Gulf. "There's a sandbar out there that's supposed to keep the sharks away from these beaches, but it doesn't work." He turned to Martin. "Do you have the briefcase?"

"Yes."

"With you?" He looked down the beach at the cars.

"No. In Veracruz."

"Ah." He pulled on his cigarette. "They almost got you last night in Tampico, huh?"

"Yes, they did. Only I don't know who 'they' are."

"The *federales*. But they didn't know what they were doing. I mean, they were not working as *federales* of the Limón government. Tony Sleep directed them. The Tampico *comandante* is an old friend of Sleep's from the Mexico City days. When Sleep realized you had discovered his little deception at the curio shop he was afraid you had already fled Tampico. He called on the *comandante* for assistance. It was an 'illegal' favor for an old friend."

"How did he know about the Ébano safe room?"

"Vicki Zubaran. Sleep 'persuaded' her to tell him before she died. He thought by some long shot you might be there, or if not you, then someone else who might give him more information, like Vicki. He would have gotten you, too, if it had not been for poor Arango."

"He had bribed the *federales* on the roadblock at the Panuco bridge," Martin explained.

"Arango was a clever boy. Everything is for sale in Mexico. It's sad, but true."

Luis looked out in the surf and bent to take a couple of turns on his heavy reel. Then he stood again.

"I know you are worried about your sister, but I can give you no information about her. I am sorry. We are fragmented right now, as so many parts of our operation are drawing to a close. Tonight it will be over. I do know, however, that your little friend Jesse is dead."

Martin put both hands in his pockets, and a tongue of surf foam came onto the sand and licked at his shoes. The seagull gave up and lofted up on a wind current and drifted back toward the village.

"And who was responsible for that?" Martin asked.

"Mr. Sleep."

"And Susannah Lyra?"

Luis shifted his eyes to Martin and then away again toward the dunes. "We thought she was with you."

"She was until early last night. We were staying together after I got the documents from Stella."

"Then she knew what you were doing?"

"Yes."

"Everything?"

"As much as I could tell her. As much as I knew."

"Madness," Luis said.

"She was my lifeline. I didn't trust GATO," Martin said sharply, aware that he was defensive about justifying his actions to this stranger. "I didn't know what I was getting into, and I thought I could always get her to send someone after me if everything fell apart down here. As it turned out it didn't work too well. I reported the Tampico thing to the GATO number in San Antonio and I told Susannah what had happened too. But when I tried to call both of them back last night, Susannah was gone and the GATO number was out of commission. I was stranded anyway. I didn't know when you people were going to contact me or where. I didn't know anything about Sleep or who was working for him. *You* could be working for him for all I know. How the hell would I know?"

Luis hunched his shoulders around a match as he lit another cigarette. The wind whipped the smoke out of his hands.

"Then you don't know where Mrs. Lyra is?" he asked, straightening up and looking out over the surf.

"When I called the motel where we had been staying, the night clerk said two men from the FBI had come and gotten her."

Luis stared at Martin, and the kindness drained from his eyes like the color from the face of a dying man. The carved features of his thin lips took on the rigidity of barely controlled anger.

"You are a *fool*, Mr. Gallagher," he said evenly. "You have given them a road map and a guide besides."

Martin exploded. He grabbed the front of Luis' shirt, jerking him close to his face. "Listen to me, you son of a bitch. I've done for you what nobody else would and have watched my friends be murdered one by one for my effort. I risked my own life against odds that I'm only just now beginning to realize were impossible. I tell the one person in this whole damn world I can trust what's happening to me and you call me a fool. I've had it with this whole sick charade of secrets, and I've got a good mind to ransom those documents for every goddam peso your government's worth."

The second Martin finished, Luis slapped his hands together into a double fist and drove them upward between Martin's arms, breaking his grip and crashing them against the bottom of his jaw. He slammed a sickening blow to Martin's stomach that turned him half around and followed it with a final chop to the kidneys that sent Martin sprawling on the sand.

Luis stood over him until he was sure Martin had caught his breath and could hear him.

"What you would *do*, Mr. Gallagher, is no longer yours to say. You are involved in something larger than your individual preferences. We do not care what you have a mind to do. Your mind belongs to GATO until you hand over those documents."

He stopped a moment while Martin coughed violently, spitting blood from where Luis' blow had driven his jaw teeth into the back of his tongue. Then he went on.

"We all belong to GATO. You say you have sacrificed your friends. We all have. Have you asked others what they have sacrificed? Do you know the extent of the agony behind the faces you have met through GATO? No. You are a stranger to this world, a sojourner who has invested nothing but a little pain. And pain is the least of it, my friend. You have no idea how much more there is to give beyond that."

Luis had been standing between Martin and the white Veracruz sun. As Martin slowly regained his breath and raised himself on one knee, he looked up, and Luis stepped aside, letting the sun strike Martin full in the face. Martin jerked his head away, his eyes filling instantly with tears as he remained in the half-crouched position in the sand.

"May we continue our conversation?" Luis asked, his voice having regained its former studied evenness.

Martin didn't answer. His temples were still throbbing from the blow on his jaw, and his lower back felt as if it had been ripped away from his spine.

"Where is the briefcase?" Luis had stepped back between Martin and the sun.

"At the hotel," Martin said hoarsely.

"Exactly where, I mean."

"Return air vent in the room."

"Does your pilot know about this?"

"No."

"Very good. Tonight I want you to bring the briefcase to me at the Castillo de San Juan de Ulúa. Are you familiar with the castle?"

Martin shook his head.

"It is only ten minutes from your hotel," Luis explained. "It is an ancient fortress built by the Spanish shortly after Cortez's arrival here. It sits on a reef island at the mouth of the Veracruz harbor and was built to defend the port. It was also used as a prison. The dungeons of Ulúa have a grim history stretching right up to the twentieth century. They were deliberately designed to flood at high tide. A nice touch of sadism by Cortez's engineers. Of course it is now Veracruz's main tourist attraction.

"A taxi will be in front of your hotel tonight at eight o'clock. Number 212. The driver will take you across the causeway to the fortress, which will be closed by then. We will have someone at the gates to let you in. Since our people will control the traffic on the causeway we need not fear an ambush. After you deliver the briefcase you are no longer obligated to GATO."

"What about the money?"

"I'll have it with me."

"I promised Kennedy, the pilot, forty thousand if he got me safely to Veracruz," Martin said, massaging the back of his neck.

"You will have it."

Martin got up carefully and knocked the sand off his clothes.

Luis stepped back. "Genaro will make sure you get back to your hotel safely. Do not leave your room until eight o'clock. I am sure Tony Sleep and Dan Lee are either in Veracruz or on their way here. There is no reason for us to take risks this close to the end."

"I don't understand why you can't just come to the hotel with me now and take the damn documents off my hands. You seem to be making this more complicated than necessary," Martin said.

Luis was lighting another cigarette, seemingly unafraid that Martin might assault him in his unguarded moment.

"I can assure you, Mr. Gallagher, that we do not play games for the game's sake. Everything is properly motivated. I will be giving the documents directly to Paco himself, and he is not going to be in a position to receive them until eleven o'clock tonight. It will take me that long to get to the point of transfer after I have them from you. I cannot take them from you now, because in the everyday world I am not Luis but someone else and I have to tend to that. No, it is best if the briefcase stays in one place, hidden, until tonight."

Martin looked at Luis standing in front of him with all the confidence in the world, his cigarette held close to his chest and one hand resting in the bib of his rubber boots. The man exuded discipline, and the lingering pain in Martin's lower back reminded him how much distance there was between his present flabby state and the military discipline of Luis. Martin had known that kind of tautness too, but that had been a dozen years ago in a jungle half a world away. In the present context he was a joke.

Luis looked toward the cars down the beach and waved at the two men looking their way.

"If you have no further questions..."

Martin shook his head.

"Then I shall see you tonight," Luis said. He did not offer his hand to Martin, but he smiled. *"Buena suerte."*

Martin turned and walked away. When he was nearly to the cars he looked back along the stretch of marbled sand. Luis was already out in the surf, his white shirt glistening in the sun against the gray waters of the Gulf.

The trip back to Veracruz along the coast highway passed quickly as Martin watched the whitecaps roll in and thought of returning to Susannah. He decided that when he returned to the hotel he would place a call to the FBI office in San Antonio and try to find out what Lee had done with her and if Stella had been located. If the Bureau wasn't forthcoming he would call Hooper. He would call everybody he knew until he got some answers.

206

It didn't seem logical to him that Luis would not know what had happened to Stella. It didn't look good.

They got to the Colonial shortly after lunch, and the tables under the arcades were crowded. Martin hurried through the maze of lunching tourists thinking it was a hell of a time to go in the front door with half the people in Veracruz watching you. He got in the first elevator that opened in the lobby. As he walked down the hall jangling the room key he thought of Kennedy and his fifty thousand dollars. He would be more than willing to fly back to Matamoros that night. They would both be relieved to leave this whole damn mess behind.

He turned the door handle and the key in the same motion and let himself in. His heart stopped. Kennedy was lying on the floor, the lower half of his body hidden behind his double bed. His face was turned toward Martin, his eyes closed. From his nostrils and opened mouth, a pudding of black congealed blood spilled onto the carpet and formed the pool in which he lay. Martin thought of the briefcase and whirled to look down at the grill as a searing blow smashed the back of his head, numbing his limbs instantly. He fell softly through an ever-darkening space filled with the heavy fragrance of gardenias and the faraway yapping of a dog.

Chapter 23

He was aware, first, that his arms and legs were tied to the sides of the bed, and next, that he was naked except for his shorts. Afraid, he kept his eyes closed as he tried to convince himself that his neck was not broken. It wasn't. He could move it, though with horrible pain at first, slightly from side to side. When he slowly opened his eyes the first thing he saw was the whirling blades of a ceiling fan above him, stirring the muggy coastal air that came in from the open balcony doors. Next his eyes fixed on the stoic Olmecian face at the foot of the bed between his splayed legs. The stout Mexican wore a short-sleeved rayon shirt with a jungle print of exotic birds and flowers. The shirttail hung loose out of his trousers.

Then Martin remembered Kennedy. He gathered all the strength in his shoulders and neck and slowly raised his head so he could see the floor beside the Mexican. There was no Kennedy, no bloodstain. His head fell back on the bed, but he had seen someone else to his right out of the corner of his eye. When the throbbing in the back of his head subsided, Martin turned his swollen eyes to two armchairs a little way from his bed.

Perched in the first chair like a large, fat quail was a smallish man in a white Panama suit without a tie. He was slightly balding and his straight stringy hair, which he combed from one side across the top of his head to the other to hide his smooth pate, was dyed coal-black, as was the thin, slightly crooked mustache on his long upper lip. His chubby arms clutched a palsied and ancient Chihuahua so frail and emaciated Martin could see its tendons stretching from bone to bone. Both the man and the dog were staring at him with anticipatory expressions, the one smiling sweetly, the other trembling uncontrollably.

Next to the middle-aged man sat a woman a decade younger and strikingly handsome. She was dressed in an *haute couture* suit of pale rose which accented a faint rubescent glow on her high, creamy cheeks. Her hair was a dark mahogany with russet highlights, her features were Spanish, and her expression was mild interest.

Martin recognized them both. He even remembered the damn dog from the bus ride.

"Well!" the little man said in a pert, effeminate voice. "We thought Felipe had bashed you dead. That would have been *un error malo*." He turned to the small pedestal table between him and the woman and took a sip from a frozen daiquiri.

"Let me introduce us," he said. "I am Anthony Sleep, and she"—he opened one hand toward the woman, "Is Madame Marie Dumeril. That beast at your feet is Felipe. And this"—he raised one of the Chihuahua's cadaverous legs and waggled a nail-painted paw at Martin—"is Pepe!" He laughed ridiculously and alone at his inane humor and snuffled slightly as he sipped again at the daiquiri.

"I noticed you were looking for Mr. Kennedy," he continued, smacking his lips. "We haven't cleaned him up, we simply changed rooms. Being a robust sort, he bled so damn much we just couldn't stay in there. Poor Pepe was absolutely quaking at the odor. Felipe would have done the same thing. God, I can't even *imagine* the amount of blood *he* would leak!"

He laughed, looking at the big Mexican in a coy, teasing manner. "So we came here, just down the hall, really. We have just lots and lots of questions, and if you will click the answers right off we can all be on our way."

He took the little piece of celery from his daiquiri and popped it into his mouth, then adjusted Pepe's gaunt body so the animal sat upright on its buttocks like a human and looked at Martin. Martin moved his tongue around in his mouth, trying to stimulate enough moisture to allow him to speak. He cleared his throat. "Did . . . did you kill her?"

Sleep was surprised by the question. "My, you *do* get right to the point, don't you? I suppose you mean Stella. What do you think? No, no, I won't do that. I won't be clever about it. No, we haven't seen her. The closest we came to her was at the Palacio del Río. Let me tell you, Marie and I *listened* to that whole episode and it was absolutely *gruesome!* Oh, God! You know, the mike was around his neck, and we heard him *gurgle!* Oh, God!" He shuddered. "But he was an ass. He had it coming, damn him. Cardinal rule: Don't get randy on assignment. I spent years training him. He was the absolute *best* at needles, and he blew a brilliant career on the commonest mistake in the business. It was embarrassing."

"He killed Cuevas?"

209

"The old bugger in the movie theatre? Certainly. He didn't like leaving his needle, though. That was my idea. We had so little time and I thought it might panic Stella into doing something stupid. I wanted to flush her out. It worked, and then Alex blew it."

"Jesse?"

"Jesse . . . ? Oh, the dwarf and his black. Well, I didn't actually have a hand in the questioning. I got some of those nice *vatos* to work for me. I didn't *mean* for them to kill those two. You see, we had this tape of you and Jesse . . . oh, but you saw Marie the morning she put the limpet mike under the pew. We had heard on the street that you and that dwarf met at the same time and place every week. Marie slipped in the cathedral and slapped the limpet on the right bench and was just leaving when you came in. You weren't even supposed to be there. People would never believe how this work depends on *luck*. Just pure luck. But we didn't learn anything that wasn't on the tape. And I left there just minutes before the police came. I couldn't believe it!"

He looked at Dumeril and shook his head in wonderment as though they had discussed it at length and were still amazed that he had managed to escape an untimely capture.

Martin turned his eyes again to the ceiling fan. He tried to ignore the Mexican between his legs. If he let his mind dwell on what the Mexican was going to do, he would be psyched out even before they began. He had to fool himself into being surprised at what was going to happen. He could hear Sleep taking another drink from his daiquiri.

"Do you have any more questions?" Sleep asked accommodatingly. "You might as well get them out of your system, because it's going to be the other way around in just a minute."

Martin heard the *chit* of a cigarette lighter and both Sleep and Dumeril began smoking. The heavy sweetness of marijuana was drawn up by the ceiling fan and circulated throughout the room. It seemed to Martin the narcotic provided the perfect atmosphere for his sacrifice at the hands of the stolid Indian. The Mexican did not smoke, and Martin assumed he had enough experience at what he was about to do that he didn't require a sedative to get through it.

Sleep stood and walked up to the side of the bed, still holding the pop-eyed Chihuahua. He let his eyes go the length of Martin's body and back, and a simpering smile pulled at his mouth. At close quarters Martin found the contrast between the withered, sinewy dog and the puffy obesity of his master to be decadent.

210

"You keep yourself in good shape," Sleep said. "Work out at a gym?" He pulled his mouth open and tucked in his chin as he smirked. A little laugh rolled around in the back of his throat.

Martin was afraid Sleep was going to reach out and touch him. He could imagine himself enduring Felipe's brutalizing, but he didn't even want to consider being fondled by Sleep's pudgy fingers.

"I'll tell you," Sleep said as if reminded that there was business to tend to. "There's really only one question we care that much about: Where's the briefcase? Of course, the CIA wanted Stella, and Paco, and this and that and so on and so on." He rocked his head from side to side to indicate tedium. "But *we* think the documents are *the* prize. We tried for the others, of course, but they called us in too late after they'd already choused around in the water and stirred things up. Now. Our basic situation is this: You have it and we want it."

If there was a signal, Martin didn't see it, but Felipe responded to something. He abruptly left his position at Martin's feet and came around to the head of the bed. He pulled a round sponge from his pocket and squeezed it tightly with one hand as he clasped a pressure point under Martin's chin with the other. Martin's mouth opened involuntarily, and Felipe shoved the sponge ball inside. He took a cigarette from a pack in his shirt pocket, lit it, took several drags off it, then blew on the burning end to clear it of ashes before he put it on Martin's right nipple.

It was not until Felipe stopped and Martin's constricted arms and legs relaxed against their bonds that he felt the blood at his wrists and ankles and realized he had been tied with fine wire.

Sleep appeared at Martin's head again.

"I hate to see you go through this," he said, contorting his brow in sympathy. He was holding the Chihuahua upright in the cradle of one arm and the daiquiri in the other hand. "If you want to talk, nod. Otherwise . . ." He shrugged apologetically.

Martin closed his eyes.

Felipe began a rash of burns around his other nipple, and when he finished he ground the cigarette out in the slight concavity in Martin's sternum. Martin's hair was drenched in sweat, and he had to fight waves of nausea that began in the pit of his stomach and crawled up his trachea before subsiding and starting again. He was afraid if he vomited while the sponge was in his mouth he would drown before they realized what was happening. He knew tension was the torturer's main device. The anticipation of what would happen next heightened the pain itself when it came. He concentrated on the whitecaps on the Gulf he had seen coming back into Veracruz that morning and on a solitary seagull riding the thermal lifts along the coast. As the gull rose he passed the horizon and ascended into the cobalt sky, going higher and higher, caught in a lift so strong that he began to disappear into the deepening indigo. When the bird was only a mote Martin opened his eyes.

"Let's just start with a simple question first," Sleep said. He was leaning close to Martin, and the Chihuahua was rearing his head back, not wanting to get any closer. "Is the briefcase in your room?"

Martin turned his head toward Marie Dumeril. She was watching him, but he might as well have been a blank wall. She appeared to be daydreaming, bored. He noticed her mouth this time; her lips were graceful, reddened in just the right shade to compliment the pink in her dress and cheeks. He took all this in and then turned back to Sleep and closed his eyes.

The explosion of electric current on his stomach lifted his whole body off the bed, and he began to vomit. His nostrils and throat filled as he gagged on the sponge and his eyes burst open and rolled upward in his head. Felipe yanked the sponge out of his mouth and slammed his head over to the side while Martin vomited and spat to keep from drowning.

"Oh, Felipe!" Sleep squealed in exasperation. "You like them to do that, don't you? You just couldn't work up to it, could you?"

Felipe's huge hands kept Martin's head mashed to the side away from Marie Dumeril until he stopped vomiting and had caught his breath. He blinked back the tears and wondered why he was still conscious. At some point he knew he would pass out, but he had no idea he could endure this much pain before that happened. Now he was afraid. How much more intense could it get before he lost consciousness? Felipe jerked Martin's head around and rammed the sponge back into his mouth. He was about to find out.

He did not know how long it lasted. Felipe put the cattle prod into his groin next. The charge was so strong it felt like a gunshot. With glazed eyes he tried to raise his head to see if a hole had been blown below his waist. He couldn't. The cattle prod struck again on the other side, and then between his legs. He blacked out.

When he woke, the room was brilliant with sunlight and he could not turn his head anywhere that it didn't hurt to open his eyes. He heard Sleep's voice far away at the end of a tunnel asking him where the briefcase was. He squeezed shut his eyes and waited. The cattle prod exploded again and again in rapid succession, plunging him into a jolting hell that stripped every screaming nerve from his body through a ragged hole between his legs.

This time consciousness didn't come of its own accord; he had to fight for it. He fought for it because he heard a shrill whistling and the whistling became a shriek and the shriek became the sound of Death sucking him down into its long dark tunnel.

So he fought. He sang to hear the sound of his own voice above the shriek and he flailed his arms, treading in the dark well of unconsciousness just above death. Did he want to live? Yes, yes. Of course he did; yes, yes, yes. He nodded his head. Yes. He saw light and he nodded frantically.

"He wants to talk, Felipe."

Martin heard Sleep's eager voice. Talk? Yes, he would talk. If talking would stop the godless Mexican, he would talk.

The sponge disappeared and Martin gulped air, great quaffing lungs full of air.

"Just relax," Sleep was saying. "Just relax. Nothing else will happen to you if you talk."

There was silence in the room as Martin lay heaving with his eyes closed. When he could finally speak, he squinted through his eyelashes into the brittle light.

"I hid it . . . nobody knows. If you kill me . . . nobody knows. I want to bargain."

"Of course, of course. Felipe! Get him whiskey," Sleep barked. The cajoling tone was gone and he had shed his wimpy act. "Go ahead," he said to Martin.

"You won't kill me." Martin found it difficult to control his vocal cords. He didn't recognize his voice. "But I don't want to be a vegetable. Nothing's worth that . . . nothing."

"Here." Sleep held Martin's head with one hand and Felipe sloshed some of the amber liquor into his mouth. When it hit his empty stomach it almost came back up, but Martin fought to keep it down.

"Where is it?" Sleep said.

"No," Martin gasped. "I'll take you to it." He fought to think straight. "I tell you now and that'll be the end of me. If that's the way it's going to be, I'd rather die without telling you. I could do that, and I would. If you want it you're going to have to let me take you to it. Then let me go."

Martin's eyes were open now, and he was squinting at Sleep

through the splinters of light. A wry smile had twisted Sleep's face.

"You really think you could resist Felipe's persuasive methods?"

Martin nodded. "I know I could. A dead man's got nothing to lose. You let me go or I'll die with my mouth shut. I can do that. You've seen others do it. I can do it too."

Sleep stood beside the bed and studied Martin's face. It was true. Torture was not as efficient a method of obtaining information as was often claimed. It all depended upon that fine, immeasurable quality within a man's psyche. For a man or woman with strong psychic reserves a successful interrogation required a skilled "surgeon" and a lot of time. Felipe was crude and lacked talent, and time was running out.

Sleep held the vulgar little dog and thought it over. With a flip of his chubby wrist he motioned to Felipe.

"Clip the wires," he commanded, and then he got down close enough to Martin's face for Martin to smell the marijuana on his breath. "You make one false move, Gallagher, and I'll blow your head to jelly. I only take risks up to a certain point, and I decide for myself where that point is." He paused, then added, "When it comes, my decision might seem a little capricious to you."

After Felipe cut the wire at his legs and wrists, Martin lay on the fouled bed with no thought of covering himself. He brought his arms stiffly in to his sides and it was as though he were forcing them into an unnatural position. His groin was so sensitive he didn't want to move his legs. Knowing now that he wasn't going to die, he found himself once again slipping toward unconsciousness. But it was coming now as a balm, and he let it happen.

He didn't know how long he had been out but it wasn't long enough. Felipe pulled him off the bed and took him into the bathroom, where he dropped him on the floor of the shower and turned on the cold water. Slumped beneath the cold spray, Martin felt his body come alive again as the blood rushed to his hands and feet and pulsed in his head. Bracing himself against the close walls of the stall, he stood, forcing himself to move, to limber up, and bring stability to his quivering muscles.

When he finally stepped out of the shower, Felipe handed him his clothes, which he put on slowly and painfully. Sleep and Marie Dumeril were gone, and Felipe took Martin down the hallway to another room. He knocked, and Sleep let them into a suite with a sitting area near the balcony. Martin noticed for the first time it was late afternoon. Dumeril was sitting in one of several armchairs around a table on which sat an assortment of liquor bottles and glasses.

Martin stiffly followed Sleep to the table, where the now serious effeminate motioned for him to sit down. Dumeril settled her eyes on him, and he was instantly ill at ease in the gaze of this striking woman. Knowing she was an assassin did not impress him as much as her extraordinary beauty. He was uncomfortably aware that his emotions were paying tribute to the wrong thing.

"What do you want to drink?" Sleep asked dryly.

"Scotch. A little water."

Sleep mixed the drink with one hand, the other still cradling the Chihuahua. Dumeril didn't move to help him but sat back comfortably in her chair holding her own drink.

Sleep handed the scotch to Martin. "All right," he said, sitting back. He breathed loudly through his nostrils in deference to his obesity. "How do you want to do this?"

Martin sipped from the squat glass Sleep had given him and avoided the stare of Marie Dumeril.

"This morning I took an early trolley ride. I didn't want to keep the briefcase with me while I waited for word from GATO about its delivery. I ended up at the fortress of Ulúa across the harbor. That's where I left it."

Sleep's face was stony. "You *hid* it there?"

"Yes."

"God," Sleep said, rolling his eyes upward. "Welcome to another Hardy Boys mystery." He clenched his teeth.

"What time is it?" Martin asked.

"Nearly seven o'clock."

"GATO was supposed to have contacted me today, I don't know how, and we were going to make arrangements for the delivery sometime tonight. I've hired a cabby to pick me up and take me to the fortress. I paid him well, and he's bribed the night watchman out there to let us in."

"What time?"

"Eight o'clock."

Sleep cut his eyes at Dumeril and idly scratched the Chihuahua's leathery underbelly. The dog half-closed its bugged eyes, enjoying it.

"You remember what I said about risks, Gallagher?" Sleep asked.

Martin nodded.

"Okay."

They sent Felipe downstairs to the café for food, and the four of them ate in silence, Felipe alone near the door. Sleep fed Pepe from his own plate of shrimp and ate with the same fingers he continued to scratch the dog with. Dumeril paid no attention to Sleep's lack of manners as she ate with her own impeccable demeanor.

Martin tried not to think about what he was going to do. A little before eight o'clock, Sleep rose from the table, took Felipe aside, and talked to him softly as the Mexican listened intently. Dumeril opened her large purse and removed a Czech Skorpion machine pistol. With a sense of unreality Martin watched as she deftly removed the curved magazine and checked over the mechanism of this ugly but deadly weapon favored by terrorists throughout the world for close-range assassination. Behind him Martin heard the snap and ratchet sounds of other firearms being checked.

The four of them went downstairs together, and Martin waited with Dumeril and Sleep in the bright lobby while Felipe went to the parking garage and brought around their blue sedan. Through the front doors Martin could see his cab waiting. When Sleep saw Felipe pull onto the lighted plaza he took Martin by the arm and they preceded Dumeril outside past the café patrons lining the *portales*. A marimba band played at another café across the plaza, and laughter echoed along the amber-lighted arches and died softly in the steamy Caribbean evening.

When they got to the cab and Martin bent down to look inside, he looked into the alert face of Genaro Novo. Novo gave a quick tip of his head.

"Are you ready?" Martin asked cryptically.

"*Sí, señor*," Novo said, and he flipped up the flag on his meter.

Sleep moved Martin aside and got in the front seat beside Novo. He turned half around with his back to the door facing the driver, making it easier for him to see in the back where Martin had crawled in, followed by Dumeril.

Novo pulled away from the *portales* and circled the plaza in front of the cathedral, past the municipal palace, and then left on Zaragoza. They passed under the palms lining the meridian across from the customs house at the docks, then started up the long slope of the bridge that spanned the railroad depot. On the other side of the bridge they entered the causeway. The bright lights of the harbor and neighboring shipyards illuminated the stone face of the fortress that sat on the reef that jutted out into

216

the mouth of the harbor. Beyond the fortress on the north side of the harbor, petroleum-storage tanks and factories that manufactured oil-field equipment cluttered the night skyline, the sparkling lights of their towers and smokestacks camouflaging the sour refuse and grim scars of heavy industry.

Martin tried to read something in Novo's eyes each time they met his own in the rear-view mirror, but the car was too dark for anything to pass between them. He saw a bar of light pass across the dash from behind and remembered Felipe. He should say something about him, though he was sure Novo knew he was there.

Martin leaned forward slightly. "Did you arrange things with the night watchman?"

"Everything is fine, *señor*."

"We have another person with us. Behind us. Will that cause any problem?"

"No, *está bien*. My friend might want more for the second car."

"Okay," Martin said. He didn't know what he had accomplished by this little dialogue, and he sat back in his seat discouraged. Sleep looked at him cautiously from the front seat. Marie Dumeril sat in the opposite corner with her hands in her lap, gripping the Skorpion pistol.

At the end of the causeway a small guardhouse protected the entrance to the island. It was only a formality. They stopped, and Novo spoke to the night watchman in Spanish. Martin strained his eyes to see through the front windshield to the parking lot in the courtyard of the fortress itself. It was the only place cars could park, and it was empty.

The parking area was small, about the size of two tennis courts. The cab moved slowly across the cinder lot directly up to the front entrance overshadowed by bulky stone parapets and turrets. Novo pulled up close to the entrance, throwing the cab in the shadows, and turned off the motor. Sleep looked out into the courtyard and turned toward his door as Felipe pulled up beside them and cut his lights.

Across the harbor the cranes on the docks churned and reeled in the night air and the city lights of Veracruz lighted the shoreline with incongruent splendor. The slur of water lapping against the fortress walls filled the silence on the reef island, and then Felipe's car door clicked open, followed by the sound of his shoes crunching on the cinder. Sleep opened his door too, as did Marie Dumeril, and for a few brief seconds the interior light of the cab lighted them from behind as each, half crouched, half standing, emerged into the darkness.

At that moment Novo whipped a gun from inside his coat and pumped three quick blasts into Sleep's lower back. Simultaneously gunfire erupted from the ramparts above the courtyard and Marie Dumeril spun around and opened the Skorpion into Novo's face as Martin flung himself on the floor of the cab. A second volley from the parapets caught Dumeril as she was swinging the Skorpion toward Martin, lifting her out of the cab door and blowing her into the darkness of the courtyard. Sleep was still alive, screaming in Spanish to Felipe, who had managed to get back into the sedan and start the motor. With his door still open he jammed the gears in reverse just as he was caught in the crossfire from the walls. The sedan spun in the loose cinder drive and skidded wildly across the courtyard until it smashed into the limestone wall near the guard gate. The small-arms fire continued for another second, plucking at Sleep's Panama suit and kicking up spumes of sand.

Suddenly there was silence except for Sleep's Chihuahua squealing hysterically. Someone ran across the cinder yard to Sleep's body, just outside the glow cast by the interior light of the cab, and shot the dog.

Martin didn't know whether to get out of the cab or stay in. He heard voices above him on the castle walls and others coming across the courtyard stopping at each of the bodies, checking them. Someone opened the front door of the cab, and Novo fell out onto the cinders. Then the back door opened and a uniformed Mexican helped Martin out.

He heard a familiar voice coming toward him in the dark, and then Luis' face came within the wash of light.

"You're lucky, Mr. Gallagher, very lucky," he said quickly. "I don't know why yu are still alive." He turned and shouted orders in Spanish, and Martin heard footsteps running in the darkness and saw flashlight beams crisscrossing in the courtyard as men hurried to follow his instructions.

Martin turned and leaned on the top of the cab. Luis gripped his upper arm firmly.

"Do you have the documents with you?"

"No." Martin was trembling, and he knew Luis could feel it. "I told them I had hidden them here and had planned to get them tonight."

"We will have to hurry," Luis said. "Is the briefcase still at the hotel?"

Again Martin nodded. Luis shouted for someone to help them,

and in a moment Martin was being half carried up a narrow stone stairway toward the castle parapets. When they emerged from the dank turret chase onto the ramparts, they hurried across the night-dampened battlements to another stairway that led them down to a stone landing beneath the sheer walls. They descended to two launches moored to the pilings, and Martin was helped into the smaller of these while Luis stood at the bottom of the stairs speaking rapidly to a *federale* officer. The launch was shoved away from the pilings as Luis started the engine.

"Tenga cuidado, capitán!" someone shouted from the darkness, and Luis steered the launch into the harbor.

The trip across the harbor was rough; the launch slapped against the water with jarring concussions that had an agonizing effect on Martin's aching body. They passed across the mouth of the harbor unnoticed in the long shadows of the mammoth tankers and freighters berthed at the sparkling piers to their right. As they approached the head of the jetty that formed the harbor's southern boundary, Felipe cut the launch out into theGulf and crossed the harbor mouth to the jetty on the opposite side. He followed it on its Gulf side, staying close enough to the granite breakwater for Martin to see the white foam of the waves crashing into the rocks. When they had nearly traveled the length of the breakwater, Luis cut his lights and steered for the ocean aquarium that sat on the seawall at the juncture of the jetty and the *malecón*.

A signal from the beach beyond the aquarium guided them to a sheltered cove below the merchant marine school. Luis stopped the launch's motor before they reached their landing, letting it shunt onto the sand in silence. They were helped out of the boat by two men in street clothes who hustled them up a rocky path along the seawall to an unmarked car waiting beneath the palms on the *malecón*.

Martin got in the back seat with Luis, who leaned forward and spoke to the other men, who had just closed their doors.

"Alberto," he said to the driver. "Go to the Colonial."

Both men shot him questioning looks.

"We don't have the documents," he explained. "There was a shootout at the fortress. Novo was killed only moments ago."

As they drove back downtown to the Plaza de Armas, Martin told the three men what had happened to him since his meeting that morning with Luis on the beach at Boca del Río. After he finished his story there was a brief silence as each man explored the ramifications of the recent developments. Then Luis reached in his pocket and handed a key across to the man sitting beside the driver.

"Miguel, this is a key to the room in the Colonial. We cannot risk letting Mr. Gallagher be seen in public again tonight."

The three of them waited in the car on the dark side of the plaza across from the brightly lighted arcades of the *portales*. On the car's shortwave radio they listened to the frantic transmissions of the *federales* from the fortress in the harbor to their counterparts in the city, who were now sharing the airwaves with several cars of Dan Lee's agents, who had arrived from Mexico City during the day as Luis had predicted. Luis and Martin had hardly reached their contacts on the beach below the *malecón* before Lee's agents were crossing the causeway to San Juan de Ulúa. Luis could only hope the *federales* on the scene would use his instructions with sufficient creativity to buy them enough time.

In the taut silence as they listened to the crackling radio and waited, Martin's wounds throbbed with increasing intensity, his attention no longer preoccupied with constant movement and escape. The inactivity stiffened his joints and dried up the pain-killing adrenalin that had saved him more agony than he knew.

Miguel emerged from the palms in the plaza, carrying the briefcase under his suitcoat, which he had draped over his arm as though he had shed it in deference to the gummy Veracruz night. Within minutes they had circled the shimmering lake in Zamora Park and were speeding down Díaz Mirón Boulevard, past the cemetery on the outskirts of Veracruz, and onto Highway 150, which led west over the Sierra Madre Oriental to Mexico City.

Chapter 24

Dan Lee sat with his socked feet on the coffee table as he watched the dove-gray light of evening close over the water of the Gulf of Mexico. He nursed a whiskey sour, which he hoped would counteract the slump toward inertia that had come over him with the dying sun and his continued failure to make progress in locating Martin or the documents.

When Lee and John Womack had deplaned at the air terminal in Tampico, Jack Whitfield had met them and told them they had been half an hour too late. Apparently Martin and his pilot had had a gun battle with the *federales* less than an hour earlier in a barrio back street and had fled to their plane at an outlying airstrip, where they had barely escaped in a hail of small-arms fire. Tampico radar had tracked them west toward Ciudad de Valles and then lost them as the plane entered the foothills of the mountain range. The *comandante* had told Whitfield the light plane had sustained heavy fire from his men and he was sure they had punctured the gas tank. He believed the plane had gone down near a small town called Tamuín and said that he was sending a search party into the hills within the hour.

Whitfield believed differently. He had checked into the pilot Martin had hired and learned he was a well-known *contrabandista* whose regular routes were those along the Gulf Coast to Yucatán. Whitfield thought the radar disappearance smacked of vintage evasive maneuvering and that Martin and Kennedy were already on their way to Veracruz. Lee agreed. As a precautionary measure they sent one agent into the mountains with the *comandante*'s search team and then reboarded their plane for Veracruz.

They had arrived in Veracruz in the dark heavy hours of the morning and taken an adjoining room and suite at the Mocambo Hotel, which sat on a terraced hillside overlooking the white beach of the same name on the south side of the city. Susannah had taken the room while Lee and his agents occupied the suite, installing the radio equipment in one of the bedrooms.

Sunrise that morning had found Lee still awake, talking periodically to his agents who were already in Veracruz from Mexico City and those who had followed them down on another plane from Tampico. No one had slept. They didn't get a break until midmorning, when two agents working with a team of *federales* located Kennedy's plane on a caliche strip north of the city. The *comandante* had been right about one thing: the Cessna Centurion had been riddled by small-arms fire. It was a fluke the plane had been able to fly at all.

Throughout the day, however, no further progress had been made. From his temporary radio headquarters at the Mocambo, Lee stayed in constant touch with his agents, two in each of the four rental cars they had equipped with the radios brought down from San Antonio. Shortly after lunch the radio operators received a message from the San Antonio office that Francisco Lyra had just boarded Mexicana Airlines Flight 206 bound for Mexico City. Lee had checked with the skeleton staff at their Mexico City office to make sure someone would be at the Benito Juárez International Airport to intercept Lyra and keep close tabs on him during the next twenty-four hours.

In the middle of the afternoon the Bureau's Houston office radioed that Senator Leonard Kahan had been found dead at his home by his wife when she returned from her regular afternoon tennis matches at the Houston Oaks Redondo Club. The Bureau had taken charge of the investigation.

In Veracruz the *federales'* cooperation had been thorough enough . . . on the surface. Saying that he had acted on Captain Ruiz Campa's instructions, the local *comandante* established roadblocks on every highway, street, and road leading out of Veracruz and encompassing the sprawling suburbs and slums. Every departing aircraft, commercial and private, was searched by *federale* teams. All outbound shipping had been put on a twenty-four-hour hold. This last accomplishment had required some muscle from Mexico City. Lee couldn't complain.

Lee stood up in his rumpled clothes and walked to the window of his suite. A three-quarter full moon had already come up over the Gulf and was balancing like a lopsided doubloon on the water that reflected a rippling swath of liquid gold all the way from the horizon to the beach below him. Below him too, on the Mocambo's terrace that curved out into the tropical night, the hotel had set up a bar and a marimba band was assembling its instruments. The promenade was gradually filling with chic guests. Two leggy girls in skimpy *tangas* came up the wide terrace steps that led to the beach and worked their way through the milling crowd to the bar. They each took drinks, then disappeared along a palm-lined gallery toward a collection of dimly lit bungalows a little lower on the hillside.

Lee turned and went back to the sofa and again put his feet on the coffee table. No, he couldn't complain about the *federales'* cooperation, yet, on the other hand, neither Lee nor any of his men had been directly contacted by Captain Ruiz Campa since they had arrived in Mexico. If Campa's absence had been a calculated snub in retaliation for his own less than enthusiastic reception by the Bureau in San Antonio, Lee would have understood. In fact, he had not anticipated as much help as he had already gotten from the *federales*. But Lee had a nagging feeling that was not the reason for Campa's absence.

With a tired tilt of his head, Lee drained the whiskey and sat the empty glass on the floor at the end of the sofa. He listened to the static on the radios in the next room and shook his head. He was having a difficult time convincing himself he hadn't lost the main thread of the investigation once again after having the unexpected break with Susannah Lyra the night before that had given him a jump ahead. They had been so close in Tampico. For the first time in his career Lee began to doubt his ability to cope with the assignment. Perhaps if he had been a more creative investigator . . . if he had been more intuitive. But then he *had* formulated an original theory. The only thing was, it looked as if he would have to wait until the end of the game to prove he was right. Only the end of the game *could* prove he was right, and if he moved on his theory before the final moments he would be moving alone. If he was wrong, his old friends Colin Weathers would have a hell of a time salvaging Lee's career when it was over.

A telephone rang in the next room, which meant there was a call from Mexico City. All other communication was coming through the special equipment brought from San Antonio. Lee stayed where he was, listening to Womack ask questions in a modulated voice too low for Lee to understand. He was conscious of his increased heart rate, and he knew the whiskey sour hadn't done it.

Finally Womack hung up the telephone and walked across to Lee as he jotted notes on a pad.

"That was Mendez," he said without excitement. "They've had a pretty frantic time trying to keep up with Lyra after he landed in Mexico City. Says Lyra acted like he knew someone was onto him and tried every trick in the book. Mendez had taken the precaution of getting help from his old private-investigator buddies, so he had things pretty well covered."

"And . . . ?" Lee was impatient. He didn't want the details now.

"They followed Lyra to the bank building on the Paseo de la Reforma. He went to a top-floor suite variously occupied by the bank's executives, kind of a home base, a private meeting place for half a dozen privileged men. He stayed about half an hour, then returned to the airport and a private hangar closed off by a chain-link fence. One of the Mendez investigators got inside and watched Lyra board a twin-engine Beechcraft—I have the number—along with several well-armed men. They took off just a few minutes ago after—"

"Flight plan!" Lee broke in, reaching for a map.

"—filing a flight plan for Puebla."

Lee rolled out the map on the coffee table. "Get Mrs. Lyra in here," he said.

When Susannah came into the suite through the adjoining door, she was wearing a Mexican-made cambric dress that she had bought earlier in the day when Lee had let her go into Veracruz, accompanied by an agent, to do some quick shopping. She had left San Antonio with no change of clothes or toilet articles. Even though she had just been awakened and had had too little sleep, like the rest of them, she showed very little of the strain except for the darkening shadows under her green eyes. Lee never wondered for a moment why Martin had risked an affair with this woman.

She sat down in an armchair across the coffee table from Lee and watched him as he finished explaining something to Womack, who then returned to the radio room.

"Mrs. Lyra," Lee said, "we've just learned your husband has left Mexico City in a private plane and has filed a flight plan for Puebla. That's sixty-five or seventy air miles. In a twin-engine plane it'll take him only a few minutes."

He moved over closer to her on the sofa and turned the map so that she could see it at a better angle.

"Do you know any reason why he might be going to Puebla? Does his bank have a major branch there? Is there someone there he goes to see often? Any reason at all?"

Susannah instinctively looked at the map as she thought and slowly shook her head. "There *is* a branch of the bank there, but I don't know of any reason why he should be going there now. Then again, I don't know why he shouldn't."

Lee had learned enough from Susannah on the flight down

and during the long, seemingly endless day to know that the end of the whole complicated mess was imminent. He had learned enough to know that Susannah Lyra had no idea of what was really happening. Though she was an intelligent woman, and could qualify as an expert in Mexican-American affairs after having lived more than a decade in Mexico City with one of the government's most brilliant young statesmen, she was nevertheless guilty of having a blind side: her husband. If she didn't know what Francisco Lyra was up to in his flight from Mexico City, Lee was not going to be the one to enlighten her. In their long conversations since her telephone call from the Flamingo Courts twenty-four hours earlier, he had gathered far more information than he had shared. Susannah's sole preoccupation was with keeping Martin out of the hands of the Limón government.

Lee shifted his eyes to the map again.

"You're right," he said, "there's no reason why he shouldn't go to Puebla. But under the circumstances there *is* a good reason why he *should* go. I've got to decide what that reason is."

He continued to study the map.

"We know Martin made it to a worn-out airstrip north of Veracruz. More than likely he's still here. He's supposed to be going to Oaxaca, but we know he can't fly there. We have his plane and, to the best of our ability, we have a fix on most of the small strips in the area from which he might be able to originate another flight. From Veracruz to Oaxaca is one hundred and fifty air miles. It's probably half again that far by car. From Puebla to Oaxaca by air is one hundred and seventy miles. If Martin started driving to Oaxaca last night when he got to Veracruz there's a good chance he got through the roadblocks, which were still being set up at that time. He would be in Oaxaca now. The ambassador will be in Oaxaca in less than an hour, if that's where he's going. And we'll be sitting right here unless we can make some decisions based on very good educated guesses."

Lee took a ballpoint from his shirt pocket and drew a straight line from Veracruz west to Puebla, from Puebla south to Oaxaca, and then back up to Veracruz to form a near equilateral triangle.

"On the other hand," he said pensively, "GATO knows that its checkpoint system has been blown. Why would they stick to it? Assuming with some certainty the ambassador knows something we don't, why is he headed for Puebla? If GATO changes the point at which Martin is supposed to hand over the briefcase, wouldn't they move that point closer to Veracruz to save time and risk? Would it be Puebla? I doubt it."

"Why not?" Susannah had moved her chair closer to the map.

"He wouldn't have advertised his destination by filing his flight plan."

"But he'd have to know the new point of exchange. Do you think the Brigada Blanca has been that successful?"

Lee shrugged and avoided the question. "And there's the problem of Tony Sleep. I have a blank there. No ideas, no theories."

Womack came back into the room. "He's way overtime in Puebla," he said. "They haven't heard from him since he left Mexico City. He's never even checked his coordinates."

Lee looked at Susannah, then down at the map. He traced a finger over the triangle he had just drawn.

"Think hard, Mrs. Lyra. Do any of the small towns or villages within the triangle mean anything to you? Do you know of an airstrip within that area that could accommodate several planes, a farm or ranch that might belong to an acquaintance where a strip might be located?"

Susannah looked at the huge deltoid Lee and drawn on the map that covered some of Mexico's most scenic mountain country and spanned three states by the same names as the cities at each of the points of the triangle. She tried to recreate trips she had taken to other cities within the prescribed area: Tehuacán, Orizaba, Córdoba, Tehuipango. In thirteen years there had been many, most of them made in airplanes, since that was a major method of travel for the wealthier politicians in this mountainous region. From the larger towns they took automobiles into the countryside. But secluded airstrips?

She spoke slowly, thinking. "There are strips at the two major archaeological sites within the triangle: Monte Albán at Oaxaca, Cerro de las Mesas south of Veracruz. We flew once to Tehuacán because Francisco wanted to show me the spas, but his pilot had to land on a road near a ranch outside the town. But we did that a lot out in the states. I don't think it would be what we are looking for."

She paused a moment, squinting at the map, and then reached out and put her finger on Orizaba. "Here," she said. "There's a very good strip here on the ranch of Silvanio Gris. He's one of Francisco's closest friends, an industrialist with extensive holdings in Monterrey and a board member of the bank. We've been to several weekend parties there, and I've seen as many as a dozen planes lined up along the strip for these occasions."

226

"Is it a caliche strip?" Lee asked, circling Orizaba.

"Oh no, it's paved. First-class. A small hangar-shed at the end nearest the ranch house, which is, maybe, six hundred yards away."

The radios in the adjoining bedroom came alive and loud excited voices crackled through the receivers. The radiomen had been monitoring *federale* transmissions as well as the four cars of the Bureau's agents.

"Captain!" Womack yelled. "We got a shootout here."

Lee jumped up and ran into the bedroom, followed by Susannah. They stood in the doorway listening to the confusion of urgent transmissions in Spanish interspersed with English, requests for locations, what was happening, and clusters of sharp popping sounds of the actual gunfire. Everyone in the suite listened helplessly as Jack Whitfield, speaking Spanish, tried to shout down the gabbling *federales* by repeatedly and persistently requesting the location of the gunfire.

The answer finally came from the dispatcher at *federale* headquarters, who was receiving phone calls from people all up and down the waterfront who were reporting seeing and hearing gunfire across the harbor at the fortress of San Juan de Ulúa. By sheer good luck Whitfield's was closest of the four Bureau cars and was already speeding across the causeway. Strangely, after the gunfire ceased, there was no communication from the fortress itself, though it was obvious someone at the site had a radio tuned to the *federale* frequency.

Lee continued to listen as Whitfield sensibly kept up a running commentary of what was happening as he approached the fortress at high speed and roared through the night watchman's gate and into the gruesome scene in the courtyard.

It took him a while to find a *federale* who would admit to being the officer in charge at the scene, and then the man seemed to be as confused as those who were just arriving. Whitfield had seen it too many times before: the collusive subordinate officer trying to cover for his superior in a situation he didn't really understand, trying to keep a bad situation from getting worse for the senior officer who had left him in the lurch. He gave up the interview with the sweating sergeant and turned to the bodies.

Everyone in the Mocambo suite listened stonily to his report.

"We got a taxicab and a Mexican-made Ford LTD. The cabby's hanging half out of his front seat with his face blown away, so I can't tell anything about identification right now. The LTD is backed into the courtyard wall with a Mexican bodyguard type shot all to hell on the inside. Outside the cab on the ground,

227

looks like they're between the cab and where the LTD had been parked, is a smallish, heavyset Anglo in his mid-forties wearing a white Panama suit. Five, maybe eight, feet from him is a good-lookin' woman, Anglo, dressed in Paris' best. Both of 'em have taken on a hell of a lot more lead than it took to kill 'em. If I had to stake my career on a guess, I'd say we got Tony Sleep and Marie Dumeril out here."

Lee stepped over to the radio and took the microphone from the operator.

"Whitfield. Do you see any signs of anybody else being there? Sleep had a meeting with somebody. Did they make it? Was he killed before the meeting took place? Search those two cars inside out. It could be there. You understand?"

"Yeah, I know, but I can't tell anything about the scene. These damn *federales* have been all over everything. Dixon's here now, and I've already got our three men going over the cars."

"*Capitán* Lee."

Lee was caught off guard for an instant and pressed the transmission button on his microphone. As though the words formed an afterimage that lingered in his mind's eye after he heard them spoken, Lee recognized the voice of Ruiz Campa.

"Campa?" Lee snapped.

"Yes, *capitán*. I am sorry I have not been able to be of personal help to you since your arrival in Mexico. But I'm sure you understand. When an investigation depends on your direction you cannot always be where you wish."

"Where the hell are you, Campa? What's the deal out there in the harbor?"

"Again, I apologize, *capitán*, for not letting you know about the details of that encounter. I had hoped it would all be over at the fortress, but I am afraid I miscalculated." Campa's voice faded, then surged again, and Lee realized he was speaking from a car radio.

"But time is short now," Campa said, "And I need your help. Gallagher and a GATO pilot are heading north on Highway 140 toward Jalapa. We are in pursuit, but we are alone and can do nothing. This is not a time to be greedy, my friend. We are going to have to work together. I am quite certain the GATO pilot is heading for an airstrip at the small town of Paso de Ovejas a little less than halfway to Jalapa. Can you get your men into planes and try to intercept them? We will continue to radio coordinates. I have contacted my people in Jalapa and they are on their way to meet us. Can you help us?"

His voice was fading as he continued to the farthest limits of his range.

"We'll be in the air in fifteen minutes. Campa, we've got a lot of details to work out when this is over. Understand?"

"*Comprendo, capitán,*" Campa said. His voice was distant, barely audible above the static.

"Whitfield? Did you get that?"

"Yeah."

"Go straight across the causeway and call me from a pay phone. Keep Dixon and his man with you." Lee then addressed himself to the other cars that were somewhere in Veracruz. "Meecham? Lewis? Did you hear me? Do the same. Call me from a pay phone. And hurry."

Lee handed the microphone back to the radio operator and walked back to the coffee table, where he crouched down to study the triangle once again. Susannah and Womack followed him.

"John, we're not going to Paso de Ovejas. When they call in I'm going to tell them to meet us south of Veracruz at the intersection of highways 180 and 150. We'll leave two of the cars there and drive to Orizaba."

He looked up at Susannah. "Can you still find that ranch and the airstrip?"

"I think so," she said. And then, "I'm sure of it."

Lee looked at the map again and spoke as much to himself as to the others. "I wasn't sure until now," he said. "Campa has been very good, but he didn't give me enough credit. That snipe hunt north of Veracruz was amateurish. It's going to cost him."

He stood and walked to the window overlooking the terrace, where the marimba band was playing to the dancers under the colored lights. Beyond them were the palms and the moon over the Gulf.

"Mrs. Lyra, this is going to be very dangerous. I'll have to be honest with you: You don't have to do it. I'll also be frank: I hope you will. You know what's at stake. I have no idea what will happen."

"You think Martin will be there, don't you?"

"Yes, I do," Lee said, still looking down at the dancers. "I think he's with Ruiz Campa and that the final transfer of the documents to GATO will be made at that airstrip on Gris' ranch. I'm not sure how much of a head start Campa has on us, but if we can't catch him on the highway we'll have to try something at the airstrip."

"I want to go," she said flatly.

Lee had known she would say that, and he hated himself. The first call jangled the telephone in the next room, and he turned to Womack as he started toward the bedroom.

"Start putting everything in the car. Make sure there are sidearms for all of us as well as rifles."

She walked to the window and looked down to the terrace, where the dancers moved to the lilting Caribbean rhythms of the marimba. It was another world she saw in the languid tropical night, a world she had been accustomed to only two days before and which now seemed all but alien to her. It had been a life she had taken for granted, and now she found herself watching the sybarites under the sparkling lights and wondered what they were thinking, how they would spend the long passing hours of the night and how it would all eventually come to an end for them, as it had for her.

Dan Lee had to speak her name twice before she heard and turned to see him folding the map. He had rolled down the sleeves of his shirt and wore a pistol in a holster strapped snugly to his waist in the small of his back.

"Are you ready to go?" he asked as he quickly grabbed his jacket from the back of a chair. "I can't think of anything you'll need."

"I'm ready," she said, and she preceded him and another agent out the door of the suite. They descended two flights of stairs and followed an outside walkway along the curve of the terrace above them. The car was parked in a small cul de sac surrounded by coconut palms only a short distance out in the pale, hazy night. Womack was waiting. In a few moments they had pulled out onto the coastal highway, leaving behind the Mocambo hotel and the pulsing tempo of the *bamba* on the terrace.

Chapter 25

When they arrived at the intersection of the two highways, one leading south along the coast to Yucatán and the other west through the mountains to Mexico City, Lee found his agents waiting beside their cars behind a roadside tavern. With characteristic efficiency, Whitfield had already transferred the contents of the four cars into two, and organized the eight agents into two teams. Including Lee, there would be eleven agents altogether, and Susannah.

They leaned against their cars in the feeble light of a backdoor lamp while trash burned in an old rusted barrel a few yards away and listened as Lee explained what he thought had happened and what he wanted to do. They would stop again in Córdoba and work out the physical details after Lee had had a chance to talk more with Susannah about the layout at the airstrip. Their maneuvering would be complicated by the necessity of having to stay off the car radios. Campa would be monitoring all broadcasts, and an American voice, or Spanish spoken with the slightest trace of an accent, would be enough to alert him.

Lee's car left first, and the others followed at two-minute intervals. They had agreed to hold the speedometers on eighty for the first part of the trip; the highway held a fairly straight course across the coastal plains, where the fertile soil and long growing season supported cattle ranches and sprawling plantations of tobacco and vanilla. The moon, now high above them, flooded the plains in a silver haze, and the snow-capped Pico Orizaba rose majestically before them more than a hundred miles away.

Lee waited until he saw the headlights of both cars far back on the highway before he turned to Susannah.

"Okay, Mrs. Lyra. Can you tell me exactly how to get to the Gris ranch from Orizaba?"

"It's been three years, maybe more," she said tentatively. Lee didn't respond, and in the face of his strained silence, she began. She described, as accurately as she could remember, the route by car from Orizaba. Lee stopped her several times to clarify a landmark or the distance between two points. He had several questions about the terrain and what the route looked like coming from the other direction. The more she talked the more she remembered, which surprised her.

When she finished, Lee silently continued to take notes, pausing from time to time to gaze out the window. Susannah had noticed that since they had left San Antonio, Lee had grown increasingly quiet as he slowly peeled back the layers of intrigue that hid the secret he pursued. With the lifting of each layer he became more sober, even morose, until at last he had revealed the answer, and found it profoundly disturbing.

Neither of the agents in the front had spoken during the time she had been talking to Lee, nor did they speak now. The tension, she knew, must be great, but she felt she deserved some kind of explanation about what was going to happen. She didn't want to be surprised at the airstrip any more than they did.

Finally she said, "Can you tell me what's going to happen?"

Lee didn't answer immediately, and when he did he didn't look at her. "No," he said.

"Can't or won't?" she responded.

"Can't," he said.

"Then why don't you tell me what you *think* will happen?" she said stiffly. "You *owe* me that."

She heard him sigh as he turned to her. "I'm sorry. Yes, I do owe you that."

"I'm frightened," she said, trying perhaps to explain her own terseness. She wouldn't have admitted it if the car hadn't been shadowy, hiding much of what he normally would have been able to see of her eyes.

"We are too," he said after a moment. "Usually when we go into something like this we have a lot more information than we have now. I'm playing a very big hunch. But I either play it or we're out of the game; there's really no choice. However, if I'm right, anything could happen." He hesitated. "I suspect there will be shooting. Since they have no idea we're going to be there, we'll have a chance to surprise them. Maybe we can do it."

"Who's 'them'?"

Lee thought a moment. "Just more hunches," he said evasively.

"If everything goes as you hope, you'll arrest Martin with the rest of them?"

"I'll have to, yes."

"And then what?"

"And then I'll do the best I can. I told you that."

Highway 150 stretched seventy miles across the coastal plains, rising gradually from sea level in Veracruz to three thousand feet as it reached Córdoba in the foothills of Pico Orizaba. The vegetation became more dense as the highway rose into the hills. Susannah peered out her window into the moonlit valleys of the coffee plantations sprawled along the slopes.

After they entered Córdoba, Womack drove through the plain square and entered a side street one block off the plaza. He and the other agent crossed to a neighborhood café and returned with four mugs of the strong black Matalargan coffee. When the other two cars arrived, everyone got out and stood in the night shadows of the jacaranda trees that hung over the sidewalk and listened to Lee give them their final briefs.

Susannah stayed in the car, feeling suddenly superfluous to the action that was about to take place. The whole feel of what Lee was planning was depressingly reminiscent of the "police actions" she had seen so often during the ten years she had lived in Mexico.

In a few minutes the cluster of agents on the darkened sidewalk broke up and the men filtered back to their cars. They avoided the plaza as they traced their way to the new toll expressway that began at Córdoba and continued all the way to Mexico City. Four miles out of Córdoba they passed through Fortín de las Flores. From there to Orizaba the highway grew steep and winding and climbed fifteen hundred feet in only ten miles.

The three cars stayed close together as they snaked upward through the mountain gorges beneath Pico Orizaba. The highway crested, then dropped slightly into the tropical Maltrata Valley and the city of Orizaba. Again they avoided the center of the city; they turned off the main thoroughfare and traveled through the residential section south of the main plaza. They passed the salt-white tower of the Moctezuma breweries and then turned onto the rural roadway that took them beyond the cotton mills at the edge of the city and into the farmland and bordering jungles of the valley.

They followed the road, which was ridiculously narrow and poorly paved, for nearly five miles before Susannah recognized the turnoff. Womack pumped his brakes twice and the two cars behind them cut their lights and slowed to a crawl as they pulled up close, and all three cars turned off onto the rutted dirt road. For a little more than a mile they crept along in the moonlight

233

as the odd mixture of high-country pines and tropical palmettos grew thicker. By the time the road took an abrupt turn to the left, the tropical forest had closed in to form a dense wall on either side of the road.

Leaning forward against the front seat, Susannah strained to see through the murky windshield. When they came to the sharp left bend in the road, Womack rolled to a stop with the car facing the forest wall before the turn.

Susannah spoke in a low even voice. "If you go straight into the jungle at this point you'll come to the escarpment after about seventy-five yards. From there you'll be able to see Gris' hacienda and the airstrip on the floor of the basin."

"Would we be directly in line with the hacienda if we went straight down into the basin now?" Lee asked.

"That's right. The airstrip is to the left, parallel with this road when it turns. After this turn the road continues along the edge of the escarpment and then drops down into the basin at the far end of the strip. Then it doubles back to the hangar at the head of the runway. The hacienda is about five or six hundred yards beyond that."

Lee sat motionless, thinking, then got out of the car and signaled to the car behind them. Two doors opened and Whitfield and another agent got out and joined him. Both men adjusted infrared binoculars around their necks as the three of them walked to the forest edge. They talked a moment before the two agents disappeared into the dusky margin of vegetation. The night was as quiet as a tomb, amplifying and carrying the faintest noises on the thin mountain air. The sweet fragrance of the luxuriant forest nourished by warm daily rains filled the car through its open windows.

For a moment Lee stared into the black jungle that swallowed the two agents, then he turned back and walked past the first two cars to the third. Again two agents with binoculars got out of the last car and accompanied Lee to the bend in the road, where they left him as they struck out at a brisk pace. Lee walked back to the car and leaned his forearms on Womack's window.

"Why don't you have the guys start taping the taillights? The jungle's heavy enough to reflect the glow as we come off the escarpment. Have them tape the interior-light button on the doors too."

Susannah sat in the car alone as Womack and the other agent took care of the details of masking the lights. Lee remained outside, walking back and forth in front of the car, impatient for the two reconnoitering teams to return. She watched him pace nervously. He concealed his anxiety with far less skill than his agents, who bore the waiting with the traditional stoicism expected of them.

When Whitfield and his partner emerged from the dark wall of the jungle, Susannah got out of the car and joined them. The pale light from the moon illuminated the Oklahoman's face enough for Susannah to tell that he was drenched in sweat.

"It's like she said," Whitfield addressed Lee, taking his wadded handkerchief from his hip pocket and smearing it across his forehead and around his neck. "But the escarpment's closer, maybe forty-five, fifty yards. The basin's long, filled with tropical forest except for what's been cleared out for the house and airstrip. The house is dark, looks vacant."

Lee turned a questioning look at Susannah.

"I wouldn't know," she said. "I would have thought a small staff would be living there."

"I didn't see anything, no dog, nothing. The hacienda is plush. The airstrip's about five hundred yards away, like she said." Then he added the punch line. "There's a car parked in front of the hangar at the head of the strip. One guy outside smoking, two, maybe three, sitting inside." Whitfield smiled at Lee. "Guess you were right."

Lee was somber. "Chuck Spanner and Cable have gone down the road. We've got to see what they find before we can move an inch. Is the undergrowth thick on the escarpment?"

"Very. I had to climb a tree to see the basin. It should be a good cushion, absorb a fair amount of noise despite the atmosphere."

At Lee's instruction the agents began dividing the ammunition and firearms, each taking a hand radio to be used after the action began. The wait for Spanner and Cable was longer than they had anticipated, and Lee was considering sending Whitfield after them when they saw a lone man walking toward them in the white seams of the rutted road. It was Spanner.

"Don't panic," he said softly as he approached them. He was huffing, the high altitude and the quick walk working against him. "I left Walt at the bottom of the road to watch them." He assumed Whitfield had spotted the car from up above and had told Lee.

"I couldn't believe it," he said when he had caught his breath enough to talk. "There's only four of them. We were close enough to recognize them with the infrareds. Campa, Gallagher, and a couple of agents, I guess. They're just waiting. Did you know the strip had lights for night landing?"

"That's new," Susannah said, and Lee knew he had come to the right place.

Spanner confirmed everything Whitfield had said about the layout of the basin. "The road follows the escarpment about a mile and a half, I'd guess. When it drops off into the basin it's not a steep decline but angles gradually, doubling back toward the hacienda. I don't think we'll have any trouble with the cars slipping on the grade, making noise kicking up gravel. Walt's at the bottom. Hell, I bet he's not two hundred yards from the car. The jungle's been cleared away from the far end of the strip so that the whole length of the tarmac is usable for approaching and takeoff."

"You mean they can take off and land from either end?" Lee asked.

"Looks like that's the way it was planned, but in reality it would be a hell of a lot more sensible to approach and take off from up the basin over the hacienda. In fact, I imagine that's the way it's done. Otherwise from the other direction you'd have to drop fast coming in and pull up fast going out. You've got palms to contend with at that end of the strip too."

"What about sneaking up on the car?" Whitfield asked. "Can it be done quickly?"

"It can be done. I don't know about how quickly. It'll have to be done on foot, and it's going to take some time for us to fan out. From what I can tell through the binoculars they don't seem to be particularly touchy."

"They're not expecting anything," Lee said. "Campa's convinced we're on our way to Jalapa, and he's been out of radio range too long to have heard otherwise. But we're not going to take them now."

Whitfield and Spanner waited for the explanation. Lee crossed his arms and rubbed an opened hand along the side of his face, where a shave was long overdue.

"It would be easier now, before the plane comes in," Lee conceded, "but it would be a mistake. There's probably a clearance signal Campa has to give before the plane will land, so we can't risk his being killed in a shootout. If we take him alive there's no doubt in my mind he would either refuse to give the signal or give the wrong one. It won't matter to him if we threaten to blow off his head. That briefcase sitting down there is tempting, but I want the whole ball of wax. Sometime tonight Paco is going to taxi along that strip, and I want to be there when he does."

"Okay," Whitfield said. "Then what do we do?"

236

Lee began to explain, and Susannah listened with increasing trepidation. It was clear the capture Lee was outlining would be a bloody affair. She knew that, because she knew how the Mexicans were going to react to what Lee had planned. She didn't believe Lee actually cared anymore. He had the edge once again. Everything was in his reach if he played it right. If he played it wrong a lot of people would be killed. After all her effort, she wasn't sure she had gotten Martin any closer to freedom and safety than when she had first begun. In fact, she feared she had guaranteed his death.

Martin was slumped against the door in the back seat. Every bone and muscle in his body was aching. He didn't know how badly he was hurt, but he knew his burns were becoming infected, and a few minutes earlier he had urinated blood. He tried not to think about what was happening inside him.

Luis sat on the other side of the car with his door open, smoking and looking out into the hazy blue moonlight that made a silver corridor of the airstrip that led straight as an arrow into the jungle and the silhouetted palm trees.

The briefcase lay on the seat between them. Martin had slept fitfully during the drive from Veracruz, but he had not been sleeping when Luis had radioed Lee that they were on their way to Paso de Ovejas and needed help. From their scratchy transmission Martin learned that "Luis" was a *federale* named Campa, that he was giving Lee as well as his own men a false lead. Was he really working for GATO, then? Or did his loyalties lie with the Brigada Blanca? When the plane arrived would Campa hand the briefcase over to GATO or the Mexican government? If it was the Mexican government, Martin had gone through hell only to find he had played the fool. Well, he just didn't care anymore. He just didn't give a damn.

They had been at the airstrip for nearly half an hour and Campa had not said a word. He had chain-smoked with his foot propped on the sill of the opened car door and stared out across the basin to the jungle-laden escarpment where the road angled down toward them. In the passenger side of the front seat Miguel dozed with his legs stretched out on the seat. Outside, Alberto also chain-smoked as he paced up and down along the runway lights.

Suddenly Alberto stopped and threw his head up like a hunting dog catching scent. He dropped his cigarette and put it out. Miguel sensed something also and sat up, his head cocked slightly sideways. Campa did not move. Then Martin heard it too, the faint, faraway drone of an airplane. Almost with one action the three of them got out of the car and joined Alberto at the end of the runway. The sound was unmistakable now, coming from the north toward Orizaba.

Then it faded away.

That seemed to be a signal for Alberto, who ran to the hangar and opened an electrical box attached to the side of the shed. He, Miguel, and Campa kept their eyes glued to the north end of the basin. Without warning, a huge twin-engine Beechcraft burst over the rim of the basin and barreled over them so low Martin could feel the vibrations in his chest.

"Now," Campa yelled, and Alberto flashed the lights for a millisecond and their afterglow lingered in the clear night like a glowworm in the grass as they watched the plane rise over the jungle at the end of the runway.

Alberto set the runway lights on half power instead of bright, and they listened to the plane bank toward the north and then begin its approach. Again the sound faded before the plane roared over the edge of the escarpment, noticeably slower this time, with its belly lights pulsing as it dropped over them and hit the tarmac with a sharp screech that split the stillness of the mountain air. The Beechcraft wheeled around at the end of the runway and taxied back toward the car.

Martin watched as the pilot cut the turbo engines and let them wheeze to a stop before he doused the lights. The passenger door swung back, and portable steps were let out on the runway. Immediately two men carrying automatic weapons came down the steps and stood on the asphalt. One of them shouted to Alberto to cut the runway lights. When he did, four more men with weapons descended the steps and fanned out under the wings of the plane. They faced outward to the darkness.

By this time Campa had turned back to the car and gotten the briefcase and was approaching the steps. As he did so, a tall lean figure backlighted from the cabin ducked out the door and came down to meet Campa with an *abrazo*. A chill washed over Martin as he recognized Francisco Lyra.

He sank back on the fender of the car and watched them, Lyra with one hand still resting on Campa's shoulder, Campa holding the briefcase. Martin could hear their voices, though he couldn't make out the words. There was an occasional burst of laughter, euphoric and at the same time expressing relief. Martin couldn't understand what he had done. Was Campa a double agent or not? He didn't know. He could feel his burns leaking blood serum now; his groin was throbbing, and his back still ached where Campa had chopped him early that morning at the beach. Was that just this morning? It seemed like a year ago. Everything had been turned upside down, and he didn't know anything anymore.

Martin watched as the two men's conversation grew more subdued. They checked their watches as Lyra seemed to explain something to Campa, and then Campa nodded toward Martin and Lyra looked his way. A few more words were exchanged, and Campa went up the steps of the Beechcraft and handed the briefcase to someone who met him at the door. Lyra looked at Martin again and started toward him.

The moonlight shining in the basin was incredibly bright, bright enough for Martin to see that Lyra was wearing an expensive suit. As he approached, he removed a cigarette from a silver case that glinted in the blue light of the moon. He stopped in front of Martin and lit the cigarette. The yellow flare revealed graying temples and crow's-feet at the corners of his handsome eyes. He blew the first lungful of smoke into the air.

"I am grateful for what you have done," he said. His voice was sincere, kindly.

"I'd feel a lot better if I knew who I'd done it for," Martin said sharply. He was confused, but he didn't want to appear weakened by it. He recognized the silly vanity of it even as he spoke.

Lyra smiled. "For Stella, for GATO. For Mexico."

"GATO?"

Lyra tilted his head forward in a courtly nod.

"Jesus," Martin said, looking down as he shook his head. "Paco." He thought of what Cuevas had said about the man, of what Susannah had said. God, Susannah. How could she not have known? She had even sympathized with what he was doing, all the time thinking he was on the opposite side of the fence. He ranked right up there with the best in the business. It was difficult to grasp what had happened, what it all meant.

"I owe you an apology, Mr. Gallagher. You have been used by us, and by your own government. I am afraid it is the nature of the business."

"What business?"

"Revolution."

"I could never take that word seriously."

"Even after what you've been through?"

"Especially after what I've been through," Martin said.

Lyra smiled. "Nevertheless, we are indebted to you. You have enabled us to make a new beginning for Mexico. We have

239

that in common, you and I. We have participated in the historical prologue. The story itself is yet to be told, but we have lived the opening pages. You will see someday. You will realize the magnitude of what has happened and you will understand."

He stopped. This was no preamble to political rhetoric, only a statement of faith by a man who had no doubts about what he was doing. The tall, reserved aristocrat was a secret dreamer, a romantic with a vision that required sacrifices that only he could make. Looking at him now, Martin wondered which had come first, the dream or the dreamer. But he knew it didn't matter. It was all coming to an end, and soon there would be no point in making such distinctions.

The two of them looked at each other. There was more. Martin knew it, and he could see in Francisco's eyes that he knew it too, but neither of them could speak to the other about Susannah. And then there was no time. Without even the faint hum of forewarning a second plane burst over the crest of the escarpment, low, at incredible speed. As the runway lights flashed on, the plane was already pulling up over the palms and banking for its return approach.

The single-engine Cessna Stationair feathered in over the hacienda and dropped quickly to the runway, taking only half the runway's length to land before it turned and started back toward them. The pilot obviously was used to tight spots. Before he cut the motor he swung the Cessna around to face the empty strip.

Francisco turned and strode toward the plane as it disgorged two, four, five armed men who quickly positioned themselves around the Cessna. Again the runway lights were dimmed, but not out, and Martin saw Stella climb out of the seat beside the pilot and run past the tail gear to Francisco. They embraced for a long while, bathed in the pulsing cherry flash of the Cessna's taillight as they stood in the middle of the tarmac between the two planes.

In that brief moment as Martin watched them, everything fell into place; the whole perplexing drama of the past four days was solved in the space of one kiss. The illogical became rational, the secret became known, and everything was in its place, except him. As he watched, they turned and started toward him with their arms around each other, and Martin could clearly see the radiant smile on Stella's face. They were halfway to him when it happened.

"Alto! Alto! Alto! No movés!"

The bullhorns boomed the warning from the jungle periphery

240

on both sides of the runway opposite the planes and echoed off the escarpment like a lingering nausea. The astonishment of everyone on the tarmac was complete, and for an instant even Lyra's elite guards remained frozen in silence. Only Francisco moved as he reflexively stepped in front of Stella and stared stoically into the dark wall beyond the lights.

"Ambassador! Campa! This is Dan Lee. You are surrounded. We will not hesitate to kill you where you stand. Please have your men throw the briefcase out of the Beechcraft and toss their weapons away from them onto the runway."

The response was instant darkness as the runway lights were extinguished. The airstrip and the surrounding jungle erupted in thunderous explosions of heavy gunfire as Stella's pilot hit the ignition on the Cessna and revved its engine to a whine. Suddenly the lights came on again, full beam, but the first hundred feet of kliegs had been kicked over on their swivels by the guards, sending their powerful beams outward against the jungle, blinding Lee's agents and exposing those who had not taken sufficient cover.

The crossfire surged murderously, and Martin, who had fallen to his knees by the fender of the car, was stunned to see Stella go down immediately, her back arching as she tried to keep her balance as she fell. Without thinking, he was on his feet springing across the tarmac, his ears ringing with screaming and convulsive gunfire. Francisco bent down and scooped Stella into his arms but got no farther than a few steps before Martin saw his shin splatter and he crumpled.

As Martin reached them, Francisco was raising himself on his elbows and looking down at his leg, which was nearly severed just below the knee. Stella saw it and started screaming, her eyes riveted to the lower leg lying at a skewed angle on the pavement. At that moment Campa's car, driven by Miguel, roared onto the field beside them, blocking the gunfire coming from the jungle on one side.

"Get her in the plane!" Lyra yelled. He hadn't blacked out or gone into shock but was removing his belt and strapping it above his wound to stop the pumping arterial bleeding. "Get her out of here, get her out of here," he bellowed as he struggled with the belt, and then he reached inside his waistband and pulled out a pistol, which he thrust into Martin's hand.

Martin pulled Stella into his arms as she fought him to stay with Francisco, and started for the plane only a few yards away. He had no idea how serious her own wound was, but he knew she was bleeding from somewhere in her back. He didn't know how much of the blood on her dress was from Francisco's leg. She continued screaming from fear and pain and stark desolation.

He flung open the Cessna's back door and lifted her onto the floor of the plane, where she clung momentarily to his neck, her eyes wild with confusion and incomprehension. Martin felt the plane move and realized with horror the pilot was already trying to pull away.

"You goddam bastard," he yelled, pulling the gun from his coat pocket and aiming it at the man's eyes. "If you don't wait for me to get that man in here I'll blow you to pieces myself."

The grim-faced pilot jammed on the brakes while Martin, near panic himself, wheeled around from the opened door and raced to Francisco, who, unbelievably, was dragging himself across the tarmac toward them as he flinched against the chunks of asphalt exploding around him. His leg was leaving a bloody snail's trail behind him. Martin jerked him up on his good leg and got him to the plane as Miguel moved the car forward with them, continuing to provide protection. Stella, less frantic when she realized Francisco would not be left behind, pulled Lyra into the belly of the plane as Martin boosted him from the ground. Lyra's dangling leg caught in the doorframe, and Martin grimly looped it into the plane beside him.

As Martin reached for the door to swing it shut, Francisco grasped his arm and locked his eyes on him. Lyra's ashen face reflected agony and his colossal determination to overcome it. And something else was there too. He seemed about to speak but hesitated, his words stymied by the moment's sad, impossible brevity. What should have been spoken, of the women they shared in the labyrinth between them, was not. Yet for an instant they both understood, then Martin pulled away and slammed the door.

In that exact instant the car exploded with a scorching blast that knocked Martin off his feet and lighted the taxiing Cessna more brilliantly than if spotlights had been deliberately thrown on the escaping plane. Martin heard a shriek and saw Miguel frantically and futilely clawing at the car door until it was too late. Death and his realization of it came at the same moment, and he stopped, sitting erect, blackened and burning.

Martin's movements were now dictated by survival reflexes alone as he scrambled on his hands and knees across the tarmac to the edge of the hangar and then to the jungle margin just behind it. The klieg lights focused on the jungle had been quickly shattered by Lee's agents, and Martin could hear Lee shouting directions over the bullhorn as Campa screamed hoarsely to his own men at the same time.

Suddenly the headlights of three cars fanned out from the road at the base of the escarpment and raced toward the landing strip. It was then that Martin realized the Cessna was still sitting in the same position, its engine idling, the pilot slumped over the controls as the flames from the burning car licked at the tip of its wing. Martin's muscles tensed as he prepared to run back to the plane. Then he saw Francisco struggle up from the floor of the plane and make his way to the cockpit, where he dragged the dead pilot from his seat and took his place in the crimson glare of the fire.

Martin watched in awe as Lyra wrestled with the controls until the engine revved to a fever pitch, fanning the flames of the car in the propeller's wash. Then the plane lurched forward and started down the tarmac, gaining speed as it burst into the section of the strip where the kliegs were still shining straight up. Chunks and chips of the plane were picked off by gunfire, and yet the Cessna hurtled on until the engine screamed and it lifted into the lighted space above the runway. But there was not enough room. They were already to the jungle at the end of the strip when Lyra strained the engine to the limit and pulled up, banking to avoid the palms. It was a futile maneuver. The banking effort became a sliding, whining careen, and the Cessna plunged into the dark jungle with a violent concussion followed by a globulous ball of fire which rose from the explosion like a red death's head hanging in the sky and lighting the carnage around them.

Appalled, Martin watched from the forest edge, where he had clawed his way into the spongy earth. He felt the heat against his face, and tears sprang to his eyes as he watched the flames reach incredibly high, seeming to threaten the stars themselves as they destroyed the two people he had felt so close to in their final desperate moments. He had tried. He had tried right up to the very end to help them. It simply was not meant to be. Stella and Francisco had seen a common vision and had fought together to make it a reality, but it was not for them to go beyond that struggle. Not now, not in this life and time.

Martin clenched his teeth and cringed at the incredible noise of the battle that still raged in the war zone of the runway. There was no letup in the ferocity of the fighting, and he was amazed to see, as if time had stood still, the three swerving cars still rushing toward the strip where the solitary Beechcraft sat shrouded in the smoke of cordite at the end of the tarmac.

He watched, unable to move or believe what was happening, while one of Francisco's guards, with calm efficiency, crouched in the flickering light of Miguel's burning car and laid the long tube of a rocket launcher over his right shoulder. Martin heard the great sucking *whoosh!* and saw the burst of fire at the rear of the tube followed by a mind-jarring *whump!* as the projectile disintegrated the first car and enveloped the second in a leprous inferno of white phosphorus. The third car plowed to a shuddering halt just at the edge of the runway. As its front doors flew open a GATO bodyguard deftly lobbed an apple-green antipersonnel grenade through an open window and dove for cover. It was too late for the horrified agents. The explosion blew the doors off the car with the agents still clinging to them.

Martin was stunned at the speed with which GATO's guerrilla-trained bodyguards had recovered the advantage and were methodically slaughtering Lee's agents. It was sickening to watch, and it was clear Lee didn't have a chance. The GATO fighters were not the kind to take prisoners or give quarter, and Campa was not inclined to restrain them, even though it was obvious what was happening. Martin caught glimpses of the double agent stooping and running back and forth across the asphalt now littered with bodies and pools of blood. Twice he slipped and fell.

Then, abruptly, the fearsome barrage stopped, leaving only the sporadic pop of small-arms fire in its wake. Martin lay on the mulchy earth and dropped his head on his crossed arms, trying to ignore the wailing and groaning of the wounded that was now more insistent than the shouted commands. Suddenly he heard his name screamed again and again and was shocked to recognize Susannah's voice coming out of the darkness from the direction of the hacienda.

He scrambled to his feet and began running toward her through the smoke, not even trying to understand why she should be in this unbelievable place. She came from the edges of the darkness, her dress a pale tea rose in the reflected fires. He embraced her, held her as she sobbed hysterically, but was unable to console her.

Then Campa found them. His face had the vacant weary look of battle shock, but he was military, he was in control.

"Please hurry," he said, making a guiding gesture with a handgun. "The plane is waiting."

Martin stopped. "Lee. What about Lee?"

Campa looked at Martin and shook his head. "Please hurry. They are clearing the runway for us."

By the time they reached the Beechcraft the gunfire was only occasional as Campa's men mopped up the last of Lee's agents hiding in the tangles of the tropical undergrowth. The cabin lights were turned off in the plane and the pilot steered to the opposite end of the field. When they turned again, the last of the bodies were being dragged off the strip, and Martin felt the surge of both powerful turbo engines as the pilot fed them every ounce of power and they bolted down the runway. The liftoff was smooth, as if there had been no emergency, no war.

Susannah wept inconsolably on his shoulder. Martin kept his eyes fixed on the scene below them as the plane banked. The few remaining runway lights had been dimmed, all three of Lee's cars were burning, and at the end of the tragic runway a single huge pyre burned alone in the jungle.

Epilogue

Martin rose from the wrought-iron chair on their private terrace of Las Brisas and walked over to the low wall topped with terra-cotta urns of scarlet-blossomed bougainvillea. He was barefooted, wore loose-fitting peasant trousers of white cotton and no shirt. The sun felt good on his bare skin; his chest and stomach had healed quickly with the attention of the best doctors GATO could buy in Mexico City. He would have no debilitating aftereffects from his ordeal with Tony Sleep.

Lost in thought, he looked down the palm-covered hillside of Punta Bruja into the emerald crescent of Acapulco Bay and the Pacific waters glistening in the brilliant sunlight. Behind him on a white wrought-iron table the cluttered mess of newspapers and weekly magazines he had been reading fluttered in the light breeze that swept up the hillside. An empty gin-and-lime glass sat on the Spanish tile beside his chair. The magazines and newspapers were still featuring the story that had dominated the news media for the past two weeks: the abrupt resignation of Mexico's President Jorge Limón (for health reasons) and the appointment of his replacement by the Chamber of Deputies in an emergency session.

It had been an unusual maneuver by the chamber, which selected an internationally prominent financier, a board member of the Banco Federal de México, Silvanio Escobar de Gris, rather than the candidate of Mexico's most powerful political party, who was already being groomed to succeed the president. With the new president, a new political party had also come to the forefront during the tumultuous events following the presidential resignation: El Gobierno Agrario Tradicional de Oaxaca. Political analysts throughout the world hailed the significant changes in Mexico as the nation's final move toward a new international maturity.

Martin looked down in the bay and watched a yellow-and-orange silk parachute billow and lift off the ivory sand of the beach as the speedboat pulling it headed straight out into the blue water. One more tourist getting a brief but breathtaking bird's-eye view of the bay from a hang glider. From the palm-sheltered cottage just below him the lively rhythms of a Brazilian *butucada* wafted up on the breeze along with a girl's mirthful laughter and the sound of water splashing in the private pool hidden behind a screen of banana trees.

Two bare arms encircled his chest from behind, and he felt Susannah's face and hair against his sun-warmed back. She kissed his shoulders and then nuzzled his neck below his ear. She held him for a moment, tightly, then moved around beside him, keeping one arm laced under his. Together they watched the sailboats in the bay.

"Just thinking?" she asked, her eyes still on the brilliant-colored sails against the blue water.

"Just thinking," he said. "Trying to make it real."

"I know," she said.

"Reminds me of Nam. All kinds of hell and horror for two weeks and then, in eight hours, it was sweet R&R on China Beach. *Guerre moderne*. The worst part of it was that after a few days, if you were lucky enough to get more than a few days, you began to forget. It didn't seem right to forget so quickly. What had happened to you, to your friends, didn't deserve to be forgotten. It cheapened it."

"You're not going to forget it," she said. "You didn't forget the war, after all, did you? Neither of us is going to forget. We'll live with this every day for the rest of our lives and it's not going to be easy. Some of it will be hard to accept, and some of it... well, I don't know if I'll ever be able to justify my part in what happened at Orizaba."

He gripped her hand tightly. "It's just that Mexico was turned upside down by all those deaths and nobody even knows they were related. *Newsweek* said Francisco was on a business trip when his plane went down in a thunderstorm in the mountains outside Puebla. In a different article, totally unrelated, they reported Kahan's 'massive stroke.' I wouldn't have known about that myself if Campa hadn't leveled with me when I started raising hell during that so-called debriefing they put me through. Lee, of course, didn't rank the national weeklies. My own newspaper said he had been killed in a car accident while vacationing in Mexico."

Susannah rubbed the side of her thumb along the raised scar at Martin's wrist as he continued. "And poor Stella is only a ghost, not mentioned in the States at all, and here in Mexico even *Proceso* only referred to her obliquely as being an activist in a splinter group of the now famous and respectable GATO. The cover-up is total, mind-boggling. Makes you wonder what this world is really like. What other horrors have been hidden?"

They watched a brief, spirited race among three sailboats that approached the mouth of the bay simultaneously. They caught the Pacific wind and sprinted a short distance toward the open sea before they broke away from each other and dallied lazily in the sunlight.

"I feel bad about the money too," Martin said.

"There's no question Stella earned it," Susannah said gently. "The way they see it she died as a war heroine. You earned it too, as far as that goes. They're grateful and feel obligated. Let it go."

"I'd like to believe that, but a stipend of this size is a hell of a lot of gratitude. If I were on the outside looking in, I'd call it hush money."

"They didn't have to do it. You could have died in a 'car accident' too."

"I guess it's academic," he conceded. "I'm taking the money; I'm not going to turn it down."

"Martin, we can't let guilt destroy us. I don't know why it happened this way, that we survived rather than some other combination of people. I'll admit it's a nasty feeling, vaguely like cheating. It's hard to explain. But we *didn't* cheat. It's just the way it happened, and I can't honestly say I wish it had been some other way."

Martin knew she was right. He was being pretty damned self-righteous about it, perhaps even hypocritical. He didn't want it to be any other way either. But he wouldn't forget. Neither of them would be able to forget how Chance had played her game, taking so many, and leaving so few behind . . . to remember.